PIERCED

A NOVEL

THOMAS ENGER

Translated from the Norwegian by Charlotte Barslund

ATRIA PAPERBACK

New York   London   Toronto   Sydney   New Delhi

ATRIA PAPERBACK

A Division of Simon & Schuster, Inc.
1230 Avenue of the Americas
New York, NY 10020

Copyright © 2011 by Gyldendal Norsk Forlag AS
English translation © 2012 by Charlotte Barslund

First published in Norwegian as *Fantomsmerte* in Oslo, Norway,
by Gyldendal Norsk Forlag AS.
Previously published in English in Great Britain by Faber & Faber.

First Atria Paperback edition October 2012

ATRIA PAPERBACK and colophon are trademarks of Simon & Schuster, Inc.

For information about special discounts for bulk purchases, please contact Simon & Schuster Special Sales at 1-866-506-1949 or business@simonandschuster.com.

The Simon & Schuster Speakers Bureau can bring authors to your live event. For more information or to book an event, contact the Simon & Schuster Speakers Bureau at 1-866-248-3049 or visit our website at www.simonspeakers.com.

Designed by Jacquellynne Hudson

Manufactured in the United States of America

10 9 8 7 6 5 4 3 2 1

Library of Congress Cataloging-in-Publication Data

Enger, Thomas, date.
 [Fantomsmerte. English]
 Pierced : a novel / by Thomas Enger.—1st Atria Books trade pbk. ed.
     p. cm.
 "Originally published in Norwegian as Fantomsmerte . . ."—T.p. verso.
 I. Title.
 PT8952.15.N44F3613 2012
 839.82'38—dc23   2012029260

ISBN 978-1-4516-1648-4
ISBN 978-1-4516-1649-1 (ebook)

PIERCED

Prologue

Jocke's Harley-Davidson is already there.

Tore Pulli parks his motorbike and removes his crash helmet. The gravel crunches when his feet touch the ground. The windows in the old factory stare blindly out into the darkness. The silence is dense and eerie.

Pulli hangs his helmet on the handlebars and walks across to the door. The hinges groan when he pushes it open. He enters warily.

"Jocke?"

His voice bounces off the walls. His boots slam against the concrete floor. Little by little his eyes acclimatize to the darkness, but all he can see is the naked floor and walls, beams and pillars wreathed in cobwebs. The October wind howls through the panes of broken glass. White clouds of frozen breath pour from his mouth.

It's almost like the old days, Pulli thinks as he moves forward. The buildup to the confrontation. He can feel the adrenaline pumping and he likes it.

His eyes are drawn to something lying on the floor deeper into the shadows. He approaches with caution and is met by a pungent smell of urine and metal. He steps in something slippery and has to take a step to the side to avoid falling over. He pulls out his mobile and uses it to light up the floor.

Then he sees what he trod in.

A body lies in front of him. The back of the bloodstained leather jacket has been slashed repeatedly. Above the collar the skull shines brightly through the shaven and tattooed scalp.

He recognizes the tattoo immediately. Only Jocke Brolenius has *Go to hell* tattooed on the back of his neck.

His mobile goes dark.

His eyes dart around and he pricks up his ears, but he hears nothing in the profound silence. The room appears to be empty, apart from Jocke—a man Pulli loathed with a passion but didn't want dead for anything in the world.

Or, at least, not now.

He bends down, grabs hold of the leather jacket, and turns over the heavy body. The face is contorted and bloody, the mouth is open. Pulli presses two fingers against the artery on Jocke's neck, but withdraws his hand at once. Jocke's throat is still warm, soft and loose like a moist, mangled sponge.

Then he sees it, on the floor. The knuckle-duster.

His knuckle-duster.

How the hell did it end up here?

He is overcome by a horrible realization. A lot of people knew about this meeting and even more saw him set out for it. Far too many knew that the knuckle-duster hung on the wall in his study. And now he has Jocke's blood on his hands, his clothes, and his boots.

Someone has set him up. Some bastard has set him up.

Pulli is about to pick up the knuckle-duster and flee the scene, but he stops himself. You touched the body, he thinks. Your fingerprints are on Jocke's leather jacket. Don't make things worse for yourself, it's bad enough as it is.

He takes out his mobile again. With bloodstained fingers he enters the number of the emergency services to call the police. You know what really happened, he says to himself. Tell them the truth and you'll be all right.

You've got nothing to be scared of.

Part I

Part I

1

It's always the same scream.

Henning Juul blinks and fumbles for the light switch. The sheet under him is wet and the air quivers with heat. He runs clammy fingers over the scars on his neck and face. His head is pounding with a bass rhythm that is pouring out from an open window in Steenstrupsgate. In the distance a motorbike roars as it sets off, then there is silence. Like the drumroll before an execution.

Henning takes a deep breath and tries to strangle the dream that still feels all too real, but it refuses to go away.

It had started off as a good dream. They had gone outside to play, Jonas and him. A thick layer of snow had covered the ground overnight. At the junction by Birkelunden Park the tramlines were reduced to just ruler-straight silver lines, and they could barely make them out. The dense snowflakes were still dancing in the air, but they melted the moment they landed on Henning's cheek.

He was pulling Jonas on the sled down Toftesgate and into Sofienberg Park, where the children looked like ants on the small hill sloping down from the church. Jonas threw himself energetically from side to side. Henning was exhausted when they finally reached the top of the hill. He was about to sit down at the rear of the sled when Jonas stopped him.

"Not you, Daddy! Only me!"

"Okay. But you know that means you'll have to pull the sled back up the hill all on your own."

"Yeah, yeah."

"Do you promise?"

"Yeeees!"

Henning knew that the wet snowflakes had a longer life span than the promise Jonas had just made, but he didn't mind.

"Give me a push, I want to go reeeeally fast!"

"Okay. Hold on tight. Let's count to three."

They counted in unison:

"ONE! TWO! Aaaand THREEEE!!!"

And Henning gave Jonas a big push. He heard the boy squeal with delight as he got under way and noticed that the other children were watching him, too, enjoying the sight of the little boy with the pale blue woolly hat hurtling toward a jump that someone had built halfway down the hill. And Jonas reached it, gained some height, but landed quickly and whooped as he turned the steering wheel to avoid colliding with a girl coming from the side. She turned around and followed Jonas with her eyes as he veered further and further to the left.

Toward the tree.

Henning saw it, too, saw where Jonas was heading, his small fists gripping the steering wheel. Henning started running down the hill, but he lost his footing. He stumbled and rolled over a couple of times before he managed to get back on his feet.

The snowflakes, the voices, and the din faded into the background as Henning mouthed a scream, but no sound came out. He looked in desperation as the other parents who were also watching Jonas stayed rooted to the spot and did nothing to help him. In the end he closed his eyes. He didn't want to see it when it happened. He didn't want to see his son die. Not again.

And Jonas was gone. As were the hill and the snowflakes, the trees and the people. It grew dark all around him. The unmistakable smell of smoke stung his nose. And even though he couldn't see Jonas, he had no trouble hearing his cries.

Henning waved his arms frantically to carve a hole in the darkness surging in front of him, but it made no difference. The intense heat scorched his face. Breathing became difficult and he started to cough.

A glimpse of light appeared in the smoke. Henning blinked and focused on the opening that grew ever larger; he could see a door being eaten up by the flames. He coughed again. Then the gap started to close up and soon the smoke covered it completely. It was burning hot and black as night everywhere. And then Jonas started to scream.

Again.

Henning exhales at the sight of the flashing red light. His eyes seek out the other smoke alarm in the ceiling. He waits for it to emit its cyclical indicator of rude health. But the seconds pass. And some more. And even more. He feels a tightness creep across his chest and spread out to his shoulders and neck. At last the second smoke alarm lights up. A quick red flash.

He flops back onto his pillow and breathes out while he waits for the monster in his chest to calm down. Eventually it resumes its normal pace. He touches the scars on his face again. They still hurt. Not just on the outside. And he knows they will keep hurting until he finds out who torched his flat. Who snuffed out the life of the best little boy in the whole world.

Henning turns to the clock on the bedside table. It's not even ten thirty in the evening. The headache that made him lie down an hour and a half ago is still throbbing. He massages his temples as he shuffles to the kitchen and takes the last can of Coke from the fridge. Back in the living room he tidies away clothes and newspapers from the sofa before he sits down and opens the can. The sound of bubbles rising to the surface makes him sleepy. He closes his eyes and longs for a dream without snowflakes.

2

"**How** long are you going to be? I want to go home."

Gunhild Dokken leans over the counter and looks across the room. A song by Jokke & Valentinerne belts out from the loudspeakers. Geir Grønningen is lying on a bench, pressing 135 kilos up from his chest while he groans. Behind him, in front of the mirror, a short sturdy man is guiding the movement of the bar with his hands—without helping him.

"We've just got a few more reps to do," Petter Holte says without taking his eyes off the bar.

Dokken turns around and looks up at the clock on the wall. It says 22:45.

"It's Friday, guys. Friday night for God's sake; it's almost eleven o'clock. Haven't you got anything better to do?"

None of the men replies.

"Put your back into it," says Per Ola Heggelund, who is standing with his arms folded across his chest at the end of the bench. Grønningen has nearly raised the bar above his head. Holte gently takes hold of the bar and assists Grønningen's trembling arms.

"One more," he says. "You can do one more."

Grønningen takes a deep breath, lowers the bar until it touches his chest, and pushes as hard as he can. His muscles quiver while Holte lets him earn every single millimeter, right until the kilos have been raised and a roaring Grønningen can return the bar to the forked holders. He pulls a face and flexes his pecs, scratches his straggly beard, and shakes his long thin hair away from his face.

"Good job," Heggelund says and nods with approval. Grønningen scowls at him.

"Good? It was crap. I can usually do much better than that."

Heggelund glances nervously at Holte, but all he gets is a sour look in return. Holte loosens his gym belt while he studies himself in the mirror. His shaven head, like the rest of him, has the deep tan of a tanning bed. He adjusts his black gloves slightly and observes the muscles under the tight-fitting white vest, nods with satisfaction as he tenses them and watches the contours in his biceps stand out. He hoists up his Better Bodies pants before he marches over to the reception counter, behind which a bored-looking Gunhild Dokken is flicking through a magazine, her fringe covering her eyes.

"Are you doing anything tonight?" Holte asks and stops in front of her. His voice is soft and hopeful.

"I'm going home," she replies without looking up.

Holte nods slowly while he gazes at her.

"Do you want company?"

"No," she replies, unequivocally.

Holte's nostrils flare.

"Are you meeting anyone?"

"That's none of your business," Dokken huffs.

After a brief pause Holte turns to Grønningen, who gives him an encouraging nod.

"It's just us here," Holte says. "I can lock up for you, if you like."

Dokken slams the magazine shut.

"Couldn't you have told me that earlier? While there was still some of the evening left?"

"Yes, but I—"

A shadow falls across Holte's face as he stares at the floor.

"Okay," she sighs, sullenly. "You know where the keys are."

Dokken goes over to a coatrack and pulls on a thin black jacket. She drops her mobile into her handbag, which she slips over her shoulder.

"Don't work too hard."

"We're not training again until Sunday."

"Wow," she says, rolling her eyes. "A day off."

Holte smiles and follows her with his eyes as she marches toward the door. A bell above her head chimes before the door shuts firmly behind her. Then she is gone in the night. Holte shakes his head almost imperceptibly before he goes behind the counter, stops the music, and takes a Metallica CD, *And Justice For All*, from the stand. He finds track number eight, 'To Live Is to Die,' turns up the volume, and fast forwards to the middle of the song.

"Still no luck?" Heggelund smiles when Holte comes back. Holte glares at him, but makes no reply. Instead he asks who is next.

"Heggis," Grønningen replies and looks at Heggelund.

"Yep, me it is," Heggelund replies, cheerfully. He goes over to the bar and removes fifteen kilos from each side. Then he sits on the bench and breathes in deeply a couple of times before he lies down and finds the point on the bar where he always places the up-yours finger. He fills his lungs with air again. Holte is back in position behind him while James Hetfield proclaims, *When a man lies, he murders some part of the world.*

Heggelund lifts the bar from the stand, the weights clang against each other before he lowers the bar and raises it again. His first lift goes without a hitch. He tries to establish a steady rhythm and his next repetition is smooth, too. Two lifts later his grunting has become more aggressive. Holte straightens his back, ensures his legs are evenly balanced before he puts his hands under the bar, ready to assist. He looks at Grønningen, who nods as he moves a little closer. From the sound system Metallica launches into the thumping riff that is the opening of "Dyers Eve."

Heggelund closes his eyes and summons up all his strength for the next repetition, but the bar refuses to move. He opens his eyes. Holte's hands have moved from the underside to the top of the bar. Grønningen is standing by the side of the bench. He sits down astride Heggelund's stomach. Heggelund groans loudly. Holte pushes the bar down and lets it hover a few centimeters above Heggelund's Adam's apple. His eyes fill with panic.

"What . . . what—"

"How long have you been coming here?" Grønningen asks him. "Two months? Two and a half, perhaps?"

Heggelund tries to say something, but all his strength goes into keeping the bar off his throat.

"Do you think we're idiots?" Holte says and eyeballs him. "Do you think we let just anybody work out with us without checking them out first?"

Heggelund can only manage some gurgling sounds.

"You've been lying to us," Holte says through clenched teeth. "You've been having us on. Did you really think we wouldn't find out that you're starting at the Police College in the autumn?"

Heggelund's eyes widen eyes even further.

"So what was your game?" Grønningen continues. "Have you been watching too much television? Did you think you could get a head start? Go undercover, like?"

"No chance," Holte takes over. "No one messes with us like that!"

"Please," Heggelund pleads as his arms tremble. Holte pushes the bar down until it makes contact with Heggelund's skin. Sparks fly from his eyes.

"So do you think you'll be coming back here?" Grønningen asks him. Heggelund squeezes his eyes shut and tries to shake his head. Tears mix with drops of sweat on his face.

"Are you going to tell anyone about this?" Holte hisses. Again Heggelund attempts to shake his head. Grønningen looks at him for a few seconds before he gets off and nods to Holte. Heggelund can barely breathe, but Holte doesn't remove the bar.

"Petter!"

Reluctantly Holte lifts the bar aided by what little is left of Heggelund's strength. He slams it back in the stand. Holte turns around and snatches a towel while he snorts with contempt. Grønningen pulls him to one side.

"You could have killed him!" he whispers. Holte doesn't reply, he merely looks at Heggelund, who is gasping for air. His cheeks are stained with tears, his eyelids heavy.

"Enough is enough," Grønningen says. "Have you forgotten everything Tore taught us?"

Holte makes no reply, he just walks off a few steps. Heggelund discreetly moves into a sitting position while James Hetfield's voice roars from the sound system. Grønningen turns around and goes back to Heggelund, who is still clutching his throat. Grønningen waits until the two of them have eye contact before he nods his head in the direction of the door. Heggelund struggles to his feet and staggers toward the exit, where the name of the gym glows at him in letters the color of blood: FIGHTING FIT.

3

A sharp light makes Henning blink. His eyes feel gritty. He rubs away the sleep and feels an ache across his lower back.

He sits up slowly. The Coke on the coffee table is no longer cold, but he takes a sip all the same, letting it fizz in his mouth. Outside, shades of blue sky merge into one another. He lets in the warm summer wind through a window in the living room. A swallow cries out, but no one answers. Behind the block of flats opposite his a yellow construction crane skims the tops of the trees.

Henning goes to the bedroom, takes two tablets from the jar on his bedside table, and swallows them dry before he continues to the kitchen where he glances at the chaotic pile of newspapers and printouts on the table. He sits down in front of his laptop, bumping into one of the table legs as he does so and jolts a mug of cold coffee with dark brown rings on the inside. He opens up the screen and is greeted by an old version of the homepage of 123news.no, before it automatically updates itself. Henning reads the main story, then he scrolls down and learns that nothing much has happened overnight. Heat waves in Europe. Russia thinks Iran will soon have the ability to develop a nuclear bomb. Two people seriously injured following a traffic accident in Hedmark. Some girl he has seen before but whose name he can't remember has had enough of her silicone breasts.

Henning checks the competition's websites as well, even though he doesn't know why he bothers because it's a waste of time. It's the same news everywhere. But this is how he starts his day. And it's what he used to do before Jonas died.

Soon it will be almost two years, Henning thinks. For most

people two years is an eternity of moments and memories stacked on top of each other. For him it's no time at all. He hasn't managed to uncover a single clue. It would have been so much easier if only he could remember something, anything from the days and weeks leading up to the fire.

The face of Mikael Vollan stares out at him from the top of the pile. Mikael Vollan, the man who bombarded businesses and private individuals with 153 million fraudulent emails sent through accounts he created using false identities. Vollan advertised pyramid schemes and other scams to trick people into paying for something that didn't exist. Henning got so fed up with receiving all that spam that he decided to check up on who was behind it and what was in it for them. Together with 6tiermes7, Henning's anonymous police source, and his good friend, the computer wiz Atle Abelsen, he eventually managed to unravel Vollan's network. When the most important pieces were in place, Henning handed over his file to the Norwegian Gaming Authority, the Norwegian National Authority for Investigation and Prosecution of Economic and Environmental Crime, and eventually Kripos, the Norwegian Serious Crime Unit, in return for a head start of a couple of hours before the long arm of the law went into action. Vollan was later sentenced to seven years imprisonment and was ordered to pay restitution as well.

Henning studies the printouts once more before he puts them away with a sigh. In court Vollan expressed both remorse and relief, glad that someone had finally put a stop to his behavior. It had become an obsession, was how he put it.

Vollan wouldn't have had any money left to pay a hit man to eliminate Henning. Or Jonas.

Henning rubs his face wearily. Something will turn up, he tells himself. It has to.

4

Tore Pulli used to enjoy looking at himself in the mirror. The ultrashort hair. The bright blue eyes. The strong nose. The dense, neatly combed beard. The sharp chin that no one had ever managed to punch without having their own smashed soon afterward. The gold chains around his neck. The tight-fitting clothes. He loved to see how his muscles bulged, how his veins swelled under the tanned, tattooed skin. No one was ever in any doubt that he, Tore Pulli, was a guy they really didn't want to mess with.

But that's not what he sees now. His clothes no longer fit his body as snugly as they once did. What was at one time a tightly packed explosion, feared and revered, is nothing but a distant memory.

Pulli turns on the tap and lets the water run until it gets cold before he bends down and immerses his face in his cold, wet hands. He rubs his eyes, dragging his fingers across his cheeks, his forehead, the frown lines and the bald patch before he dries himself with a white towel. Are you ready? he asks the face in the mirror, Are you really going to go through with this?

Veronica looks back at him from the picture on the cork notice board. As always she looks straight at him with her lovely youthful smile. And as always he wonders how she keeps going.

Pulli sits down on the narrow pine bed, rests his elbow on his knees, and cups his hands under his chin. His eyes wander to the rubbish bin overflowing on the gray linoleum floor. An ashtray, a lighter, and a remote control are lying on a stool in front of him. His best friends. And surrounding him, his four worst enemies.

Resolutely he gets up and walks out into a corridor almost as long as a handball pitch only narrower and with tables and seating arrangements, benches and chairs, placed either side of thick yellow lines. He nods briefly to the guard in the armored glass cage, points to the telephone, gets a nod in return before he walks, unwillingly, to the table on the opposite side. A gray telephone sits on top of a dark red plastic cloth. Stacks of writing paper, envelopes, and forms are lying next to it. Pulli looks at the wall clock. Twenty minutes max.

He lifts the receiver, but puts it back immediately. Have you done everything you can? he wonders. Is there really no one else who can help you?

No. There are no other options left.

5

Henning's back is damp with sweat as he stops at the corner outside Café Con Bar. Across the road Vaterland Park lies like a lung between Oslo's Plaza Hotel and the aggressive main road to Grønland. Nearby, a steady stream of people hurry across the uneven cobblestones. The traffic roars angrily.

Henning takes off his rather scruffy jacket and finds a vacant table. If Erling Ophus hadn't insisted on meeting in the city center, and preferably near his old workplace, Henning would never have chosen to sit in a place where people rush by.

Henning has interviewed Ophus many times before, but he has never met him in person. By the time Ophus turns up at a crime scene, the flames have usually died down and the journalists have gone home to write up their story. Henning was surprised that Ophus was prepared to meet with him on a Saturday rather than enjoy his leisurely retirement in Leirsund.

It doesn't take long before Henning spots Ophus across the road. The retired fire investigator wisely waits for a green light before he crosses. Henning stands up, takes a few steps toward Ophus, and holds out his hand. The tall, stately man in the short-sleeved white shirt and dark blue trousers smiles and shakes Henning's hand firmly.

"Hi," Henning says. "Thank you for coming."

"No, thank you. My wife had planned for me to spend the day on all fours in the flower bed; you've given me a good excuse to come into town and perhaps catch up with some old colleagues later. If they're at work, that is."

Ophus smiles and lets go of Henning's hand. He gestures to a chair on the opposite side of the table and they sit down.

Ophus looks as if he has just come down from a mountain

hike, albeit even more energetic than when he set out. The skin on his face is fresh and clean-shaven with a warm glow of summer. The lines in his forehead are wavy and deep. He has a distinctive mole on his left cheek, but his face would be poorer without it.

A waiter with bed hair and large bags under his eyes comes over to them.

"Would you like something to drink?" Henning asks his guest.

"A cup of coffee would be nice."

"Two coffees," Henning says to the waiter, who turns around instantly without saying a word. Henning holds up his new mobile. "Would you mind if I record our conversation?"

"No, no. That's fine."

Henning presses the red button in the center of the active screen and checks that it starts recording.

"As I explained to you on the telephone," he clears his throat, "I'm working on this case."

"Yes, so I gather."

Henning is about to ask his first question when his mobile rings.

"I'm sorry, I have to—"

"That's all right," Ophus says and holds up his hands. Henning looks at the number. *Unknown.* He ignores the call.

"Let's try again," he smiles. "So you worked as a fire investigator all your life?"

"That's right," Ophus says, proudly. "I guess I've investigated more cases than anyone else in Norway. The insurance companies were keen to snatch me up when I retired, but once I had decided it was time to stop, I wanted to stop completely. Though I have to admit I'm starting to regret my decision."

"Too much weeding?"

Ophus nods and smiles as he accepts the clattering china cup from the sleepy waiter.

"What is the most common cause of a domestic fire?"

"Carelessness," Ophus replies and slurps his coffee greedily. "Around one in four fires is started by naked flames, cigarettes and candles. People are careless with ashes, it doesn't cross their minds that something could still be burning or smoldering long after the flames have burned down. Then you have people playing with lighters and fireworks, of course. Things like that." Ophus gestures eagerly.

"A fair number of fires are caused by people boiling a kettle dry or overheating a cooker or covering electric heaters. These days we all have so many electrical products and the quality varies enormously. Around twenty percent of all fires are caused by faulty electric goods."

Henning leans across the table.

"What about arson?"

"Roughly ten percent of all fires are started deliberately. We never succeed in identifying the cause of around double that number. And finally some fires are caused by lightning or people immolating themselves."

Henning makes a quick note on the pad lying in front of him.

"Is it difficult to investigate a fire?"

"Yes, very much so. Most of the time the fire will have wiped out any evidence there might have been. Besides, even the most experience investigator never stops learning."

"And the police must investigate all fires by law, am I right?"

"Indeed they must."

Henning's mobile rings again. *Unknown* is calling him a second time, he notices, but he continues to ignore it.

"How do they do that?"

"Eh?"

"How do the police go about investigating a fire?"

"Have you ever heard about the Five Es rule?"

"No, what's that?"

Ophus smiles and takes a run at it: "Evidence, Examination, Evaluation, Elimination, and Enforcement."

Henning grins.

"How long did it take you to come up with that?"

"Weeks. No. Months!"

Ophus smiles again. Silence falls on the table while Ophus drinks his coffee. Henning looks at his notes.

"So approximately ten percent of all fires are arson?"

"Around ten percent, yes."

Henning nods. He feels the scars on his face burn as if they were being licked by flames. Slowly, he looks up at Ophus.

"My flat burned down two years ago," Henning says and looks down again. "I lost my son."

"Oh, how awful."

"That was when I got these."

Henning points to his scars.

"I had to jump through a wall of flames to get to my son, but—"

He doesn't manage to complete the sentence. He never does.

"I think the fire was started deliberately."

"What makes you think that?" Ophus asks after an unashamed slurp of his coffee. Henning cringes. He is only too aware that his argument is low on evidence.

"I don't know, really. It's a hunch I have, a gut feeling, call it what you will. And then there is—"

Henning breaks off, thinking there is no point in telling a man like Ophus about his dreams and the images he sees in them. He shakes his head softly.

"It's just something I believe."

Ophus nods quietly while he raises his cup to his lips.

"When did it happen?"

"Eleven September 2007."

"That's after my time, sorry."

Henning gives him a deflated look before lowering his gaze.

"What did the police say? I presume they investigated the fire?" Ophus looks at him over the rim of his cup and narrows his eyes.

"Yes," Henning says. "And they concluded that the cause of the fire was unknown."

"But you believe it was started deliberately?"

Henning tries to straighten up, but he slumps immediately and hugs himself.

"I've no idea how it could have been done," he admits.

Ophus finally takes a sip of his coffee and puts down the cup with a bang. "What did the police report say?"

"I've never seen it myself, but I've heard they concluded that the fire most likely started in the hallway."

"Did the fire start while you were at home?"

"Yes."

"Any sign of a break-in?"

"Not that I know of."

"Did you lock the door?"

"I don't remember. I've no memory of anything that happened in the days and weeks leading up to the fire, but I think so. I always used to lock the door even when I was at home during the day, but I can't remember if I locked it that evening."

"Didn't you have smoke detectors fitted?"

The rhythm of Ophus's questions and Henning's answers breaks down. The cobblestones stare back at him accusingly.

"I did have one, but the battery was dead and I—"

Henning tries to look up while he gulps.

"And the police found no foot- or fingerprints, no other evidence, DNA—"

Henning shakes his head.

"And yet you still believe that someone started a fire in your home?"

"Yes."

Ophus leans back in his chair. At that moment Henning's mobile rings for the third time. Henning glances irritably at the display. *Unknown.*

"I'm sorry, I—"

"Go on, answer it. I'm in no rush."

"Is that all right? Are you sure that—"

"Yes, absolutely. I don't mind."

"Thank you, I'll—"

Henning waves his hand without quite knowing why. Ophus nods sympathetically. Henning takes the call.

"Henning Juul?"

"Yes?"

"Henning Juul, the reporter?"

"That's me, yes. Who is this?"

"My name is Tore Pulli."

Henning straightens up and says hi.

"Do you remember me?"

"I know who you are. What's this about?"

Pulli doesn't reply. Henning moistens his lips in the silence that follows.

"Why are you calling me?" he asks.

"I've got a story for you," Pulli says.

"What kind of story?"

"I can't tell you over the phone."

"All right. Listen, I would like to talk to you, but I'm a bit busy right now. Could I get you to call me back later? Preferably during office hours?"

"I can't—"

"Great," Henning interrupts him. "Thanks very much."

He ends the call and smiles quickly at Ophus who is watching the increasingly busy traffic. Henning exhales hard.

"I'm so sorry," he says and is rewarded with another understanding smile.

"But back to our conversation," Ophus says, looking at

Henning. "I have to be honest with you. If the police investigation has made no progress in two years, there's little that can be done now. Finding fresh evidence is out of the question. I assume your flat was demolished or renovated following the fire?"

"Yes. Other people live there now."

"So any evidence is gone for good. And there are many ways to torch a flat that are impossible to detect. Unfortunately."

Henning nods silently. They sit there looking at each other until Henning looks away. He knows he has to find the person or persons who set fire to his flat and get them to admit it. It is the only thing that will satisfy him.

His eyes wander to the junction.

"So you think someone was trying to get you? Kill you?"

"Yes."

"Why?"

"Well, that's the big question. I don't know. I don't even know where to begin."

"And this happened two years ago?"

"More or less."

Ophus looks at Henning for a long time.

"Don't you think they would have made a second attempt?"

"What do you mean?"

"Has anyone tried to kill you since?"

"Not that I've noticed."

Ophus doesn't reply, but Henning can see what he is thinking all the same. *It would suit you to be arson, wouldn't it? So you can blame someone other than yourself?*

They listen to the traffic.

Eventually Ophus says. "I don't think there is very much I can do to help you."

"That's what I was afraid of," Henning replies, quietly.

"You mentioned that you hadn't seen the police report. Perhaps there is something in that which could be useful to you? I might be able to get you a copy of it, if you like."

"I don't know if it will make a difference, but . . . but why not?"

"They owe me a favor down at the police station. I'll see what I can do."

"Thank you so much, I really do appreciate it."

Ophus straightens up, but Henning is aware that his eyes are still on him. He can't bear to look him in the eye. So he says without raising his gaze:

"I don't want to take up any more of your time than necessary, Ophus. Thank you so much for meeting with me."

"Not at all. You're welcome to contact me if you think of anything else."

Henning smiles and nods. They shake hands before Ophus gets up and heads for the junction. He passes a man leaning against the whitewashed wall sucking at a thin hand-rolled cigarette. The embers barely alive.

6

Ørjan Mjønes presses his forehead against the window of the United Airlines plane and looks out over Oslo. Green trees surround Ekeberg Restaurant on the eastern slope of the city. Nearer the city center people lie outstretched, sunbathing on the grass in Fjordbyen. The roof of the opera house sparkles like an ice floe in the sunshine. Below the belly of the plane the redbrick towers of Oslo Town Hall stick up toward him like rotten teeth.

The airplane glides slowly through the quiet air. The captain announces that they will be landing in a few minutes. Mjønes closes his eyes. It has been a long journey. A return trip to Bogotá, changing in Newark both there and back, and he hasn't managed a wink of sleep the whole time. He had to make do with a thirty-minute power nap on a bench while waiting for the flight back to Oslo. Soon he will have spent thirty-five hours in the air. It has been exciting. It has been exhausting. But it has been worth it.

It all started five days ago when he saw his fictitious contact name in the subject field in an advert on the website finn.no. Later the same day he called the number listed in the advert, which was answered by a voice he hadn't heard for almost two years. Bearing in mind the rage in the voice the last time the two had spoken, Mjønes hadn't expected to hear from Langbein ever again, but they agreed to meet at the bottom level of the multistory car park under Oslo City Shopping Center. Mjønes walked as far west as he could until a sharp voice from behind a pillar ordered him to stop. A long shadow stretched out across the concrete.

Mjønes did as he was told and looked around. He could hear tires squeal in the distance, but he saw no one.

"It has been a long time," he said, but Langbein made no reply. Instead, a legal-size envelope was slid along the ground toward him. Reluctantly, he bent down to pick it up. He took out a photograph. There was a big red cross covering the face of the man in the picture. Mjønes's jaw dropped.

"You're kidding me."

"No."

Mjønes looked at the photograph again, took out a sheet of paper that had been inserted behind it, and skimmed the text. Then he shook his head and spoke the words he rarely allowed himself to utter:

"That's impossible."

"Nothing is impossible. And if you hadn't screwed up the last time, there would be no need for this job."

Mjønes was about to protest, but he knew that Langbein was right. He was haunted by the incident. Mistakes are bad for his reputation. And yet he said:

"It's too risky."

The turn in conversation catching him completely by surprise.

"In my office there is an envelope identical to the one you are holding in your hands. With one sole exception. It also contains a picture of you."

"Of me?"

"Yes, of you. If you don't take the job, you become the job."

Mjønes was about to go behind the pillar to confront Langbein, but the sight of an arm and the mouth of a pistol stopped him in his tracks.

"If I'm not back in fifteen minutes that envelope goes to the next man on the list. But I want you. I thought it would be an appropriate way for you to correct the mistake you made last time. Besides, you'll be well paid."

Mjønes tried to shake off his initial shock.

"How much?"

"Two million kroner. Twenty-five percent up front, cash. You'll get the rest when all the loose ends have been tidied up."

Mjønes said nothing for a long time. He was contemplating the level of difficulty, his options. He scratched the back of his head and rubbed his nostrils with two fingers. Then he said:

"I'll do it for three."

A few seconds of silence followed. Then Langbein said:

"Done."

An intense rush surged through Mjønes's body, but he didn't have time to savor it. The next moment a suitcase was pushed in his direction.

"It must happen quickly and quietly. No traces. No questions. And no mistakes this time."

Mjønes nodded. Ideally, he would have liked plenty of time to plan, but he had always been good at thinking on his feet. In his head he had already come up with one possible scenario. But he had no time to ask Langbein any more questions, because immediately afterward a car door slammed shut. And when Mjønes walked around the pillar, Langbein was gone.

Mjønes thought about what he was being forced to do for several minutes. Langbein could be bluffing, but even before the threats and the money were mentioned, Mjønes had already made up his mind. It was an opportunity to redeem himself. To be generously paid for it as well was simply an added bonus. Besides, it was a long time since he had taken on a job of this magnitude and his fingers were already itching. All of his senses seemed heightened. He felt so much more alive.

Five days go quickly, Mjønes thinks, and prepares himself for landing. So much has happened in that time. And yet so little. Perhaps that's why he has been unable to sleep. Perhaps his body can't relax until it's all over. Nor will he have much time to rest when he gets home. The operation begins in a few hours. Everything must be in place.

The airplane lands and half an hour later Mjønes is on the train to Oslo. He thinks about the small box in his suitcase, about the plan he has come up with. It's daring. It's fiendish.

But if it works, it's pure genius.

7

Henning stares out the window while silence fills the space between the walls. The facade of the white building opposite him is streaked with brown trails of grime. His gaze continues down toward windowsills and intricate decorations. But he doesn't look down. Not all the way down. He never can.

Behind a window without any curtains a woman is pacing back and forth. She is talking on the telephone, gesturing angrily. Henning thinks about his conversation with Erling Ophus. Ophus is right, of course. Simply believing that the fire was arson is a sign of desperation. There has to be something he can investigate. But what?

Perhaps it's true that he is only looking for another explanation so he doesn't have to face the truth. And whether or not it was arson, nothing will change the fact that he could have saved Jonas if his eyes hadn't been stuck together with melted skin. If he hadn't slipped on the wet railing. If he hadn't been so bloody—

A vibrating sound from the kitchen table makes him turn around. He doesn't feel like talking to anyone right now, but the eight numbers on the display arouse his curiosity. He presses the green answer button and puts the mobile to his ear.

"Is this a better time?"

Tore Pulli's voice is deeper than Henning managed to register in the noisy street in Grønland.

"Eh, yes, I think so, but—"

"Eleven September 2007."

Henning stops.

"What did you say?"

"I know what happened that day."

Henning feels a sudden rush of heat to his forehead. Something sharp stirs in his stomach, his throat tightens. He tries to swallow.

"You lost your son," Pulli continues.

"Y-yes," Henning replies in a weak and dry voice. "I did. What do you know about it?"

"So now you're prepared to listen to me? Now you've got time for me?"

"Yes, I've got time to talk to you now," he says, rather more combatively this time. "What do you want? Why are you talking about my son?"

"I've a story for you."

"Yes, so you said. What does that have to do with my son?"

Henning is unaware that he is standing on tiptoes.

"Nothing. Not directly."

"What do you mean? And cut the bullshit, Pulli, I'm starting to get bored—"

"Do you know who I am?"

"Yes, I told you when we spoke earlier today. What about it?"

"Then perhaps you know why I'm calling."

Henning racks his brains. He doesn't remember reading anything about Tore Pulli since returning to work earlier this summer. Before Jonas died, the former enforcer was still in the newspapers, often depicted with a broad grin on his face and usually accompanied by his glamorous model wife.

"No," Henning says.

Pulli starts to laugh.

"What's so funny?"

"Sorry, I just—"

He leaves the sentence hanging in the air.

"You just what?"

"So you don't know that I'm inside?"

"No."

"Okay, I guess you've had other things on your mind in

the last two years. But I'm calling you because you're a good reporter. You're good at finding things out."

"Do you know anything about the fire in my flat?"

There is a long silence. Then Pulli replies:

"Yes."

Henning stands as if rooted to the floor, no longer on tiptoes. Pulli's deep voice drills into him. There is something about the depth of gravity in it. He is not joking.

"Are you there, Juul?"

"What do you know about the fire?" Henning demands to know and fails to hide the aggression lying right under the surface. "Did you start it?"

"No."

"So who did?"

"Before we talk about that, I want you to do something for me."

"What?"

"You obviously don't know why I'm in jail. When you've found that out we can talk again."

Outraged, Henning starts to pace around the flat.

"You can't just expect me to—"

"I'm only allowed twenty minutes of phone calls per week, Juul. I need a few minutes with Veronica as well."

"What do you know about the fire?" Henning shouts and stops right in front of the piano. "What do you want from me? Why are you calling?"

There is a short silence while Henning holds his breath.

"Because I want you to find out who set me up," Tore Pulli says, slowly. "I want you to find out who should be sitting in here instead of me. If you can do that then I'll tell you everything I know about the fire in your flat."

8

Henning puts down the mobile, runs his sweaty hands through his hair, and resumes pacing up and down the living room floor. How the hell could a man like Tore Pulli know anything about the fire? What exactly does he know and why hasn't he said anything before?

If it hadn't been for the fact that Pulli was in prison, Henning would have called back immediately, grilled him, and refused to let go until all his questions had been answered. But he can't simply march down to Oslo Prison, knock on the door, and demand to be let in. First Pulli must add him to a visitor's list, then Henning has to apply for permission to visit, and then the prison authorities will check his criminal record. And even though he is a journalist, it can take days, weeks even, for permission to be granted.

But then it strikes him that one important question has just been answered, perhaps the most important of all. Somebody knows something. Perhaps the fire in his flat was started deliberately after all?

Rattled, Henning sits down in front of his computer and googles Pulli's name. He can't remember the last time his heart beat so fast. A second later the search engine brings up a list of thousands of hits. Henning sees Pulli's mug shot, somber photos of him outside Oslo Court and inside the courtroom in conversation with people Henning can only see the backs of.

Pulli cuts a towering figure. Thick ox neck, broad shoulders, a huge chest and biceps the size of Henning's thighs. His body matches his voice. Dark, big, terrifying. In some of the earlier photos he has pierced eyebrows. Together with the rings in his ears they reinforce his thuggish appearance, a look he clearly abandoned when he announced his new career as a property developer.

Henning clicks on an article from dagbladet.no.

PULLI GETS 14 YEARS AND LAUGHS

Friday last Tore Pulli was sentenced to fourteen years in prison for the murder of Joachim "Jocke" Brolenius.

Joachim Brolenius, Henning mutters to himself and tastes the name. Never heard of him. He reads on:

> The high-profile property speculator Tore Pulli smiled and shook his head in disbelief when he was sent to prison for fourteen years in Oslo Court Friday morning for the murder of Jocke Brolenius. His lawyer, Frode Olsvik, told dagbladet.no that his client received the verdict with composure, but that he continues to maintain his innocence.
>
> "My client has already decided to appeal," Olsvik says. This means a whole new hearing in the appeal court. No date has yet been set for Pulli's appeal.
>
> Jocke Brolenius was found murdered in a closed-down factory building at the top of Sandakerveien on 26 October 2007. The Swedish enforcer is believed to have been beaten up with a knuckle-duster before being killed with an ax. Pulli's fingerprints were found on the knuckle-duster and the victim's blood was found on Pulli when he was arrested.
>
> The court chose to ignore the fact that the murder weapon has never been found as well as Pulli's claim that Brolenius's blood was on him because he was trying to help him. Pulli has always strongly denied any involvement with the killing though he admits arranging to meet with Brolenius.

When summing up the judge took into account Pulli's past as an enforcer, especially since Brolenius's jaw had been broken, a type of injury Pulli was known to inflict on his victims when he worked as a debt collector. At Ullevål Hospital this particular kind of injury had become known as a Pulli Punch and the Institute of Forensic Medicine (IFM) found that Brolenius's jaw had sustained this kind of fracture.

In addition to fourteen years' imprisonment Pulli was ordered to pay compensation and restoration to his victim's parents totaling 256,821 kroner.

Henning rereads the article. Who was Joachim Brolenius? What was his relationship to Tore Pulli and why were they meeting?

Brolenius was killed on 26 October 2007, Henning reads. Only six weeks after the death of Jonas. At that time Henning was in Haukeland Hospital, and all he can remember doing is staring at the wall. He avoided newspapers like the plague. People, too, as far as he could.

Henning scrolls down to the article's list of links and clicks the first one:

PULLI SUSPECTED OF MURDER

The celebrity Tore Pulli has been arrested on suspicion of killing a Swedish criminal.

Henning reads on:

The call came in around 23:30 Friday evening. Oslo police were called to an old factory where the Swedish enforcer Joachim "Jocke" Brolenius had been found murdered. The celebrity Tore Pulli, who has himself a past as a hard-hitting enforcer, alerted the police that he had stumbled on the body, but found himself arrested for murder.

The background or the motive for the murder is unknown. For the moment police have released very little information, but they have told TV2 that evidence was found at the crime scene. The TV channel's expert commentator, Johnny Brenna, who previously worked as a detective for Oslo police, says it is most likely a revenge attack. He refuses to speculate on what could lie behind it.

Henning finds a Wikipedia article about Pulli.

Tore Jørn Pulli (born 19 June 1967 in Tønsberg) is a well-known Norwegian ex-enforcer and former member of a biker gang who, in 2008, was convicted of the murder of the Swedish enforcer, Jocke Brolenius. Pulli became well known in Norwegian media when he started dating the former glamour model and now model agency owner Veronica Nansen. They married in 2006. Pulli took part in an episode of the topical news quiz *Nytt på nytt,* among others.

In a rare interview with Dagens Næringsliv in the spring of 2007, Pulli claimed to have collected approximately 75,000,000 kroner for clients during his time as an enforcer "just by breaking a few jaws." He has never referred to himself as an enforcer, but sees himself as a broker. Before he was convicted of murder he bought and sold property in Østlandet, making considerable profits.

Henning looks up from the screen. *"Just by breaking a few jaws,"* he repeats to himself. Why would an enforcer known for using his fists to solve problems ever kill anyone with an ax?

Henning skims several other articles about Tore Pulli. He clicks on an article headlined *Pulli promises million-kroner reward* and reads:

> Convicted killer, Tore Pulli, has offered a reward of one million kroner to anyone who comes forward with information leading to his acquittal.

"Wow," Henning exclaims. He clicks on other articles on the same subject without finding anything indicating an avalanche of tip-offs. What does that mean? he wonders. Surely someone must know something?

I want you to find out who should be sitting here instead of me.

Well, that's not going to be easy, Henning thinks to himself, when not even a million kroner could entice anyone to come out of the woodwork. And the prosecution appears to have had a strong case. It was widely known that Pulli had invited Brolenius to a meeting at a place where they wouldn't be disturbed. Pulli's fingerprints were found on the knuckle-duster. He had Brolenius's blood on his clothes and Brolenius had been beaten up in a way that had Pulli's MO all over it. Four bullets that were hard to dodge.

So what happened?

Henning picks up his mobile and rings Bjarne Brogeland. The inspector replies after only a few rings.

"Hi, Bjarne, it's Henning Juul."

"Heeey!" Brogeland replies in a voice that reminds Henning of a stag party.

"Are you busy?"

"Not more than usual given it's a Saturday. We're on our way to Paradise Bay. Have you been there?"

"Eh, no."

"Lovely beach, great water. How about you? What's new?"

Henning places his thumb and index finger on the corners

of his mouth and lets them glide down toward his chin. He hasn't spoken to Brogeland since the Henriette Hagerup case, the girl who was stoned to death in a tent on Ekeberg Common earlier that summer. Given how the case was cracked, Henning feels entitled to call in a favor or two from the police.

"I'm working on an old story."

"That doesn't surprise me, but for God's sake. It's Saturday! Don't you ever stop?"

"It doesn't feel like a Saturday," Henning says and realizes he can't remember when he was last aware that there was a difference between the days of the week.

"The sun is shining, Henning. Buy yourself an ice cream. Get some fresh air!"

"Mm. Listen . . . did you ever have anything to do with the Tore Pulli case?"

The voices of excited children in the background can be heard through the receiver. Henning tries to shut them out.

"No, I was still working on organized crime at the time. Why?"

Henning pauses for a moment, not sure how to reply.

"Oh, I was just curious."

"You're never just curious," Brogeland scoffs. "What are you sniffing around after this time? Does it have anything to do with his appeal?"

"His appeal?" Henning replies and frowns.

"Yes, it's being heard in a couple of weeks, if I'm not mistaken."

"Is it? No, it doesn't have anything to do with that. Or, at least, I don't think so."

Henning holds his breath for a moment.

"The guy is guilty as hell," Brogeland says.

"How do you know?"

"Does the name Jocke Brolenius mean anything to you?"

"Just about."

"Then you probably know that he killed Vidar Fjell?"

Vidar Fjell, Henning thinks and runs the name over his tongue. It sounds familiar.

"No?"

"I thought you had a photographic memory?" Brogeland teases him.

"My camera is broken."

Brogeland laughs.

"You certainly haven't lost your way with words. But here goes: Vidar Fjell managed a gym called Fighting Fit in Vålerenga. He was murdered a couple of months before Brolenius. Or perhaps a bit more. Pulli worked out at Fighting Fit and was a good friend of Fjell's."

Henning is aware that his cheeks are burning hot.

"Why was Fjell killed?"

"I don't remember."

"But Brolenius was a Swedish enforcer, am I right?"

"Yes. The Swedish gangs dominated Oslo quite considerably at the time, you probably already know that. Alisha—don't go up there, you could kill yourself if you fell down!"

Brogeland's voice disappears for a moment. Henning remembers the case now. Fjell was killed not long before Jonas died. He had done a little bit of research on the story, but he can't remember when he stopped.

"But if Brolenius was killed to avenge the murder of Fjell, did anyone later avenge Brolenius?"

"There was a rumor going around that somebody had knocked over Vidar Fjell's gravestone, I seem to recall, but nothing more than that. I don't suppose there was much point in carrying out a revenge attack once Pulli had been arrested. Why are you working on this story now?"

"I don't know if I am."

"Hello, you're calling me on a Saturday."

"Yes, I'm . . . sorry."

"Yeah, right. Tore Pulli had this woman, I recall. Damn—"

"What?"

"Why is it always the biggest arseholes who get the hottest chicks?"

Henning makes no reply.

"Anyway, talk to Assistant Commissioner Pia Nøkleby," Brogeland continues. "She's totally in charge of the case. And all other cases, for that matter."

"Good idea."

"But wait until Monday, please," Brogeland hastens to add. Henning says *hmm* and hangs up.

It's not going to be easy, he thinks. Murders and revenge killings in gangs that are practically impenetrable—especially if you're a journalist. But if Pulli is innocent then someone managed to kill Jocke Brolenius in a style that framed Pulli. That in itself was no simple task. The killer would have to be devious and without scruples. And this killer would almost certainly not like it if I tried to stir up the past.

9

The distant headlights of a fast car weave their way in between the tree trunks and cast a white veil over the approaching autumn. Ørjan Mjønes grips the steering wheel hard and checks the mirrors to make sure he isn't being followed. It would be something of an achievement if he was, he thinks, given the speed he is traveling.

The clock on the sat nav shows 02:15, and it is some time since he left the nearest main road. A loud but brief rumble under the tires tells him he has just driven over a cattle grid before the tires resume spraying gravel at the verges.

Mjønes knows that the others have already arrived. It has been a while since they last worked together, but he knew they would be just as ready for action as he was. Flurim Ahmetaj is there because he knows everything about computers and surveillance equipment and has easy access to it. Durim Redzepi because nobody is better at getting in and out of someone's home than he is. And Jeton Pocoli because he is a master at following people. In addition, he has bedroom eyes and a bad-boy image, which makes it easy for him to chat up Norwegian women. The reports he has supplied so far suggest that these skills in particular will prove useful.

As far as these men are concerned, it has always been a matter of showing up to a table already set, to a plan already laid, and they do what they are told to and paid for. This has never motivated Mjønes. He lives for the craftsmanship. The preliminary work, gathering pieces of information, fitting them into a bigger picture, planning for the unexpected. It is during this phase that he feels alive. And when everything works according to plan, his plan, it makes him delirious with happiness.

His favorite pastime is reading about himself in the newspaper afterward and being absolutely certain that the police will never be able to catch him.

Mjønes slows down, turns into a narrow track, and a red-painted cabin appears a couple of hundred meters farther down the road. He pulls up next to two motorbikes and a dark blue BMW Estate. Mjønes smiles and shakes his head, takes a long look at the desirable car before he steps out onto the makeshift car park. He glances at the cabin where the light is still on and the murmur of conversation fills the night.

Mjønes takes out the cage and the backpack from the boot of his car. He walks over to the cabin, doesn't bother to knock, but firmly pushes down the door handle and enters. The arm of a short, thin man on the sofa reaches swiftly for a pistol lying on the table in front of him. He cocks the weapon and points it at Mjønes.

Twice in one week, he thinks. It's becoming a habit.

"Relax, Durim, it's only me."

Durim Redzepi looks at Mjønes for a few seconds before he lowers the pistol. Mjønes smiles and takes a few steps inside. Playing cards and chips are spread across the oval table. The smoke from countless cigarettes hangs like a blue cobweb across the room.

"Who is winning?" he asks and sets down a cage where a cat with rust-colored fur is dozing on its stomach. He also removes his backpack.

"Flurim has the most chips," Redzepi says in broken Swedish. A man with a mohican turns to Mjønes. His broad smile reveals a pointed silver stud in his tongue. The men's attention reverts to their game.

"Hurry up, it's your turn," Ahmetaj says with the same East European Swedish accent, addressing a compact man in gray tracksuit bottoms who is leaning on the table while he contemplates his next move. A hairy stomach is visible under his white

T-shirt. Jeton Pocoli taps his nose with his index finger before he puts down two cards and pushes all his chips to the center of the table.

"I'm all in."

The men around the table stare at him in disbelief.

"You're bluffing."

Pocoli shakes his head.

"Screw you."

Redzepi runs his hand over his stubble-haired head, throws his cards on the table, picks up a can of beer from the floor and lifts it to his lips. Ahmetaj looks at Pocoli, searching for signs of bluffing. He scrutinizes him for a long time before he heaves a sigh, looks at the chips in front of him, grabs a large chunk of his own pile, and shoves them into the pot.

The last card is played. Ahmetaj's hopeful look dissolves instantly.

"For fuck's sake!" he groans and tosses aside his cards. "Just my rotten luck."

"Luck, or the lack of it, has nothing to do with it," Pocoli gloats as he scoops up the chips with a broad grin. Mjønes laughs and goes over to the kitchen in the corner. He looks at the messy row of empty beer cans and takes out a plastic carrier bag from one of the drawers. One by one the cans disappear into the bag.

"Okay," he says when he has made the place look reasonably tidy. "Have you done everything I told you?"

"Do you have the money?"

Ahmetaj doesn't look at him, but interlocks his fingers at the top of his mohican. It shines even in the modest lighting of the room. Mjønes opens his backpack, takes out a wad of banknotes, and runs his finger quickly over them. Fifty notes. He takes out another five wads and throws two to each man.

"If we pull it off, you'll get the same again," Mjønes says while the trio around the table counts their money. Ahmetaj nods happily.

"The equipment is over there," he says, pointing to a black bag.

"What about his email? His mobile? His bank accounts?"

"Already taken care of."

Mjønes nods and looks at Pocoli.

"Anything specific I need to know?"

"I'll brief you later."

"Okay."

Mjønes's eyes shift to Redzepi.

"I'm ready when you are."

Mjønes nods again. Everything is as it should be. He sees no point in explaining the plan to them in detail even though he is itching to do so. They are supplying a service. End of story. And yet he can't resist giving them a preview.

"Why did you bring the cat?" Pocoli asks him.

Mjønes smiles.

"To check that I didn't buy a pig in a poke."

Mjønes laughs at his own joke, but the card players stare blankly at him.

"Right, I realize you don't speak Norwegian. But I promise you, you've never seen anything like it. It's quite—"

A contented smile plays at the corners of his mouth. He puts his hand inside the backpack and produces two identical boxes the size of a matchbox, which he puts down on the table.

"What are they?" Redzepi asks.

Mjønes touches the first box with his index finger.

"Piercing needles," he says.

"And the other?"

Mjønes smiles and opens the second box.

"You really don't want to know."

With reverential movements he takes out an ampoule sealed with a small plastic cap. He unscrews the top, takes out a piercing needle and dips it in the clear liquid with the utmost care. He holds the needle with the tip pointing upward. The needle gleams.

"Who wants to do the honors?" he asks and looks at them before he nods in the direction of the cat. The eyes around the table light up immediately. He assesses them in turn.

"Durim," he decides. Redzepi smiles and gets up. Mjønes hands him the needle.

"Watch yourself."

Redzepi takes a step backward and is extra careful to avoid the point of the needle.

"No screwups this time."

Mjønes looks at him long and hard. Beads of sweat force their way out of the pores of Redzepi's forehead. He pinches the needle so hard that his knuckles go white.

Calmly, he approaches the cat in the cage. Behind him the others get up and move closer. Redzepi's look is one of deep concentration.

He opens the cage and looks at the sleepy animal that barely raises its eyelids to look back at him.

"Meow," Redzepi says, softly.

Then he aims the needle at the cat's neck.

And pricks it.

10

Henning wakes up early Sunday morning after a dreamless sleep. He goes to the kitchen to make some coffee. While he showers he turns over in his mind the information he found on Tore Pulli the previous night.

Pulli's parents died in a car crash a few days after his eleventh birthday, and it was left to his grandparents, Margit Marie and Sverre Lorents, to try to turn young Tore Jørn into a good citizen. The boy's life had, however, already taken a wrong turn. As the youngest member of a tagging gang, he constantly had to prove his place. In his early teens he was involved in a series of minor burglaries, he started smoking cigarettes, moved on to cannabis, and was quick to start fights. He drove a moped long before he was legally allowed to. His path to the biker gang was a short one. And it was at that point that he took up bodybuilding in earnest.

One evening when Pulli and his biker friends had been drinking heavily, Fred Are Melby, a notorious enforcer, came over to Pulli and started talking to him. Pulli, who was eighteen or nineteen years old at the time, thought this was cool until Melby's fist connected with his temple and floored him. Pulli quickly got back on his feet and proceeded to beat Melby to a pulp, including breaking his jaw with a lightning-fast jab with his elbow.

In the days that followed Melby's discharge from the hospital, Pulli was expecting some form of retaliation, but it never came. Instead, Melby offered him a job and promised to teach him everything he knew about the business. Pulli had gotten his foot in the door. Melby encouraged him to perfect his fast-elbow move, thus establishing Pulli's signature trademark. Later Pulli discovered that the initial provocation had simply been a kind of initiation test.

For six years he worked as a debt collector. Loan sharks and dodgy builders knew they could trust him, and as his reputation started to precede him, he no longer had to resort to violence to collect on his clients' behalf. As soon as people heard Pulli had been hired, they paid up. However, brute force alone wasn't enough even though Pulli regarded his body as a temple and never touched a drop of alcohol. He soon learned the importance of charisma, and the combination of strength and knowledge was—in his eyes—unbeatable. For that reason he read not only all the literature about weapons and combat techniques he could get his hands on, but also biographies of famous war heroes and personalities. Pulli enjoyed huge respect within his circle and in the course of time he came to be a wealthy man.

His grandfather, Sverre Lorents, who had worked as a carpenter all his life, advised Pulli to invest in property and he entered the market at a favorable time. He reinvested the money he made in larger ventures, which provided him with even greater profits and enabled him to continue down the same road. Soon he no longer needed to rely on his enforcer activity to make a living. Nor was it beneficial to his legitimate business interests to have at least one foot firmly anchored in the criminal underworld. In 2004 he shelved his knuckle-duster, or more precisely, he hung it up on the wall in his study. And then he met Veronica Nansen. They married two years later and the tabloid press regarded their wedding as the highlight of the year.

Today Nansen owns Nansen Models AS—a company that soon became a popular supplier of girls and models for a variety of glamorous assignments. Before that she had earned her living as a high-profile model and hosted a reality TV show that promised to give young, skinny, and very ordinary girls the chance to make a living from their looks.

Henning would not normally call anyone on a Sunday, but given that the matter affected both him and Tore Pulli, he has no scruples disturbing Veronica Nansen slightly later that morning. After many long rings the telephone is answered by a woman whose voice is rusty with sleep.

"Hi, sorry for disturbing you. My name is Henning Juul."

Henning's other hand drums the table impatiently while he waits for her to reply.

"I don't know if Tore has—"

"I spoke to Tore yesterday," Nansen says sharply. "I know who you are."

Her words sow a seed of guilt without him quite knowing why, but he shakes it off.

"So you know that I'm also—"

"I know that you're giving Tore false hope. It's the last thing he needs right now."

"False—"

"As far as I'm concerned he's free to seek comfort in a pipe dream that someone outside the prison walls will ride to his rescue, but I've no time for people like you."

"People like me? You don't even know what I—"

"Oh, yes, I do. You're attracted to mysteries, aren't you? Riddles nobody has managed to crack, and now you want to turn up and save the day."

"Not at all—"

"Tore doesn't need this now."

"So what do you think he needs?"

"He needs to prepare himself for his appeal. He should be trying to find out how to challenge his sentence rather than—"

Nansen fails to find a suitable ending.

"So he's guilty?"

"Did I say that?"

"No, but—"

Nansen interrupts him with a snort.

"If you had known what I know, you would have done Tore a favor and turned down the job. He has been through enough."

Henning changes tactics.

"Have you ever been to prison?" he asks and hears that she is about to reply, but he interrupts her. "Have you sat in a room no bigger than a broom cupboard where your door is locked at eight forty every night knowing you won't be able to leave until seven o'clock the next morning?"

Her sigh is heavier and more labored than he had expected.

"No, but—"

"Sometimes hope is the only thing that keeps you going," he continues. "If Tore believes I can help him then I don't think—with all due respect—that you should try to oppose it."

His comment verges on the pompous, but it works. He thinks.

"I'm just trying to be realistic," she says, eventually.

"Okay, I understand, but could we at least have a chat about his case? You probably know him better than anyone and perhaps you know more about the case. And just so you know, I haven't decided if I'm going to take this job yet."

"You're right," she says, quietly after a long pause. "Sorry, I didn't mean to be so abrasive. It's just that—"

"Forget it," Henning says. "Is there any chance that we could meet? Today preferably, if that's all right? I know it's Sunday and all that, but—"

"Could you be here in half an hour?"

Surprised at her sudden cooperation, Henning looks at his watch.

"I can."

11

"Can we play the snake game? Please, please, pleeeeease!"

Thorleif Brenden hears his daughter's voice from the bedroom while he takes out plates from the kitchen cupboard. Glasses and cutlery are waiting on the table with cold cuts, cheese, orange juice, and milk. The oven is on. A saucepan with water and eggs splutters on the cooker, but the sounds from the bedroom drown out even the dulcet tones of Norwegian songbird Marit Larsen from the Tivoli radio on the windowsill.

The snake game, Thorleif thinks and smiles. The kids never get bored with it even though Elisabeth has been playing it with them for years. First with Pål, then with Julie. And now with both of them. Thorleif hears a hissing sound and the expectant squeals from the children who are hoping—or dreading—being bitten by their mother's hand snaking toward them under the duvet. The game usually ends in tears either when Julie is kneed in the stomach or her eye is poked by a stray finger. Even so the tears are always forgotten by the next time.

Thorleif bends down and sees that the bread rolls are golden brown on top. He turns off the oven and takes them out. His stomach rumbles with hunger. The eggs are almost done so he goes through the living room and into the bedroom. *Hissssss.* He can hear suppressed giggling that could erupt at any minute.

"Breakfast is nearly ready," Thorleif says just as the snake strikes. The room is filled with panicky squeals of laughter.

"Just a bit more!" Pål pleads.

"The eggs will go cold."

"Just two more minutes! Please!"

Thorleif smiles and shakes his head while he looks, unsuccessfully, for Elisabeth's eyes somewhere in the sea of bed linen.

Hisssss.

The room explodes in new shouts of glee.

Marit Larsen has long since finished singing when Thorleif cuts the bread rolls in half and puts them in a brown wicker basket.

"Smell my hands, Daddy. I've washed them."

Julie toddles into the kitchen, climbs up on her Tripp Trapp chair and holds out her hands to him. The tears from the snake game are still fresh on her cheeks. He puts the basket on the table and sniffs them.

"What a good girl you are."

Her face broadens into a smile. Across the table Pål's eyes take on a wounded expression.

"You never tell me I'm a good boy when I wash my hands."

"That's because you're eight years old, Pål. You learned to wash your hands a long time ago. By the way, have you washed them this morning?"

Pål doesn't reply, but his sulky face gradually changes into a mischievous smile.

"Then you go and do it straight away."

Pål gets up and runs to the bathroom. He bumps into Elisabeth who is coming from the opposite direction.

"Remember to dry your hands properly!" Thorleif calls out after him. "And hang up the towel when you're done, please."

He looks at Elisabeth. The night still lives in her eyes, but her face instantly lights up when she sees the breakfast table.

"Oh, how lovely," she beams as she admires the food. "Candles and everything."

Thorleif smiles.

"What would you like to drink, Julie?" he asks his daughter.

Pål runs back in and sits down. The water is still dripping from his hands.

"Milk, please."

Thorleif takes a glass and is about to fill it.

"No, juice," she says. "I want juice."

"Sure?"

Julie nods adamantly. Pål leans across the table and helps himself to half a bread roll before he grabs his knife and tries to slice off the top of his egg.

"Who boiled the eggs?"

"Daddy," Julie replies.

Pål groans. "Mum is better at boiling eggs."

"Absolutely," Thorleif replies. "Mum is better at everything."

"Not at spotting roe deer," Julie points out.

"No, definitely not when it comes to spotting roe deer," Elisabeth joins in. "Once we saw twenty-five of them along the road when we drove home from Copenhagen. Twenty-five!"

"Is that true?"

"Absolutely! Daddy was the first to spot nearly all of them."

"Is that true, Daddy?"

Thorleif nods and smiles proudly as he removes the top of his egg.

"And not just roe deer. Cows and sheep, too."

"And wind turbines," Elisabeth interjects. Thorleif smiles and sprinkles a little salt on the scalped egg. Around the table the rest of the family help themselves to rolls, butter, cheese, jam, and cold cuts.

"So," Thorleif begins. "What are we going to do today? Any suggestions?"

"Can we go to the cinema?" Pål asks.

"I want to go swimming," Julie counters.

"We've been doing that all summer. Can't we go to the cinema? It's been so long! Please."

"Going to the cinema is expensive," Elisabeth says. "Or it is if we all go."

"Mum is right," Thorleif says. "What would you like to do today, Mum?"

"Bogstad Farm is open to visitors. I saw it in the paper. Perhaps—"

"Is it?" the children shout in unison. "Can we go there? Please! Can we? Can we?"

Elisabeth studies the children for a little while before her eyes find Thorleif's.

"Do you really think Bogstad Farm is cheaper than going to the cinema?" he smiles.

"No, but we can't spend the whole day indoors when the weather is so nice."

"We want to visit the farm, Daddy. Please. Pleeease."

Thorleif looks at his children in turn.

"Okay," he says. The children whoop and start jumping up and down on their chairs immediately. "But then you need to eat a big breakfast first. One bread roll each, at least. Do you understand?"

"Yes, Daddy!"

Thorleif takes a bite of his bread roll, feels it crunch between his teeth while he looks at Elisabeth, at all of them, one after the other. It's Sunday morning. Everyone is happy.

Can life get any better?

12

Ullevål Garden City lies in the borough of Nordre Aker and was built shortly after the First World War as a residential area for the working class. The intention was that the workers would leave their tenements in favor of bigger houses with their own patch of garden, but it didn't take long before the better-off hijacked the idyll. Since then house prices in the area have been among the highest in Oslo.

It's a lovely part of town, Henning thinks, as the cab comes to a halt on John Colletts Plass. Living in Ullevål Garden City bestows a certain status on its residents even though he doesn't think that was the reason Tore Pulli and Veronica Nansen bought a home here. The properties are well maintained, plants climb up the walls, and the whole neighborhood is characterized by expensive gardens and attractive cafés.

It doesn't take him long to identify the brick building where Nansen has chosen to remain despite her husband's jail sentence. Perhaps it's about holding on to what they had? Henning rings the bell and is admitted immediately. He wheezes as he climbs the stairs to the second floor, where the front door has been left open for him. He enters a hallway where a large wardrobe is concealed behind spotless mirrors. Further into the flat a chandelier sparkles from the ceiling even though no light is coming from its bulbs.

Veronica Nansen, wearing loose-fitting gray jogging pants, a pink top, and a thin gray zip-up hoodie, appears in his field of vision. She has a pink baseball cap on her head and her ponytail dangles from the back.

"You found it, I see," she says and smiles briefly.

"Oh yes," Henning says, still panting, and smiles. His scars stretch and he is aware of her looking at them as they shake hands. His skin feels young, like the skin of a child.

"Coffee?" she asks.

"Yes, please," Henning replies and follows her into the kitchen. There are warm gray slate tiles on the floor, an integrated wine storage unit, a heating cupboard for plates, a steam oven, a sophisticated espresso machine, and two stainless-steel ovens, one of them extra wide. The island in the center of the kitchen alone is bigger than Henning's bedroom.

"Let's sit down here," Nansen says, indicating tall slim bar stools with shiny chrome legs and bright yellow seats and backrests. "The living room is a mess," she says, and it sounds like an apology. Henning, who always feels ill at ease in the presence of expensive objects, scales the chair and tries to make himself comfortable. Clumsily, he rests his elbows on the surface of the table where a bowl of brightly colored fruit is tempting him.

"Nice house," he says. "Or rather—nice flat."

"Thank you."

Her voice is devoid of enthusiasm. She is probably used to being complemented, Henning thinks and watches her while she starts the espresso machine and finds two cups. She is shorter than he had imagined and refreshingly free of makeup. He had assumed that a woman for whom every pavement is a catwalk, or at least once was, would make an effort to pose in male company, but Veronica shuffles her feet and slumps slightly. Her hunched shoulders make her look as if she has a puncture. Perhaps her guard is down when she is at home? Henning thinks. Perhaps that's the one place where she allows herself to be exactly who she is.

Soon the aroma of freshly brewed coffee spreads across the kitchen. Henning thanks her when she puts a cup in front of him.

"Tore said you're a journalist?" she says, half-asking half-accusing, and sits down opposite him.

"Yes. I work for 123news."

"'1–2–3 News—as easy as 1–2–3?'"

"Yes, I'm afraid so," Henning replies.

Nansen takes out a packet of cigarettes and a lighter from the pocket of her hoodie. She offers Henning a cigarette, but he shakes his head.

"Good place to work, is it?"

"No," he replies and smiles quickly.

"Why not?" she says and lights up. Henning stares at the flame.

"I don't know if I would like it anywhere in the media, to be honest."

"So why are you in this line of work?" she asks and blows out hard blue smoke through pursed lips.

"It's the only thing I'm good at."

"I don't believe that. Everyone has hidden talents."

"In that case my talents are very well hidden."

She smiles.

"Isn't there something you would like to do?"

Henning hesitates.

"I like making music. Playing the piano."

"So why don't you do that?"

"I'm not good enough."

"Says who?"

"Says me."

A furrow appears on Nansen's brow when she takes another drag of her cigarette.

"Also it's been a while since I last played, so—"

"Didn't you just say that you enjoy playing?"

"Yes."

"So why haven't you played for a while?"

Nansen fixes him with her eyes.

"Because . . . because I can't bear it."

Henning looks down, surprised at how quickly they reached

such an intimate point in their conversation. And the fact that they got there at all.

"It reminds me of my son," he says, quietly. "And what . . . what—."

Henning can hear how desperate he sounds.

"Tore told me what happened."

Henning looks up.

"Did he? What did he say?"

"He said that you lost your son in a fire."

"Did he say anything else?"

"No."

Nansen doesn't elaborate. She looks at the smoke that wafts randomly from the embers of the cigarette.

"He hasn't mentioned my son before?"

"No. Why would he?" she says.

Henning can't think of a suitable reply. Nansen takes another tight-lipped drag.

"You really should try to play again," she says, blowing the smoke right up in front of her face. "For your own sake. You never know, you might surprise yourself. It might do you good."

"I don't think so," he says.

They drink coffee in silent seconds.

"And you run a modeling agency?"

"Yes," she says, matter-of-fact. "Someone has to look out for them."

"Is there that much to look out for?"

Nansen smiles faintly.

"The things I've seen—one day I'll write a book about it."

"Really?"

She nods and sucks the cigarette again.

"Are you busy?"

"Not at the moment. It has been tough what with the recession and all that. I've had to lay off a lot of staff recently and that's never much fun. Tore being convicted of murder didn't exactly help, either."

Her face darkens.

"How has it been . . . since?" Henning asks. Nansen sighs.

"It has been tough, I won't lie. I haven't had the energy to go out much."

She looks down. He can barely make out the contours of her face in the warm light from the kitchen window.

"But," she says and straightens up. "I'm boring you talking about myself. What do you want to know?"

"As much as possible." Henning smiles.

"I don't really know how to begin," she says, looking at him. Her ponytail winds its way down one side of her neck like a blond snake. Her eyes, ice blue and sharp, contain something Henning can't quite fathom.

"I've done some homework on the case," he begins. "I understand that Tore was arrested at the crime scene and that he had arranged to meet Jocke Brolenius there?"

Nansen nods, takes a final drag and stubs out the cigarette, grinding it into the ashtray.

"Why did Tore ask Brolenius to meet with him?"

"How much do you know about Vidar Fjell and all that?"

"I've read that the murder of Jocke Brolenius was regarded as revenge for the murder of Vidar Fjell."

Nansen nods again.

"Vidar had worked with the Drug Rehabilitation Service for many years. Young addicts who were trying to get clean were encouraged to work out in his gym."

"You're referring to Fighting Fit?"

"Yes. Christ, what a name," she says and rolls her eyes. "Anyway, Vidar received grants from the council so he could look after disadvantaged youths."

"Isn't that The Inner City Project?"

"It's part of it, certainly. Vidar taught them what workouts to do, how to work out, and he tried to give them a sense of belonging. A couple of the young people he helped even ended up working there. Vidar was a really great guy."

Nansen lights up another cigarette.

"And he had a zero tolerance policy as far as dope, steroids, and all that was concerned. If you messed about with drugs in his gym, you were out on your ear. But Jocke Brolenius didn't give a toss about that. He even tried to recruit some of the kids Vidar had managed to straighten out."

Nansen curls her lips around the cigarette and sucks greedily.

"Because of who Brolenius was, he was given a friendly warning first. But he didn't listen so Vidar threw him out."

"And Brolenius took offense?"

"Oh, yes."

Henning recalls that Fjell was attacked in his office and that he died of a brain hemorrhage as a result of the injuries he sustained. The fact that he was a hemophiliac and wasn't found until the following day by one of his staff didn't exactly improve his chances.

"Why didn't the police arrest Brolenius?"

"They interviewed him as far as I know, but he denied having anything to do with the murder."

"And there was no incriminating evidence?"

"No," Nansen replies, crossing her feet while she leans back. "But everyone knew it was him. When the police failed to do their job, it didn't exactly calm the troubled waters down at Fighting Fit. But Tore put his foot down. He knew exactly what Brolenius was like and who his friends were, and he wanted to prevent a bloodbath. That was why he invited Brolenius to a meeting. To see if the two of them could settle the conflict."

Henning tries to visualize the scenario.

"Why did he think he could do that?"

"I don't know. I tried talking him out of it because I thought it was a crap idea."

"Did a lot of people know about this meeting?"

"Yes, a fair number, I think. Everyone was talking about it, both here and at the gym. Tore eventually managed to convince them that nothing good would come from killing Brolenius. He asked them to trust him."

Henning looks at her pensively.

"So what do you think happened?"

"I think someone got there before Tore, killed Brolenius, and ran off before Tore arrived."

"That sounds risky."

"Yes, perhaps. But they succeeded."

"They?"

Henning raises an eyebrow.

"Yes, I don't really know why I say that. But somehow it sounds more likely than him or her."

Henning turns his head and looks across the kitchen. A long pause follows.

"On the phone you said to me that *'if you had known what I know, then you would have done Tore a favor and turned down the job.'* What did you mean by that?"

Some moments pass before she answers.

"It suits a lot of people very well that Tore is where he is."

"And what do you mean by that?"

Henning attempts a smile, but Nansen's stern armor remains intact.

"Let's start with the police," she says and blows smoke out into the room with an air of resignation. "They've been trying to get something on Tore for years. And when the opportunity finally presented itself, they grabbed it with both hands."

"And did they have any reasons for wanting to get Tore?"

Nansen taps the ashes off her cigarette with an angry index finger.

"No one is saying that Tore was a choirboy, at least not until he stopped working as a debt collector. But he didn't kill Brolenius. He was trying to keep Brolenius from getting killed. But when the police discovered there was evidence that implicated Tore, it suited them perfectly. It meant they didn't have to look for anyone else."

"So the police deliberately failed to investigate important leads? Is that what you're saying?"

Nansen sucks in one last drag before stubbing out the cigarette.

"The police force is riddled with incompetent two-faced idiots."

The glance she throws out into the room is bitter, but she doesn't elaborate. Henning considers the wisdom of discussing this particular topic with her.

"So who could have killed Brolenius—if Tore didn't do it?"

"It must have been one of those morons Tore surrounded himself with."

"You're referring to his friends at Fighting Fit?"

She nods and looks away.

"Tore's so-called friends," she says, acidly. The darkness in her eyes is still there when she continues: "How many of them have visited Tore in prison, do you think?"

Henning looks at her quizzically.

"Just one," she says, holding up a single finger in the air. "Just one."

"And that is?"

"Geir. Geir Grønningen. I suppose you could say he's one of the more decent of that bunch. He's still a moron, though. And that was one of the reasons I was so skeptical when you called."

"In what way is he decent?"

"Geir has been trying to help Tore ever since he was first arrested. But he hasn't managed to find out a damn thing. And then you turn up out of nowhere and—"

She interrupts herself.

"Sorry, I didn't mean to—"

"Don't worry about it," Henning says. "But Grønningen, who is he? What does he do?"

"I think he still works as a debt collector, not that I have much contact with him these days. He also works as a doorman in a strip club in Majorstua. Åsgard it's called, or something like that."

"Who runs Fighting Fit now?"

"A guy called Kent Harry Hansen."

"Is he okay?"

"Well," she says after a short pause, "I don't really know how to answer that. There certainly isn't much left of Vidar's old gym, that much I can tell you."

"What do you mean?"

Nansen looks at him for a little while before she continues:

"I think Kent Harry is happy to look the other way when it comes to drugs. I also think people call him up when they need some muscle. And there is a lot of that in the gym."

Henning nods again.

"Do you have any more names?"

"There's Petter Holte, Tore's cousin. He works as a doorman at Åsgard and is a wannabe debt collector, though I can't imagine Kent Harry would ever dare to use him. Tore certainly never did even though Petter was always pestering him."

Nansen looks him straight in the eye as she explains.

"When Tore was still involved with his old life, he got so many requests he had to outsource some of his work for a while. He passed on several jobs to Geir, that much I do know, but never to Petter. Petter had a temper."

Henning, who has forgotten to drink his coffee for several minutes, raises the cup to his lips again.

"There are plenty of other morons down at the gym," Nansen goes on. "Or at least there used to be. I don't have very much to do with them these days."

Henning looks out of the window. Outside in the street a tram glides past.

"Let's say for the sake of argument that Tore is innocent," Henning says, looking at her. "That means someone managed to beat up and murder Jocke Brolenius, a hardened criminal, something which in itself is no easy matter. But not only that, the same person also made it look as if Tore did it?"

Nansen doesn't reply. She just looks at him.

"It would require brains," Henning says, tapping his forehead. "And a level head. Do you think any of the people you've mentioned so far fits that description?"

"I don't know," she says, quietly.

"You keep referring to them as morons."

"Yes," she says. "But that is mostly because I hate everything they stand for. Everything they are."

"You blame them," he says. "That's understandable."

She sighs and takes out another cigarette.

"It's just so bloody frustrating," she bursts out. "I know that Tore is innocent and there is not a damn thing I can do about it!"

She squeezes the lighter hard.

"And you don't have any theories about who could have done it? Anyone who would have wanted to make life difficult for Tore or avenge the murder of Vidar Fjell?"

She shakes her head.

A long silence ensues.

"So what do you think?" she says and looks up at him. "What do you think you can do?"

"I don't know," Henning says and exhales heavily. "But I think I'm going to need my gym bag."

13

"**Are** we nearly there yet?" Julie Brenden whines. She tries to wriggle out of her car seat, but the seat belt keeps her in place.

"Not long to go now, darling," Elisabeth replies, turning around. "Isn't that right, Daddy?"

"It's just over there," Thorleif says as the popular Bogstad Lake, where people go swimming in the summer and skiing in the winter, appears behind the trees. On the far shore the manicured fairways of the fashionable Oslo Golf Club sparkle in the late-summer sun.

"Oh, dear," Elisabeth exclaims as they turn into Bogstad Farm. "We're not the only one who thought of this."

Thorleif looks at the sea of cars parked outside the farm. He lets the car roll across the thick cobblestones. There isn't a single vacant parking space to be seen.

"I'll drop you off outside the entrance and then I'll look for somewhere to park," he says.

"That would be great."

He drives them as close as he can, stops, and helps Julie out of her car seat.

"I'll be with you very soon," he says to Elisabeth. "Keep your mobile on so I can find you."

Elisabeth doesn't seem to hear him, instead she extends her hand toward the children and waves them eagerly over to her. Julie jumps and skips across the cobblestones. Thorleif is about to repeat his request when he notices a dark blue BMW right behind him.

"Oh, sorry," he says, holding up a hand apologetically. He quickly gets back in the car and drives off. Soon he is back on the road. It'll be a long walk back, he concludes. Both sides of the road are wallpapered with cars. The BMW is still right up his back.

A car park appears to his left. Expectant-looking families are getting out of their cars. I'll try my luck here, Thorleif thinks and turns into it. He drives slowly across the gravel while scouting for a vacant space.

There! A single vacant space. He presses the accelerator and slips in before someone else grabs the space. Triumphantly, he turns off the engine and sits there for a while feeling the sun heat the car. Thorleif removes his seat belt and as he does so he looks in the rearview mirror. The dark blue BMW is quietly blocking him in. The driver appears to be staring at him. Thorleif tries to work out if the man wants something from him, but that doesn't appear to be the case.

As Thorleif gets out, the wheels of the BMW dig into the ground and tear it up. Thorleif follows the car with his eyes as it turns right at the end of the car park and accelerates toward the exit. He notices the driver's fair skin and ponytail. The car indicates left and drives off at speed toward Oslo.

14

Human beings are creatures of habit. They have their fixed rituals, which they repeat every day, every week, every year. Henning is one of those creatures. In the past, before Jonas, he might visit a restaurant or somewhere similar, and if he used the toilet there more than once, he would inevitably find his way back to the same cubicle. He might even wait for it to be vacant if it wasn't when he first arrived.

Veronica Nansen told him that Tore and his friends worked out every Sunday at one o'clock in the afternoon and that you needed a good reason not to show up. When Henning stops outside Fighting Fit in Kjølbergveien, the time is a little past one thirty. If I'm lucky, he thinks, that ritual is still being honored.

The name of the gym is printed in red letters against a black background on a filthy glass door. The carpet inside is purple. Henning walks up to an imposing reception counter. Three tiny potted plants have been placed at random on the counter next to an index of workout cards and a till. A computer screen lights up the face of a short-haired woman who is staring at it. Two white cupboards in a corner behind her are stocked with protein drinks and dietary supplements.

Henning waits patiently for her attention. The receptionist, whom he had initially classified as a woman, isn't particularly feminine. She has rings in both eyebrows and wears black makeup around her eyes and on her lips. The muscles in her biceps are defined in a masculine way. When she finally looks up at him, she pushes her chest up and out. She is even wearing a T-shirt advertising a deodorant for men. He notices she has thin, encrusted scars running diagonally down her forearms.

Whether they were made by an angry cat or something else Henning can't determine without making it obvious that he is staring. The infected needle scars around the major veins in her elbow joint, however, are unmistakable.

Henning says hi and attempts a smile.

"Hi," she replies.

"My name is Henning Juul. I work for 123news."

No response, only a dull stare.

"I'm working on a story about gyms. I don't mean gyms that belong to the big chains, but the independent ones that survive despite the fierce competition. I thought it was about time that someone wrote about you, too."

He flashes a smile as false as the Rolex watches on Karl Johansgate, but it will have to do.

"And that's why you are here? On a Sunday?"

Her voice is hoarse as if something is stuck in her throat.

"Eh, yes. I'm writing a lot of other stories this week and as I happened to be in the neighborhood, I thought I'd—"

Henning realizes he is struggling to convince even himself so he shuts up. The woman says nothing, she just stares at him.

"Is Kent Harry Hansen here?"

"No."

"Oh, no," he says, excessively positive. "So where is he?"

"Some people have better things to do on a Sunday than work."

"Fair point," Henning says and smiles again.

The girl's fixed mask remains intact.

"I was wondering, is there anyone from admin here today?"

"I'm the only one."

"And you are—"

"I'm just the receptionist."

Henning looks around.

"How about Geir Grønningen—is he here today?"

"He doesn't work here."

"No, but I've heard that he uses this gym?"

"So what?"

"I need a quote or two. Why people work out here and blah blah blah. It makes the article sound better."

The girl behind the counter looks at him before she nods in the direction of a row of exercise bikes by the windows. A man in a white vest is pedaling at a sedate pace while looking at a screen on the wall.

"That's him?"

The girl nods. Imperceptibly.

"Okay, thanks for your help."

Henning attempts an ironic smile, but her attention is already elsewhere. He crosses the large room where white and black equipment in all shapes and sizes compete for floor space. Music blasts from the loudspeakers. The weights ring out. Grunting and bellowing alternate. The sound of testosterone, Henning thinks. No one here looks as if it bothers them that brute strength on its own is pointless if you can't run a hundred fifty meters without getting out of breath. Many of the stomachs on display are bulging, but not from muscle.

"Geir Grønningen?"

Henning puts his hand on the bike's handlebars. A tall man with long thin hair turns to face him. He has a wispy beard around his lips and chin. And here was Henning thinking the age of grunge was long gone.

"Hi," Henning goes on.

Grønningen's only reply is to pedal more slowly. Henning gets on the vacant exercise bike next to him and discovers too late that his feet don't reach the pedals, but he refrains from adjusting the seat. Instead he sits there dangling his legs.

"Do you mind if I have a chat with you while you warm up?"

Grønningen looks straight ahead. Henning fixes his eyes on him until he turns around. "My name is Henning Juul," he continues. "I'm a journalist with 123news. I've just been talking to Veronica Nansen."

Grønningen turns his head slightly.

"She told me that you've been trying to find out who—"

"Are you out of your mind?" Grønningen hisses and looks daggers at him before quickly glancing around. "You can't just come in here and—"

"Why not?" Henning says as frown lines appear on his brow. "We're just having a chat."

"You don't understand," the big man says. "Get out before anyone sees you."

"You're quite right," Henning says, feigning ignorance. "I don't understand."

Grønningen gives him a look of exasperation. Neither of them says anything for a while, but Henning refuses to release Grønningen's eyes. Finally, Grønningen gives in.

"Do you know where Jarlen is?"

"No, but I can find out."

"Wait there and I'll have a chat with you later."

"Okay. When?"

Grønningen rolls his eyes before he faces Henning again.

"When I'm done here. I can't cut my workout short just because you turned up."

"So give me a time."

Grønningen glances surreptitiously around again. Then without looking at Henning, he says:

"Give me a couple of hours."

"A couple of hours it is."

Henning looks at the clock on the wall behind the reception counter, nods to Grønningen, and climbs off the exercise bike. On his way to the exit, he smiles at the girl behind the counter and gives her a thumbs-up before he walks outside and back into the heat.

15

Thorleif Brenden wakes up with a start and looks around. There is light all around him. From an open window that overlooks the courtyard the sound of children shouting enters and exacerbates his headache.

He gets up and goes to the kitchen. Then he fills a glass with cold water and swallows the contents with rapid gulps. He groans with satisfaction. The next moment the door is flung open as if Kramer himself from *Seinfeld* is about to make an entrance. But it is only Julie with Elisabeth at her heels.

"Hi, Daddy! I need the loo."

"Okay, sweetheart," he smiles and looks at Elisabeth. "Remember to close the door behind you."

"Okay," Julie replies.

"And afterward you must tell Daddy what you've just learned, promise?" Elisabeth calls out after her daughter.

"Yeees!"

Elisabeth smiles and looks at him tenderly.

"Hi," she says in a soft and affectionate voice. "Did you have a good sleep?"

Thorleif shakes his head and refills his glass.

"You certainly look as if you have."

"How can you tell?" he asks her.

"Your eyes are swollen. As if they've relaxed properly for once."

"It's probably just an allergic reaction."

"Oh, you poor thing. You shouldn't have joined us on that horse and cart ride. Have you taken your medication? Do you feel better for it?"

"A bit, perhaps."

Elisabeth strokes his cheeks and gazes at him as if he were a baby. Then she kicks off her shoes. He can hear Julie singing happily through the open bathroom door.

"Are you going to fix the alarm today?"

"What?"

"The burglar alarm. We must get someone in take a look at it."

"Oh, right."

Thorleif had already forgotten that the alarm had, unexpectedly, not worked when they came back from Bogstad Farm.

"Daddy," Julie shouts as she comes storming out of the bathroom. "Do you know something?"

"No."

"I've learned to ride my bicycle!"

Her sense of triumph is written large across her face.

"Really?"

Julie nods, bursting with pride.

"Do you want to see, Daddy? Do you want me to show you?"

Thorleif looks at Elisabeth. Julie's parents are bursting with pride, too.

"Of course I want you to show me, sweetheart. Hang on, let me just put my shoes on."

16

Henning walks across the golden brown floor of Jarlen. A wall painted red at the top and white at the bottom welcomes him to the restaurant. The wall sconces look like hats someone thought it would be amusing to turn upside down. There are white cloths and napkins on the tables, but hardly any customers eating at them.

Henning picks a table in the middle of the room, orders a Danish-style beef burger with potatoes, vegetables, and pickled beetroot for no other reason than he likes Denmark and the Danes. While he waits for his food, he looks out of the window at the five-meter-high wall across the road.

Oslo Prison.

He is somewhere inside it, Henning thinks, the man with information about the fire. The time until he meets Tore Pulli face-to-face can't come soon enough.

Henning is still feeling uncomfortably full after his meal when Geir Grønningen shows up two hours and fifteen minutes after their brief chat at Fighting Fit. He has showered and is wearing tight leather trousers and a white T-shirt that strains over his belly. His steps are measured and decisive and his arms hang well away from his upper body, as if something has been stuffed under his armpits. He has long hair that falls loosely over his shoulders, but his hairline has retreated high up his forehead and made room for deep frown lines.

Henning gets up when Grønningen appears.

"I don't think we managed to introduce ourselves properly earlier," he says and holds out his hand. "Henning Juul."

Grønningen shakes his hand reluctantly.

"You've got a nerve," he says as he sits down.

"Why is that?"

"Walking straight into the gym and talking to me about what I—"

Grønningen breaks off, looks around, but all he sees is a noisy family with children at a table farther away.

"You're lucky no one saw you," he continues.

"I am or you are?"

Grønningen doesn't reply.

"So no one knows that you're trying to find out who set Tore up?"

Grønningen looks at Henning. His lips form the beginning of an answer, but Henning sees that he opts for an alternative reply.

"Turning up at the gym and asking questions about people isn't very smart," he says archly. "People might think you're trying to set them up."

"And they've developed this paranoia because they've been law-abiding citizens all their lives?"

"You know what I mean."

"I think so. But I wanted to talk to you because Veronica said that you've tried to help Tore while he has been inside."

"I've tried and tried," he says and looks down.

"So you haven't found anything out?"

Grønningen studies his napkin in detail.

"Not much, no."

"That probably explains why Tore rang me yesterday," Henning says and waits for Grønningen to look up. Which he does half a second later.

"Did he?"

"Yes. He asked for my help. Since you're clearly trying to help him, too, I thought we might be useful to each other."

Grønningen snorts with ill-concealed contempt, but it's loud enough for Henning to hear it.

"I get it," he continues. "You don't know if you can trust

me. And no one has claimed the one million kroner reward yet. But you can relax, Geir. I don't care about the money. I have my own reason for doing this."

"What reason would that be?"

"This is how we do it," Henning says and waits until he has Grønningen's undivided attention. "I tell you everything you want to know about me and why I'm here, and then you tell me what you know about your friend's case. I'm interested in anyone who knew Tore. Who they were and what they stood for."

Grønningen directs his dark brown eyes at a floral arrangement on one of the console tables.

"I don't snitch on my mates," he says in a mournful voice that suggests he has just betrayed a lifelong principle.

"I'm not asking you to. All you have to do is tell me a bit about Tore and how he got on with his friends, how they treated each other. You don't have to talk about what they got up to if you don't want to. And just to make it clear: I'm only interested in this story. If I should stumble across anything else while I'm sniffing around, I'll leave it alone."

Henning is surprised when he realizes that he actually means it.

Many seconds pass without Grønningen saying anything. At regular intervals he looks at Henning before his gaze breaks away. The waiter comes over to their table. Grønningen orders a Wiener schnitzel with extra potatoes and vegetables. When the waiter has gone, Henning leans across the table.

"My son died," he says, and a lump forms instantly in his throat. "I tried to rescue him from my flat. Somebody set fire to it."

Henning tries to swallow.

"Tore says that he knows something about what happened that day. He has promised to tell me what it is—if I help him. That's the only reward I'm looking for. I'll do anything to make

Tore tell me what he knows. No matter what that is or where it takes me."

He pauses for effect. Grønningen stares pensively at the table.

"And it's fine if you don't want to help me help your friend. But I promise you, Geir, I'm not going to go away. Not now, not ever."

Henning notices that his voice is trembling. Even so Grønningen remains silent.

"You don't happen to know something, do you?" Henning continues after a pause.

"Eh?"

"About the fire in my flat?"

"Me?"

"Yes, you—given that you and Tore are such close friends. If Tore knows something then it's not inconceivable that he might have told you."

"He didn't."

Henning concentrates on Grønningen's eyes. At the table farther away a family erupts in a collective giggling fit. Grønningen quickly turns in their direction before resuming his study of the napkin in front of him. He picks it up and spreads it out.

"How was he?" he asks.

"Tore? I don't know. I've never met him so I don't know what he was like before. And I didn't speak to him for very long."

"I haven't spoken to him for a long time."

"Why not?"

"He's only allowed one visit a week and Veronica gets first pick. That's all they've got, the two of them, so the rest of us tend to leave them alone."

Henning refrains from saying anything for a while. He senses that Grønningen has started to open up.

"It has been difficult to talk about Tore since he went to

prison," he says. "Nobody really wants to and in a way we've put it behind us. I've tried to find out where everyone was the night that Jocke Brolenius was killed, but people were either with each other or they were out of town."

Henning nods.

"But you knew that Tore was meeting Jocke Brolenius?"

"Yes, several of us did. He came to the gym to work out before he drove up to the old factory."

Henning picks up a jug on the table and fills his glass with water. He looks at Grønningen to see if he wants some and Grønningen holds out his glass without nodding.

"Can you describe Tore to me?" Henning asks as he pours the water. "I mean from a friend's perspective?"

Grønningen sighs and starts to reminisce. Suddenly he breaks into a smile.

"The first time I met Tore, he punched me in the face."

"Why?" Henning asks, mirroring his smile.

"Because I had just put Tore's cousin in hospital for chatting up my girlfriend. Petter was just a boy then, so Tore had to step in. He broke my jaw."

Grønningen touches his face and briefly strokes the beard that decorates his chin.

"When I came to, he squatted down in front of me and said: *I look after my own. I just want you to remember that.*"

"And from then on you were best mates?" Henning asks in disbelief.

"Well, not straight away. But he saw that I had what it took and that's why he recruited me for—"

"The enforcer business?"

"Call it what you will. He put me up for the odd job here and there. In time we grew to be best mates even though there were lots of contenders for that role."

"How come?" Henning asks and sips his water.

"Tore was a popular guy. And he was feared as well. Being

around Tore gave you a certain status. Everyone looked up to him. He got whatever he wanted. And I'm not just thinking of his job, but . . . other things."

"What things?"

"One day we were watching some reality TV show when Veronica appeared on the screen. And Tore said: *"I want her!"* And that's what happened."

Henning twirls the glass in his hands.

"And did he get whatever he wanted in the property business, too?"

"Yes, on the whole."

"Did he have any enemies in the property business?"

"I'm sure he did, but I doubt if any of them would have gone to so much trouble to get rid of him. It would have been simpler just to have him killed."

That sounds very reasonable, Henning thinks. Tore's meeting with Jocke Brolenius was an internal affair that had nothing to do with his legitimate business activities.

"I understand Tore met with some resistance when you discussed what to do about the murder of Vidar Fjell?"

"Not just some."

"Who shouted the loudest?"

Henning folds his hands and leans closer.

"Irene Otnes. Vidar's girlfriend. She made it clear that she wanted revenge and there was no shortage of volunteers. Petter was one of them. But Tore put his foot down. All hell would have broken loose if we had picked a fight with a Swedish gang."

"Was anyone apart from Irene Otnes out for blood?"

"We all were."

"I mean was anyone especially incensed and did they express their anger or disgust at Tore because he *didn't* want revenge?"

Grønningen mulls over the question.

"Robert."

"Who is he?"

"Robert van Derksen. A martial arts instructor. He was a good mate of Vidar, but Tore and Robert weren't exactly best mates. Or they weren't then."

"Why not?"

Grønningen breathes out.

"One night, three or four years ago, we went to the opening of Order @ The Bar in the city center. Veronica was there with some of her models. Free drinks. You know what these events are like."

"Robert helped himself—quite liberally you could say—and I'm not just talking about the drinks. It looked as if he thought the girls were free, too. Tore didn't like Robert pawing Veronica's girls and told him to lay off—for all the good that did—and when Tore took him outside to cool down a little later, Robert tried to hit him. Tore saw the punch coming a week in advance."

Henning raises an eyebrow.

"Didn't you just say that van Derksen was a martial arts instructor?"

"Yes, but he was shit-faced that night. When he sobered up and heard what had happened he felt humiliated. Things between the two of them were never the same again."

"So Robert van Derksen had a motive for killing Jocke Brolenius *and* setting Tore Pulli up?"

"Yes."

"But could he have broken Brolenius's jaw? In the style of Pulli?"

"Yes, definitely," Grønningen replies without hesitation before he adds: "It's not that difficult. All it takes is a bit of practice."

17

Henning decides to walk home from Åkebergveien, an exercise usually conducive to thinking. And he has much to digest after his meetings with Veronica Nansen and Geir Grønningen, especially the information Grønningen gave him about Robert van Derksen. According to Grønningen, van Derksen claimed to be with a woman on the night that Brolenius was killed, although Grønningen was ashamed to admit that he had never double-checked his alibi. Van Derksen had a habit of replacing his women frequently and Grønningen hadn't been able to remember which particular woman he had been with at the time. *And I'm not sure that Robert would be able to remember either,* as he put it.

When Henning comes home he visits hardenever.no and finds a picture of Robert van Derksen showing off an oiled torso, a six-pack, and rippling muscles in his arms and legs posing in combat style. Henning reads about the courses he teaches—karate, tae kwon do, and krav maga—and realizes that he can't simply turn up on van Derksen's doorstep and ask if he murdered Jocke Brolenius. He could sign up for one of the courses and ask if van Derksen would teach him the Pulli punch, but such questions rely on familiarity and trust. And both take time—which Henning doesn't have.

There must be another way, he thinks and rings the contact number listed at the bottom of the screen.

"Hi, my name is Henning Juul from the Internet newspaper, 123news. Am I speaking to Robert van Derksen?"

"You are," van Derksen replies, sounding bored. His voice is lighter than Henning had expected, bordering on meek.

"Sorry for disturbing you on a Sunday, but I'm working on

a story about Tore Pulli. I understand that the two of you knew each other well?"

There is silence.

"I've got nothing to say about Tore."

"You don't need to say anything about Tore," Henning is quick to add, scared that van Derksen might hang up on him. "I'm more interested in the murder of Jocke Brolenius. I think there may have been a miscarriage of justice and that Tore might be innocent," Henning continues. The seconds pass.

"Why do you think that?"

Henning waits a few more moments before he replies: "Because certain things in the case against him don't make sense. The murder weapon has never been found, for one. And if Tore really wanted to kill someone, I don't think he would have left his calling card behind at the crime scene."

Another silence.

"What do you mean?"

"The Pulli punch," Henning continues, feeling himself warming to his subject. "Brolenius's fractured jaw. I think that someone with strong fists wanted it to look as if Tore killed Jocke Brolenius."

Henning lets his words take effect. Many long seconds of silence follow.

"Are you still there?" he asks, eventually.

"You need to call someone else," van Derksen says. "I've got nothing to say to you."

And the line goes dead.

Henning looks at his mobile as if it could tell him why van Derksen went from being interested to cutting him off. Perhaps he got nervous? Henning thinks. Or perhaps he just didn't want to talk to a journalist?

Henning reviews the information he has obtained during the day. It's a fair amount. But he still can't work out how Pulli knew that he was back at work. As far as Henning is aware, prison inmates don't have Internet access. Did someone tell Pulli? In which case who could it have been? Neither Veronica Nansen nor Geir Grønningen gave the impression of ever having heard of Henning before.

Henning googles his own and Tore Pulli's name on the Internet, but finds only stories he wrote years ago. Henning pulls a face. Something doesn't add up, he thinks. His reputation is not of sufficient caliber for an inmate with whom he has never spoken to call him up out of the blue to ask for his help. There are private investigators who would happily take on this kind of work and Pulli has enough money to pay them. Henning types the words "private investigator" and googles it with Pulli's name, but he isn't rewarded with helpful hits this time, either.

Given that a reward of one million kroner is on the table, there can only be two reasons why no one has come forward with information that could free Pulli. Either the real killer is so smart he hasn't aroused even the slightest suspicion among his own people, or Tore Pulli is guilty and is merely putting on a show.

Henning butters a slice of crisp bread and eats it while he walks up and down the living room. His eyes stop at the dark brown piano. As always the lid is closed. He doesn't want to look at it, at everything it represents. But then he hears Veronica Nansen's voice. He takes one hesitant step toward the piano before he pauses. Then he takes another toward the piano stool. He pulls it out. Slowly, he sits down and visualizes the keys trapped under the lid, tempting ebony and ivory.

He opens the lid with great care. His stomach lurches just at the sight of the keys. Silently, he folds back the lid as his eyes glide from side to side. He remembers how his fingers used to run off, finding their own ways and following any path they liked, repeating movements and sequences until slowly but surely they formed wider roads in an increasingly familiar terrain. He loved how the tone colored the walls, how the sound and its resonance opened up parallel worlds the moment he closed his eyes.

Henning places his fingers on G7, one of his favorite chords; he didn't know that's what it was until he pressed the same keys on a digital piano many years ago, an instrument that was hooked up to a computer, and the name came up on the screen. He has learned the names of his favorite chords Cm7 and Eb7(B5), chords that cry out to be followed by pure tones. But he was searching for contrasts, exploring the relationship between harmony and discord, believing that something pure and right would emerge out of the dissonance and the friction, something that would grow stronger and transform even disharmony into harmony. Often he would hit random keys until he stumbled across something he liked, something to which he could add side chords and compose a melody around.

Now he barely hears the tones, not to begin with, but they grow, they force their way inside him and compel him to listen, to let the notes resonate, and he gets a strong urge to strike them down again so they can lift him up and away from time and space, but his fingers seize up, he is unable to lift them, and gradually every note in the chord blends with the others to create a mélange of sound that vibrates and cascades. Soon all that is left is chaos, which quietly dies away.

Henning retracts his hands with effort. He realizes he hasn't been breathing for a while. Then he closes the lid.

18

Monday morning Henning hangs up his jacket at the office and looks at Iver Gundersen's face. As always it displays traces of the night before. The bags under his eyes are puffy. His cheeks and chin are unshaven even though some areas show evidence of a razor. His long hair falls like a fringed scarf over his shoulders. The fibers on the elbows of his cord jacket are frayed.

Henning nods quickly in Iver's direction, thinking he can detect a hint of Nora's moisturizer across the table. Damn coconut.

"Good weekend?" Iver says without looking at Henning.

"It was all right."

Henning registers a nod, but doesn't feel the need to reciprocate. He sits down, turns on his computer, puts down his mobile, removes some papers from his desk, and types in his username and password. Other journalists start to arrive. Henning hears sleepy grunts, chitchat, someone laughs. He has no idea how he will be able to concentrate on work today.

He only managed a few hours' shut-eye before going to the office. His sleep was fitful and he woke up with a pounding headache that has yet to release its grip on him. However, he managed to do some research last night that he hopes will be useful during the day. The question is simply when.

"Coffee?"

Iver gets up. Henning shakes his head even though he quite fancies a cup of coffee. Iver lingers for a moment before he hurries to join the queue, occasionally stealing a glance at the national news section where Henning is sitting. He looks away whenever Henning looks back at him.

Henning remembers how Iver, in the weeks that followed the Henriette Hagerup story, was very happy to accept pats on the back when he didn't think Henning was watching. But his smug and self-satisfied facade disappeared whenever Henning entered his field of vision. Iver's eyes took on an unfathomable expression. Gratitude, possibly, mixed with guilt and a kind of shame because Henning knew the real truth. And for that very reason there was also irritation and even resentment. Ever since Iver returned from his holidays, they have only exchanged small talk, but Henning senses that something unspoken hangs in the air between them.

"The Eagle is in a bad mood today," Iver says when he comes back.

"Who is?"

"Heidi. She dropped by earlier."

"Right."

The Eagle, Henning thinks. Good nickname. He clicks on the publishing tool and opens some websites.

"Are you ready for the morning meeting?" Iver asks as he sits down.

"I've tried and tried, Mrs. Blom."

Iver quickly presses some buttons on his mobile before he puts it down. He stares vacantly into space before he suddenly turns to Henning.

"Who the hell is Mrs. Blom?"

Henning meets Iver's puzzled face.

"I keep hearing people talk about her, but I've no idea who she is. I doubt that anyone does."

"Why—because you don't?"

"No," Iver says a little shamefaced. "But nowadays people use all these expressions without knowing what they really mean or where they come from. Once in a blue moon. Fit as a fiddle. Not on my nelly. I've tried and tried, Mrs. Blom. I find it really quite irritating."

Henning looks briefly at Iver before he says:

"It's a term intended to express moderation or reservation."

"Yes, I get that, obviously. But who is Mrs. Blom?"

Again there is silence between the desks.

"It's a line from *Carousel*," Henning says, reluctantly.

"Eh?"

"It's a comedy by Alex Brinchmann. There is no mention of a Mrs. Blom in the script, but the actor Per Aabel ad-libbed during rehearsals. And it stayed in."

Iver sips his coffee.

"That's all there is to it, seriously?" he says, sounding incredulous as he turns his mug in his hands.

"That depends entirely on how you look at it. Do you want me to go through the other expressions?"

Iver stares at Henning for a long time, initially with amazement, until he realizes that Henning isn't joking. Iver looks at his watch.

"We haven't got time," he says, getting up. "The Eagle awaits."

19

Entering the TV2 building in the middle of Karl Johansgate, Oslo's main street, has always instilled in Thorleif Brenden a feeling of being part of something important. It has nothing to do with the size of the building; it is the knowledge of all those people working in one place toward a common goal, and yet in fierce competition with each other. He feels proud when he nods to the receptionist, when he swipes his staff card through the reader with practiced ease and enters the lift, greeting producers, editors, reporters, and anyone else there with the same purpose: creating programs that will enlighten or entertain the people of Norway.

Thorleif remembers his first weeks working for TV2 and how he would look at everyone, surreptitiously, to see if he recognized them. And he did, of course. Everywhere. Glamorous TV personality Dorte Skappel, without makeup and in jeans. Journalist Oddvar Stenstrøm, for once not wagging his finger at a hapless guest. News anchor Pål T. Jørgensen, just as well-groomed off camera as he is on. Everyone who was anyone was there. And they were all normal people.

Thorleif began his TV2 career in 2000 after nearly five years of studying in the U.S., where he obtained a bachelor's degree in film and TV and started a master's in documentary filmmaking, which he never completed. He much preferred working to writing even though he has always enjoyed the latter. For a man with his background, getting a foot in the door at TV2 was fairly easy. The corporation always needed freelancers with his skills, and to begin with he worked thirty days every month. Even in February—or at least that was how it felt. In the end he had to slow down. It wasn't a realistic long-term plan, especially after he started seeing Elisabeth. And certainly not once Pål was born.

In 2002 he covered someone's leave of absence and he was offered a full-time employment contract the following year. Since then, he has worked for various departments within the corporation to avoid doing the same thing every day. However, he mostly works for the news desk. He has been to Afghanistan, Iraq, Chechnya, and several African countries—places where history is being written. He has helped tell their stories, risking his life on occasions. The trip to Kenya in 2008 was a particularly bad time.

It was just after the election. Several hundred Kikuyu had sought refuge in a church in the town of Eldoret because no one could make up their mind who had won. A furious mob set fire to the church and between fifty and one hundred people were killed, many of them children. Anyone who tried to escape was hacked to death with machetes.

Thorleif was working on the day it happened and the international news editor decided that TV2 should cover the situation because it was starting to look like another Rwanda. Accompanied by the seasoned war correspondent Frode Greverud, Thorleif packed his camera and sound equipment and set off. Having landed in Nairobi, they traveled to Eldoret the next day. They could only travel during daylight because it was impossible to know what or who you might bump into at night.

They had talked to local people and the Red Cross in advance and learned where it was safe to go, but on their way to Eldoret they came across a bus of refugees. Thorleif and Greverud stopped and decided to make a feature about them. This delayed them by forty-five minutes, which meant they didn't reach Eldoret before sunset. Three kilometers from the town the darkness was total. Either side of the road were lines of narrow, rickety houses. Suddenly they saw that the road had been deliberately blocked with hundreds of rocks. It was impossible to drive through.

Twenty to twenty-five men approached their car with

gleaming machetes. Thorleif looked at Greverud, a man with years of experience in areas torn apart by conflict. He didn't know what they should do, either. They were unable to drive on or reverse. The driver they had hired for the trip was black, but fortunately he was from a neutral tribe, otherwise he and possibly they, too, would have been hacked to death.

The men let them pass and the next day they visited the church. There they spoke to two young men who claimed to have witnessed the massacre. Thorleif and Greverud didn't notice anyone approaching, but soon found themselves surrounded by twenty locals. Foreign visitors were exotic; the cameras and microphones were attracting attention.

Suddenly they heard a gunshot. Then another and another. The bullets whizzed over their heads. Total panic broke out. Greverud signaled to Thorleif that they had to get out of there, but there were only two dirt roads, one leading directly toward the shooter while the other would take them farther into the bush. The men they had been interviewing ran that way. Greverud pulled Thorleif into the car where they took cover.

But the gunman came closer. For a few frantic seconds they sat as if frozen in the front of the car. Should they drive in the direction of the shooter or follow the people being shot at? They decided to drive toward the gunman, make themselves known to him, show him that they were white. When the car was only a couple of meters from the gunman, he stopped. They saw that he was carrying a Norwegian AG-3 battle rifle, of all things. There was no chance of escape. Thorleif was convinced he was about to die. It would take the gunman three seconds to shoot them down. Possibly not even that.

But rather than kill them, he crouched down behind their car. Thorleif filmed the gunman as he shot at the men they had just been interviewing, footage that was broadcast on TV2 later that day. The shooting was a personal vendetta by a soldier from another tribe. But the fear of death which overcame

Thorleif when he thought the gunman was going to kill them was impossible to describe. He has tried since using pen and paper and in conversation with others, but he has never succeeded. It happened so quickly. Once when he was young he was in a car that aquaplaned on the motorway at a hundred fifteen kilometers an hour. Three seconds later the car had come to a standstill with broken windows in a thicket of bushes and trees. Nor had he on that occasion managed to think anything at all before the crisis was over.

Later that day in Eldoret, Greverud and Thorleif visited a hospital where they filmed a man who had had half his face destroyed in an acid attack. "Show the world," he said. "Show people what is happening here." And it's moments like that when Thorleif understands the value of his work. Its importance. To uncover cruelty, draw attention to it, expose it to the world so that the global community can take action.

Not long afterward two Nobel Peace Prize winners visited the area to broker a cease-fire. The conflict was resolved. It was unlikely to be as a result of the footage Thorleif had shot, but it might have contributed to saving some lives. Shortly after returning to Norway he went to Parliament to interview opposition politicians who were unhappy about the state of Norwegian roads and he felt like throwing up.

Today probably won't involve a trip to Eldoret, Thorleif thinks as he takes a seat at one of the vacant workstations in the technical department on the second floor. None of the producers or photo editors is there. A quiet day in the office is not to be sniffed at.

Thorleif goes on the intranet and finds DeskPlanner to see if anyone has booked him for a job today. At the moment it looks quiet, but he knows things can change without notice.

"Hi, Toffe."

Thorleif turns around. Guri Palme strolls into the room with her trademark elegant ease. It's as if the room expands.

She always has an infectious, rather seductive smile on her face. Palme looks around.

"I was actually looking for Reinertsen, but—"

"I've just come in," Thorleif says. "I haven't seen him yet."

"No? Perhaps you could come on a job with me?"

"Certainly. What's it about?"

"Nothing fancy, we're just visiting a solicitor who is working from home today. But we need to leave in fifteen minutes."

"Okay. Will you be needing anything specific for the recording?"

"No. And anyway, you always have the coolest sound and camera equipment so—"

Thorleif smiles, watches her go over to the watercooler and press a button that releases a plastic cup. Her blue jeans fit snugly around her ankles and thighs. Her jacket only covers half her bottom so that he can just about make out what it conceals. The art of suggestion. Guri Palme masters it.

"Listen, you might know how to go about this," Thorleif says, swiveling around on his chair so that he is looking directly at her.

"What?"

"You've been a crime reporter for a while. Have you ever needed to identify a car registration number?"

"Yes, I have. Lots of times. Why?"

Thorleif hesitates.

"I'm just curious."

"You can send the number to a text-based service, but I can't remember their number off the top of my head. Anyway, it might be easier to go on the website for Brønnøysund Register Centre."

"Please, would you show me?"

"Sure," she smiles and marches over to him. Thorleif rolls his chair aside to make room for her. As Palme leans over the keyboard her blond hair falls forward, but she tucks the tresses behind her ears so they don't obstruct her view. She smells of something lovely. Thorleif doesn't know if it's her shampoo or perfume. Not that it matters. It's a good smell.

"Here you go," Palme says, turning to face him. "You type in the number in that field there," she says, pointing at the screen. "Then you press *enter* and abracadabra you'll get a page with information about the car."

"Wow," he says. "That's brilliant. Thank you so much."

"No problem. But make sure you're ready. Fifteen minutes."

"Okay. I'll meet you in the car park."

Palme disappears, but the scent of her lingers behind. Summer sky and meadows, he thinks. What a woman.

He ends his reverie to focus on the task in hand. He remembers the registration number of the annoying BMW and types it in, then he presses enter. A new window opens. He reads:

As of 27.09.2009 the following liabilities were registered in respect of vehicle registration number BR 65607: Security for unpaid balance of the purchase of the motor vehicle. NOK 763,910.00. Click on the date for further information about liabilities.

Thorleif clicks on the date.

Submitted by 1134291 DNB Bank Car Financing
  Loans Administration Department, PO Box 7125
  5020 BERGEN

Relating to person/business:
  Ravndal, Anthon
  Bekkestuveien 13a
  1357 Bekkestua

"Anthon Ravndal," Thorleif says and looks up the man's telephone number. "Good to know."

20

"**Your** turn, Henning."

He looks up and meets the sharp eyes of national news editor Heidi Kjus. Henning hasn't noticed it until now, but Heidi has had a haircut. Short and modern, though he doesn't really know why he thinks it looks modern—how would he know? And for once her makeup doesn't look like war paint.

"Eh?"

"What about you? What's in your notebook today? We have been through Iver, Rita, and Jørgen. You were paying attention, weren't you?"

"Of course."

"What have you got for us today?"

Henning looks down at the notebook he brought with him to the meeting mainly for show. The top sheet is blank. He considered writing down Tore Pulli's name, but decided it wasn't an obvious story. Not yet.

"Well, I'm not really sure," he begins.

There is silence all around him. The eyes of everyone in the meeting room make the skin on his forehead tingle.

"There's not much happening at the moment."

"So nothing for us today, either, Henning?" Heidi Kjus asks.

"It's very quiet out there. It has been an uneventful summer."

Kjus looks at him over the rim of her glasses and pushes them further up her nose. He hasn't noticed the glasses until now, either.

"I'm aware of it," she says. "But then you have to go out and find the news. We can't just sit here hoping for stories to drop into our laps. We need to chase them. Talk to people. Our circulation has been lousy this summer."

"It always is."

"Yes, but—"

"I have an appointment later today," he continues and takes a sip of his coffee. "I'm meeting a source."

It's the oldest reporter excuse in the book, but it usually works.

"Which story is this?"

"I can't tell you anything at this stage."

Heidi interrupts herself at the beginning of a sentence.

"What did you just say?"

"If I get what I'm hoping for from my source, it could turn into a story. But until then I'm keeping my mouth shut."

"Just so," Heidi says, offended, and shakes her head almost imperceptibly, but enough for everyone around the table to register it. She draws a long hard line under Henning's name on her sheet. "Then you're on cuttings duty until further notice."

Henning's jaw drops.

"Cuttings duty?"

"Yes. You know what cuttings duty is, don't you?"

"Yes. Of course I do."

"There's no one from the cuttings team here today. Ill health, holiday, blah blah. Plus Egil is taking time off in lieu. I'll send you NTB's list shortly, Henning, and the list of today's stories to everyone else."

Henning sees that Iver is grinning from ear to ear.

"Quick, quick," Heidi says, making get-out-of-here gestures with her hands. "I'm off to an editors' meeting and half the day has gone already."

Chairs are pushed back and they stand up. Henning is the last to leave. "Cuttings," he mutters to himself. Lucky me. Another time he might have kicked up a fuss or spent a minute or two before the meeting inventing a story, a follow-up—anything—to give Heidi the impression he was busy. But cuttings duty is practically a no-brainer. He can spend the time between cutting and pasting stories doing further research on Tore Pulli and the people around him. Henning knows he has barely scratched the surface.

21

The secretary's friendly smile reaches all the way down the handset. Henning thanks her and waits for her to route the call through the switchboard at the offices of Johnsen, Urne & Olsvik. Henning has been there before, but now that Heidi has put him on cuttings duty, he doesn't have the time to visit Frode Olsvik, Pulli's solicitor, in person.

He produces two stories during the first two hours of his day at the office, one about bad weather hampering the search for survivors after a plane crash in Pakistan, which has so far claimed the lives of one hundred fifty-eight people, and a brief eight-liner about four men charged with the gang rape of a woman in a basement flat in Nordstrand last weekend. News agency stories all of them. Henning forgets all about them when Olsvik's well-upholstered voice winds its way down his mobile. Henning introduces himself.

"Good morning, Juul."

"Hi. Do you remember me?"

"I do," the lawyer says and clears his throat. Frode Olsvik is a defense lawyer who would have fit right into an episode of *LA Law* in the late eighties. He wears tailor-made suits, suspenders, and treats his guests to a large selection of single malt whiskeys from crystal carafes in his drawing room. But despite working long hours he appears to have both a happy wife and well-adjusted children. The latter is something Henning snapped up from other crime reporters who are Facebook friends of Olsvik.

"My condolences," he says. "I heard about your son. How are you?"

"Thank you, I'm not too bad."

"I saw that you had returned to work."

"Where did you see that?"

Olsvik laughs.

"Even though I don't have much time for your paper, I do occasionally socialize with your boss. It's nothing personal, you understand."

"Perfectly. Can you spare a minute?"

"One, yes, but no more. My next client is due shortly."

"Okay, I'll try to be brief. It's about Tore Pulli. How long is it until his appeal will be heard?"

"Let me have a look—"

Fingers leaf through a diary.

"We're starting next week. Why? Are you planning a feature on him?"

"I don't know to be honest. But could I ask you a question first, please? Off the record, did he do it?"

Olsvik laughs out loud.

"You know very well I can't answer that question, Juul."

"Haven't you ever asked him?"

"I never ask my clients that question. They are legally entitled to a good defense whether they're guilty or not."

"But Pulli claims that he is innocent and that he was set up?"

"He does."

"What do you think about that?"

"What do I think about that?"

"You must have met some villains in your time. Many of them must have assured you that they were innocent and most of them would have been lying through their teeth. Given Pulli's past, then—"

"I can't discuss that with you, Juul," Olsvik cuts him off.

"Okay, fair enough," Henning replies. "What's Pulli's explanation as to why his fingerprints were found on the knuckleduster?"

Olsvik delays his reply for a few seconds.

"Haven't you read the verdict?"

"No, I . . . I haven't gotten that far yet."

Another silence.

"Well. It was Tore's knuckle-duster. His old one."

"Which he used when he was an enforcer?"

"Yes. He claims that someone must have stolen it."

"When?"

"He doesn't know."

"But it was his knuckle-duster that was used during the attack?"

"Yes. Traces of Brolenius's skin and beard were found on it."

Henning thinks about this and he grabs a pen by the notebook without quite knowing why. Heidi appears from around the corner. Henning lowers his voice.

"The murder weapon was never found. What was Pulli's explanation for that?"

"Pulli thinks it's inconceivable that the prosecutor would believe that he would hide the murder weapon elsewhere only to return to the crime scene later. That was one of the reasons why we appealed the verdict immediately."

Henning ponders this.

"Will you be introducing any new evidence for the appeal? Information that wasn't available the first time around?"

"Not at the moment. Juul—I have to go—"

"Just one last quick question if I may, Olsvik."

Olsvik sighs theatrically before agreeing.

"Has your client ever spoken to you about . . . about me?"

"About you?"

"Yes?"

"Why would he do that?"

"I don't know. But has he ever done so?"

"Eh, no. Not that I can remember."

"Has he ever mentioned my son?"

"Your son? No," Olsvik says. "Why do you ask that, Juul?"

A clammy, lonely feeling overwhelms him.

"Forget I asked. I was just curious."

22

Henning informs Heidi before he leaves for the police station. On his way he calls Pia Nøkleby. She is by no means the only assistant commissioner at the police station, but he has had more contact with Nøkleby than anyone else there since his return to work.

"Hi, Pia, it's Henning Juul."

"Hi, Henning."

"Do you have a couple of minutes?"

It takes a while before she replies: "Yes, I think so. What's it about?"

"Would you come outside, please?"

"Outside where?"

"Out on the grass. I'm outside the station."

This is a lie, he hasn't gotten there yet, but it will take her some time to get down from the fifth floor.

"Now?"

"Yes, please. I'm bored standing here on my own even though the weather is nice."

Another pause.

"I'm due in a meeting very shortly, but—"

"I've bought you an ice cream."

Lie number two.

"Have you now? But I'm on a diet."

"On a diet? You?"

"Ha-ha."

Henning laughs even though he knows it sounds false.

"Okay, give me a couple of minutes. I feel in need of a break."

"I'm on the bench to your left as you come out. Hurry up, your ice cream is melting."

"Yes, all right, I'm on my way."

Nøkleby walks briskly past a group of smokers occupying their usual spot a short distance from the main entrance. A blue cloud of cigarette smoke rises toward the sun. Henning waves when he sees her.

As always the assistant commissioner is in uniform and her sunglasses emphasize her bone structure. Henning hasn't noticed it before, but she is actually rather attractive. Distinctive cheekbones, not too defined, just enough to endow her face with shape and character. When she comes closer, he sees that her skin is unblemished and lightly tanned. She has no bags under her eyes though he knows how hard she works. Her dark hair is cut short over her ears and neck and combed into a neat side parting to the left without a fringe to block her view. Her glossy hair has a touch of auburn. She fills out the uniform, not too much, but not too little, either.

Nøkleby sits down next to him.

"Hi, Henning."

"Hi."

He hands her the ice cream, strawberry soft ice in a cup he bought in a kiosk across the road.

"I took a wild guess that you liked strawberry."

"All girls like strawberry," she says and smiles.

Henning watches her rip off the cellophane from the spoon that comes with it. She raises the cup to him.

"Thank you very much."

"Don't mention it."

"Are you trying to bribe me?"

"Yes. Is it working?"

"Let me taste the ice cream first and then I'll tell you."

Henning smiles again as he watches her scoop out the soft ice. She swallows a mouthful and closes her eyes.

"Not bad. Not bad at all."

Henning laughs. Nøkleby raises her eyes toward the avenue that leads up to Oslo Prison.

"I presume you haven't come here just to eat ice cream?"

Henning takes a bite of his own ice cream.

"I've started looking into the case of Tore Pulli," he says and swallows. Nøkleby eats another spoonful and looks at him.

"There was evidence at the crime scene indicating that Pulli did it while other clues pointed elsewhere. I'm just curious: did you consider other suspects?"

Nøkleby smiles indulgently.

"We didn't just find one piece of evidence and build the case on that alone—if that's what you're implying."

"It wouldn't be the first time."

"Not since I've been here." Nøkleby licks her lips and puts down her ice cream.

"Some of Tore's friends wouldn't agree with you. They go as far as to claim that the police have been hunting Tore for years."

"Hunting?"

"Yes, trying to frame him."

"For God's sake," she scoffs. "Anyone who says that has been watching too many American movies. The police in Norway don't frame people, Henning."

"The press regularly bring stories about substandard police work, inappropriate charges, evidence going missing, being planted even—in some cases. Do you really think it's that strange that people in the street don't have total faith in the ethical and moral integrity of today's law enforcers? That some people might think that a case such as Pulli's is as much about face-saving as it is about the truth?"

Nøkleby doesn't reply. Her arms are folded across her chest. The color of her cheeks has darkened. For a while they watch the green area outside the police station. Near the pavement a man is pushing a lawnmower up and down.

"It wasn't my intention to criticize you, Pia," Henning says after a long pause.

"No, I know."

"Pulli called the police himself, didn't he?"

"Yes."

"And you trawled the neighborhood looking for the murder weapon?"

"Obviously."

"Why did Pulli return to the crime scene to call the police?"

"Probably because he couldn't find his knuckle-duster."

Henning looks at her for a long time.

"Do you think that sounds convincing?"

"No, not totally convincing, but plausible. I'm perfectly aware that a man like Tore Pulli realized that he would have a problem explaining himself after killing Jocke Brolenius. It was widely known that he had asked Brolenius for a meeting. That's why he concealed the most important piece of evidence against him, the murder weapon, before coming up with this conspiracy theory that someone stole his knuckle-duster and gave Brolenius a Pulli punch to fit him up for something he hadn't done."

"You're forgetting that Pulli tried to prevent Brolenius from getting killed in the first place."

"Yes, I've heard that story, too. It could have been his plan all along, getting people to testify that he had been working to avert a bloodbath so we were more likely to buy his conspiracy theory."

"But you didn't."

"No."

"Something of a gamble, I must say."

"You may be right. But you're forgetting that Brolenius very likely killed Pulli's friend. No one can convince me that Tore Pulli didn't want revenge."

Henning nods quietly.

"And there's one more thing: during his initial interviews Tore Pulli claimed that he turned up at the factory exactly at the agreed time of eleven o'clock that night and that Brolenius was already dead when he arrived. But Pulli didn't call the police to report the death for another nineteen minutes. So tell me this: Does it take nineteen minutes to discover a body and call the police or does it take nineteen minutes to kill someone, conceal the murder weapon, and then return to the crime scene to pick up anything you may have forgotten?"

Henning doesn't respond immediately.

"But in that case why call the police at all?"

"Because he had come to the conclusion that showing his hand was his best chance of getting off. He knew he would be our prime suspect. But nobody bought his story."

Nøkleby gets up.

"Pulli did it, Henning."

Henning doesn't reply.

"I've got to get back," Nøkleby continues. "If you're going to write about this, I want copy approval if you quote me. You haven't made any notes."

He nods.

"Thanks for the ice cream," she says. "It was really good."

"And quite sickly."

She smiles, waves, and walks away. Henning gets up, too. He shakes his foot, which has gone to sleep, and watches her stride toward the entrance at a brisk pace. He notices with a certain degree of fascination that he likes what he sees.

23

On his way back to the newspaper, Henning reviews his conversation with Pia Nøkleby. She has a point. If Pulli is adamant that he arrived at the factory at the agreed-upon time, he has a problem explaining the nineteen minutes. Henning wonders if he can trust him at all.

He gets himself a cup of coffee, sits down by his desk, and starts thinking about Vidar Fjell. Who was he really?

Henning finds out that Vidar Fjell's parents, Linda and Erik, live in Lillestrøm. Erik is a professor in Nordic studies and works at the University of Oslo, but he can find no information about Linda other than a home telephone number, which she shares with her husband. A rusty female voice answers after a few rings.

"Hello, it's Henning Juul from the Internet newspaper 123news. Can I have a few minutes of your time?"

"That depends," she replies with that buttoned-up, brusque voice that many people switch to the moment they realize they are speaking to a journalist.

"It's about your son."

There is silence.

"Why are you writing about Vidar? Now?"

"I don't know yet. I'm working on a story where Vidar's name keeps cropping up. I—"

"What kind of story?"

"Tore Pulli's appeal."

Linda Fjell snorts.

"Vidar is dead. That's bad enough without you journalists bringing it up all the time."

"I—"

"I don't want to talk about Vidar," she interrupts him sharply.

"What about your husband then? Is he at home?"

"No," she replies swiftly.

Henning can hear that she is about to hang up.

"I'm sorry to call you about this," he says quickly. "I don't know you and I don't know your husband. But I know how you feel. I've lost a child myself."

There is silence. Henning closes his eyes, tries to will away the images that surface whenever he mentions Jonas. Scenes he never saw but which he can't stop imagining.

"I know what it's like," he says gently. "And nothing helps."

He can hear her breathing, heavy and tortured.

"So how do you manage?" Linda Fjell asks him after a pause.

Henning is incapable of replying straight away.

"Who says I'm managing?" he whispers, finally.

When he continues his voice is soft and slow.

"But I try to make my boy as alive as I can. For me that means thinking about him as often as I can bear it. I talk about him when I get the chance. And I talk to him sometimes—even if it's just inside my head. If I don't do that then I might as well be dead, too. I still draw breath just to keep the memory of him alive. It deserves that. And he deserves it.

Neither of them says anything for a while. Henning feels in need of a shower.

"Is it okay if I ask you some questions about Vidar?"

Linda Fjell heaves a sigh.

"Okay," she sniffs.

"Good. Thank you so much."

"I don't really know what you want to know, but—"

"Perhaps you could begin by telling me something about your son?"

"Ah."

"Perhaps we could start with the place where he worked," Henning says to help her get started. "His gym."

"Fighting Fit," she says, proudly. "It was the apple of his eye. He did everything himself, almost. He was never tempted to sell out to a chain or anything like that. No, not Vidar. He always wanted to do things his way, ever since he was little. Did you know that his gym was a place where young people who had been in trouble could work out?"

"Yes, I knew that."

"Vidar practically dragged them in off the street. At his funeral they were queuing all the way out to the cemetery. There wasn't room enough in the church. Vidar had so many friends."

Henning can hear how she grows with every word.

"Did he have a lot of close friends, too?"

"Yes, he did."

Linda Fjell reels off the names Henning was expecting to hear. Robert van Derksen, Geir Grønningen, Petter Holte, Kent Harry Hansen. But not Tore Pulli. Henning asks if Tore was one of Vidar's close friends.

"No."

"Pardon me for asking," he says after a short pause. "But how do you know that?"

"Because real friends are there for each other."

"And Tore wasn't?"

"No."

"In what way was he not there for Vidar? After all, he was convicted of avenging your son's killing."

Linda Fjell snorts.

"Is that how you prove what a good friend you are? By killing people? I'm talking about something completely different. Some years ago Vidar had problems at the gym, money trouble. The rent shot up and the grant the council gave him through The Inner City Project wasn't enough to cover it. Tore had so much money he didn't know what to do with it. Vidar went to see Tore to ask for his help. And you know what he replied? He said no, that's what he said."

"Are we talking about a lot of money?"

"I don't know. I never knew the actual sum involved, but it was definitely not more than Tore could have managed. And do you know what Tore did next? He bought himself a brand-new motorbike. He already had three or four or whatever! Dear God."

Henning notes down the word "mean" on the pad in front of him.

"How did Vidar take it?"

"How do you think? He was upset, obviously."

"Hm."

An uncomfortable silence ensues. A few minutes later, when Henning ends the call, he is left with the feeling that Pulli might not have been all that popular—even before Vidar Fjell was killed.

24

The first time the Brenden-Haaland family marked the start of a new school year by eating out, Julie had just been born and they were forced to abandon their celebration before the waiter had even brought the menus. Little Julie screamed her head off and refused to be consoled. At home they could cope with a crying baby, but in public was another matter.

The following year was more successful. Thorleif managed to eat almost half his food before they had to leave. The third year was even better when Julie insisted on having her own meal and swallowed four or five mouthfuls before declaring she had had enough. Today, as Pål proudly announces that he is now in Year Four, Thorleif is actually starting to think that his family can behave like civilized people in a restaurant and enjoy a meal without ruining the experience for the other diners.

They follow a petite young woman with short hair down the stairs at Pizza Di Mimmo and are seated in the farthest possible corner. Once they have ordered, a sort of calm descends upon their table.

"Do you know what happened to me today?" Elisabeth says with an animated expression.

"No?" Thorleif replies.

"I was interviewed."

"Who by?"

"*Aftenposten,* I think it was. It was one of those 'Your say' features."

"I didn't know *Aftenposten* still did that."

"Neither did I."

Elisabeth beams.

"The topic was crime and immigration, I think. Or maybe

it was the other way around. Or it might have been organized crime, I don't know. Anyway, I was asked if I or anyone in my family has ever felt threatened. I answered no, of course."

"Did they ask you anything else?"

"I can't really remember."

Thorleif looks at her while she thinks about it.

"Yes, now I can. The question was: how far are you willing to go to protect your family?"

Thorleif looks at her.

"Is this a joke?"

"No."

"And what did you reply?"

"What do you think? I would do whatever it takes, of course. Wouldn't you?"

Thorleif nods slowly. He used to laugh at people who claimed they would do whatever it took to protect their girlfriend or children—or both. He seriously doubted they meant what they said or had any idea what it might involve. So he never used the expression himself.

Not until he had children of his own.

"When are they running it?" he asks.

"Tomorrow, I think."

"Then we had better get up early," he says and smiles. In the mirror the short-haired waitress approaches with bouncy steps. He straightens up a little and looks at Julie's expectant face. She makes only sporadic contact with the seat underneath her. Pål licks his lips. Thorleif gazes at his children. Right until something deep inside him starts to melt.

25

The knife-sharpening business, Skjerpings, is located in Kurveien in Kjelsås, a northern suburb of Oslo. Kurveien is a street where yellow concrete blocks press against the mountainsides. White and blue terraces stick out like open drawers. Outside the ground-floor flats, privet hedges struggle to conceal tiny gardens where barbecues and tricycles occupy most of the grass.

At the end of the street a Nissan Micra with Skjerping's logo and web address on a sticker on the left rear window is parked on the drive in front of a garage. At the top of a small hill to the left Henning can see a large, black log cabin.

He takes a deep breath and starts walking up the steps. When he reaches the cabin, he can see the blue water of Oslo Fjord on the horizon. The whole city lies at his feet. It strikes him what an incredibly beautiful city Oslo is—as long as you look at it from afar.

At the front of the cabin he finds a doorbell labeled skjerpings.no. Soon he hears footsteps coming down a staircase. The door is opened.

"Hi," a woman with long red hair says. Pretty dimples. Lots of attractive freckles. She doesn't look like someone who could have taken out a man like Brolenius. But if somebody kills your boyfriend, Henning thinks, there are no limits to what you can do. Especially if you earn your living by making murder weapons even sharper than they already are.

"Are you Irene Otnes?"

"Yes, that's me. Can I help you? Do you have some tools you need sharpened?"

"No. I was wondering if I could have a chat to you about Vidar Fjell?"

Her warm smile vanishes instantly.

"My name is Henning Juul, and I work for the Internet newspaper 123news."

Otnes frowns.

"Why do you want to talk about Vidar now?"

"I'm working on a story about Tore Pulli. His appeal is coming up and much of the evidence against him is circumstantial. It is based on his relationship to Vidar. I was . . . working on other things when he was killed, but now I'm back and I'm trying to get an idea of what happened."

She looks at him. A cat rubs itself against her legs before it darts out onto the flagstones.

"If it's convenient? I really need your help."

Otnes hesitates before she nods.

"We can sit over there," she says, pointing to an arrangement of plastic chairs. A parasol casts a dark shadow over the gray flagstones.

"Thank you so much."

Otnes goes back inside to get a jacket and comes out again. Henning smiles as they sit down.

"Lovely house," he remarks.

Otnes beams with pride.

"Thank you."

"And very unusual for Oslo. A proper old-fashioned log cabin. Do you live in this enormous house all on your own?"

"I have my cat," she replies and smiles quickly as a gust of wind takes hold of her hair. An awkward silence passes between them.

"So you run a knife-sharpening business?" Henning continues.

"Yes, I do. It's not very common, especially if you're a woman. And these days people just buy new knives when their old ones get dull. The throwaway society. We have it too good in this country."

Henning nods in agreement.

"Is it mainly knives you sharpen?"

"Yes."

"What about axes?"

"No, hardly ever. If someone had brought in an ax, I think I would have remembered."

"And you don't remember an ax?"

"No. Why do you want to know about that? I thought you were here to talk about Vidar?"

Henning pauses briefly before starting in again.

"I have to be honest with you, Irene. I didn't just come here to talk about Vidar. The circumstances surrounding his death seem quite clear. I'm more interested in what happened afterward. With Jocke Brolenius and Tore Pulli."

"Yes, that's when it all fell apart," she says and shakes her head softly.

"How do you mean?"

"I'm thinking of the discussions we had in the weeks that followed."

She shakes her head again.

"You were very outspoken, I understand, seeking to avenge Vidar's murder?"

"Yes, I was angry and upset. But I look at it from another viewpoint now. After Brolenius was killed, I realized it made absolutely no difference. I was still upset."

Henning nods.

"I've heard that Vidar came to Tore to ask for financial help for Fighting Fit. Is that true?"

"It is, yes."

"But Tore said no?"

She shakes her head in contempt.

"Tore liked to think of himself as a big shot, you know. He

took his business very seriously. He wouldn't make any investment unless there was a guaranteed profit at the other end."

"Did Vidar and Tore fall out over it?"

"No, it would have taken a lot more than that. They had known each other a long time."

Henning nods quietly.

"Do you think Tore is guilty?"

"I don't really know how to answer that."

"A simple yes or no would suffice."

Henning attempts a smile.

"I don't think I want to say anything about it."

"Why not?"

"Because of Veronica. I don't want her to read about me in the paper. We're friends, you understand, and I've always supported her. I wouldn't want her to find out that I don't believe her husband is innocent."

"This won't appear in the paper, I promise you. So you believe he did it?"

She looks at him for a while before she nods.

"Because?"

"Because Tore has always been good at wrapping people around his little finger. And I know that he lies about all sorts of things."

Henning moves to the edge of the chair.

"Such as?"

"Everything from little fibs and white lies to outright deception. Vidar used to get so annoyed with him because of it. When Vidar set up Fighting Fit, Tore was around and he helped out a bit. Whenever Vidar asked Tore if he had done something, picked something up, or called the plumber, Tore would say yes, he had done it, but then it turned out that he hadn't done it after all. It happened all the time."

Henning feels his stomach lurch.

"I could go on. Cinema tickets, hotel rooms. Once Vidar

was helping out a musician friend of his who was looking for a rehearsal space and Tore said he could fix it. And when Vidar asked Tore if he had taken care of it, Tore replied that everything was sorted. But when the guy turned up to practice, the room was already occupied. The man who ran the place had never even heard of Tore."

She shakes her head.

"People who do that really irritate me," she declares.

Henning nods and reasons that if you lie about the little things in life then the path to the really big lies isn't a very long one. Once again he is overcome by a feeling that Pulli is playing him.

"Do you know Robert van Derksen?"

Otnes snorts.

"Have you seen his Facebook profile, perhaps?"

"I'm not on Facebook."

"He has posted some very impressive photos of himself, shirtless and glistening with oil."

She pulls a face and shakes her head. Henning thinks about the photos van Derksen had uploaded of himself on hardenever.no.

"So he likes showing off?"

"Oh, yes. And he is extremely fond of the ladies. He even tried it on with me."

When they wind up their chat a little later, Henning concludes that Otnes is still bitter, but at the same time she is also starting to come to terms with Fjell's death. There was no hatred in her eyes when she talked about Tore. Nor when she spoke about Brolenius. And he can't see why she would keep secrets. If she had known who Brolenius's real killer was, she would have told someone. Especially if she could have earned herself one million kroner by doing so.

The afternoon is warm and pleasant and Henning decides to walk all the way home to Grünerløkka. It takes him an hour and he stands under the shower for a long time when he gets back. He eats a slice of bread with jam while he checks his emails, scrolling quickly through the one hundred and twenty-eight new emails in his inbox. Heidi Kjus has sent some round-robin emails, he sees. Directives and targets. The memos she has carefully composed disappear with just a hard tap on the *delete* button. He instantly feels better for it. His mood improves even further when he discovers an email from Oslo Prison.

> From: Knut Olav Nordbø kon@kriminalomsorg.no
> Subject: <<request for visit—Tore Pulli>>
> To: Henning Juul <henning.juul@123news.no>
>
> Your application has been processed and your request to visit has been granted.
>
> There is still considerable press interest in connection with the forthcoming appeal, but Tore has indicated that he would like to meet with you as soon as possible. If you are available as early as tomorrow—Tuesday—he would like to meet with you at 10 o'clock.
>
> Kind regards
> Knut Olav Nordbø
> Liaison Officer, Oslo Prison

As soon as tomorrow, Henning thinks, pleased. Perhaps then he can finally get some answers.

26

Aftenposten is lying on the doormat right inside the front door. Thorleif picks it up and quickly flicks through the news section, then arts and finance, but he sees no "Your say" column, not on the back page—where it used to be—or in connection with any of the articles inside the newspaper itself. He goes through it again in case he was too sleepy and bleary-eyed to spot it the first time, but the result is the same.

He takes the newspaper to Elisabeth, who is still in bed.

"Are you sure it was *Aftenposten*?"

"Eh?" she grunts from under the duvet.

"*Aftenposten*. I can't find your interview."

Elisabeth pushes the duvet aside and looks at him. Her eyes are two narrow lines.

"Are you sure?" she mumbles.

"I've gone through the whole sodding newspaper twice."

He gives her the paper. Elisabeth sits up and starts leafing through it herself. Thorleif is aware of a pressing need for coffee so he doesn't wait for her to finish, but goes to the kitchen, finds a filter, and measures out coffee and water. Shortly afterward Elisabeth comes plodding.

"I couldn't find it either," she yawns.

"Are you sure it was *Aftenposten*?"

Elisabeth thinks about it.

"Fairly. Perhaps it wasn't for today's edition," she says and yawns again. "Perhaps it'll be in tomorrow. They might not do "Your say" every day."

It is possible that things have changed since the days Thorleif trotted up and down the streets of Eidsvoll on the lookout for potential interviewees who rarely or never agreed to be photographed or answer any of the idiotic questions, which the editorial team had thought up. But on the occasions it was his job to find people in the street for "Your say," it was always for tomorrow's edition. It was usually the last thing he did before going home.

But Elisabeth could be right. Perhaps the column has simply been moved and will appear in the evening edition or later in the week? He bends down and finds some sandwich bags.

"Did you ring the burglar alarm people yesterday?" Elisabeth asks, as she shuffles around.

"Eh?"

"The burglar alarm. We have to get it fixed."

"Oh, right. No, I forgot."

"Don't forget to do it today, please."

27

At any given time there are three hundred ninety-two inmates in Oslo Prison divided between Botsen, Bayeren, and Stifinneren—also known as A, B, and C block. Henning is due to visit Botsen, which consists of a main building with wings spreading out in a fan shape in addition to some smaller units. Everything is constructed in red brick. The prison—especially the entrance—is familiar to most Norwegians thanks to the famous Olsen Gang films, which traditionally opened with Egon Olsen walking out of the prison and down the avenue after being released—having already planned his next master stroke while inside.

Henning's pulse quickens as he walks up the same avenue. He isn't usually nervous before interviewing or meeting someone, but today he is.

Heidi Kjus welcomed his idea of talking to Pulli. She said—no surprise there—that she had been thinking of suggesting it herself, but no one at the morning meeting, not even Iver, looked as if they believed her. Henning has practically forgotten about it when he presses the button on the intercom outside the prison and introduces himself. Seconds later the door slides open. Henning is met by a man in jeans and a stonewashed shirt who introduces himself as Knut Olav Nordbø. He has short hair, a mixture of brown and gray, neatly combed and parted to one side. He has no beard, but his skin is slightly flushed with some liver spots and moles. Nordbø exudes a vapor of stale nicotine and yesterday's tipple. Red wine would be Henning's guess.

He is ushered through an old door and down some stairs to a passage where he hangs up his jacket. Once Henning has handed over his mobile and press card, Nordbø disappears into a room. A short while later he returns with a visitor's card that Henning pins to his shirt.

"There we are," Nordbø says kindly and guides Henning through two heavy concrete doors to the visitors' rooms.

"That's it?" Henning asks. "No body searches, no nothing?"

"Those are the rules," Nordbø says. "The penal code states that all inmates are entitled to meet representatives of the press to promote their case. And the system is based on trust."

"But in theory I could smuggle in all sorts of things?"

"Indeed you could. But we would rather you didn't," Nordbø smiles. "If you wait in there I'll go get Tore."

"Okay."

Henning enters a small and narrow visitor's room with a gray linoleum floor, yellow walls, and a rectangular window with green and white curtains. A black leather sofa has been placed below the window. A tall plant is gathering dust on the floor. At one end of the room there is a small, sad-looking box of plastic toys. He opens a green cupboard directly opposite and finds faded green sheets and hand towels.

It doesn't take long before he can hear footsteps. Nordbø is the first to appear.

"I'll leave you two to chat," he says and smiles. Henning nods by way of a thank you and watches as Nordbø steps aside to make way for a mountain of a man who enters the room. Henning represses the urge to bombard the man with questions and stares at him instead. Tore Pulli is almost unrecognizable. He must have lost at least fifteen kilos. His steps are tentative. He wears a red baseball cap that doesn't match any of his other clothes. Green shirt, blue tracksuit bottoms.

Henning takes a step forward as he thinks about everything he has read and learned about Tore Pulli recently. The enforcer, the businessman, the friend, the liar. Which one of them is he now?

Pulli transfers a steaming cup from his right to his left hand and extends his free hand to Henning. Henning shakes it and looks him straight in the eye.

"Hello," he says. "Henning Juul."

Pulli's handshake is firm and warm.

"So this is what you look like," Pulli says.

"What were you expecting?"

"Well, I don't know really."

"Most people feel awkward when they see my face."

"I've seen worse."

Pulli walks past Henning and takes a seat on the leather sofa by the window. Henning takes the chair opposite the coffee table and watches Pulli as he dunks a tea bag up and down in the steaming water. His hand movements are gracious and measured. His shirtsleeves have been folded up to his elbows and on the upper side of his right forearm he has a tattoo of a woman's face with long wavy hair. Pulli always used to have a deep tan, but now his skin is pale. He takes off the baseball cap and reveals a scalp almost free from hair that he scratches quickly before putting the cap back on.

"So," Pulli says, carefully sipping his tea. "I presume you've found—"

"Before we start talking about that," Henning interrupts him. "I have a question. Or rather it isn't a question, more a demand. If I'm to help you or try to help you, you have to give me something first."

Pulli puts down the cup and smiles coyly.

"Give you something?"

"When you called me last Saturday, you said you knew something about what happened the day my son died. I need to know if I can trust you, if what you say holds true or if you're just messing with me."

"I think you may have misunderstood," Pulli says and gives Henning a condescending look.

"Not at all. You need my help. I need yours. Give me something, anything, which I can check out so I'll know if there is more where that came from."

Pulli looks at Henning in disbelief, but he says nothing.

"What guarantee do I have that you'll scratch my back if I scratch yours first?" Henning continues.

"You have my word."

"Yes, that's all very well, but I know nothing about what your word or code of honor is worth, especially when you have nothing to lose. And you came to me, an investigative reporter who hasn't been particularly active in the last couple of years, and that makes me suspicious. You already know that my son is dead, that there was a fire in my home, and you're dangling the world's biggest carrot in front of me. How can I be sure that you aren't just playing me because you're bored with the color of the walls in here? I need to know if this is a scam, Pulli."

Pulli takes a sip of his tea and puts down the cup.

"If I tell you everything I know now, you've no incentive to help me."

"If you're innocent, then yes, I do. I don't like miscarriages of justice."

Pulli smiles again.

"I can't wait that long."

"What do you mean?"

"If I tell you everything today, you'll be chasing that lead until you can't get any further, and in the meantime you won't give a damn about me. Besides, I'm not sure that you'll get very far or live very long."

Henning looks at Pulli.

"So we're talking about dangerous people?"

"What do you think? You're no use to me if you're dead and I don't have very much time. My appeal is about to be heard."

"Okay, I hear what you're saying. But—"

"It was raining," Pulli says. "That day."

Henning looks at him for a few seconds before he snorts.

"Thanks, I already knew that. Anyone could have found that out."

"I was sitting in a car outside your flat that night. The windscreen wipers were going all the time."

"Why were you there?"

"That's not important right now. The point isn't why I was there."

"So what is the point?"

"The point is that I saw someone who had no business being there enter and go through to the courtyard."

A knot tightens in Henning's stomach.

"How do you know he had no business being there?"

"Because I know who he is."

Henning straightens up a little.

"Who is he?"

Pulli smiles.

"Nice try, but this will have to do for now."

"No, it bloody won't! How did you know he had no reason being there?"

Pulli sighs.

"He didn't live there and as far as I know, he didn't know anyone in the building either. It wasn't his kind of neighborhood."

"But he knew me or he knew who I was?"

Pulli looks away before he takes another sip of his tea.

"I don't know."

"Come on, of course you do. I can see it in your face."

"No."

Henning studies Pulli for a long time.

"How did you know I lived there?"

"Eh?"

"You were sitting outside my flat, you said, and you knew that I lived there. How did you know that?"

"There were stories about you in the paper in the days that followed. I put two and two together."

"Just so," Henning says, reluctantly. "This man, where do you know him from?"

"That's enough."

"No."

"I'm not giving you any more."

"How did he get in?"

"Eh?"

"Into the courtyard. Did he break in? Did he have a key? Did he ring anyone's bell?"

"It was difficult to see from where I was sitting. But he gained entry. And that's all I'm going to give you. This time."

"Was he carrying anything?"

Pulli sighs again.

"A bag."

"Black? Blue? White?"

"I couldn't see. It was dark. And that's it."

Henning snorts again.

"You could easily have made up everything you've just told me."

"Are you calling me a liar?"

"Not necessarily, but we have an inherent problem. I can't check what you've just said. A man entering the courtyard as it was getting dark? Come on, Pulli."

"I'm telling you the truth"

"Yes, I heard you the first time."

"Look at me," Pulli says, leaning forward aggressively. "Do I look like a liar?"

Irene Otnes's words come back to Henning as he examines Pulli's face. He hears his breathing quicken as he focuses on the eyes, staring deeply into Pulli's irises.

"I don't know," Henning says, at last.

"No, you don't, do you?" Pulli says, wearily and leans back.

"You'll have to make up your mind what your son's life is worth. I guarantee that you'll be interested in what I know. If that isn't enough for you, I suggest you leave now."

Pulli looks away. He's angry, Henning thinks. Either that or he's a brilliant actor. Henning inspects Pulli a little longer before he nods.

"Okay," he says.

28

Thank God it's nearly lunchtime, Thorleif Brenden thinks and hugs his stomach, which has been troubling him recently. He hopes he isn't coming down with something.

His computer pings to alert him to an incoming email. Thorleif leans toward the screen, minimizes a webpage, and brings up his inbox. He doesn't recognize the sender, but the title in the subject field makes him open the new email:

"Elisabeth—survey"

The email has an attachment, a photograph. He downloads it. Elisabeth appears, talking to someone whose profile he can only just make out. She is holding up one hand, but not high enough to cover her face like she often does when she is talking or explaining something. The picture has a date stamp in the bottom right-hand corner.

Thorleif's eyes widen. It was taken yesterday. It must be Elisabeth's "Your say" interview, he thinks. The man she is talking to is wearing a black leather jacket and dark trousers. He has no distinguishing features apart from his height and ponytail. The man must be at least two heads taller than she. Why would anyone send him this picture?

Thorleif is about to call Elisabeth to ask if the picture has also been sent to her when he clicks to close it and sees the sender's email address, Murder@hushmail.com. He looks up. Murder? As in *murder*? What on earth—"

Thorleif leans back in his chair and tries to remember what Elisabeth told him about the interview, the questions she was asked. Crime and immigration, was it? Or organized crime, Elisabeth hadn't been entirely sure. Now what was it the interviewer had wanted to know?

Have you or your family ever been threatened?

How far would you go to protect your family?

Is someone playing a joke on them?

"Are you coming for lunch, Toffe?"

A colleague walks past him, but Thorleif doesn't register who. He stares at the picture.

"Toffe?"

"Coming," he replies, absentmindedly. A cold wind chills him. He looks at the man with the ponytail. Didn't the man who drove the BMW the other day have a ponytail? Don't they look a bit similar? He looks at the email again and sees that it comes with an acknowledge receipt request.

The next second his work telephone rings.

Thorleif's attention instantly switches to the ringing telephone. The display merely shows . . . *calling*. He decides to ignore it. Somewhere in the open-plan office a door slams shut. The telephone refuses to be silenced. Thorleif stares at it. Reluctantly, he reaches out and lifts the receiver, but he says nothing.

"Thorleif?"

"Yes?" he replies eventually in a feeble voice.

"Have you opened the photo?"

The Swedish accent has a strong hint of Eastern Europe.

"I know what you're thinking. The answer is yes," the voice continues. "We know. We know quite a lot about you, Thorleif. Or perhaps I should call you . . . Toffe?"

Thorleif quickly glances around the room. Only his work colleagues ever call him Toffe.

"Who are you?" he stutters. "What do you want?"

"We need your help."

"My help?"

"Yes. Your help. Soon you'll find out why. And when we ask you to be ready, Toffe, then you'll do what we tell you. No questions asked."

"B-but—"

"And Toffe, if you care about your family at all, you'll keep your mouth shut. Do you understand what I'm saying?"

Thorleif nods.

"I can't hear you, Toffe."

"Yes, yes, yes," he nods again. "I understand."

"Good. We'll be in touch."

29

"I'll set this to record if that's all right with you," Henning says and holds up his mobile. Pulli nods and leans back in the leather sofa, crossing his legs.

"Before we begin there's one thing you need to be absolutely clear about," Henning says, looking hard at Pulli. "If I'm going to be able to help you, you need to answer every single question I ask you. That means no secrets. Nothing. Agreed?"

"Sure," Pulli says and shrugs his shoulders.

"Okay. Good. Then we'll start with Jocke Brolenius. Who was he?"

Pulli lifts the teacup to his lips.

"A Swede, like most Swedes in that business. Brutal and totally unscrupulous."

"But he worked out with you?"

Pulli nods as he slurps.

"Jocke was a guy who took up space. He was quite cocky and tough, liked to brag if he had beaten up someone in a particularly nasty way. Not to everyone's liking, if you know what I mean. And he had other business interests."

"Yes, I've heard about those. How could you be sure that he had killed Vidar Fjell?"

"Who else could it have been? A few days before Vidar was killed, the two of them had a massive row. Several people heard Jocke threaten Vidar."

"And when Vidar was found dead that was when the trouble started?"

Pulli nods before he goes on to tell him about the discussions at the gym and at home in his flat where he finally managed to convince everyone that he would sort out the problem alone.

"But wasn't it a bit risky to meet that night—just you and Jocke? After all, you knew what he was capable of?"

"Yes, but my name and reputation were still worth something then. And I knew Jocke quite well. He and I had agreed to come alone and unarmed. I've seen enough gang wars to know that people often get their retaliation in first to beat their opponent to it."

"And that was what you were trying to prevent—a gang war?"

"Yes. It might have been quite a naive attempt at diplomacy, but I felt I had to give it a try."

Henning nods again.

"So according to you what happened the day Jocke Brolenius was killed?"

Pulli takes off his baseball cap and scratches his head before replacing the cap.

"I don't suppose there is much I can say that I haven't said already. I was due to meet Jocke at eleven o'clock, but when I arrived he was already dead."

"You saw no one else in the area? No one coming in the opposite direction?"

"No. And I was only meeting Jocke, no one else, so I wasn't expecting—"

"You said in court that you arrived to meet Jocke precisely at the agreed time, but you didn't report his death to the police until nineteen minutes later. How do you explain the gap?"

Pulli looks down.

"I don't think I can. I must have lost track of time."

Henning looks at him for a few seconds.

"That doesn't sound very convincing."

"No, I know. But I have no other explanation for it."

"You're quite sure that you were on time?"

"Yes, of course I bloody was. I was never usually late for meetings and I certainly wouldn't screw up such an important one."

"But all the same," Henning persists. "Nineteen minutes. That's quite a lot."

"Yes, I . . . I know. But I give you my word: Jocke was dead when I arrived. And remember, I spent a little time checking that he really was dead so that must account for some of it."

Henning nods slowly and studies Pulli. He looks sincere, Henning thinks, and decides to continue the conversation on Pulli's terms.

"I'm sure you've spent a lot of time wondering who could be behind this."

"Believe me, I've checked the archives," Pulli says, tapping his forehead with his index finger. "I certainly had plenty of enemies, but I don't know if any of them were smart enough to frame me."

"Not even Robert van Derksen?"

Pulli looks up.

"Why do you ask about him?"

"Oh, I was just curious. I heard that the two of you didn't really get on. And he was a good friend of Vidar, as far as I understand."

"Robert is a jerk," Pulli says with contempt. "He has an IQ deficit."

"But he did know your elbow technique?"

"Yes, I taught it to him a hundred years ago."

"And yet you still don't think he could have done it?"

Pulli shakes his head.

"Robert is so full of himself that he would never have been able to pull a stunt like that without boasting about it."

Henning nods.

"Were any of the others jealous? Or resentful of your status, for example?"

"No, we respected each other. I've always believed that if you treat people with respect, then they'll respect you back. I've done some things in my life that I'm not very proud of and I'm quite sure that some people envy me, but to go to such extremes?" Pulli says, and makes a sweeping gesture with his hand out into the room. He shakes his head wearily and drinks more tea. Henning looks at his notes.

"So what's with the knuckle-duster?"

Pulli starts to laugh.

"To start with I haven't worked as a debt collector for years. But even so I can't remember the last time I used the knuckle-duster. I probably did a bit in the beginning before I discovered that my elbow had given me something of a reputation, and all I had to do was roll up my sleeves and people would pay. Why would I turn up to the meeting with Jocke with my knuckle-duster? It makes no sense at all. Somebody obviously nicked it from me. But nobody in court cared about that. They had their nineteen minutes."

"Did you report the theft?"

"No, I didn't even know the knuckle-duster was missing then."

"And your flat hadn't been burgled in the days or weeks before?"

"No."

"Did you have a lot of visitors?"

"Yes, people came over practically every single day."

"So anyone could have taken the knuckle-duster?"

"Yes."

"Who has keys to your flat?"

"My nan has one in case we lose ours, but she is eighty-seven years old and lives in Enebakk. And even if someone had nicked her key, it wouldn't have done them much good. The flat has a burglar alarm. Veronica and I are the only two people who know the code."

The key to the flat, Henning says to himself and drifts off for a moment. He remembers what Erling Ophus, the fire investigator, asked him, if Henning had locked the door on the night of the fire or if there were any signs of a break-in. If Pulli is right and someone gained access to Henning's courtyard, it suggests that this person had a key. But Henning has only one set of spare keys and he keeps them at his mother's. And she never leaves the house because her smoker's lungs confine her to the kitchen, where she sits with a bottle of St. Hallvard in front of her all day.

Something beeps. Henning looks around.

"It's that time again," Pulli says and takes out an object that looks like a pen. "I've got diabetes. I need insulin several times a day."

Pulli presses the pen against his trouser leg and pushes down the top of it.

"I've always wondered if that hurts," Henning says.

"You get used to it," Pulli replies and returns the pen to his breast pocket. "Nowadays I hardly ever feel it."

"Is it the same with piercings? I seem to recall that you had some before you became a property developer."

"Yes, it's a bit like that."

They smile quickly at each other. There is a knock on the door. Nordbø sticks his head around.

"Time's up," he says, apologetically.

"Okay," Henning replies, looking at Pulli. The bags under his eyes seem even heavier. "We need to talk further. I've many more questions for you."

"I have to do some media interviews in the next few days," Pulli replies. "But yes, we need to meet again."

They get up and shake hands before Henning is escorted out the same way he came in. Just like Egon Olsen he walks out and back into freedom. He realizes how good it feels not to be surrounded by concrete walls.

30

Thorleif turns his attention away from the roofs outside the kitchen window and gazes at Elisabeth across the dinner table. She looks back at him quizzically.

"Would you pass me the salt, please?"

Thorleif finds the bowl of Maldon salt next to his knife and hands it to her before he resumes staring out of the window. He sees nothing. Something gray, perhaps. Around him cutlery clangs against plates, children eat noisily.

"Hello, what planet are you on?"

He turns to Elisabeth again.

"You haven't said one word during dinner."

"No, I'm . . . I'm not very hungry."

"Right. So just because you're not hungry, you can't talk to us?"

Her eyes pin him down.

"I'm not feeling very well," he whispers and looks at her. There is no change in her face to suggest sympathy. Perhaps she can tell that he is lying? Though he isn't really. He feels terrible. His stomach is in constant turmoil. Everything he eats seems only to pour gas on the fire burning below. Since he came home he has been to the lavatory three times. Four times while he was at work.

He had summoned up the courage to ring Anthon Ravndal just before he left work, but it didn't make him feel any better. He doesn't know what he had expected, if he would get straight through to the Swedish-speaking East European or if Ravndal was the man behind the wheel of the car which appeared to follow him the other day. The same man who probably interviewed Elisabeth.

"Are you the owner of a BMW estate car with the registration number BR 65607?"

"Eh, yeah. What's about it? Have you found it?"

Ravndal's voice went from being skeptical to hopeful in one second.

"Found it? What do you mean?"

"My car was stolen four days ago. Are you calling from the police?"

"Stolen?"

"Yes! It was—Who is calling? What's your name?"

Thorleif was tempted to hang up immediately, but he couldn't do it. Instead he introduced himself and explained how he had seen the car, but without mentioning his suspicions.

"The car is probably halfway to mainland Europe by now," Ravndal said. *"The last thing the police knew was that it passed a toll road in Vestfold."*

They finished the conversation and agreed to keep in touch should either of them find out what had happened to the car.

"The guy who interviewed you," Thorleif says, interrupting Julie who is in the middle of a story about a number game at her nursery. "Did he give you his name?"

Elisabeth turns to look at him.

"I know a few people on *Aftenposten*," he says by way of explanation. "Perhaps it's someone I know?"

"If he did, I don't remember what it was," Elisabeth says.

"And you can't remember what he looked like either?"

"Well, he was certainly very tall. Dark hair. He looked a little like Furio from *The Sopranos*."

"The Italian with the ponytail?"

"Yes. The one Carmela was so keen on. He never did anything for me personally, but—"

Elisabeth eats a mouthful of her cod fillet, then piles potato with melted butter and sliced carrots onto her fork.

"Did he speak Norwegian?"

"What do you mean?"

"The man who interviewed you. Did he speak Norwegian?"

"Of course he spoke Norwegian! Hello—he works for a Norwegian newspaper. What kind of question is that?"

In that case there must be more of them, Thorleif concludes and pokes at his food. The voice on the telephone made it very clear that Thorleif must not talk to anyone. But how will he manage that?

"Did you remember to call the security company today?"

"It was a really busy day at work," he lies. She rolls her eyes at him. "You're welcome to fix the alarm yourself, if it's so urgent," he adds.

"You know very well I haven't got a clue about such things."

Thorleif doesn't reply.

"By the way, I'm going out tonight. Perhaps you remember that?"

"Eh?"

"I'm going out and you're putting the kids to bed."

"Oh, yes."

"Had you forgotten that, too?"

"No," he replies, reluctantly.

"For God's sake, Thorleif, I told you several days ago!"

"I'm sure you did. It's not a problem, you go out if you want to. What are you doing? Where are you going?"

"It's my mums' night out tonight."

Thorleif sends her a baffled look.

"With the other mums from Pål's football team," she explains. "You dads should do it as well. It's good fun."

Thorleif doesn't reply, but locks his eyes on a spot on the doorframe behind her. Thank God she's going out, he thinks. That way he won't have to lie to her more than necessary.

31

As soon as Henning gets home, he sits down at the kitchen table and plays the recording of his conversation with Pulli. He listens to it a couple of times and notes down items to follow up. He registers with irritation that he forgot to ask a couple of important questions.

It dawns on him that he should make a chart of the key people in Tore Pulli's life to make it easier for him to keep track. He tears a sheet off the pad and starts writing.

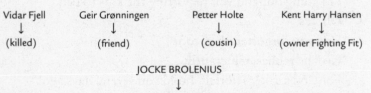

TORE PULLI
↓
Veronica Nansen (wife)

Vidar Fjell	Geir Grønningen	Petter Holte	Kent Harry Hansen
↓	↓	↓	↓
(killed)	(friend)	(cousin)	(owner Fighting Fit)

JOCKE BROLENIUS
↓
Swedish enforcers

In addition there are Irene Otnes and Robert van Derksen, various girlfriends and boyfriends, the staff at Fighting Fit, people who work out there, other friends who might potentially know something. There are just too many of them, Henning thinks. He really needs help. Pulli's appeal is coming up very soon.

Henning recalls the conversation he had yesterday with Frode Olsvik, Pulli's lawyer. The first question Henning asked him was *do you remember me?* because they hadn't spoken for a long time. Pulli asked Henning the very same question during their telephone conversation last Saturday, but Henning didn't think anything of it at the time. Now that the question has resurfaced, the choice of words intrigues him. Is it really what you would say if you were a celebrity and you hadn't spoken to the media for some time?

Henning shakes his head. No, you would say: *do you know who I am?* Pulli's question indicates a kind of relationship that belongs in the past. So why would Henning remember Pulli?

Brogeland jokes that Henning has a photographic memory. It's not all that far from the truth. Henning has forgotten a great deal, but he rarely forgets a face and a name. The only thing he can't remember clearly—with the exception of the memories of his late father—are the weeks before Jonas died.

Henning looks up from the sheet. Is it possible that Pulli and I had something to do with each other in those weeks? Could that explain why Pulli was sitting outside my flat that night?

32

Thorleif jumps when the door opens.

"Hello, Daddy," Julie says, her hair wet and tangled. She is stark naked.

"Hello, sweetheart. Bath time with Martin again?"

She nods eagerly.

"What happened to your clothes?"

She stops, her face takes on the *oops* expression.

"I forgot."

"Then go back upstairs and get them."

"But it's Martin's bedtime."

"Then we'll have to get them tomorrow. Come on, let's go to the bathroom. It's your bedtime, too."

"But I don't want to go to bed."

"It doesn't matter what you want, sweetheart. You're going to bed."

"But, Daddy. I haven't had any dinner yet."

Thorleif sighs.

"Okay. What do you want?"

"Crisps."

"Crisps? But Julie. What day is it today?"

She thinks about it.

"Saturday?"

"Nice try," he laughs. "You can have crisp bread. Or an apple. Your choice."

"Ahemmmm. An apple."

"An apple it is. But afterward it's straight to bed. Okay?"

"Okay, Daddy."

"Sit down, then."

"But Daddy. I need to put my pants on first."

He laughs again.

"You go put on some pants and while you do that I'll peel you an apple."

She races into her bedroom where one drawer after the other is opened and closed with a bang. Soon she comes running back, yanking her Hello Kitty pants as high up her waist as she can. Suddenly she stops and pulls a face that quickly transforms into deep toddler distress.

"What happened?" Thorleif says anxiously and rushes over to her. Julie is clutching her big toe as the tears flow. He realizes immediately what the problem is. Those damned cracks in the floorboards, he thinks, everything gets stuck in them. They have been talking about getting them fixed for ages, but they never have the money. Thorleif consoles his daughter as best he can. Soon the crying subsides.

When Julie has sat down and taken the first apple slice, his mobile beeps on the windowsill. Thorleif picks it up and sees that he has a text from an unknown number. A feeling of nausea spreads through his body. He downloads the photo. The contours of a dimly lit room gradually emerge. Several glasses on a small, round table. A painting on the wall at the back. The details are blurred, but he can make out a group of smiling women. His eyes stop at the woman in the center.

Elisabeth.

He looks at her more closely than at any of the other women in the photo.

The football mums.

A message appears under the photo:

Your wife is lovely. Do you want her to stay that way?

33

Thorleif is pacing up and down the living room floor, constantly checking his watch and his mobile. It's almost eleven thirty. Bloody woman, he thinks. Why the hell isn't she back yet?

She hasn't answered a single one of his calls. Typical! Every time Elisabeth leaves the house, especially when she is out with a girlfriend or three, it's as if the rest of her world ceases to exist. In many ways he envies her ability to switch off. Thorleif feels compelled to check his mobile at regular intervals. But not so Elisabeth. And especially not now, when he needs her more than ever. What on earth is keeping her?

Once the children were asleep Thorleif considered going out to look for her to reassure himself that she was still in one piece, but he decided against it. If they found out it would only make matters worse. And where would he look? Elisabeth never told him where she was going. She could be anywhere in Oslo.

Thorleif looks at his watch again. I have to do something, he thinks. What if something has happened to her on her way back? What if they have talked to her, threatened her even?

Downstairs the front door slams. Thank God, he thinks. It has to be her. The sound of footsteps gets louder. On the other side of the door Thorleif hears the familiar jingling of keys. He opens the door and pushes it hard against her.

"Oh!" Elisabeth exclaims. "You frightened me."

Her breath is saturated with alcohol.

"Has it never crossed your mind that people might need to get hold of you when you're out?"

Elisabeth is about to step inside the flat, but she stops.

"Eh?" she says, looking vague. "Did you try to call me?"

"Yes, I tried calling you! Several times. Didn't you check?"

"No, I—"

Thorleif huffs and marches angrily into the kitchen.

"And hello to you, too," she says and closes the door behind her. Thorleif turns on the tap.

"Was it something important?" she asks as she kicks off her shoes.

Thorleif fills his glass with water.

"What's happened? Is everything all right?"

"No, everything is not all right!" he shouts when he has swallowed a mouthful.

"Well, go on then. What is it?" she says, following him into the kitchen. "Has something happened to the kids?"

"No, they're—"

Thorleif wipes his mouth and turns away, unable to look her in the eye.

"Well, tell me then. What's happened?"

Thorleif hesitates for a long time.

"Nothing," he says at last. "Only I got . . . scared."

"Scared? Why?"

He shakes his head.

"Oh, forget it. I just think you should pick up when I call or text you."

"But Thorleif," she says and mimics Julie's voice as she takes a step closer. "I like having fun, Daddy. Don't you understand?"

"Yes, but—"

"I need a bit of space from time to time, too."

"I know, but our life and what we have together—it's . . . it's—"

He shakes his head.

"There are times when I need to tell you something important or I need a quick answer and then it's bloody irritating that you don't pick up!"

"I know. I'm not very good at it."

"No."

"I'll try harder. Okay?"

She takes another step toward him. Her eyes are inviting. Thorleif looks at her with reawakened tenderness. He pulls her close and holds her tight for a while.

"Did you have a good time?" he says, pushing her away from him.

"It was great. But I think I might have had too much to drink," she says, taking the water glass from his hands.

"Yes, I can smell it," Thorleif says, waving his hand under his nose. He grows serious again, desperate to ask if she noticed anything suspicious or anyone watching them, but he drops it. Instead he looks at Elisabeth gulping water and gasping for air when she has emptied the glass.

"Poor Hilde," she says when she gets her breath back. "She was rather embarrassing. She doesn't get out much these days. And there was this guy who, well, I don't know—"

Thorleif looks straight at her.

"I think he fancied one of us. He bought us all a round. Several rounds."

"Did he?"

"I'm sure I'll pay for it in the morning," she says and rolls her eyes.

"What did he look like?"

"Eh?"

"The guy who was buying the drinks? What did he look like?"

"I can't really remember. Why do you want to know?"

"Well, I—"

Thorleif evades her eyes.

"Calm down, it wasn't me he was interested in. Chance would be a fine thing."

"Hey, hey, don't talk about yourself like that. I won't have it."

Elisabeth smiles through swimming eyes.

"Did he speak Norwegian?"

"Did he speak Norwegian? Why do you keep asking me that?"

"I don't think I do?"

"Yes, you do. Earlier tonight you asked if that journalist from *Aftenposten* spoke Norwegian. Have you gone mad? Why do you keep asking me if everyone I meet speaks Norwegian?"

"I—"

He looks down.

"I don't think he said anything, so I don't know. He just sat there, smiling and looking at us, nodding and raising his glass. That's all I remember. Oh, hang on. He was slightly chubby. Balding. He looked like he thought he could pull, if you know what I mean. Fancied himself. But relax—he's not my type."

Elisabeth looks at him and smiles. Thorleif looks at her dark hair, which falls loosely over her shoulders when she doesn't put it up. At her tempting mouth.

"Seriously," he says, pulling her close again. "You mustn't ever say such negative things about yourself. Do you hear?"

Elisabeth closes her eyes and smiles.

"You're the best, the most wonderful woman in the whole world," he whispers to her.

She opens her eyes again and kisses him on the lips. Her lips taste of stale alcohol. But it doesn't matter.

"Thank you," she says, tenderly.

Thorleif swallows to make the lump in his throat go away. And he realizes as he looks deep into her eyes and it's late and they are tired, that his girlfriend has never been lovelier.

34

The morning meeting has already begun when Henning rushes into the meeting room on the ground floor. News editor Kåre Hjeltland is sitting at the end of the table with Heidi Kjus diagonally opposite him.

"Hi, Henning," Hjeltland shouts as Henning arrives. "Good to see you. Climb on board, climb on board."

"Sorry, I'm late," he says. "Something . . . something came up."

"Not to worry, not to worry."

Heidi glares at him as he sits down. Henning spent some time earlier this morning looking for old telephone records because Telenor only stores files online for three months, but he found nothing. Nor would the Data Retention Directive have been much use since he is looking for information that is more than a year old.

"We were just discussing today's stories, stories, *stories,*" Hjeltland shouts as a twitch takes control of his face. Henning has never got used to the news editor's Tourette's. The fact that his hair stands out on all sides does little to lessen Hjeltland's comical appearance.

"Have you got something you want to add?" he yells, looking at Henning.

Henning clears his throat, aware that everyone's eyes are on him.

"No, I—"

He looks at Heidi.

"I don't mind being on cuttings duty today as well, if the cuttings team is still short-staffed."

"Cuttings duty?" Hjeltland exclaims. "Why on earth would

you want to be on cuttings duty? You're going out, Juul. To work. Chasing scoops."

Heidi's cheeks redden.

"All right, I'll do that then—"

"Okay. Great," Hjeltland says and checks his watch. "I've another meeting, *meeting*," he hollers. Henning struggles for a second or two to suppress an involuntary laughter and sees that Iver Gundersen is doing likewise. Hjeltland storms out of the door closely followed by Heidi. Henning is the last to leave with Iver right in front of him.

"He ought to be called Holler," Iver jokes. "Holler and The Eagle. They would make a great team."

"Good film title."

"Yes. *Starsky and Hutch. Thelma and Louise. Holler and The Eagle.*"

They walk back up to the second floor and return to their desks. Henning looks at Iver, who loses himself in the screen. Perhaps Iver can help me, Henning thinks. He's smart enough. He contemplates asking him for a moment. Then he shakes his head.

Thorleif simultaneously loves and hates dropping off Julie at nursery in the morning. He hates it because sometimes she starts to cry when he leaves. And he loves it for the very same reason. At home Elisabeth is always her favorite. Julie wants Mummy to put her to bed, to read to her. But at nursery she only wants him.

Today, fortunately, there are only smiles. He hugs her for a long time and whispers in her ear that Mummy will pick her up at four o'clock as usual. Then they go through their good-bye ritual.

"I love you," he says. "All the way to the moon."

"I love you all the way to the sun. No, to Morocco!"

"Ah," Thorleif says. "That's very far away."

She nods and squeezes him hard until he has to free himself. He waves to her again and again and again. Even when he is back at the car park outside the Ladybird Nursery he has to wave and wave and wave toward the window where she always stands. As usual he blows her kisses as well. And he gets one back. As he always does.

Kids, Thorleif thinks and opens the car door. The only thing they ever care about is the next treat or the next game. The dangers that lurk out there in the real world never cross their minds; all that matters is getting sweets on Saturdays.

He checks the time and sees that he is running late. He is just about to start the engine when the door on the passenger side is pulled open and a man sits down next to him. Thorleif turns in his seat and is about to protest when he realizes who the man is.

The BMW man.

Furio.

Thorleif nearly has a heart attack. The man looks unperturbed.

"Drive," he orders him.

"But—"

"In—"

The man checks his watch.

"—three minutes a friend of mine will enter a school not very far from here. He will sit down in the canteen. With regular intervals he will go to classrooms thirty-eight and thirty-nine, where Elisabeth Haaland is teaching today—with the exception of period four when she has a free period. Your behavior today will determine whether or not she makes it home from work. Do you understand what I'm saying to you? Are you listening?"

Thorleif nods feverishly and swallows hard.

"Drive."

Thorleif turns the key in the ignition with trembling

fingers. The car starts. Nearly. He makes a second attempt and this time the engine roars. Thorleif's cheeks are flushed. He tries to breathe, but it is difficult.

"Drive," the man says for the third time. Thorleif puts the car into first gear. The car jumps when he releases the clutch. He maneuvers out from between the other parked cars and parents with children, spare clothes and lunch boxes in their hands. Thorleif lets the car roll down the hill toward a junction.

"W-which way?" he stammers.

"That's what's so great about this," the man says. "You can choose."

"Choose?"

"Yes."

"I-I don't understand."

"It's a simple choice. If you turn left, your wife will die. If you turn right, the four of you will still be eating tacos on Friday."

Thorleif is speechless. *Your wife*. He indicates right. The man smiles.

"Good," the man says. "Wise choice. Now you'll call work and tell them that you're ill today."

"Ill?"

Thorleif changes from first to second gear.

"Yes. Ill. But that you'll be well enough to return to work tomorrow."

"But—"

"If you can't remember the number, then I've got it on my mobile."

Thorleif stares at the man who smiles again. As cold as ice. Thorleif eases out the mobile from his inside pocket. He scrolls down to the number for TV2 with shaking fingers and presses *call*. He wedges his mobile against his left shoulder as he steers the car into the central lane. He can feel his pulse throb in his neck. He stops at another junction and looks at the car next to him. A woman in the passenger seat meets his eyes. In a manic moment he wonders if he can warn her, but realizes immediately how hopeless it would be. What would he signal? How? With what?

Guri Palme picks up at the first ring.

"Hi, Guri, it's me, Toffe."

"Oh, hi, Toffe."

"Hi. Listen, I'm . . . I'm not feeling very well today."

"Aren't you?" she says, sounding concerned. "I'm sorry."

Thorleif squeezes his eyes shut.

"Nothing serious, I hope?" she continues.

"I threw up this morning, but I'm absolutely sure I'll be fine tomorrow."

"Are you really? I can probably get Trude to find someone else for tomorrow."

"No, no, I'll be all right."

"Are you sure?"

"I'll be fine."

"Okay. Good. I hope you feel better soon."

"Thank you."

He ends the call and hyperventilates. The man next to him claps his hands.

"Bravo," he says. "I liked the bit about throwing up. I'm starting to think this is going to work out just fine, Toffe. You're good at improvising. That's very promising. Take a right up there."

That man points toward the upcoming roundabout. The emerging autumn colors of Frogner Park glow in the morning sun.

"I've got another very important question for you," the man says and turns to Thorleif. "Which do you prefer: pedestrian or cyclist?"

35

Henning is working his way through a pile of papers on his desk. It takes him only minutes to establish that none of the printouts or notes that have been lying there since Jonas died can be linked to a story that relates even remotely to Tore Pulli. He simply can't recall who he interviewed around that time. Nor are any of the notes dated.

There has to be something, he thinks, something that will remind him of what he was working on in the weeks leading up to the fire. He found nothing significant in the archive, only standard news stories about a robbery, an assault, and a couple of court verdicts. Isn't there anyone he can ring? Talk to?

For a brief moment he considers calling Nora, but dismisses the idea instantly. When they were married they worked for rival newspapers and hardly ever discussed details of the stories they were investigating. And they had been separated for months when Jonas died. Nora would get hysterical if she were to discover that Henning is digging up the past that she is making a determined—albeit counterintuitive—effort to slam the lid on it by trying to find happiness with Iver.

My tapes, it suddenly occurs to him. The old recordings I made of my sources so I could quote them and use them as evidence in case someone kicked up a fuss after the story had been published. Perhaps there was something on them? The ones he has made since returning to work are in a driftwood cupboard in the kitchen in his flat. But what about his old tapes?

He pulls out his desk drawers and sees at once that they are empty. They had different desks before the refurbishment, he recalls, and gets up, walks past the coffee machine and around the corner to where the national news section used to be. But the old workstations are no longer there.

Henning returns just as the news editor is finishing a telephone conversation.

"The old office furniture we used to have," Henning says and gets Kåre Hjeltland's attention. "Do you know what happened to it?"

"Retired along with the office bike—I rode them all to death, ha-ha," Hjeltland says and folds his hands behind his head. His armpits are wet. Henning tries not to look at them. "Oh, the furniture? Not a clue. Why do you ask? Thinking of giving your flat a makeover?"

"No."

"Try asking Ida. I think she was in charge of the refurbishment."

"Okay. Thank you."

"Nice day for a drive, isn't it?"

Thorleif doesn't reply.

"I love driving. I never listen to the radio. I like the silence around me. It helps me think. Don't you agree?"

Thorleif glances at the man next to him, but he says nothing. He can see something shiny in his inside jacket pocket. The man is wearing gloves. The speedometer shows one hundred kilometers per hour, the legal limit exactly. Every time Thorleif nudges the speed up above one hundred ten kilometers, the man leans over and checks the speedometer, a movement always followed by a look of concern.

"Careful now," he says. "You don't want the police to pull you over, do you?"

Of course I bloody do, Thorleif thinks every time. He has considered doing something insane like drive the car into a ditch in the hope that only he survives. But fear makes him cling to the steering wheel. His heart refuses to beat in a steady rhythm.

He has asked the man what he meant by *pedestrian or cyclist*, but the man merely smiled and ignored his question. However, there is something which troubles Thorleif more than that. The man has made no effort to conceal his face. Isn't he scared that Thorleif will recognize him later or point him out to the police?

The answer when it hits him is as simple as it is brutal. They don't care. When this is over, they won't need him anymore and then they will kill him. That is why it doesn't matter if Thorleif knows the man's real identity or remembers his face.

"Where are we going?" he asks.

They pass the exit to Holmestrand going south on the E18.

"We're not there yet. You just carry on driving. And stick to the speed limit."

The man's mobile beeps. He takes off his glove and presses some keys. When he has finished, he puts his hand on the armrest and looks out of the window. Thorleif alternates between looking at the road in front of him and the landscape where the trees are starting to take over. But today he sees no deer lowering their heads toward the ground. Only short, rust-colored wheat stubble and white plastic-covered big bales that look like giant marshmallows scattered across the undulating fields. The man puts on his glove again.

One hour later they exit toward Larvik.

"Take a left in that roundabout," the man says, pointing at a sign for Fritzøe Brygge Shopping Center. "And go into the multistory car park."

Thorleif drives his Opel Astra slowly down to the basement level, which amplifies every sound and movement. He passes a dark wooden entrance that leads to the shopping center where today's special offer from Meny is fish cakes at 49.90 kroner per kilo. A dozen cars are parked, but there are plenty of vacant spaces.

"Park over there," the man says, gesturing toward a dark blue BMW. Thorleif drives closer, steering the car around white supporting pillars, and sees the estate car. It's the same color as the one he saw outside Bogstad Farm, but the registration plates are different. Thorleif looks at the man who smiles slyly.

"Park now and then we will swap cars."

Thorleif maneuvers into the bay and turns off the engine. A heavy silence fills the car. In the distance a door slams with a bang before an engine starts. They get out of the car. He is met by a smell that reminds him of a ferry deck. There is a constant humming above him. The man goes over to the passenger side of the BMW, opens the doors, and tosses the keys to Thorleif. Caught off guard, Thorleif only just manages to catch them.

"You want *me* to drive?"

"Let's find out what you're made of," the man says, and his voice echoes against the walls. He grins. "In you go."

36

They have left behind Stavern and driven past horse paddocks, onion fields, and a free church when Thorleif is told to stop in a bus layover opposite a maize field where the crop reaches waist height. Beyond them, far away in the horizon, the Strait of Skagerrak opens wide toward Denmark. White horses on the surface of the water chase boats, big and small. Above them white and dark gray clouds drift along without bumping into one another.

"Do you want me to turn off the engine?" Thorleif says. The sun is roasting him through the window. The man next to him looks at an old garage with rusty doors and a black sheet-metal roof. He turns his whole body toward Thorleif.

"Earlier today I asked you which way you wanted to go. Remember?"

"Y-yes."

The man points ahead where the road bends left in a long, soft curve.

"A few hundred meters further ahead there is another junction. Technically, you can't turn right there, you'll have to go straight across it, but I'll ask you all the same. Right or left?"

"W-what?"

"Right or left?"

"But—"

"Right or left?"

"I don't know! Which way do you want me to go?"

"You remember how it was earlier today. I'm asking you one last time: right or left? Left—your wife dies. Right—you can still eat tacos—"

"Right," Thorleif replies, quickly. "I'll turn right, okay! Why don't you just tell me which way you want me to go? I'll do anything to save my wife! My girlfriend!"

"Good, Toffe, I want you to hold that thought: You'll do anything to save your wife—your girlfriend. Great. Now start driving. Stick to route 301."

"What are we going to do when we get there?"

The man doesn't reply. Thorleif sighs and puts the car in drive. He pulls out into the road again, calmly increases his speed to sixty kilometers, and follows the long curve to the left, toward the sign for the 301. He brakes in the bend before continuing straight ahead and accelerating up a small hill. The narrow road continues to wind its way through dense forest interspaced with onion and potato fields on both sides whenever the landscape opens up. No cars come in the opposite direction. Thorleif clutches the steering wheel. Tiny side roads turn off to the right, toward farms and cottages he can't see.

"Pull up over there."

The man points to a faded brown fence enclosing a plot that doesn't appear to be named but where gravestones stick up from the well-tended grass. Thorleif parks in between two birches whose branches offer them shade.

"What do we do now?" Thorleif asks.

"We wait. You can turn off the engine now."

They sit in silence for several minutes. They hear the sound of a car approaching. A black cat runs along the edge of the road before it shoots off in between the rowanberry bushes. The car appears, zooms past them before it falls silent once more. Soon afterward a tractor comes along. Then two cyclists. Thorleif notices that the man follows them with his eyes with considerable interest.

Suddenly he leans forward and says:

"Perfect."

"What is?"

"Check your side mirror."

Behind them a man with a headset on his head and wearing dark blue running trousers and a blue jacket comes jogging. His pace is leisurely.

"Wait until he has passed us."

Thorleif waits, he watches the jogger in his mirror, sees him overtake the car. The jogger pays no attention to them, he just disappears around the next bend. The minutes pass.

"Okay, start the engine."

"What are we doing?"

"Just do as you are told."

The engine growls menacingly.

"What you want me to do?"

"Drive. Faster."

Thorleif pushes down on the accelerator a little more. The car gains speed. The jogger appears around the next bend. He has reached the foot of a long sloping hill that twists like a snake.

"Faster!"

The man leans forward.

"Why?"

"Because I want you to hit him."

"I can't drive into him. I'll kill him!"

"Faster!"

Thorleif obeys, gripping the steering wheel. His thoughts bounce up and down like a roller coaster. What does he do now? Surely he can't run over someone deliberately?

They pass a house and a sign advertising a sculpture exhibition.

"There are people living here," Thorleif yells.

"So what?"

"What if they see us? What if there are other cars behind us or coming toward us?"

"Think about your wife. Think about what we're going to do to her if you don't run him over."

"I can't do it," he screams.

"Of course you can!"

The tears well up in his eyes and make it difficult for him to see clearly. Thorleif closes them and tries to blink away the wetness, but the tears keep flowing. He struggles to breathe. The engine emits another roar as they gain on the jogger. The fields open up on both sides of the road, and there is a smell of onion, of bloody onions, while Thorleif's heart feels as if it is about to jump out of his chest. He hears himself cry out as his hands twist the steering wheel in the direction of the jogger. I'm going to hit you, Thorleif thinks, I'm going to hit you now.

He closes his eyes and waits for the car to react to the collision with a human being and the loud crash that will follow as Thorleif takes the life of an innocent man. But the crash never comes. The wheels of the car never stray across the edge of the tarmac where the gravel starts, where thousands of onions are neatly lined up. Thorleif opens his eyes again. Only a few meters ahead of them the road goes into a double bend, and they are about to plow into a field where the red-tinted flowers of the potatoes still display the remains of summer. Thorleif tries frantically to regain control of the car, to get it back on the road. He hears a quartet of tires scream as the car hurls itself to the left just as they come into the bend, and Thorleif clings to the steering wheel while he pants and tries to straighten up, gasping and frantically turning the wheel. Behind them the jogger has stopped. He waves his clenched fists at them.

You failed, Thorleif mutters to himself. You failed the test.

He stares at the man who has already pressed a number on his mobile, which he is pressing against his ear.

"Hi, it's me," he says and sends Thorleif an icy stare. "He screwed up. Kill his wife."

37

A bunch of keys that editor in chief Ida Caroline Ovesen has lent to Henning is jingling in his hands. One of the keys fits the lock of a basement storeroom, where all superfluous office equipment was dumped during the refurbishment until someone found a suitable home for it. "It'll probably stay there forever," Ida remarked.

She had no idea where his cassette tapes might be. The refurbishment had been chaotic and many staff had helped clear out the offices. This impression is reinforced when Henning enters a room filled to the rafters with chairs, desks, old computers, boxes of wires and cables, mice and mouse pads, ring binders and bookcases, workstations and monitors.

Henning moves a chair, clambers to the first desk, and opens its drawers one by one, but they are all empty. The desks are identical and none of them has his or any of his colleagues' names on them, so he has no other choice but to go through all of them and keep his fingers crossed that he might have some luck for once. He clears a path, taking one drawer at a time and slamming it shut as soon as he has looked inside. Soon he has built up a rhythm, but it produces no result.

Perhaps the drawers were emptied first, he speculates. He closes his eyes and imagines being the person who cleared out and removed the tapes from his desk. Could they have been put in a separate box? Bundled together with tape, even? Henning opens his eyes and locates the packing crates, but soon realizes that the filing system used is the one known as chucking stuff in any old box. Ten minutes later he has rummaged through all of them without finding a single audiocassette.

He looks around again. At the rear, behind the storage

crates, he can see an unvarnished pine shelving unit filled with old stationary, letterhead paper with 123news' old logo, envelopes, pens, even umbrellas and white T-shirts. Henning works his way across to it, stepping over a dusty computer monitor in the process, and starts scanning the shelf in front of him at eye level. Nothing of interest. He stands on tiptoe and takes down a box from the top shelf. As he does so its bottom falls out and the contents cascade around his feet. He bends down and feels twinges in his back and hip, pain that sometimes returns as a reminder—as if he could ever forget the slippery railing and the fatal flagstones two floors below, but he grits his teeth and searches through the rubbish that someone decided was worth keeping. Papers for SKUP conferences. union agreements. A computer mouse. Three pens that are unlikely to work still. He removes two half-empty boxes of drawing pins that have fallen out—and spots a pile of cassettes held together with yellow tape. The initials HJ have been written on the side followed by a question mark.

Henning smiles. So someone did pack them, he thinks, delighted, as he counts eight cassettes each containing four hours of recording time. He realizes immediately that he will be unable to concentrate on anything else until he has listened to all of them. Perhaps he could ask Heidi Kjus for a few days leave?

His thoughts are interrupted by his mobile ringing. The caller is unknown, but Henning answers.

"It's Tore Pulli. Olsvik said you wanted me to call you?"

Henning stands up and feels his back ache.

"Yes. Eh, great."

He tries to organize his thoughts, but ends up asking the first question that comes into his head.

"How do we know each other?"

The seconds pass without Pulli replying.

"The first time we spoke, you asked me if I remembered

you. That's not a question you ask someone you've never met or spoken to before. But I have no memory of us meeting. I remember nothing from the weeks or days before my son died. So I was wondering, did we have any contact around the time of the fire at my flat? Did we know each other?"

The seconds tick away while Henning grows increasingly agitated.

"I read somewhere that you weren't in the habit of giving interviews, Pulli. Was I trying to arrange an interview with you? Was that the reason?"

Pulli doesn't reply.

"Was I working on a story where you were one of the players?"

Still silence.

"Why were you outside my flat that night? And I mean, really?"

Pulli sighs.

"I can't tell you anything about that, Juul."

"Why not?"

"I just can't. The telephone in here is being monitored."

"I don't give a damn about that."

"No, but I do."

"If you want my help, you have to not care about that."

Pulli sighs. As does Henning when Pulli takes a long time to consider his response.

"I can't tell you on the telephone," he says, eventually.

"Then tell me this," Henning counters aggressively. "How did you know that I was back at work?"

Another silence.

"Great," Henning snorts. "I can't be bothered with this. Good luck with your appeal."

38

"No! Don't do it, don't do it, please, don't do it!"

Thorleif grabs the man's left shoulder and pulls him.

"Watch the road!"

The car has swerved out onto the gravel at the edge of the tarmac. Thorleif lets go of the man and forces the car back on the road. The moment he is in control of the car, he pleads with the man again.

"Don't do it! I'll do whatever you want, please, give me another chance, please, don't hurt her, don't kill her!"

"It's too late, Toffe. You had your chance."

"No, it can't be too late! I'll do what you want me to. Whatever it is. Please."

Thorleif is crying. The man ignores him.

"Please," he begs him as he bangs the steering wheel. They reach the end of the road. Thorleif stops the car, rests his head on the steering wheel, and sobs.

"Turn right," the man says quietly as he turns to Thorleif. "There is a car behind us. Turn right," he repeats, his voice firmer this time.

Slowly, Thorleif straightens up. A swirling mist is dancing in front of his eyes. He doesn't see where the car is heading, he merely registers that it is accelerating. I've killed her, Thorleif thinks in despair. It's my fault. Soon she'll be leaving work for the last time. She'll never see the children again.

The children, he thinks. My God.

"Please," he repeats, weakly. "I'll do anything. Anything. I promise, I'll get it right next time."

But the man doesn't respond.

Thorleif drives quietly. The road is narrow with grass on

both sides right up to the tarmac. The colors around him merge, churn, and spin inside his brain. Again his head slumps forward against the steering wheel as he weeps. The car almost comes to a halt. The man reaches over and takes the wheel, making sure that they stay on the road. Then he looks at Thorleif.

"Okay," he says, calmly. "I'll give you a second chance."

Thorleif lifts his head quickly and stares at the man; he never would have thought he would experience such a genuine and profound sense of gratitude toward someone who only a few minutes ago had tried to make him kill another human being.

"Thank you," he says, relieved. "Thank you so much."

His breathing is rasping as he closes his eyes and mouths a silent thank you.

"Have you calmed down now? Are you fit to drive?"

Thorleif blinks away his tears and nods.

"Okay. Then drive."

Thorleif sniffs and wipes his face on his sleeves, his cheeks are burning hot. Sweat is pouring from his forehead and his hair. They drive past a large greenhouse just begging for kids to throw stones at it.

"Do you want me to turn around?" he stutters.

"No."

"But what . . . where—"

"Just drive back to the multistory car park. Stay on this road."

"But don't you want me to—"

"Not now."

Thorleif tries to compose himself. He wipes sweat and tears off his face and presses the accelerator. An infinite feeling of relief washes over him. The trials have ended. At least for now. At the same time he can't stop panicking about what will happen next, what he will have to do and to whom. But why does it have to be him? What has he done?

Twenty minutes later they are back in the multistory car park under Fritzøe Brygge Shopping Center. Thorleif parks next to his own car.

"What happens now?" he asks when the BMW has come to a standstill.

"Now you go home. And when you get there, you act normal. You don't tell anyone what you did today. We have contacts inside the police. If you try to warn anyone, we won't just kill your wife."

Thorleif is speechless with shock.

"Now go home."

"But what do I—when do you want—"

"We'll contact you again. Now go home."

Thorleif stays in the car.

"Why are you doing this to me?" he asks, quietly.

The man doesn't reply.

"Okay," Thorleif says with a sigh and opens the car door. He gets out and walks around to his own car. The window on the BMW's passenger side is rolled down.

"Drive safely," the man says. "We wouldn't want anything to happen to you. And if you try to harm yourself, we'll make it even worse for your family."

"I understand," Thorleif nods.

"And Thorleif," the man says, looking at him, "you should seriously think about fixing the cracks in your kitchen floor."

39

As soon as Thorleif has left the multistory car park he calls Elisabeth, but she doesn't answer her mobile. Thorleif looks at his watch. She is probably still teaching, he thinks and joins the E18 toward Oslo. On his way home he calls her at regular intervals, but she doesn't pick up until he passes Sandvika.

"Hi," she says, anxiously. "What's happened?"

Thorleif closes his eyes. He is so relieved to hear her voice that he almost bursts into tears. He takes a deep breath and regains some sort of composure. He thinks carefully before he answers.

"Nothing."

"For God's sake, Thorleif, I have eight missed calls on my mobile. I thought something had happened to the kids!"

"It's nothing."

"You can't do this to me."

"Where are you?" he says, trying to distract her.

"Where am I? I'm at work, of course. Where are you? I can hear you're in the car."

"Eh, yes. I'm working, too."

"Why did you ring me eight times?"

"Because . . . could you do me a favor?" he says.

"Yes, of course, but—"

"Could you pick up the kids today? I'm going to be a bit late. I think."

"Hello—I pick them up every day! Why would you ask me to do that? You don't need to call me eight times to ask me to do something I do every day already. Have you gone completely mad?"

"No. It's just that—."

He shakes his head at himself.

"Just drive carefully. Okay?"

"Drive carefully? Jesus Christ, Thorleif, you're sitting in our car! What is wrong with you?"

"Nothing, I'm just joking," he says quickly, hoping that will suffice.

"When will you be back?" she sighs.

"I'm not really sure."

"No, I didn't think so. If you're later than five, we'll go ahead and eat without you."

"Okay. Take care. I—"

He can't complete the sentence so he hangs up. He regrets it instantly. He should have warned her, told her to look over her shoulder, be on her guard. But what if they are bugging his mobile? Or both their mobiles? They must have been in his home since the man in the car knew about the cracks in the kitchen floor. Thorleif feels sick just thinking about what else the man has seen. The children. Their lives.

I can't talk to anyone about this, Thorleif concludes. I can't and I don't dare. But how do I get myself out of this nightmare? I can't just do what they want since they are clearly going to kill me afterward. First I kill, then I am killed. No, he says to himself and feels the car accelerate.

He has to come up with something.

40

The queue at the off-license in Grønland Basar is never very long. Henning buys two bottles of St. Hallvard and walks out into the mix of aromatic spices that always fills the air in this part of Oslo. His most recent conversation with Pulli replays in his head while he walks. *I just can't,* Henning mimics. At the time Henning meant it when he said that he could not be bothered to waste any more time on a man who is used to getting what he wants and who, according to Irene Otnes, also has a habit of lying. But Henning knows he has nowhere else to go. And he hopes it gave Pulli something to think about until the next time.

As always he finds his mother in the kitchen with a lit cigarette between her fingers. Another cigarette is burning in the ashtray next to her.

"Hi, Mum," he shouts, trying to drown out the sound of the radio. "Losing My Religion" is playing on P4 for God knows how many times, he registers.

"How are you?"

She glances up from the newspaper in front of her. Her face is seething with irritation.

"Look at this," she snorts. "Look what they have done to my newspaper."

Henning goes over to the kitchen counter and puts down the bottles. Today's edition of *Aftenposten* is scrunched up at the bottom.

"How annoying," he shouts and tries to smooth out the crinkled paper. She sweeps his hand away with a dismissive gesture. R.E.M. finish singing and the voice of an intense female speaker fills the kitchen. Christine Juul looks at him.

"Did you get the liqueur?"

"I did."

"Would you—"

She waves her hands in the direction of the cupboard. Henning opens it and takes out a glass. He removes the top of one of the bottles and is about to pour the first soothing drops into the glass when he stops.

"This glass is filthy, Mum."

Her eyes shoot sideways, toward him, but she says nothing. Henning turns on the tap, waits for the water to warm up before he washes and dries the glass, but then he discovers that the tea towel is damp. He sniffs it, pulls away from it quickly and looks at her.

His mum needs a carer, he thinks. Someone who could help her with the basics. She can't manage on her own. It's either that or she has given up. He doesn't have the energy to decide which is worse at this particular moment in time. His sister, Trine, can obviously never spare a single minute of her precious minister for justice time.

Henning puts the glass in front of his mother where a fawning *Se og Hør* feature about Trine and her husband just happens to lie open. *"We want kids!"* screams the headline.

"Did you buy cigarettes?" she asks as she knocks back the liqueur.

"No, you didn't say anything about—"

"You didn't buy cigarettes?"

Henning is shocked by the anger in her voice, which is soon replaced by a coughing fit that tears holes in her lungs. He puts his hand on her back and is about to slap it, but she wiggles away from him, pointing to the home respirator on the kitchen table near the wall while she hacks almost to the point of throwing up. Henning pushes the machine closer, attaches the mask over her nose and mouth with a blue strap around her head before he switches on the device. Soon her breathing calms down. Minutes later only spasms of her cough remain. She sits like this for some time, slowly breathing in and out.

Henning waits until her shoulders are no longer heaving before he slips out and locks the door behind him. Outside he can still hear the sound of the machine that is keeping her alive—for the time being, at least. And he catches himself wondering if he will feel sad the day she dies.

41

Suddenly his duvet feels suffocating and hot—even though he was shivering with goose pimples a minute ago. In the living room Pål is racing across the floor with Endre, one of his new classmates, close behind.

Thorleif went straight to bed when he came home blaming a stomach upset. He knows he would not have been able to look at their faces without collapsing with terror. His family would think that he had gone mad, something which, now that he thinks about it, is close to the truth. What the hell is he going to do? They are watching his every move. The man with the ponytail told him they even have contacts within the police. Is there anyone at all who can help him? Is there some way he could raise the alarm?

This leads him to another thought. When did the burglar alarm stop working? Sunday? The days of the week are a blur to him, but he thinks it was Sunday. Could someone have been in their flat while they visited Bogstad Farm?

He is startled by a thud on the wall. He hears squeals of laughter coming from the living room. Pål's laughter always makes him smile. Footsteps disappear and new footsteps approach. The bedroom door opens. Thorleif jumps again, then he sees Julie stop on the threshold. Even the sight of her pout is enough to take his breath away.

"What is it, sweetheart?"

"Pål says I'm rubbish at drawing."

"Does he now?" Thorleif says in a gentle voice. "Don't listen to him, my love. Pål is just showing off for Endre. You're great at drawing. Did I hear Mummy say that you've learned to draw hearts?"

Julie's face explodes in a smile.

"Can I show you?"

"Yes, please!"

Little feet patter across the floorboards. Thirty seconds later she returns to the bedroom holding a sheet of paper in her hand.

"Look, Daddy."

Beaming with pride she shows him the heart drawn in fat red pen.

"Well, I never," he enthuses. "What a fantastic heart."

"Would you like me to draw you one?"

"Would you?"

Another broad smile followed by running feet. Thorleif straightens up and looks at the heart. It resembles a pair of buttocks. But it is a heart. The finest heart he has ever seen.

It gives him an idea.

"Julie?" he calls out.

"Yeees?"

"Why don't you bring your coloring pencils in here? Then I can watch you while you draw?"

"Would you like that, Daddy?"

"Yes, absolutely. Perhaps I could do a bit of drawing myself?"

"Yeees!"

Shortly afterward she comes running across the floor. Thorleif hears her drop the box and all the colored pencils fall out and roll across the floor.

"Oh," Julie cries out.

"Never mind, my love," he says. "Just pick them up again."

"You need to help me."

Thorleif sighs in the knowledge that the job will never be done unless he gets out of bed and picks up every single pencil with the possible exception of one or two. So that's what he does, he gets up. His whole body aches, but it is reenergized by his idea. He goes out into the living room and can see no sign of Pål, Endre, or Elisabeth.

"Come on," he says, picking up the last pencil. "We need to find something we can rest the paper on so we don't accidentally draw on the bed linen. Or Mummy will be cross."

"We're going to draw in bed?"

"Yes. And we'll build ourselves a tent so we can sit inside it and draw. Won't that be fun?"

"Lots of fun!"

"Come on."

He nudges her, picks up two newspapers from the coffee table, and crawls back into bed. They cover themselves with both duvets. Thorleif sits upright so the duvets form a wall around them. Julie puts one newspaper under the paper she is going to draw on.

"Listen," he says to get her attention. She doesn't respond, she's busy deciding which colors to use. "Do we have any crisps?"

Now Julie looks at him.

"But, Daddy. It's not Saturday."

"No, I know. But we could pretend," he whispers. Julie's face lights up.

"Run off and get some. Make sure nobody sees you. Or at least not Mummy."

"Okay, Daddy."

Her feet dart across the floor. She soon returns with a crumpled bag in her hands. Her face is glowing. Julie climbs back into bed and gives the bag to Thorleif. He opens it and offers it to her first. Julie takes out a single crisp that soon crunches between her teeth. She smiles again.

"Take care not to leave crumbs," Thorleif whispers. "Mummy mustn't find out what we've been up to, do you understand?"

Julie sends him a conspiratorial smile and nods her head as she munches happily. Thorleif takes the bag and helps himself to some crisps. The salt stings his taste buds and almost makes them curl up. He holds out the bag to Julie while he looks at her. She takes some more crisps and carries on drawing. One heart after another. Red and yellow, black and purple.

"Daddy, are you crying?"

"No," he sniffles.

"So why are your cheeks wet?"

"Because—"

He looks at her for a long time, at her swift movements, her tangled hair, the traces of tomato sauce at the corners of her mouth. He removes a strand of hair from her eyes.

"It's going to be really good," he says, pointing to her drawing.

"What are you going to draw, Daddy?" she asks him.

Thorleif looks at the red heart and turns over the paper before he looks up at the ceiling, scanning the room for something small and round that might be a camera. But he sees nothing. Even so he bends down and speaks carefully into her ear.

"I'm going to draw a car," he whispers. "A really fine car."

42

Henning buys a baguette from Deli de Luca on his way home and eats it as he walks. The thought of what awaits him makes him speed up.

Heidi let him have the rest of the week off though she couldn't refrain from sighing heavily when he refused to give her a reason. Instead she said: "Fine. You need it. You look dreadful."

Henning said nothing.

Back in his flat he sits down on the sofa, takes out the mini cassettes with his initials on them, peels off the tape, scrunches it into a ball, and throws it on the kitchen floor. None of the tapes are labeled with a date or year, and it's impossible to see if some of them are more used than others.

Henning finds his old tape recorder in the driftwood cupboard, plugs in the power cable, and inserts the first cassette. Soon he hears his own voice.

What did you think of Statoil's handling of this matter?

The reply is provided by a female voice he can't identify.

Statoil's promises concerning my role and the company's self-imposed obligations in respect of human rights were false and misleading. This individual case is symptomatic of a greater problem.

Henning fast forwards. The woman's voice follows him for twelve minutes and thirty-six seconds before another woman's voice appears after a short break. Henning recognizes the voice immediately.

The man was stabbed in the chest. He has been taken to Ullevål Hospital, but his condition is unknown. His attacker appears to be a woman and she is now in police custody.

The voice belongs to Assistant Commissioner Pia Nøkleby

and is professional and grave as it always is when he asks her for a quote or two on the record. Henning fast forwards through a story about sexual abuse of schoolchildren before he works out that this tape must have been recorded at least one year before Jonas died. He finds a marker pen, puts a big black cross on that cassette, and inserts the next.

It's going to be a long night.

43

The feeling just before it happens is always the worst, when the body knows it needs to vomit, but tries to fight the inevitable. And then it happens anyway, violently. Thorleif throws himself forward while his stomach contracts and expels what little is left in his gut into the lavatory bowl. His intestines contort repeatedly, but nothing more comes out of his mouth.

He hacks a couple of times and lets the saliva drip, but avoids looking down. The smell rising up toward him is enough. Tears press against his eyelids. Thorleif gets up, sniffs, and flushes the lavatory. The sound of running water ricochets against the wall and inside his head, where it jolts around, stirring up a chaotic mix of thoughts and emotions. His legs struggle to support his body. He staggers over to the sink and turns on the tap.

Thorleif recalls what he told Guri Palme yesterday. *I was sick this morning.* It had been a white lie, but less than twenty-four hours later it proves to be true. Will he be able to go to work today?

He washes his face. He looks at the water dripping from his eyebrows and beard. You won't be able to run over anyone. You'll never be able to kill another human being. The very thought is enough to send him back to the lavatory bowl. He tries to ignore it, but there it is again, he recognizes the revolting feeling, it's only a matter of seconds now and then it comes. He leans over the lavatory bowl, hugging the china. The mere smell is enough to make him gag, but only saliva comes out. Saliva and mucus. He kneels down, spitting.

Soon he gets up again, splashes water on his face a second

time, checks his watch: five thirty am. He is due at work in four and a half hours.

He has to pull himself together.

Henning falls asleep around three o'clock in the morning and for once Jonas doesn't haunt his dreams. Some hours later he is woken up by his mobile ringing, but when he answers it no one is there.

Henning drinks a mouthful of tepid Coke and opens the curtains. He goes to the kitchen and tips what is left of yesterday's pot of coffee into a mug and puts it in the microwave. While he waits for the coffee to heat up, he looks at the cassettes on the kitchen table. Six of them are marked with big black crosses. The notepad next to them is filled with notes and names, but Henning's pulse doesn't quicken as he looks at them with fresh if still half-asleep eyes.

The microwave oven beeps. Henning takes out the mug and sips the hot liquid carefully. He sits down and puts on his headphones again. With slow and still sleepy motions he inserts the seventh cassette, presses *play,* and listens. He hears his own voice. Boring questions. Bland answers. *Have you any idea of the motive?* Fast forward, fast forward, fast forward. He drinks more coffee and presses *play* again. *So what is your next move in this case?* More fast forwarding before he stops again. More play. He hears a man's voice: *they might kill me.*

Henning looks up. He rewinds to the start of the sentence and presses *play* for the umpteenth time. *I'm risking my life meeting you. If they find me, they might kill me.* Henning presses *stop* again.

He recognizes the voice as belonging to Rasmus Bjelland and soon puts a face to a story. All it takes is a few Internet searches to refresh his memory.

Bjelland was convicted of drugs smuggling in the early

nineties. He was given a prison sentence, Henning recalls, seven or eight years. When Bjelland was released, he started working as a carpenter without notable success. A limited company he set up, Bjelland Bygg & Bolig, went bankrupt after trading for only eighteen months.

As many other bankrupts at the time, Bjelland decided to try his luck in Brazil, more precisely in Natal—a pearl on the Atlantic coast and a city with eight hundred thousand inhabitants. In the spring of 2006 *Dagens Næringsliv* reported how the city was becoming a haven for Norwegian criminals. For years dirty money had been poured into various construction projects, later sold to Norwegians desperate for some sun and easily tempted by the favorable prices and generally low cost of living. They didn't know that the million-kroner construction projects were financed and controlled by criminal gangs who never filed a tax return in Norway. Even members of notorious gangs such as B-gjengen and Svenskeligaen invested in the Natal property market.

In 2004 Rasmus Bjelland married a Brazilian woman. She was responsible for attracting investors while Bjelland handled the construction side. Together they managed to build some smaller residential complexes that made them sufficient profits to reinvest. However, the people already running the show in Natal were perfectly happy with the existing setup and resented the arrival of yet another property shark trying to get a share of their market.

On an autumn day in 2006, one of Bjelland's business partners was found shot and killed outside the fishing village of Ponta Negra, an undeveloped area where Bjelland and his wife were planning their biggest project yet. Police concluded that the man, who was found with three bullet holes in his forehead and cash in his pocket, had been the victim of an armed robbery. Bjelland was terrified.

The story, uncovered by *Dagens Næringsliv,* formed the basis of a huge Norwegian-Brazilian police operation. On 9 May 2007, two hundred thirty police officers in Natal carried out Operation Nemesis, the biggest raid the authorities in the province of Rio Grande do Norte had ever undertaken. They searched thirty-three flats and offices looking for documents to prove fraud and money-laundering and confiscated items with a value of three hundred million kroner. At the same time, in Oslo, eighty police officers carried out Operation Paradise and raided various locations associated with money-laundering in Natal. While fourteen people were arrested in Natal, eleven were remanded into custody in Oslo. Seven people were later charged by Norway's serious fraud office, Økokrim.

Rasmus Bjelland and his Brazilian wife were not among those arrested, though their office was turned upside down. This led to suspicions that Bjelland had been in cahoots with the police prior to the raids and that the search of his office was purely for show. It didn't take long before a price was put on his head and Bjelland went into hiding.

Rumors that a minor Norwegian property tycoon in Brazil now headed the hit list of several organized crime gangs soon reached most news desks, and Henning knew that Bjelland would not be easy to find. One day, however, he received a tip that Bjelland had settled with his creditors in Norway and applied for witness protection—a request granted to only a few people since Kripos set up the program in 2004.

After several phone calls back and forth Henning finally tracked down a middleman who agreed to pass on a request for an interview, but it was turned down point-blank. Nor did Bjelland take Henning's bait that the article could serve as a preemptive defense brief. Henning had practically given up when the middleman contacted him and told him that Bjelland had changed his mind.

One overcast day in the summer of 2007 they met at Huk Beach. Henning remembers a man who was scared of the shadows and ready to do whatever it took to appear innocent and unjustly accused. In theory, talking to Norway's most-wanted man was a scoop, but Henning was left with a bad taste in his mouth—not because he necessarily believed that Bjelland was lying, but because he was allowing himself to be used as Bjelland's mouthpiece. Another of Bjelland's demands was that Henning would not write anything about his application for a new identity, which was currently being processed, since it would make him look even more suspicious, nor would he tell the readers that Bjelland was planning on staying in Norway. Henning had had to bite on this bullet, too. He even remembered the headline. *I'm no snitch.*

Perhaps that's the answer, Henning thinks to himself. Maybe the people who were looking for Bjelland thought that Henning knew Bjelland's location since he had managed to interview him. But why torch Henning's flat?

Perhaps they had made previous attempts at contacting Henning before opting for a more drastic approach? For all Henning knows, they may not have meant for anyone to die, only for Henning to become more cooperative. No matter what their motive was, it wouldn't have worked. Henning never knew the identity of the middleman. Their only point of contact had been through an anonymous email address.

Henning looks up his own story on the Internet. With the benefit of hindsight he sees that it was definitely a good one. He took a fine picture of Bjelland from the back with a hood covering his head, looking out across Oslo Fjord. Mysterious and appealing. The story offered hitherto unpublished information. Reading his old article again stirs a memory in Henning of the man he was before Jonas died. He can hear the hunger in his own voice in the hunt for the big story. He recognizes the feeling, not because he plans to write anything about Jonas, but because he senses he might have hit on something.

He checks the Internet for more recent information about

Bjelland, but his searches generate no hits. That must mean his application for a new identity was approved, Henning thinks. In other words, Rasmus Bjelland could be anywhere in Norway with a new face. Finding him again would be practically impossible. Nor is there much to suggest it would serve any purpose.

B-gjengen or Svenskeligaen, Henning thinks. He knows there aren't many members of Svenskeligaen left in Oslo. And he can't knock on the door of B-gjengen and ask them if they were behind a fire in a flat that led to the death of a six-year-old boy. He has to come up with another way to approach them.

But how?

The answer is obvious, though it goes against the grain and holds little appeal for Henning.

Tore Pulli.

44

Before Thorleif unlocks his car he stops and glances around. Cars and buses zoom up and down Bygdøy Allé. Pedestrians are quietly using the pedestrian crossing, but nobody is walking down Nobelsgate in his direction. His hands tremble as he opens the door and gets in. He checks the rearview mirror. Sees nobody.

He takes a breath, starts the engine, and drives toward the center of Oslo, where he finds a parking space in Kirkegaten. The engine has just stopped when there is a bang on the windscreen. Thorleif is startled and jumps, but all he sees is a man in tracksuit bottoms and a white T-shirt walk away from the car at a leisurely pace.

Then Thorleif notices the yellow Post-it note attached to the windscreen. He gets out, searches for the man, and sees him disappear around the corner. He doesn't look back. Thorleif snatches the note and reads what it says.

Oslo Cathedral. Five minutes.

A wave of panic sweeps through him and he has to make an effort to breathe. It's starting again. He leans forward and supports himself against the hood of the car while he tries to calm down. He stands like this for a while before he straightens up and takes a deep breath. Then he walks up Kirkegaten in the direction of the cathedral, whose spire and verdigris green top soar toward the open sky. His footsteps are feeble, reluctant, as if deep down he is hoping they will refuse to lead him to his executioner, acquire a will of their own, and carry him to safety. Thorleif looks up at the pedestrians coming toward him, trying to make eye contact, but nobody returns the looks he gives them. I'm on my own, he thinks. I'm the only one who can deal with this.

He crosses Karl Johansgate and continues toward the cathedral while he wonders if he can stop himself from crying. The cathedral door is open, he sees as he crosses the street by the taxi rank on Stortorvet. He enters the darkness and is instantly mesmerized by the silence that always fills a church space.

He hears mumbling, sees fingers pointing up at the ceiling, at the stained-glass windows and the paintings. He checks his watch. He needs to be at work in five minutes. He swears quietly to himself and instantly feels remorseful in view of the location and his surroundings. His shame evaporates when he detects the smell of leather behind him. He spins around and stares right into a grave face. The same face he learned to fear yesterday.

They remain opposite each other for a while. The man looks at Thorleif for a long time before he nods and walks further into the cathedral. Thorleif follows him. They sit down on a bench. The man waits until a group of Japanese tourists have moved on. Then he slips one hand into the inside pocket of his leather jacket and takes out a box. He opens it with care and shows it to Thorleif.

"W-what's that?" Thorleif whispers, looking down at it. Reluctantly, he realizes that he is intrigued.

"This," the man says, reverently. "This is a piercing needle."

45

"**Are** you all right?"

Thorleif looks up at Guri Palme's concerned face.

"You're as white as a sheet. Are you sure you're okay to work?"

"Oh, yes," Thorleif groans and forces a smile. "I'll be fine. But I think I might not start the editing today."

"Fine, it's not going out until Saturday, anyway," Palme says, sympathetically. "Are you really all right? You look terrible."

"I'll be fine," he assures her.

Palme scrutinized him for several seconds before she puts her hand on his shoulder.

"Good. It's a big day today."

They get into a white Peugeot 207 with TV2's familiar "2" and the letters ENG 12 on the right-front wing and drive off. He is numb; it's as if the body sitting in the car doesn't belong to him. He can't feel the seat underneath him.

He looks out of the window, searching for something he can focus on and lose himself in, but he finds nothing. Only children in the park, people in cafés. Life passing by. He recognizes the mood from this morning. Something is brewing. He starts to feel dizzy. The little box he was given is burning a hole in his inside pocket.

Thorleif hears the man's voice inside his head:

There is no reason why you can't go home from work today. You just have to do one small thing for us. If you do that you'll be able to carry on with your life just as it was before. If you don't, we'll not only kill you, but also your children.

Thorleif closes his eyes.

The car stops. The ground feels soft as he gets out. Ole

Reinertsen, the other cameraman, opens the boot. Both of them pick up their camera and recording equipment. Thorleif slings the lighting kit over his shoulder and soon feels his forehead flush with heat. The camera feels heavier than usual. The details around him lose substance and float past. He lets himself be guided through doors and finally into a room. He stares at the gray linoleum floor, feeling trapped by the white-painted concrete walls.

"Okay," Guri says. "We'll probably need fifteen minutes to get ready. Or what do you think, Toffe?"

He nods. He hears a kind male voice reply that that's fine and that he will be back. Thorleif is the last person to enter the room. He puts down his bags, his tripods, and his camera. The room is small and narrow. A beech and glass table stands in the middle. The curtains have a pattern that looks like butterflies.

"What do you think?" Reinertsen asks him. "Two lights and a camera right behind Guri, roughly here?"

Reinertsen makes a square with his hands. Thorleif nods.

"And I'll be filming him as he enters."

"Mm."

"Could you pass me the tripod, please?"

Reinertsen points to the tripod. Thorleif does what he is asked. Behind him, Palme is marching up and down the floor with notes in her hands that she alternately looks at and away from. Thorleif's work absorbs his attention for several minutes; he rigs the Panasonic 905 and finds a microphone and an XLR cable. Normally he would have said: *I just need to attach this to you,* and the interviewee would instantly forget that they were wearing a mike. But Thorleif doesn't know if he will be able to say that today.

He tries to concentrate on the lighting. Three lights, perhaps a spot at the back to create an illusion of depth by contrasting objects. The light coming from behind is too sharp. He will have to close the curtains. Put a dedolight in front, perhaps, with a chimera attachment. It'll be fine. The chimera will disperse the light and soften it. If he dims the dedolight, the color will be warmer.

Rigging the lights distracts Thorleif and briefly makes him feel better. But in less than ten seconds the task facing him consumes him again.

Fifteen minutes later he is ready. He takes a deep breath, reaches inside his pocket, takes the box, opens it, turns away, places the needle in his left hand with the greatest of care, closes the box and puts it back. Do everything, he thinks. You have to do everything.

Near him a door is opened. He sees Palme's face light up. She has put on her camera face. She smiles. Extends her hand. Thorleif struggles to stop his knees from knocking. You'll never be able to do it, a voice inside him whispers. You'll fail. You'll never succeed.

The room contracts. Thorleif presses his fingers together. His feet refuse to be still. The air grows clammy and difficult to inhale. Palme nods and smiles, she practically curtsies. "Thank you for coming. We're delighted to start the Dypdykk series with this interview."

A shadow appears in the doorway. Thorleif looks up. Dark, conspicuous tattoos. A woman's face on a forearm.

He meets the eyes of the towering shadow. The man holds out his hand. Thorleif takes it, hears the man's voice, deep and thundering.

"Tore Pulli."

Thorleif's hand disappears inside the huge fist. He barely has enough strength to return the handshake. He looks up and says feebly:

"Thorleif Brenden. N-nice to meet you."

Part II

46

The fan on the windowsill whooshes noisily, but still loses its battle with the quivering heat. The heat moistens Henning's face as he leans over the kitchen table and scrolls through a Google search. Hundreds of articles about Rasmus Bjelland. More irrelevant hits than useful ones.

The vibrating of his mobile makes him turn his head. It's Iver. Henning decides to ignore the call, but the mobile keeps twitching and buzzing. Finally, Henning hits the green answer button with irritation. A couple of seconds pass.

"Hello?"

"Mm."

"Is that you, Henning?"

"Yes."

"Really? It doesn't sound like you. Never mind . . . listen, have you heard the news?"

"No?"

"You won't believe it. You know Tore Pulli? The ex-enforcer?"

Henning sits up in his seat.

"Yes, what about him?"

"He's dead."

The noise from the street disappears. The heat gives way to an icy blast. The space Henning is staring at narrows and contracts. His heart beats faster and faster until he swallows and inhales sharply.

"W-what did you say?"

"Tore Pulli is dead."

Henning puts his elbow on the table and runs his hand across his face, letting it come to a rest on his forehead. His eyelids slide shut. He hears Iver say something, but the words refuse to sink in. All he can think about is Jonas. And his faint hope. That, too, has been extinguished.

"Dead how?

"Jesus Christ, what kind of question is that?"

"How did he die?"

"I don't have all the details yet. He appears to have just dropped dead, I believe, completely out of the blue. But you haven't heard the worst. Or best, depending how you look at it. He died while he was being interviewed by TV2."

The table moves in on him.

"Unfortunately it wasn't a live broadcast, otherwise we could have had a ball with it."

Henning stares at the dents and scratches in the tabletop. The veins in the wood expand, they grow darker and deeper.

Who on earth will help him now?

"When did it happen?"

"About an hour ago. It's completely—"

Henning plugs in the mobile's headset and puts it down, he holds up his hands in front of his mouth and nose so they form a closed triangle.

"Are you still there?" Iver asks.

"I'm here," Henning mumbles into his hands.

"Are you coming in or what? I could do with some help here."

"No."

"But you're supposed to be working today and—"

"I'm taking a day's leave."

"But I—"

Henning presses the red *off* button and buries his face in his hands.

47

Thorleif Brenden is shaking all over as the TV2 car drives slowly down the cobbled avenue leading away from Oslo Prison. Everything is out of focus.

Guri Palme in the front seat turns around to check on him.

"How are you doing, Toffe?"

Her voice makes him jump.

"F-fine," he replies.

"Are you sure? You don't look it."

Thorleif doesn't respond. He is trying to forget Tore Pulli's eyes, but it's impossible. They turned cold and still as if someone had covered them with a moist membrane. Saliva and mucus dribbled from his mouth and mixed with something white and foaming. His hands started to quiver and the twitching spread to each body part like an infection. Then Pulli slumped on his side where he lay shaking for a few seconds before silence descended on him like a blanket.

"We should expect to be called in to make a statement later today," Palme continues.

A statement, Thorleif thinks, alarmed, and feels his face become burning hot. He knows that he will never be able to give a false account of what happened. His voice will falter and his eyes will become evasive. He is sure the police will grow suspicious and wonder why he is so nervous. They will want to question him further. In the end he will crack. And he knows what the consequences will be.

The man in the black leather jacket told him he could go home after killing Pulli and everything would carry on as normal. But how can it? He has taken the life of another human being. And what guarantee does he have that they really will leave him alone now that the job is done? Thorleif saw the man's face, he knows that the man had accomplices to bring about Pulli's death. Do they think that threatening Thorleif's family is enough to make him keep his mouth shut forever? What if the police see through him and the choice is taken away from him?

In the park below the police station, Thorleif sees an Asian man wearing light summer clothes. The man is walking his dog. He reminds Thorleif of a guide he and a friend had when they were in the Caucasus Mountains trying to find their way from Laza to Xinaliq in Azerbaijan. Thorleif closes his eyes and recalls how they hiked through a deep gorge between grassy mountains, waded in water up to their knees through fast-flowing rivers, and were met by sheepdogs foaming at the mouths when they finally arrived early one afternoon. The shepherd who ran out from under a tarpaulin didn't mind that they threw stones at his dogs to keep them at bay. The toothless man even invited them inside his shelter for a cup of tea before he started banging on a bucket and singing shepherd songs in Ketch.

The village had only one telephone, Thorleif remembers. All the men came out from their huts to watch them communicate with the outside world. The village children followed them, too, all eager to show them the brick house where they would be sleeping that night. The father of the house came out with his oldest son, welcomed them warmly in Arabic, and took them straight down to a pen where Thorleif picked out a lamb that was slaughtered a few seconds later.

Afterward they had a warm footbath and a meal of sharp, home-made sheep's cheese that they washed down with tea. Behind a curtain little girls sneaked a peak at the men's world. At night the couple's bed was made ready for them. Thorleif will never forget feeling like a royal traveler in the Middle Ages.

He opens his eyes again. There is so much he hasn't done,

so much he hasn't seen. So many things he has yet to show his children.

Ole Reinertsen drives into TV2's underground car park and parks the car. Thorleif is the last to get out.

"You go on without me," he says as he slams the door shut. Palme turns to him.

"Where are you going?"

"I . . . I just need to get something from my car."

She looks at him for a moment before she nods. Thorleif goes out the same way the car drove in, out into the daylight where the building across the road offers him a little shade. He thinks about Elisabeth and the children and of what he is about to do. And he has an epiphany. Sometimes it's infinitely harder to live than to die.

48

Henning glares scornfully at the computer screen where the story about Pulli's sudden death is making headlines. Fat white font against a black background. No photos. There are never any photos in the breaking news section, only a small square in the top left-hand corner that says *breaking news* in tiny red letters.

It feels as if the walls are trying to crush him into tiny pieces, so he gets up and leaves the flat, moving quickly down the stairs once he has locked the door behind him.

The heat hits him as he steps outside. Three teenagers are sitting on a bench beneath a window in the courtyard, smoking. They look up at him as if he is insane, but Henning ignores them. He hurries past them out into the street and the dry summer dust. He walks past the old sail loft, which gives the street its name, and turns into Fosseveien. Cars drive by slowly. A grown man on a skateboard grins broadly as Henning moves out of his way.

He finds an empty spot on the grassy slope opposite Kuba Bru and watches the River Aker flow by lazily. Around him people are laughing, drinking beer, barbecuing, or soaking up the sun.

They're alive.

While the wrong people die.

Henning lies down and stares up at the sky. Tore Pulli is dead. He is gone. It's weird, but it feels as if he has lost a friend. And when he thinks about it, perhaps he has.

Thorleif is reminded of Will Smith and the film *Enemy of the State* as he walks out into Karl Johansgate. Smith played a lawyer who was unaware that he had microphones and transmitters all over his body. Even his watch and shoes had been fitted with high-tech equipment, which meant that Jon Voight's team of NSA agents knew absolutely everything Smith did. The film's tagline was *"In God we trust. The rest we monitor."*

Thorleif doesn't know how sophisticated the technology the man with the ponytail and his fellow thugs are using is, but they seemed to know a great deal about him, and Thorleif can't afford to take any chances. He glances over his shoulder before walking into the nearest budget clothes shop, where he buys five pairs of socks, four pairs of underpants, a pair of long dark trousers, a pair of shorts, three white T-shirts, a thin cotton jumper, and a denim jacket. Then he finds a shoe shop and buys a pair of trainers. He uses the lavatory at a Burger King restaurant to change and leaves all of his old clothes behind.

Before going outside again, he waits in the restaurant for a few minutes and watches everyone around him, including the people on the street, until he feels confident no one is waiting for him or keeping him under surveillance.

It takes him only seconds to cross the street and enter Arkaden Mall, where he buys a black baseball cap. Afterward he finds the nearest ATM and withdraws as much cash as he can, first using his Visa card, then maxing out his previously untouched MasterCard.

Thorleif tries to suppress the urge to run when he exits on the other side of Arkaden. He walks briskly in the direction of Byporten Shopping Center, enters through a revolving door, and continues up two escalators while people rush around him. He passes a café, several clothes shops, and makes eye contact with a pretty shop assistant at Handysize before passing a supermarket, a bookshop, and a kiosk. He has arrived at the forecourt of Oslo Central Station.

Leaving behind everything and everyone like this is pure madness, he thinks. But what choice does he have? If he stays, he will very likely be killed, probably today. If he is interviewed by the police, they will surely break him in the end and then his options are confessing to the murder and claiming responsibility for it or telling them everything. If he chooses to talk or if the police make him, the man with the ponytail will hurt Elisabeth and the children in ways he can't bear to think about.

The only sensible solution, Thorleif concludes, is to do what he is doing now. Get the hell out of Oslo. He wonders how long it will be before he is reported missing. Guri and Ole will wonder why he never returned to the office. They will try to call him on his mobile, but will get no reply. They might ring Elisabeth to ask if he has come home though they will probably put that off for as long as they can. But it will be sometime tonight, Thorleif thinks. Before that he needs to have found himself a place to hide. Until then his job is to make himself as invisible as possible.

Thorleif has reached the large departure boards at the station. An anthill of people is milling around. It is impossible to determine if any of them are watching him. He just has to hope that his diversion tactics have been successful.

Buses are out of the question. Too claustrophobic and too slow. So he checks the list of InterCity trains. Skien, Lillehammer, Bergen, Halden, Trondheim. The train to Bergen departs in nine minutes, he sees. The one to Göteborg in eight. With his pulse throbbing in his neck, Thorleif rushes over to one of the numerous red ticket machines. He types in the letters and feeds money into the slot.

"The train to Eidsvoll is ready to depart from platform number ten."

Thorleif snatches the ticket and sets off. The train leaves in four minutes. And he still has one more thing to do.

49

When Ørjan Mjønes catches sight of his own reflection in the shop windows, he has to make an effort not to grin. Everything went according to plan. His plan. And no screw ups this time.

It was bloody brilliant.

But it's not over yet. The home leg remains. Getting rid of Brenden and picking up the rest of the money. After that he will leave Oslo for good. He can't risk staying here or returning later if Brenden's absence proves problematic.

Mjønes laughs to himself. Problematic?

He has yet to decide on a destination, but it will be far away. He feels a strong urge to go to the woods and sleep under the trees for weeks. He could do that, of course, but not in Norway. And he certainly isn't going to a place with cheap cocktails and scantily clad women as easily accessible as the beach. That kind of life has never appealed to him.

Once he has collected the cash, he won't need to work. Not for a long time. The question is how long he can manage without it. Idleness gives him cabin fever. His brain needs stimulation and work makes him feel alive.

Around him people are rushing with briefcases in their hands or dragging suitcases behind them as they throw swift, panicky glances at their watches or mobiles. Mjønes has nothing but contempt for those who subject themselves to this every day for a whole lifetime. It is so humdrum.

Mjønes has never been attracted to a life of respectability. As a teenager, he carried out ram raids most weeks. It was easy to do and the cops were always completely baffled. Why should he be stuck in some dead-end job earning 180 kroner per hour when he could easily make a quarter of a million in a weekend?

He had a girlfriend once who tried to turn him into a law-abiding citizen, but he only lasted a couple of months. Every day he would sit in an office trying to sell some rubbish while his body ached to be elsewhere, casing a joint, on a job, mapping and planning. His mother had asked him several times why he couldn't respect the law like everyone else, but that wasn't who he was. He enjoyed destruction, he got a thrill from stirring things up, he sought out excitement and action precisely so that life wouldn't be so bloody boring. It wasn't society that turned him into a criminal. It was a life he had chosen for himself. And if he had the chance to live his life all over again, the result would have been exactly the same.

His inside pocket vibrates. Mjønes takes out his mobile and answers it.

"We've a problem," Jeton Pocoli says.

"Go on?"

"Number One. I don't know where he is."

Mjønes's smile freezes. He transfers the mobile from one hand to the other, pulls a face, and rubs the bridge of his nose with his thumb and index finger.

"Where did you lose him?"

"He went into Burger King. I walked up and down outside for five to ten minutes, but I started to worry when he never reappeared. I went inside to look for him. I found his clothes in the gents."

Mjønes says nothing.

"Which Burger King was it?"

"The one at the bottom of Karl Johansgate."

"Close to Oslo Central Station?"

"Yes. That's where I am now, but I can't see him."

Mjønes considers this as he looks at his own reflection in the window of GlasMagasinet.

"Okay," he says, eventually.

"What do we do?" Pocoli asks.

"I'll ring you back. Stay where you are."

Mjønes ends the call before Pocoli has time to reply and rings Flurim Ahmetaj straight away.

"Speak," says the Swedish Albanian.

"Has he called Number Two yet?"

"No."

"Has he called anyone at all?"

"No."

"Can you see where his mobile is now?"

"No, but I can find out."

"Do that. And check his bank accounts. Number One has done a runner."

"Right."

Mjønes looks at himself while he processes the news. Gradually, a fresh smile emerges on his face.

"It's no big deal."

"Eh?"

"It doesn't matter. Number One is about to make the biggest mistake of his life."

50

There is a strange noise inside his head.

Is it the sound of the sea? He can definitely hear waves crashing.

Henning swallows, but the sound refuses to go away. It's as if he has been to a concert where the noise level was too loud. He blinks as well, but the people around him still look weird. They blur and dissolve. Their voices mingle. The grass under him seems to come closer. An ant climbs up on his hand. It looks as if it is about to crawl inside his skin when Henning flicks it away and gets up. He stands there, swaying. The first steps hurt, the next ones are even worse. He turns away from the sun and lets it burn his neck instead. He carries on walking. The fence, where's the fence? Tarmac under his feet again. The whoosh from a bicycle racing past grabs hold of him just as a fresh, sharp pain begins under the soles of his feet. When he puts pressure on them, they feel wet.

Nearby something bounces.

"Oi!"

Henning is startled and looks up.

"Stop the ball!"

He sticks out his more painful foot, feels something hit it and come to a halt. Someone runs toward him. Henning keeps the ball in place under his foot. He sees a boy with long blond hair. Ice blue eyes. There is something familiar about them.

"Thanks," the boy says. He is eight, maybe nine years old. "Can I have it back, please?" he asks. Henning looks at him.

"What's your name?" he hears himself say.

"Fredrik."

Henning takes a step to the side for support, tries to make eye contact with the boy, but can't manage it. Instead he rolls the ball toward the boy, who kicks it up and catches it with his hands, but drops it instantly.

"Yuk, it's covered in blood!"

The ball rolls away. Henning tries to work out where it has gone, but he can't. He only registers that the boy is leaving. The stinging pain under his feet grows more intense. He looks down. It's not until then he realizes that he is wearing slippers.

Thorleif has always experienced a sense of calm when traveling by train. There is something infinitely serene about gazing idly through a window. If his eyes follow the tracks, the world rushes past. If he looks out at the landscape, everything seems almost stagnant. It's something that has always fascinated him. But not now.

Today he can't be bothered to look for deer or admire the fields or the passing mountains. Instead he closes his eyes and tries to clear his mind. It proves to be impossible; he can't stop reliving what he has done. On his fingertips Thorleif can still feel the tiny hairs on Tore Pulli's body as he attached the microphone to the tight T-shirt. The needle in the palm of his hand, clammy and smooth. The startled look in Pulli's eyes as he—

Thorleif can't bear to complete the thought. He wonders what everyone will think in the next few days. Especially the children. Elisabeth will probably tell them that Daddy had to go abroad for work and that she doesn't know how long he will be away. But how long will she be able to keep that up? Pål is eight years old and he is a bright boy. He will soon guess that something is wrong. I need to let them know that I'm in one piece, Thorleif thinks, tell Elisabeth not to worry. But how will he manage that if their flat is being monitored? What if they have bugged Elisabeth's mobile? I can't risk it, Thorleif concludes. I can't risk them suspecting that she knows where he is.

So what the hell can he do?

She might still be at work. Perhaps he can call the school office and—

Damn, he doesn't have a mobile. He looks around, sees several of his fellow passengers fiddle with their mobiles. Perhaps he could borrow one of theirs? He dismisses the thought instantly. A conversation of that sort must be had in private and no sane person would hand over their mobile to a man who says he needs to go away to make a personal call. The best he can hope for is to wait until he leaves the train and look for a public telephone.

If he is to get hold of Elisabeth before she finishes work today, he needs to take action soon. Should he stay on the train until its final destination? Or is it better to get off along the way, at a smaller station? It will be easier to keep track of what is going on in a small town, fewer people around. However, if he is discovered and someone comes after him, he will be making their job easier.

An ad above the luggage shelves further away attracts Thorleif's attention. He looks at the pictures and reads the caption. *Get your dream cabin now*. Under the caption there is a scenic photo of mountains and open spaces, white, beautiful, and dramatic with small dark cabins dotted around the landscape. It says Ustaoset at the bottom as if the ad promotes a film starring the Norwegian winter.

Thorleif straightens up in his seat. The ad reminds him of Einar Fløtaker, a childhood friend with whom he lost contact after they both had children. But Thorleif will never forget the trip they made as teenagers many, many years ago to Einar's family's cabin in Ustaoset. It was the height of winter, Thorleif recalls, and it was down to minus 30°C when they arrived. Once they got off the train, they had to walk quite a distance from the station, lugging their supplies and skis before they reached it. Inside the cabin it was minus 12°C before they got the fire going, and it wasn't until the next day that they could take off their coats and walk around in normal indoor clothes.

The cabin is probably still there, Thorleif thinks. And I can't imagine that anyone is using it at the moment.

51

The footsteps stop right in front of him. Henning blinks and looks up, sees red shorts and a naked torso. Gunnar Goma is smiling down at him.

"What are you sitting here for?" his neighbor asks him, cheerfully but surprised. Henning looks around. He is slumped on the stairwell.

"I . . . I don't know," he replies.

It's like waking up in the middle of a dream. Or perhaps he is dreaming? No. If he had been, his feet wouldn't have been hurting.

"How long have you been sitting here?"

"I'm . . . I'm not really sure."

Their voices echo between the walls.

"I was just going out for a run and then I find you here. I thought you were a ghost."

Henning tries to get up. The pain shoots through his feet again.

"It looks as if you've stepped on some glass."

"What time is it?" Henning stammers.

"Time? I don't know, I never look at the clock these days. I look outside to see if it's light or dark, hot or cold. That's all a man my age needs to know."

"Mm."

Henning wants to pull himself to standing, but the banister is on the opposite side of him.

"Do you have some disinfectant upstairs?" Goma asks him.

"I think so."

"Okay, you can't stay here. Take my hand."

Henning looks up at him.

"Take my hand," Goma repeats.

Henning finds Goma's face and eyes, discovers a determination and a gravity he hasn't seen there before. He never would have thought that he would need help up the stairs by a seventy-six-year-old bypass patient naked from the waist up. Nevertheless he holds out his hand and staggers to his feet. He moves likes a drunk. They take the stairs one step at a time. Goma wheezes. His old hand feels rough and full of cartilage. Working hands, Henning thinks. All the time he can hear someone sawing, hammering, or hitting something in the courtyard.

They reach his flat. Henning fishes out his keys and opens the door, allows himself to be led into the hallway. He stops, looks at the folding steps and the smoke detector, then he looks at Goma.

No, Henning tells himself. This is a job you need to do on your own.

He thanks his neighbor for his help.

"Don't mention it," Goma says.

Henning looks down.

"Sorry, I don't really know what . . . what happened—"

Goma holds up his hands.

"Don't worry about it. We all have our senior moments. I once came round just as I was about to go into Kondomeriet. I don't know how I ended up in front of a sex shop."

"Is that right?"

"Yes. But once I was there, I obviously had to go in and—"

"Yes, thank you," Henning interrupts him and holds up his hand. A long moment passes in silence. They look at each other.

"Can I offer you a cup of coffee or something?" Henning asks.

"No, thank you, I'm off to Sultan's to buy tomatoes."

"Some other time perhaps?"

"Yes, I would like that."

Goma looks at him for a long time.

"Right. Got to go. You take it easy now."

"You too."

52

It has just gone five o'clock when Thorleif gets off at Ustaoset Station on wobbly legs. He stops and surveys the area, looks at what must be Hallingskarvet mountain range up to his right. The peaks are covered by velvety circles of mist. Dotted randomly around the landscape below are cabins, big and small, in a range of colors. In front of him the mountain hotel with its brown and red cladding takes up a fair amount of space. There are several apartment blocks close to the hotel. Route 7 winds its way toward Haugastøl and Bergen in parallel with the railway tracks. Across the tracks there is a little lake with fish that sparkles in the late-afternoon sunshine.

Thorleif starts to walk. It is hot. He gets even hotter when he realizes it's too late to call Elisabeth. She is bound to be home by now, probably busy feeding their starving children and irritated that he isn't back yet or answering his mobile.

Normally she would have gone to the gym on a Thursday night, but now she will have to stay at home. Otherwise he could have tried calling her there. But she won't be going tonight even if she could find a babysitter at short notice. Isn't there anyone else he can call? No one he can get to visit Elisabeth or who could bring her to a neutral place?

Calling her sister or any of their parents would set any number of alarm bells ringing. And if he had been the one hunting someone, apparently with access to unlimited funds, the first thing he would have done would be to check with their next of kin or friends to see if there had been any sort of contact. One of the football mums, perhaps. But Thorleif barely knows who they are or what they are called. Nor does he have their numbers. Besides, it occurs to him, it would be stupid to get even more innocent people mixed up with this. You'll just have to wait, Thorleif concludes, until Elisabeth is back at work. This means she faces an unbearable evening and night.

As the train drives on toward Bergen, Thorleif follows a man and a woman who also have business in Ustaoset on a Thursday afternoon. They walk separately. Thorleif takes care to lag behind them while simultaneously looking as if he knows his way around. As if it was quite natural for him to get off the train right there, right now.

He leaves the platform, crosses route 7, and walks down toward the gas station. Ustaoset's only supermarket greets him with the words "Lebensmittel" and "Groceries" displayed on top of each other on a white wall. Thorleif tries to visualize the road to Einar's cabin, but all he can recall is that they passed the shop, the gas station, and the kiosk before taking a right. So that's what he does now though he has yet to recognize anything. It doesn't help that the darkness and the snow back then have been replaced by bright afternoon sunshine and dry Indian summer colors. He walks past a block of flats with five garages under a large brown building with a red roof. Otherwise it is all cabins. Everywhere. And an enormous car park with rows of blue posts lined up with space for one car between them.

Thorleif follows the gravel road until he reaches a crossroads. There is a sign saying *Prestholt* to the right, via a road called Nystølvegen. Next to it are more signs on top of each other, all signposting cross-country ski routes, such as *Embretstølen, Geilo o/Prestholt,* and *Prestholt o/Eimeheii.* No, Thorleif thinks. It doesn't ring any bells.

So he decides to continue straight ahead as a car comes toward him on the gravel road. Thorleif pulls down the baseball cap and stares at the ground. He steps aside until the car has passed him and carries on until he reaches a gray building with a sign saying *Presttun.*

Presttun, Thorleif thinks. That sounds vaguely familiar.

Spurred on by this he walks on, following the red sticks along the roadside put there in case the snowfall is so deep that the snowplow drivers can't see the road. He remembers them struggling up the same hill, expelling clouds of beery breath. He hears rhythmic hammering coming from a building site, but he doesn't see anyone.

One hundred meters later he stops and looks across the slope to the right. Cabin after cabin and occasional young birch trees rise from the ground. Doesn't he recognize the black cabin halfway up the slope? Red roof and windowsills. A small outhouse nearby. Yes, that's it, Thorleif says to himself and speeds up.

He soon reaches it. It's not a big cabin, but now when Thorleif sees it again he remembers what it looked like on the inside. Pine walls and pine furniture everywhere. A small galley kitchen. A sofa with red cushions. Oil cloth on the table. Square windows with red and white curtains.

It probably hasn't changed on the inside, either, he thinks and takes another look around. The cabin looks deserted. The surrounding cabins look empty, too. He walks up to it, stops and peers inside through a gap in the kitchen curtains. Thorleif has never burgled anyone's house, he has barely done anything illegal his entire life and he feels uneasy knowing he is about to do so now, especially to someone he knows. He tries to persuade himself that Einar and his family would understand.

Thorleif walks around to the back of the cabin, remembering how Einar told him that the Fløtaker family forgot their key one Easter. They had to call out a local locksmith who in return for a substantial fee made sure their holiday wasn't completely ruined. Einar's father, who was tightfisted, promised himself that this would never happen again so he devised an alternative way into the cabin to be used in an emergency. As a result, the door of the woodshed was always left unlocked. At the end of the woodshed a new door was fitted that led to the toolshed and larder, from which you could enter the kitchen through a hatch with a padlock. And Thorleif remembers Einar telling him that the key to that padlock was hidden in a small rusty tin can.

Thorleif pushes down the handle of the door to the woodshed, but he has to lean heavily on it before it opens. He looks around one last time before he enters and walks to the next door. The shelves and benches in the toolshed are packed with old skis, ski poles with snow guards, snowshoes, spades, tins of paint, and various tools. Then he sees the tin can. Rusty but intact. He picks it up and shakes it.

The key rattles inside.

And Thorleif realizes that he is smiling for the first time in several days.

53

Henning is sitting on his battered Stressless armchair balancing his laptop on his thighs and resting his legs on a footstool in front of him. He has cleaned the cuts under his feet and applied a sterile bandage. He can feel that the healing process has already started.

The last few hours seem a blur to him. All he can remember clearly is his telephone conversation with Iver. Then nothing until he found himself coming to in the stairwell. And it's not the first time that his body has short-circuited like this. What on earth is wrong with me, he wonders.

It's almost six thirty pm so he turns on the TV. The commercial break is followed by the logo for TV2 News. He turns up the volume as he sees Tore Pulli's tall figure in the same doorway where Henning himself met Pulli only a few days ago. A breathless female voice announces that convicted killer Tore Pulli collapsed and died in Oslo Prison today. The picture disappears while the theme music is turned up a few notches before it fades away. The next headline story is introduced. Henning doesn't listen to it, but sees images of a concertinaed train with smoke rising from it. The final headline story is given five seconds to tantalize the viewer before the camera cuts to the studio where news anchor Mah-Rukh Ali welcomes the viewers to tonight's program. Henning turns the sound up even further.

Former enforcer Tore Pulli collapsed and died in
Oslo Prison earlier today. Pulli was being interviewed by
TV2 when he died.

Ali stares into the camera. The feature begins, but there are no pictures from the prison. Instead they cut right to a green screen with a photograph of prison spokesman Knut Olav Nordbø next to a telephone. He makes a nervous attempt at telling the people of Norway what has happened, but for the time being he can't release any information about the circumstances.

The feature moves to the open air where a reporter is ready and waiting outside the entrance to the prison, clutching a microphone close to his face. He reiterates the facts of the case before addressing Prison Governor Børre Kolberg. He can't shed any light on what has happened, either. Then back to Mah-Rukh Ali in the studio, who explains that viewers can see the final pictures of Tore Pulli on the nine o'clock news later that evening. In addition, they can read an interview with TV2 journalist Guri Palme, who was about to interview Tore Pulli when he died, on TV2's website.

Henning turns down the sound, flips open the laptop, and connects to the Internet. The homepage of 123news downloads itself. The breaking news logo has gone and been replaced with a standard headline accompanied by the media's favorite photo of Pulli, the mug shot of him that cold October evening almost two years ago where his eyes are wide, his mouth open, and his face displays a gawping expression.

Henning experiences a sinking feeling, not just at Pulli's death, but also as he recalls the disappointment and incredulity in Iver Gundersen's voice right before he hung up on him. Looking at all the stories Iver has written makes Henning feel even worse. Under the lead story there is a plethora of links, all with relevant and recent titles. Henning clicks on the lead story, which still has no headline other than the obvious one.

The first thing that strikes him as he scrolls down the article is that Iver has done a great job. He has tried to dramatize today's events, written it in present tense, and even produced a timeline. He concludes by reminding the readers what Pulli had been convicted of, complete with fact frames. The main text has been broken up with a large picture of Veronica Nansen, but she has yet to respond to 123news's requests for a reaction.

Henning sees that the news desk has pasted in TV2's interview with Guri Palme. *The shock of my life* is the headline. Neat, he thinks, producing an Internet exclusive so promptly and then refer to the story during a live broadcast. Synergies is the posh word for it in TV circles. But he doesn't click on it because he already knows what it's going to say.

Iver has also spoken to Pulli's solicitor, Frode Olsvik, who explained that he visited his client only a few hours before the interview and that there was nothing to suggest that he was unwell. Henning sighs, thinks about Pulli and hankers for a cigarette for the first time in ages. But he only needs to visualize his mother slumped over the kitchen table with the oxygen tank humming next to her and the urge goes away. What a life, he thinks. What a death.

At least Pulli's was quick.

54

It's not until he is inside the cabin that it occurs to Thorleif that the property might be fitted with a burglar alarm. However, the power is switched off and he can't see any devices on the walls that indicate a connection to a security company.

It takes him a while to locate the circuit breaker in a fuse box on an external wall. Fortunately, the water is already connected so he doesn't need to search for a stopcock among the heather, bushes, and stones that make up the rugged Ustaoset landscape.

On his way back he plunders the larder for a tin of lamb casserole, which he heats up even though he isn't hungry. The meat, potatoes, and carrots turn out to be juicy and tasty and gradually he feels his strength return, but his conscience continues to trouble him. He can't bear the thought of what Elisabeth must be going through at home where she is probably pacing up and down the floor absentmindedly answering the children's questions. That the man with the ponytail and his accomplices might be watching her at this very moment doesn't improve Thorleif's mood.

When he has finished eating, he notices that the light in the sky is starting to lose its intensity. The shop is probably shut now, but it doesn't matter now that he has a meal. He won't need anything else until tomorrow so he spends some time making himself at home. The cabin is fitted with an earth closet and there are instructions on the bathroom wall that he reads before using it. Afterward he showers in lukewarm water and dries himself with a towel he finds in one of the bathroom cupboards. Soon he starts to feel better.

There are plenty of books and other types of reading

material in the cabin. He also finds a map of the area that might come in handy. In the toolshed he noticed both fishing equipment and several boxes of hooks. If I'm to stay here for a while, Thorleif thinks, perhaps I should try to catch a trout or two.

There is a television in the cabin, but he decides not to switch it on. The glare from a TV screen can easily be seen from the outside, even from afar. Initially he considers not switching on any lights at all in order not to alert the neighbors—should any have arrived during the evening, but it's not a viable long-term solution. I can't just lock myself in, he thinks. I have to find out what is going on—if anything is, what the police are doing, what the media is saying. How will I be able to do that?

The hotel he passed on the main road will definitely have Internet access and, given the time of year, the guest computers are unlikely to be in great demand. But can he really run the risk of going there?

Thorleif thinks about the man who forced him to kill Pulli and asks himself if it's true that he knows nothing about him. He must have said or done something that Thorleif can use to his advantage. They spent several hours together. There has to be something he can do without compromising his family or himself. Think, Thorleif, he says to himself. You have to think.

He inhales and realizes at that moment how exhausted he is. He goes to one of the bedrooms and lies down, covering himself with the pale blue duvet without putting on bed linen first, and closes his eyes. Minutes later he is asleep.

55

Iver Gundersen lets himself into his flat and heaves a sigh as he dumps his shoulder bag on the floor up against the wall. He kicks off his shoes, goes over to the fridge to get a beer, flops into an armchair in the living room, and turns on the TV. He downs most of the beer in four gulps, then drinks a few more mouthfuls. He realizes that one beer won't be enough tonight.

He should really have been with Nora, but he hasn't got the energy to play the lover after working twelve or possibly thirteen hours. All he can manage is to let the evening come. He wouldn't be able to lie next to Nora, sensing her expectation of intimacy, their arms wrapped around each other, her breathing wafting across his face as they sleep. She can't sleep, she says, unless she is burrowing into his naked arm or shoulder. Preferably while snuggled up to his throat.

Nora also happens to be a particularly restless sleeper; her arms and legs sprawled all over the place or brutally flung aside, often without warning. And when he wakes up, early as he always does when he sleeps at her place, she will cling to him until he spoons with her, holding her, gently caressing her back and side. It's never enough. No, Iver thinks. He definitely hasn't got the energy for that performance tonight.

She was annoyed, of course, Iver could hear it in her voice. Or not annoyed as such, more disappointed. But at least Nora knows what it's like to be with someone who doesn't care what day of the week or what time it is when a story breaks. Not that there is much left of that particular side to Henning Juul.

They never discuss her, but even so Iver knows that Henning finds it hard to have to work alongside the man who replaced him. Iver has never asked Nora if she still has feelings for Henning because he can tell from looking at her. Anything else would be strange given how their marriage ended. Never stir up a hornets' nest, Iver reminds himself. Not if you don't want to get stung.

He sits up when TV2's nine o'clock news begins. He saw how the channel hinted at footage of Tore Pulli's death during the early-evening news, clever clogs. He always enjoys seeing pictures of a subject he himself is covering. Live images of a person only seconds before their life ends adds an extra dimension to a story. He turns up the volume and hears Guri Palme's dramatic voice over the broadcast.

TV2 has nothing new or spectacular to report about the death itself, Iver soon ascertains, but then again they don't have to. They already have the cream. He sees Guri's panicky, clumsy reaction, how she disappears off screen and calls for help. There is nothing fake about her behavior. This is reality TV at its best.

It is some years since Iver and Guri were at Oslo Journalist College together. Guri was the kind of girl who would have her hair styled for the school photo, who asked the stills photographer to include her cleavage in head shots, and who would spend a week on a tanning bed before a recording, whether it was college work or private. She went to the gym four times a week, at least, concentrating on her stomach, bottom, and legs.

But she was also bright, Iver had spotted that immediately, and ambitious. Two very helpful attributes if you want to get ahead in their profession. And it didn't take many bonding beers with lecturers or media personalities before Iver understood that Guri had an appetite only for men who could further her career.

Consequently, he was rather mystified when he started noticing Guri's probing eyes on him, her penetrating gaze, her too quick and false giggling whenever he made a remark that could generously be interpreted as amusing. There were brief, furtive glances over piles of books in the reading room. And the inevitable happened. After a drunken night on the town they collapsed into bed together—without any clothes on.

They were never an item, far from it, but while they were at college they hooked up every now and then to take full advantage of each other. It was good and uncomplicated. It's like that with some people, there is an indefinable attraction. A spark whenever you look at each other and you can't help but give in to it.

After graduation they started job hunting. Guri had had a student placement at TV2, and to begin with she took all the shifts she could get there. But she was looking for her break, the scoop that would make her name. One night after they had expended some excess energy and were lying in bed pillow talking, she shared her concerns with him. *I need a scoop,* she sighed, blowing smoke up toward the ceiling. Her forehead was glistening. In the glow from the outside light forcing itself through the curtains he was momentarily lost in her smooth skin that fitted snugly over her jawline.

Perhaps I can help you, he heard himself say and regretted it immediately. But there was no way back. At the time Iver was brimming with confidence having already broken several stories that had made the headlines. And as is often the case when a reporter has written several high-profile stories, the reporter becomes noticed and people bring them tips that lead to more scoops.

One tip he hadn't yet managed to investigate—and neither did he know when he would find the time to—concerned an employee in a construction company in Sørlandet who had—allegedly—received a number of private gifts from a subcontractor as a kickback for securing the subcontractor in question work on a road-building project worth billions. Guri found out that the employee, a forty-seven-year-old man from Vennesla, was one of the construction managers on the project, and the "thank-yous" he had been given included a private garage at his home address in addition to several deposits paid into his bank account at various intervals. In total the gifts were worth just over 300,000 kroner. The forty-seven-year-old had tried to cover up the bribes with fictitious invoices.

Guri created a stir, wrote several excellent follow-up articles about corruption in Norway, and interviewed the world's leading nongovernmental anticorruption organization, Transparency International, which announced later that year that Norway was the most corrupt country in Scandinavia. Guri also secured an interview with the Norwegian-born French magistrate and politician Eva Joly, a famous anticorruption scourge, and the topic was hotly debated both in *Tabloid* on TV2 and on other news channels. It might not have been a major scoop, but it helped Guri get noticed. Shortly afterward TV2 offered her a permanent contract. She had arrived.

Guri started dating a senior TV2 executive, Iver met Nora, and since then they have stayed out of each other's beds. But Iver knows that the spark is still there, a delicious tension that simmers between them. And Guri is well aware that she owes him a favor.

The picture of Tore Pulli freezes on the screen as Prison Governor Børre Kolberg tells viewers that he can't discuss Tore Pulli's medical history before the journalist announces that an autopsy will be carried out on Pulli's body, as is standard procedure when a death is unexplained. Iver turns off the TV, lights a cigarette, and mulls it all over before he picks up his mobile from the coffee table and finds Guri Palme's number among his contacts. He stares at her name for a while before he presses *call*. And he thinks it's definitely just as well that he isn't with Nora right now.

56

After hours of mindless TV watching Henning's brain starts to work again. At eleven o'clock that evening he opens FireCracker 2.0—the program Henning's source within the police wrote a couple of years ago for their confidential two-way communication—and checks to see if 6tiermes7 is logged on. The minutes pass. Then there is a *ding dong* sound as if someone had rung the doorbell.

Henning's fingers hit the keyboard.

MakkaPakka:
Do you know what killed Pulli yet?

6tiermes7:
Come on, what do you think?

MakkaPakka:
That it's way too early. Was there any blood at the crime scene?

6tiermes7:
No.

MakkaPakka:
Anything at all suspicious?

6tiermes7:
Not that I know of.

MakkaPakka:
Police interviews?

6tiermes7:
They haven't got that far yet.

MakkaPakka:
Why not?

6tiermes7:
TV2 refuse to release the tapes without a warrant. But here's something interesting for you. A member of TV2's staff has gone missing.

Henning sits up.

MakkaPakka:
Someone who was there when Pulli died?

6tiermes7:
Yes.

MakkaPakka:
Who is he?

6tiermes7:
His name is Thorleif Brenden. He's a cameraman.

MakkaPakka:
Any previous convictions?

6tiermes7:
No, or he would never have got into the prison.

MakkaPakka:
Okay, but do you know anything about him at all?

6tiermes7:
No. He hasn't put a foot wrong his whole life.

MakkaPakka:
So what are you doing about it?

6tiermes7:
Nothing at the moment. He hasn't been missing for very long. But we'll put out a missing person bulletin, I imagine, if he doesn't turn up over the weekend.

Interesting, Henning thinks. Very interesting indeed.

MakkaPakka:
Now for something completely different: do you know where Rasmus Bjelland is these days?

6tiermes7:
Didn't he apply for witness protection?

MakkaPakka:
Yes. That's why I'm asking.

6tiermes7:
No. Not a clue. Do you want to talk to him again?

MakkaPakka:
Not really sure. But I wonder if the people looking for Bjelland might be behind the arson attack on my flat. Knowing if he is still alive would be a good start.

6tiermes7:
It could take some time. I might not be able to come up with anything.

MakkaPakka:
Okay. I'll just have to be patient.

6tiermes7:
Stay healthy.

MakkaPakka:
You too.

57

Though it is late in the evening, the weather is still warm. Ørjan Mjønes lights a cigarette, blows smoke out through his nose. He is just about to take a second drag when the public telephone on the street corner starts to ring. Mjønes squashes the embers with the tips of his fingers and puts the cigarette back in the packet. He goes inside the telephone booth and lifts the handset.

"Hello?"

"Congratulations."

Langbein's voice is flat.

"Thank you."

"Have you tied up all the loose ends?"

Mjønes hesitates.

"Not all of them, but—"

"What do you mean?"

"It's not a problem. I'm in control, there's nothing to worry about."

"I'm paid to worry."

"Yes, but you can trust me."

"I've made that mistake once before."

"Okay, I understand why you say that, but it's never going to point back to you or the deal that we have."

"I don't like loose ends."

"Neither do I. That's why I'm going to fix it."

"I'll call you in seventy-two hours. If your problem has gone away, you'll get the rest of your money."

"But—"

"Same number. Same time."

Mjønes doesn't have time to protest before the line goes

dead. He hangs up the handset hard, shakes his head, and walks out into the night, relighting his cigarette.

A big part of him is tempted to let Brenden run, let him play his own game since he evidently doesn't understand how this works. Brenden has ruined everything for himself. Brenden killed Tore Pulli. If the police should ever manage to discover how Pulli died and if they suspect that he might have been murdered, they will be looking for Brenden precisely because he is missing. They will probably want to interview him anyway, for the same reason. It doesn't look good to disappear on the day that you were in a room with a convicted killer who collapses and dies. And if the police find him, Brenden will be too scared to talk. He knows that his family will be harmed if he reveals anything about the duress he was subjected to.

The best solution, Mjønes thinks, would be to give Brenden enough time to start yearning for his family and his old life. He has no experience of lying low. Sooner or later he will have to come out or someone will find him. The cash Brenden withdrew also won't last forever regardless of how careful he is. And when the media starts running their missing cameraman stories or the police decide to issue a warrant for him, the chances that someone will recognize him are high.

But seventy-two hours, Mjønes thinks. That's not a lot. And Brenden showed initiative when he got rid of his clothes and left his mobile on a train to Eidsvoll without getting on himself. Brenden is keeping his cool. And that's why he has to die. Preferably within the next seventy-two hours.

Mjønes takes a drag and stubs out the cigarette in a nearby bin before he turns his attention to the cab rank and picks out a white Toyota Prius. It's time, he decides, to stir things up.

58

The cuts to his feet throb all the way from Grünerløkka to Grønland, but Henning alternates between putting his weight on the heels and the balls of his feet so as not to aggravate the injuries more than necessary. It works to some extent.

At the office he hangs up his jacket on a coat hook by the grid of desks and chairs that is the national news desk. A quick glance across the room tells him that neither Heidi Kjus nor Kåre Hjeltland has arrived yet. Iver Gundersen, however, is already behind his desk. Henning nods to him, sees that his eyes look bright and contented. He probably got laid last night, Henning thinks. Or this morning.

"I thought you were taking today off as well?" Iver snipes.

"Yes, but I . . . I wanted to join in."

Iver looks at Henning for a few seconds before he replies: "How nice of you."

Henning sits down. The room starts to fill with voices from a television screen and the sound of stiff fingers across reluctant keyboards. He switches on his computer and leans back, he sees Iver drink from a cup that he puts down so hard the coffee washes up the inside walls.

"Listen, I've got something to show you," Iver says.

"Eh?"

Iver looks around to check that no one is close enough to overhear.

"We need to discuss it in private. Is now a good time?"

"Time?"

"I know the morning meeting is about to start, but we need a quick review. In my opinion."

Henning shrugs his shoulders, he feels more like ringing Brogeland to check if Thorleif Brenden has turned up during the night, but he decides it can wait.

"Why not," he says.

"Great. Come on."

Iver takes a CD, gets up, and walks briskly past the coffee machine where a small queue of bleary-eyed journalists has formed. Henning tries to walk as naturally as he can to avoid awkward questions he doesn't feel like answering.

They go to a meeting room where four chairs are arranged around a table. A computer is pushed up against the wall. Iver closes the door, walks over to the computer, and moves the mouse to wake up the screen. He types in his username and password and hits the *enter* key.

"Sit down, would you," Iver says. "Take a seat, please, would you? People standing make me nervous."

Henning does as he is told.

"What is it you want to show me?" he says.

"Just wait."

Iver inserts the CD into the computer and double clicks on the icon that appears on the right-hand side of the screen. He drums his fingers on the table while he waits for the file to open. Soon the screen is filled with light coming from a doorway. Henning sees a familiar woman's face on the other side of the door. And then he realizes what they are looking at.

"How the hell did you get hold of this?"

"That specific piece of information is something I need to keep to myself," Iver smiles without taking his eyes off Guri Palme. Henning is forced to admit that he is impressed.

"Which version is this?" he asks. Iver's smug world champion smile appears to be glued to his face.

"What do you mean?"

"Have TV2 edited it?"

"No, this is raw footage. Or at least I think it is. This is just the footage from one camera. Something went wrong with the other recording, I think."

Tore Pulli's massive body comes into focus. He is wearing jeans and a tight T-shirt. Pulli shakes hands with Guri Palme, who can just about be seen. She is wearing dark blue jeans, a white top, and a short suede jacket. Her cleavage is clearly visible in the slanted camera angle. Pulli doesn't smile, he merely looks her in the eye, but can't resist the temptation to look further down.

Palme ushers him into the room and Pulli follows her. He stops and greets the other man from the TV2 crew. Could it be Thorleif Brenden?—Henning wonders and sees how the man helps to seat Pulli, attaches a microphone to his T-shirt, and connects a cable from the microphone to the camera opposite. After that he adjusts Pulli's sitting position slightly. From then on the camera focuses exclusively on Pulli.

"*Are you ready to start?*" Palme asks. "*Would you like a glass of water?*"

Pulli doesn't respond. He looks nervous, Henning thinks and stares at Pulli's restless eyes.

"*Tore Pulli, thank you for talking to us.*"

Pulli's head lolls forward, but he tries to lift it up.

"*You've been convicted of murder, but you maintain your innocence and claim that someone set you up. Who set you up?*"

Pulli still doesn't reply. Henning leans forward. Gravity seems to be forcing Pulli's head down to his chest and he starts to sway. Henning sees something that looks like fear in Pulli's eyes before the spark in them fades away. Iver turns up the sound a bit more.

"*Pulli, are you feeling all right?*"

Pulli alternates between swaying from side to side and rocking back and forth. He starts to shake all over, his eyes roll into the back of his head, and his face turns blue. The cameraman captures it, he zooms in on Pulli's face, then he zooms out again. Pulli's convulsions increase before he keels over on his side and lies on the sofa in spasms. Then he stops moving. His eyes take on a glassy stillness.

"Toffe, what the hell do you think you're doing? Just carry on filming, will you?"

Iver starts to laugh.

"What is it?"

"They'll want to cut that bit."

"Which bit?"

"The bit where she tells Toffe or whatever his name is to carry on filming."

Henning watches the chaos that ensues, he hears Guri Palme shout: *He collapsed! He just collapsed!* as she bangs on what Henning assumes to be a door with her bare fists. Shortly afterward a woman enters the room. She orders everyone to leave. Palme starts arguing with Knut Olav Nordbø.

"We need to get out of here!"

"I have to call an ambulance . . . the police . . . they . . . I—"

"Yes, but we can't stay here now!"

The camera wobbles before the screen goes blue. Iver lets the CD play for a few seconds, before he stops it.

"Well, that didn't take long," he says and exhales hard. An acrid smell of stale coffee and Pall Mall cigarettes reaches Henning's nostrils.

"What are you thinking?" Iver asks.

Henning looks at him. It feels weird to sit in a small room with Iver, just the two of them, discussing a story. Henning leans forward and rests his elbows on the table.

"I don't really know," he says and thinks about Thorleif Brenden. "There is not much we can do about the death itself except await the result of the preliminary autopsy report. And you dealt with everything else yesterday."

"So you did read it," Iver smiles happily.

Henning doesn't reply.

"But his case," Henning begins and realizes instantly that he has gone too far to turn back. The knowledge of what it involves makes his heart beat faster and harder.

"You're referring to his appeal?"

"Yes, or the reason there was an appeal to be heard in the first place. I've a good mind to review the whole case," Henning says, surprised at the determination in his own voice.

"What do you mean?"

Since the moment Henning heard that Pulli had died, he has gone over what Pulli said to him when they met in prison. *I guarantee that you'll be interested in what I know*. And the more he thinks about it, the more convinced he is that Pulli wasn't lying or trying to scam him. It's only human to want to think well of the dead, but he feels sure that Pulli had something on someone. And bearing in mind how many people he knew, it's likely that others knew it, too. If I'm to find out what it is, Henning thinks, I have to get to know Pulli better.

"Pulli always maintained his innocence," Henning continues.

Iver scoffs and smiles.

"Pull the other one, Henning," he says, sounding jaded.

"What if he was telling the truth?"

"A guy like Pulli? I refuse to believe that. He has nineteen minutes he failed to account for."

"Yes, I'm aware of that, but there are other aspects of his case which are highly suspect."

"Such as?"

"Such as why a former enforcer who didn't even use his knuckle-duster when he went debt collecting, would take his old museum piece with him to what was supposedly a peaceful meeting."

"He was losing his touch."

"Seriously, Iver."

"Yes, but why not?"

Henning is about to say something, but stops himself.

"I'm not saying that he didn't do it, but that it wouldn't hurt to take a look. Something about this case isn't right."

Iver scratches his sparse beard.

"It's going to take forever, Henning. And besides, we don't know if it'll get us anywhere. Plus we're going to upset a lot of people."

"I know, but it's worth doing some work on the story for that reason alone. On the side."

Iver looks at Henning with an expression of skepticism in his eyes.

"Why is this suddenly so important to you?" he says.

Henning doesn't reply straight away.

"I just think there is a good story here," he says, at last. "And I . . . I don't think I can crack it on my own."

Iver stares at Henning who looks steadily back at him. Neither of them speaks for a while.

"Besides, you owe me," Henning declares.

"What did you say?" Iver gasps.

"The Henriette Hagerup story," Henning reminds him. "I handed it to you on a plate and I know it opened doors for you. Is it just the two job offers you have received since then? Or did more come in during the summer?"

Iver stares at Henning with incredulity.

"But that's all right," Henning tells him. "I'm going to work on this story with or without your help."

Iver looks down. A long, awkward silence ensues.

Finally he nods.

59

Thorleif wakes up with a start. He looks around, but doesn't recognize his surroundings.

Then he remembers where he is.

He quickly flips back the duvet and sits up, heaving his legs over the edge of the bed so his feet touch the dark brown wooden floor. There is a yellow bedside table next to the bed underneath a small window where white curtains make an unsuccessful attempt at keeping out the light. Thorleif runs his hands up and down his face, looks around for his mobile and sighs when he remembers that he deliberately left it behind on the Eidsvoll train. He has no idea what time it is except that it must be morning. At home he would have shuffled to the bathroom and woken himself up under the shower.

Home.

He wonders what Elisabeth and the children are doing. Perhaps Julie is playing and having fun at nursery. Perhaps Pål is tumbling about in PE as he always does on Friday mornings. Elisabeth is unlikely to have gone to work. If he knows her well, she will be too upset. But if that's the case then he can't contact her and he is afraid to call her at home.

Thorleif goes to the living room where he carefully opens one of the curtains and looks out of the window. The cabin lies halfway up the slope with breathtaking views across Ustaoset and Ustetind at the end of the lake and the open terrain. It feels good to rest his eyes on the horizon. He sees a tiny airplane. Flocks of birds. A car drives down the gray snake of tarmac. Someone is walking from the gas station to the hotel.

Even though Thorleif isn't hungry he knows that he has to eat something. He won't be very much use to himself if his head and body aren't working. He potters sleepily to the larder and checks his supplies. Nothing very appetizing. A few tins of lamb casserole. Peas and ham. Tinned pineapple. He can see he has food for a couple of days, but there are no dried foods, cold meats, or beverages. He will have to go shopping.

It occurs to him that the weekend is about to start. People who have finished their summer holidays might already be contemplating getting their cabins ready for the winter season. Many love the vivid autumn colors that have started to emerge. There is bound to be considerably more traffic over the weekend, Thorleif thinks. Consequently he should buy enough food to last him at least two days. If not longer.

Soon he is leaving the cabin the same way he came in, through the kitchen, the larder, and the woodshed. The fresh mountain air feels good on his face. He walks at a steady pace down to the main road and into what he, with a little generosity, can call the center of Ustaoset. He climbs the gray concrete steps and enters the shop that he quickly sees is a cross between a Clas Ohlson home store and an Ica Supermarket. On entry he is met by a display of all sorts of handy tools. Spades, mops, overalls, wellies, snowshoes even though the snow is a couple of months away.

The first thing Thorleif does is check the newspapers. Tore Pulli's death is on the front page of both *VG* and *Dagbladet*. *Aftenposten*, too, features Pulli's death. As does *Bergens Tidende*. The local newspaper, *Hallingdølen*, leads with the unusual rise in break-ins in cabins in Ustaoset recently and how the Ustaoset-Haugastøl area has been particularly badly affected. Thorleif's stomach lurches, but he tries to shake it off by wandering around the aisles with the shopping basket. He fills it with a bag of ready-sliced bread, a tub of cream cheese, two cartons of juice, and a large block of milk chocolate. He also picks up both tabloid newspapers on his way out and says a quick thank-you to the man behind the till when he gets his receipt.

Thorleif is about to leave, but turns around.

"Excuse me, do you happen to know if there is a public telephone nearby?"

The man laughs.

"No, we don't have those in Ustaoset."

"I thought they were everywhere."

"Not anymore."

"Oh, right, no, I don't suppose they are. I forgot my mobile, you see. Is there anywhere around here you can make calls if you need to . . . if you haven't got one?"

"You could try the hotel and see if they can help you," the man says without the smile leaving his lips.

"Thank you."

Thorleif leaves the shop and makes his way to the main entrance of the hotel, but when he gets there the door is locked. He tries it again without success. He presses his face against the glass in the door, but sees no movement inside.

"Damn," he says and looks around while he decides what to do next. How on earth can a hotel be shut in the middle of the day? Feeling despondent and even guiltier toward Elisabeth he wanders back to the cabin. There he spreads cream cheese on some bread slices and reads the papers without finding anything to suggest that Tore Pulli's death is being treated as suspicious. But much could have happened since the tabloids went to print. If I'm to know what is going on, Thorleif thinks, I need completely different methods.

60

Heidi Kjus gets up as Iver and Henning appear from around the corner looking as if they are about to join the queue of coffee-deprived early birds. Henning can see what she wants to say long before she says it, and yet he still lets her make her first management mistake of the day.

"Where have you been?"

"We went out for a cigarette," Henning mutters.

"What did you say?"

"Sorry," Iver says and holds up his hands. "It's my fault. Henning and I have just had a meeting to prepare for the morning meeting with you."

"That meeting was supposed to start ten minutes ago! And not just because of me, but because of everyone else in the department. Wasting other people's time shows a lack of respect."

"Yes, we know. Sorry. It won't happen again."

Heidi turns her attention to Henning.

"What are you doing here today? I thought you were taking today off as well?"

"Yes, but I decided I would much rather be here," he replies, making no attempt to cover up his irony. Out of the corner of his eye he sees Iver smile.

"Okay, fine. But are you ready now? Have you finished your little chat?"

"Yes."

"Good. Henning, will you be joining us?"

"Obviously. It's the highlight of my day. Do I have time to make a quick phone call first?"

"To whom?"

"It'll only take a minute."

She checks her watch and sighs.

"All right, then. But be quick."

Heidi and Iver are sitting alone in the meeting room when Henning enters.

"So tell me," Heidi says. "What are you doing about Tore Pulli?"

Henning and Iver look at each other.

"The preliminary autopsy report will probably be ready sometime today," Iver says.

"Okay. Anything else?"

Iver and Henning exchange glances, but neither of them says anything.

"Is that it?" she asks, suspiciously.

Henning clears his throat.

"One of the people present when Pulli died has gone missing."

Iver and Heidi both look at Henning.

"Missing how? Has he done a runner?" she asks.

"Nobody knows yet. I've just been speaking to the police. He was supposed to turn up at the station to make a statement last night, but no one has seen hair or hide of him since yesterday, since Pulli died."

"Do the police suspect him of anything?"

"Not at the moment. But they would very much like to know what he has been up to."

"What's his name?"

"Thorleif Brenden. He's a cameraman."

"Perhaps the shutter went down for him?" Iver jokes.

"An experienced cameraman who has covered wars and atrocities all over the world? He goes AWOL just because he sees the man collapse and die in prison?"

Iver says nothing.

"Besides, he lives with his girlfriend and their two children," Henning adds.

"There could be a perfectly reasonable explanation for why he is missing," Heidi suggests.

"Sure, but it's still a remarkable coincidence."

Heidi makes a quick note on the pad in front of her.

"Okay," she says in her summoning-up voice. "We need some scoops, boys. Real news. It's been a long time."

61

Iver Gundersen places another steaming cup of coffee on his desk and sits down. An avalanche of emails has arrived since he last checked, but not one of them is from Nora. They always say hi to each other in the morning, especially if they haven't spent the night together. He sent her a few lines just before Henning turned up, but she has yet to respond. He guesses she is still sulking and checks his mobile. No messages there, either.

He finds her number and lets it ring for a long time, but there is no reply. With a dawning realization that she may not only be sulking but also be mad at him, he decides to leave a message. Before he starts to talk, he glances around, quickly checking that there is no one in the immediate vicinity. He hears the beep at the other end.

"Hi, it's me. I wanted to ask you about tonight. If you haven't got plans I was wondering if you would like to go to the cinema? Or out for a meal somewhere nice? That would be . . . nice. As I didn't make it last night and . . . eh—"

Iver looks up and sees Henning limp out from the lavatories.

"Eh, okay, call me. Or send me an email. Okay. Take care."

Iver hangs up just as Henning sits down. Iver looks at him.

"How did you know Brenden was missing?" he says.

Henning looks up.

"You didn't come to work yesterday," Iver continues.

Henning still makes no reply.

"You also knew that he has a girlfriend and two children, that he is an experienced cameraman, et cetera. How did you manage to find all that out?"

Henning looks at Iver for a few moments before he says:

"None of your business."

"None of my business?"

"Do I ever ask you where you get your information from?"

"No, but—"

"No, precisely. Why don't we agree how best to develop this story?"

Iver hesitates before he nods.

"As far as Tore Pulli is concerned," Henning says, "the police are awaiting the preliminary autopsy report before they do anything. It's also too soon for them to take action in respect to Brenden. But we ought to have a chat with TV2."

"I know Guri Palme a bit," Iver says. "I could try to speak to her."

Henning looks at him for a couple of long seconds.

"Okay. I'll see if I can get hold of Brenden's family. Unless they've already appointed a spokesperson. Everybody does, these days. Do you still have the CD?"

Iver looks around his desk.

"What about it?"

"I want to have another look at it."

"Okay. But be discreet. I don't want anyone else seeing it."

"Fine. Do we have something we can feed to the monster?"

"Pulli's funeral, probably. It'll be a glorious mix of celebrities and villains."

"Yes, but I wonder if we'll be able to mention anyone by name. Plus it would take up a lot of time."

"Yes. Stupid idea."

"No, we should still go. And if we're to get to the bottom of this story, there are a couple of people we need to talk to. Kent Harry Hansen is one for them. He is the manager of the gym where Tore Pulli used to go and it's where most of Pulli's friends hang out."

"Okay. I'll see if I can get hold of him."

"Fine. If you want to talk to him face to face it might be

wise to do it away from the gym. They're not very fond of visits from the press. In fact, it might a good idea to tread carefully among those guys."

"I've taken a walk on the wild side before."

"Yes, I know. You have that I'm-invincible-because-I'm-a-journalist look. It will vanish once you've had your head kicked in."

Iver scrutinizes Henning.

"I know you've just told me it's none of my business, but how the hell do you know all this? Where Pulli worked out, the kind of people who go there, their names, et cetera?"

Henning stops.

"I did a bit of research last night' is all he says.

"Yes, you could say that again."

Henning shows no sign of wanting to elaborate. Instead he says: "If you get hold of Hansen, I've got some suggestions as to what you should ask him."

62

Henning finds the meeting room as empty as it was earlier that morning, closes the door behind him, and inserts the CD. He puts on headphones and concentrates on Pulli's face while observing everything that happens in the room, the movements of the cameraman, the cables, the gobos. Henning didn't find any photos of Brenden on the Internet, but he thinks he must be the man with practically no hair and a goatee. Underneath his khaki photographer's waistcoat he wears a red T-shirt with a logo Henning can't make out.

He is reminded of a question his mentor Jarle Høgseth used to ask him, especially when Henning muttered phrases such as *I don't understand* or *I'm stuck, this isn't going anywhere.* Høgseth always made him look at the problem again from different angles.

What does it mean to understand? he would sometimes ask him.

To know something, perhaps, to appreciate its implications.

There are two ways of looking, Henning. If you don't look properly, you'll never see anything. But if you look a little less, you can also see much more.

Høgseth went on to explain his philosophy, which Henning has applied to every aspect of journalism ever since.

All journalists focus on the speaker because that's the reason they are there. But it's often much more rewarding to study the person next to the speaker or their spouse for that matter, to see how they react. It's about spotting something no one else is paying attention to.

Henning watches Brenden as Pulli enters. They nod and shake hands before Pulli sits down. The camera follows Pulli's movements. Brenden comes into view again. He attaches a microphone to Pulli's T-shirt, runs a cable from his body in the direction of the camera before he puts his hand on Pulli's back and pushes him a little closer to the table. Brenden's physical contact with Pulli lasts ten or perhaps fifteen seconds. Then only Pulli can be seen on the screen.

Henning rewinds the recording and replays the scene. He plays it a third time before he hits the *stop* button and zooms in on Brenden's left hand. It is clenched even while he clips on the microphone. Henning studies the hand more closely in slow motion. It remains clenched. When Brenden leans toward Pulli to make him straighten up, both his hands are behind Pulli's neck. Suddenly Pulli glances sideways, toward Brenden, but Brenden merely steps away from Pulli, still with his fist closed.

"Hm," Henning mutters to himself and rewinds the recording again and stops it just as Pulli looks at Brenden. Henning stares into Pulli's eyes. Then he calls Brogeland to ask if the police have seen the footage.

"No, we haven't got the recording from TV2 yet. I think it's coming later today."

"Okay. Call me when you've seen it. There are a couple of things I need to talk to you about."

"What things? Can't you just tell me now?"

"I need to check something first. Have you spoken to Thorleif Brenden's family yet?"

"Ella Sandland spoke to his girlfriend late last night."

"And what did she say?"

"The usual, that they hadn't argued, that he would never just stay away like this."

"So he hadn't been behaving strangely up until the time he was going to film Pulli in prison?"

"I don't know."

"Okay. Call me later today, would you?"

"I'll see what I can do."

63

"It's beyond me how you can live like this."

Ørjan Mjønes marches into the inner sanctum of Flurim Ahmetaj, a room that serves as his center of operations, living room, and also bedroom or so it would appear. A duvet is scrunched up on a mattress under the window, which is covered with a black blind. The only source of light in the room is coming from three computer monitors lined up next to each other.

"That's how I like it," Ahmetaj says in Swedish.

Plates with crumbs and cold pizza crusts are piled high on his desk. The floor space by the computer tower is covered with Coke bottles, empty as well as half-full ones.

Mjønes finds an office chair and rolls over to the desk. He looks for somewhere to put down his mobile, but gives up.

"You wanted to show me something?"

Ahmetaj slurps from a 1.5-liter Coke bottle and lets out an unashamed burp.

"Check this out," he says and plays a video on the screen. From a bird's-eye perspective they see people walk quickly in and out of a Burger King restaurant. Mjønes looks at Ahmetaj.

"I know a guy who knows a guy who does security for Burger King," Ahmetaj says in broken Swedish. "You wouldn't believe what people will do in exchange for a couple of grand—which you now owe me, by the way."

"I'm sure we can sort that out," Mjønes smiles.

The camera is mounted under the ceiling with the lens overlooking the tills and the entrance. At the bottom-right corner a counter shows the time as being 12:38:04.

"Look at him," Ahmetaj says, pointing to a man who walks quickly into the restaurant. In his hand he holds a big white plastic bag that appears to be full of clothes.

"That's Brenden," Mjønes says.

"Okay. And now look, a few minutes later."

Ahmetaj fast forwards the recording until the counter shows 12:43:26. A man in a white T-shirt is standing with his back to the camera glancing nervously around and carrying an identical but slightly less bulging plastic bag.

"Brenden again," Mjønes says, getting excited now.

"Are you sure?"

"Yes. It's the same hairstyle and posture."

Brenden leaves Burger King making sure he is looking at the ground and shielding his face with his hand as he does so.

"Okay," Mjønes says. "From his bank statement we know that he went into JeanTV in Arkaden Mall and bought something that cost 399 kroner."

"A hat, maybe."

"Yes, that was my first thought. Or a baseball cap. And since he ditched his mobile on a train leaving Oslo Central Station, it's highly probable that he himself traveled in another direction around the same time. Can you find out which other trains left then?"

"Okay."

Ahmetaj's fingers fly across the keyboard.

"Wait a moment, I've got a better idea. Can you give me a printout of the best picture you have of Brenden?"

Ahmetaj clicks again and replays the video. He waits for Brenden to turn his head. His face appears in profile. Ahmetaj freezes the picture, takes a screen dump, and opens the file in Photoshop where he adjusts the colors and the contrasts. Then he hits *Crtl+P*. The sound of a printer warming up comes from somewhere under the desk. Mjønes bends down, kicks away an empty Coke bottle, which in turn knocks over several other empty bottles. He pulls a face as the dust rises.

"What are you going to do?" Ahmetaj asks when Mjønes reappears with a sheet of paper in his hand.

"I'm going to play cops and robbers," Mjønes replies and grins.

64

In American TV crime dramas, male pathologists are short and fat while female ones have long legs and are as immaculately groomed as only newly divorced women can be. Both sexes have complicated private lives, but as far as Henning knows, Dr. Karoline Omdahl fits none of the above categories. When he wrote a story about a day in the life of a pathologist some years ago and used Dr. Omdahl as his subject he learned that she is married with three grown-up children and has a passion for golden retrievers. The numerous photos of dogs, children, and grandchildren Dr. Omdahl displayed in her office made it easy for Henning to bust every myth and cliché about the profession of forensic medicine. Even so, he couldn't stop himself from spicing up his feature with references to smelly corpses, stomach contents, and open chest cavities.

In Norway forensic autopsies are performed almost exclusively by forensic pathologists. Forensic medicine has become so specialized that general pathologists no longer have the competencies required to carry them out. Dr. Omdahl does, however, and she replies after several long rings. Henning introduces himself and asks if she remembers him.

"Oh, hi," she says, surprised. "Yes, of course I do."

"Good to talk to you again."

"Likewise."

"How are the dogs?"

Henning hears her drink from a cup and swallow.

"Why, thank you, they're fine. Yash had an infected paw last week, but it seems to have cleared up now, fortunately."

"Glad to hear it. Do you have a couple of minutes?"

A few seconds of silence follow.

"That depends on what it's about."

"It's about Tore Pulli."

She falls silent again.

"I can't discuss him with you, Juul."

"No, I know. But have you finished his autopsy?"

"The police have requested a forensic autopsy, yes, and we've made it our top priority. That's all I can say."

Henning nods.

"How long will it be, do you think, before the preliminary autopsy report will be available?"

"It'll be ready later today."

"Okay. What exactly goes into a preliminary report? What do you look for?"

"We open up the body and carry out a macroscopic assessment of the organs. We check for internal damage, possible stab injuries, gunshot wounds, and so on."

"And what about the final report?"

"That contains toxicology information and analyses of blood and other fluids, possibly a DNA analysis. In addition we always take tissue samples from various organs; these samples are collected as a matter of routine, but we will also take samples of any discoveries we make during the autopsy. All of this goes into the final report.

"I understand. How long will it be before the final report is ready?"

"It can take up to a couple of months."

Months, Henning thinks. Practically a lifetime.

"Speaking generally, what could be the reason why an otherwise healthy forty-two-year-old man suddenly drops dead?"

"It depends on what you mean by otherwise healthy. You can carry many potentially fatal conditions without being aware of it. An electrical defect in your heart, for example. If that happens, you'll need highly sophisticated medical intervention within minutes or you'll die. These conditions can strike without warning."

"Sounds sinister."

"An artery in your brain might burst or an artery in your chest or abdomen might rupture. This can sometimes be caused by a vessel degenerating through disease while in other cases the blood vessel may look healthy and still burst. Or you could suffer a blood clot in a central artery in your brain, your heart, or a sudden bleed in your brain tissue."

"I think I get the picture," Henning says. "In this case it looks as if Tore Pulli suddenly began to experience breathing difficulties. Does that fit in with any of the causes you've just mentioned?"

"It might."

"If I were to tell you that he didn't appear to be in control of himself or his muscles, either, what would you say?"

"That his death could still be attributed to any number of reasons. It's possible that he was poisoned, though in this case it would be highly unlikely."

"Why?"

"Because he died in a prison."

"Yes," Henning hears himself say. "But if it turns out that he was poisoned, how will you know?"

"I'm not sure that we would."

"But if you suspected it?"

"Then we would ask the Institute of Forensic Toxicology to carry out further investigations. They never attend the actual autopsy, they just get the samples. But if this turns out to be a case of poisoning, and I want to emphasize that I'm merely speculating here, then I would assume that we're talking about some sort of nerve toxin."

"He couldn't breathe or move just before he died."

"Quite so," Dr. Omdahl replies, slowly.

"What are you thinking?"

"No, it's just that—and I want to stress again that *if* it were a case of poisoning—then we might be talking about a combined neuro- and cardiotoxic substance, but speculating is a waste of time. We need to examine him first."

"I appreciate that and I have no intention of speculating in my newspaper, either. But how many types of such poison exist?"

"Oh, several. Dozens. Hundreds. The Institute of Forensic Toxicology is much better placed to answer that question. They report to the Institute of Public Health now. Their full name is the Department for Forensic Toxicology and Intoxicating Substances Research."

"Okay, I think I might give them a call."

"You do that."

"How will the body look if it was poisoned?"

"A pure nerve toxin that paralyzes the respiratory system will cause you to suffocate while your heart is still beating. Your skin and mucous membranes will probably turn slightly blue. If we are talking about a combined neuro- and cardiotoxin, it's likely to cause heart *and* respiratory failure and then there will be no external signs whatsoever. All you're likely to see are possible signs of suffocation if the respiratory system is affected before the heart stops."

"Okay," Henning says. "It sounds as if we'll just have to wait and see."

"Yes, you've got it."

"Thank you so much for your help."

"You're very welcome."

Henning ends the call and looks up. At the monitor in front of him Pulli is staring at Brenden. There is something wounded in his eyes.

Henning starts rubbing his arms. He doesn't know why, but the image makes him shudder.

65

Iver Gundersen looks at his watch. Kent Harry Hansen was meant to have turned up twenty-five minutes ago. Iver has investigated plenty of stories where the source gets cold feet and decides that they don't want to talk after all. Words in print can be mighty, especially when you are the one who will be held accountable for them later, regardless of whether you wrote or spoke them.

Iver would not have thought that of Hansen, who had said on the phone that he would be happy to talk about Tore as long as they could meet in Sagene, close to Hansen's flat. This is why Iver is waiting at La Casa Spiseri, a restaurant that tempts him with the smell of tapas.

He can't be bothered to do the return journey straightaway so he orders a club sandwich and a beer from the waitress who is only too happy to respond to his warm gaze with a smile. I ought to bring Nora here, he thinks. The whitewashed plastered walls, large red floor tiles, and tables in matching colors lend the place a rustic charm.

She finally answered his calls, thank God, and said that dinner and a movie "sounded cute." Cute, Iver snorts. Who the hell says cute to their boyfriend? He wonders if she ever said it to Henning.

A glass with condensation on the outside and a refreshing amber liquid on the inside arrives at the same time as a compact man with a tanned face and very short white hair. His T-shirt, which has the Fighting Fit logo in white and red colors printed on the black material, fits tightly across his paunch. His belly button can be seen in the upper circle of the second *g*. On his forearms Hansen has black-ink tattoos that draw the eye up to his biceps, which bulge so much the sleeves of his T-shirt look as if they are in danger of cutting off the blood supply. His biceps remind Iver of muscular thighs. His left earlobe has studs that look like diamonds, but Iver refuses to believe they would have cost more than a hundred kroner.

"Sorry I'm late," Hansen says as he approaches Iver with swaggering, vigorous steps. Iver gets up and sticks out his hand.

"I got your text, but a guy wanted to buy our entire stock of Gainomax Recovery and I had to order some more before I left. And then loads of people turned up for their workouts. Plus Gunhild was late coming back from her lunch break as usual. Have you been waiting a long time?"

"I decided to stick around."

Hansen takes Iver's hand and squeezes it hard. He sits down, knocking into the table so the beer in Iver's glass jolts.

"Do you want something to eat or drink?"

Iver sits down again, moving his mobile away from his glass as he does so.

"What you've ordered looks good, but I think I'll pass. I'm meeting a customer later today. A cup of coffee would be welcome though."

Iver holds up his hand and makes eye contact with the waitress.

"Would you get us a cup of coffee, please?" he says softly, followed by a smile. She smiles back at him as she leaves. Hansen moves closer and plants his elbows on the table. Iver does the same in an attempt to balance out the table's weight distribution, but is nowhere near as successful.

"I should offer you my condolences first," Iver says.

"Thank you."

"You knew each other well, I gather?"

"Yes," Hansen sighs mournfully and looks down. "Rotten business."

Iver nods, uncertain how to phrase the questions he has
prepared in advance. It occurs to him that it might be a good
idea to warm Hansen up with questions he already knows
the answers to before revealing the real reason he is here. It
takes some minutes; he learns that Tore was a great guy, the
undisputed leader, and that "no one would dare to mess with
Tore." Iver can't quite make up his mind whether Hansen really
believes his own bluster or whether he only says it because Pulli
is dead.

Once the coffee arrives and the waitress has left with a flir-
tatious smile, Iver leans forward. He remembers Henning's
warning that it might prove difficult to crack open this story.
For that reason, Iver thinks, resorting to more drastic measures
could be necessary.

"How's business?" he asks.

"Not too bad."

"Do you still get people coming in off the street?"

"No, not as many as we used to."

"Why not?"

"Things changed after Vidar's death."

"But you still get financial support from The Inner City
Project?"

"Yes, we do. And I still employ staff who are a part of that."

Iver stops the rhythm of his questioning.

"And how is your other business?"

Hansen looks at Iver.

"What other business?"

"The one with no paper trail?"

Iver clenches his right fist and punches it into his left palm.
Hansen stares at Iver for a few seconds before he starts to
laugh.

"What are you talking about?"

"I've heard that you run some of the enforcer business in
Oslo from Vidar Fjell's old office. Is that right?"

Hansen continues to smile.

"Okay," he says. "You're one of those."

Iver doesn't reply, he merely waits for an answer.

"If you had done your homework before coming here then you would know that Fighting Fit isn't mixed up in that. We never were. And we never will be."

"That's not what I've heard."

"Then you've heard wrong."

The smile on Hansen's face is gone.

"So you deny that you run an enforcer business? That you use Fighting Fit as a front for—"

"What the hell is this?" Hansen interrupts him. "Why are you really here? I thought we were going to talk about Tore?"

"We are. That's what we're doing."

"It seems more like harassment if you ask me, and you can forget about writing something that repeats what you just said in your paper or—"

Hansen points his index finger at Iver.

"I wasn't going to," Iver replies. "But if you agree to help me, I might decide to forget about it. I'm trying to find out who really killed Jocke Brolenius."

Hansen stares at Iver for a long time.

"Tore Pulli claimed that he arrived on time for his meeting with Brolenius, but he didn't call the police until nineteen minutes past eleven o'clock. Could he have been delayed by something that happened at your gym that night?"

Hansen shakes his head, but his short hair doesn't even move.

"Consider this a piece of friendly advice, Gundersen. Don't go around making allegations you can't prove. It's not a very clever thing to do."

Iver looks at the grave eyes in front of him and feels a shot of adrenaline spread through his body.

"Are you saying you know who really killed Jocke Brolenius?"

Hansen pushes back his chair, gets up, and glares at Iver before putting his hands on the table and leaning forward. Iver tries to stay where he is, but he can't help moving his head back.

"You're playing with fire," Hansen says quietly, and jabs his finger at Iver's face. Iver tries hard to pretend that he isn't scared. Then Hansen straightens up, heads for the door, and slams it hard on his way out.

66

Elisabeth Haaland stares at the ceiling, but sees nothing, only a pale gray fog. She doesn't know if she can cry any more, but every time she imagines Thorleif or thinks about him, what he is doing, where he is, the knot in her stomach tightens and she bursts into tears. Her thoughts repeat in a never-ending spiral without producing a single answer.

What will she tell the children?

The police aren't much help yet because not enough time has passed since Thorleif went missing. But she could hear it in the voice of the female police officer who called half an hour ago, the one who rang yesterday, that they no longer regarded it as a straightforward missing person case. Why else would she ask if Thorleif had had anything to do with Tore Pulli, including before the interview? What was she insinuating?

Elisabeth stretches out her arms behind her and buries them under the pillow. Her fingers stop when they touch a sheet of paper. She pulls it out.

"Julie's heart," she whispers to herself, holds up the drawing, and looks at the fat red lines Julie drew at nursery. Her daughter has decorated every scrap of paper and every newspaper she has come across since with hearts. Elisabeth turns over the sheet and sees the car. And she sees that Thorleif drew it.

Why would he do that, she wonders and sits up. He never draws with Julie because according to him he is so bad at it. But now he appears to have drawn a picture of a car. And why did he leave the drawing under her pillow?

The car looks like a BMW. The registration plates are clear to see. Her gaze glides down toward the words written in

Thorleif's inimitable penmanship. Elisabeth raises her hand to her mouth. And she jumps the next moment when someone rings the doorbell.

The sun hits Henning's face as he leaves 123news's offices at 9 Urtegata. He takes out his mobile and calls Iver who gives him a quick summary of his conversation with Hansen.

"So he didn't punch you in the face?"

"No, but he clearly wanted to."

"I told you to take it easy with those guys."

"I know."

"Have you spoken to any of the others?"

"No, not yet. But I'm about to call TV2."

Henning nods as he holds up his other hand. A cab across the street indicates and pulls up at the pavement.

"Good. We need a few more angles."

"I found a picture of Tore Pulli and a guy named Even Nylund on the Internet earlier today. Nylund runs a strip club in Majorstua. Åsgard it's called, or something like that."

"That's where Geir Grønningen and Petter Holte work," Henning says and dashes across the street in between two cars.

"I could try going over there tonight."

"Great idea."

Henning gets into the cab.

"What about you? Where are you going?"

"I'm going to pay Thorleif Brenden's girlfriend a visit."

67

The cab stops right outside the Italian School in Bygdøy Allé. Henning walks down a side street and searches for Brenden's apartment block in Nobelsgate. He passes courtyard gardens with withered plants, finds the building marked B, and presses the bell labeled *Brenden & Haaland*.

Henning looks around while he waits for an answer that never comes. Perhaps she's asleep, he thinks. Or trying to sleep. He called Elisabeth Haaland at the school where she works, but they told him that she was off ill today. He tried her mobile, which rang several times before switching to voicemail. Henning knows it is unlikely that she will open the door to him, but he thought it was worth a try and set out anyway. He rings the doorbell again. Another thirty seconds pass before a shattered female voice answers.

Henning introduces himself.

"I'm sorry to disturb you, but I would really like to talk to you about Thorleif. It will help you and your family if 123news can publish a detailed account of Thorleif's last movements. It could prompt people to come forward, which might lead to his being found."

All Henning hears is a click down the other end. Damn, he mutters to himself and waits a few seconds before he presses the bell once more. There is only silence and the hum of city life behind the walls and the trees. Henning swears again even though he knows it is rare for relatives to want to talk to the press at this stage.

Henning refrains from pressing the bell a fourth time. Haaland has enough to worry about, he decides when at that moment the door opens in front of him. An ashen-faced woman looks at him, her eyes and skin marked by tears and despair.

"Elisabeth Haaland?" he asks.

The bags under her eyes are enormous. Her hair has been gathered in a messy ponytail. No makeup. She pulls her jacket protectively around her and marches past him.

"I know this is a bad time," Henning says. "But I wouldn't have come here if I didn't think it was important."

Haaland ignores him. Henning hurries after her, gritting his teeth in response to the pain coming from his hips and feet as he struggles to keep up with her.

"Please, just listen to what I have to say."

Haaland stops and spins around.

"They made him do it," she says and stares at him wild-eyed.

"What?"

"Thorleif didn't do it."

"Didn't do what?"

"Isn't that why you're here?"

Henning makes no reply, but he looks perplexed. Haaland doesn't elaborate, she just turns around and walks on.

"How do you know?" he says, rushing after her.

"Because he told me," she says without turning around.

"Have you spoken to him?"

She doesn't reply, but continues marching down the street. Henning starts to run even though the soles of his feet are screaming.

"What are you saying, Elisabeth?"

"I'm going to the police."

"I'll come with you," Henning says, panting. "Perhaps we could talk while we walk? Or can I take you there in a cab?"

She glances at him over her shoulder; she doesn't nod, but neither does she reject him. Henning tries to increase his speed as they reach Bygdøy Allé. Three cabs are waiting at the far side of the junction. Haaland gets into the first one. Henning stops outside and looks at her. She returns his gaze.

Then she nods.

Henning gets into the back. The cab pulls out before he has even had time to tell the driver that they are going to the police station. Henning hands over his credit card and leans back.

"What's going on, Elisabeth?" he says, trying to get his breath back.

Haaland doesn't reply, she looks at him with eyes that instantly well up. She strangles a sob and shakes her head, but can't stop the tears that keep flowing.

"What did you mean when you said that they made Thorleif do it? Are you referring to what happened in Oslo Prison yesterday?"

She gives him a quick look, but says nothing. She doesn't have to.

"Who made him?"

"I-I don't know who they are."

"Has anyone threatened him?"

Henning can't decide if she is shaking her head because she doesn't know or if fear has taken control of her body.

"What's happened?" he says again in an even softer voice.

Another shake of the head.

"Has Thorleif been behaving strangely recently?"

Henning can see that she thinks about it before she nods.

"In what way?"

She composes herself and dries her wet cheeks.

"He has been very distant. He spent a couple of days in bed this week because of a stomach bug and he kept calling to ask me to do the things I already do every day."

Again she wipes the tears from her face.

"Has he done anything else unusual?"

"He drew a picture of a car."

Henning lets her have all the time she needs.

"And he put the picture under my pillow."

"Why do you think he did that?"

She shakes her head again while she opens her handbag and takes out the drawing. Henning's eyes widen as he sees it. He reads the words Thorleif Brenden wrote at the bottom.

If anything should happen to me, go to the police and tell them to look for Furio. I don't know what he will make me do or why, but I have to do what they want in order to protect you.

"Who is Furio?" Henning asks as he feels his heart beat faster. He used to live for moments like this.

"I'm not sure," Haaland says. "But I've met him, I think. He interviewed me a couple of days ago."

"Is he a reporter?"

"He said he was, but now I don't think so."

"Why not?"

"Because the interview he did with me was never published."

Henning studies her.

"Which newspaper was it?"

"*Aftenposten.*"

"And this man was called Furio?"

"No," she says, looking down. "But he looked like Furio, the character in *The Sopranos,* if you've seen that."

Henning nods.

"Do you mean the type or did he specifically resemble Furio?"

"Both."

Henning ponders this.

"Do you remember anything else about him?"

"No."

"What kind of questions did he ask you?"

"He wanted to know how far I would go to protect my family. It was supposed to be for a survey in the newspaper, but—"

Again she shakes her head.

"And you told Thorleif about the interview?"

Haaland nods tearfully.

"But this Furio guy appears to have been in contact with Thorleif *after* you were interviewed?"

"Yes, wouldn't you think so when you look at this?"

Henning examines the drawing.

"Yes," Henning says. "Did he speak Norwegian?"

She looks up at him at once.

"Why does everyone keep asking me that?"

"What do you mean?"

"Thorleif has been asking me the same question several times in the last few days. If the people I had come into contact with spoke Norwegian. I thought he had gone mad. Why do you want to know?"

"Because Tore Pulli was convicted of killing a Swedish enforcer," Henning says, gravely.

"And you think his friends used Thorleif to take revenge on Pulli?"

"I don't know," he says.

There is no reason why they would want to do that. Pulli was already in jail and according to his lawyer there was no new evidence in the appeal that might lead to him being acquitted. And even if there had been, all that would mean is that Jocke Brolenius's real killer is still out there. So why kill Pulli? Pulli must have had other enemies, Henning thinks.

"Has anyone else around you been acting strangely?"

"I don't think so."

"And no other unusual events have occurred?"

"No."

Henning nods slowly to himself. There is silence for a few

seconds. The cab slows down on Henrik Ibsensgate as they drive toward the National Theatre.

"Our burglar alarm," Haaland exclaims and looks up.

"Eh?"

"A few days ago our burglar alarm stopped working."

"When was this?"

"I don't remember. Last Sunday, I think."

"What happened? How did you discover that it had stopped working?"

"We had been out on a day trip, we tend to do this on Sundays and we set the burglar alarm and lock the flat before we leave. But when we came back, the alarm wasn't working. Its power had been cut. Thorleif promised to fix it, but—"

She starts to cry again. Something occurs to Henning. The media has free access to prison inmates. The only item reporters are asked to hand over when they arrive is their mobile. No one is searched. Someone must have known about the interview, must have known which TV2 staff would be visiting the prison. It follows that the people who wanted Pulli dead must have identified and coerced whoever would be best placed to carry out the killing for them. The question is what they intend to do with Brenden afterward, something which, now that he thinks about it, might explain why Brenden has gone missing.

It doesn't bode well for Brenden, Henning shudders and looks at Haaland again. She dries her face.

"Can you remember when Thorleif's behavior started to change?"

"A couple of days later, I think. I'm not really sure."

There is silence for a few more seconds as the cab approaches the police station.

"This is a really important lead," Henning says, pointing at the drawing. "You need to tell the police everything you know, tell them about the burglar alarm, everything you remember about this Furio character. They will probably ask you to help them make an E-fit."

"I don't know if I can," she says and starts to cry again.

"They'll help you," Henning assures her and puts his hand on her shoulder. "They're very good at such things."

Haaland nods and tries to pull herself together as the cab stops outside the police station.

"Will you be writing about this?" she asks him.

"It's my job."

"No matter what you write then please don't say anything that makes Thorleif sound guilty. I know what people think when they read the papers. I don't want my children to hear what their father might have done at their school or in nursery. Will you promise me that?"

"If you like I can give you a call and read the article to you before it's uploaded."

"I don't know if I have the energy," she says, weakly. "Besides you look—you look—decent."

Henning grins.

"Can I have that in writing, please?"

Her tearful smile fills him with compassion.

"I have to go," she says. "They're waiting for me."

"Okay. Don't give up, Elisabeth."

"I'll try not to," she says and gets out of the cab.

68

Ørjan Mjønes has to stop himself from laughing out loud. Everyone he meets on his way into Oslo Central Station quickly averts their eyes when he pretends to look them up and down. He can easily understand why someone would want to join the police. Having the power to make people shrink the moment they see a uniform even though they haven't done anything wrong. When you think about it, it is ridiculous.

He goes over to the ticket office, nods to a woman behind the glass, and asks to speak to "someone in charge"—a safe bet since all offices have a manager. She gives him a name he doesn't catch, but further into the office a corpulent man gets up from a chair. The man grabs hold of his belt and hoists up his trousers, peers out through the glass, and walks reluctantly toward the door. Soon he joins Mjønes outside.

"Detective Inspector Stian Henriksen, Oslo Police," Mjønes says, holding out his hand.

"Terje Eggen. How can I help you?"

"We're looking for this man," Mjønes says, holding up the picture Flurim Ahmetaj printed out for him. "He is wanted in connection with a murder and we have reasons to believe that he was here at Oslo Central Station around one o'clock yesterday afternoon. We also believe that he left Oslo on a train that departed around that time. I need a list of all one o'clock departures."

"I'm sure that should be possible. Do you mean one o'clock precisely?"

"A few minutes either side would be fine. Let's say between twelve fifty and thirteen ten, then we have a margin to work on."

"Okay."

Eggen disappears back inside the glass office. Mjønes waits outside until he returns a few minutes later with a printout. Mjønes studies it and nods sternly.

"I also need a list of ticket inspectors working on those trains. I want to start with the trains going farthest and I'll contact you again if I need the names of anybody else."

"I'll need to ring around to get those for you. It could take some time."

"I can wait."

Eggen is about to go back inside the glass office when he stops and turns around.

"There are more than five hundred cameras at the station," Eggen says, looking up. "There is bound to be a recording of him."

Mjønes improvises.

"My officers are looking into that, obviously. However, it's not enough to know which train he boarded. We also need to know where he got off. And I believe that the ticket inspectors are best placed to answer that question."

Eggen nods.

"I'm sorry, I didn't mean to—"

"Not at all."

Mjønes smiles. Pretending to be a police officer is great fun.

69

Even though the working day is far from over, Henning tells the cabdriver to take him home to Grünerløkka. Perhaps he should have checked with Heidi Kjus first, but even she knows that he works just as effectively from home as at the office.

As the cab bumbles over the potholes at Schous Plass junction, Henning thinks about Jocke Brolenius. What if his murder is related to Tore Pulli's death? Does anyone in Pulli's circle have the means to hire a guy like Furio?

How about Veronica Nansen? Now that Pulli is dead she inherits a huge pile of money. But is she really that cold and calculating? She didn't strike Henning as a psychopathic gold digger. Nor can he see that she had any motive for killing Brolenius and framing her own husband, unless there is more to her than meets the eye. So who else could it be?

None of the people he has met so far appears to have had the means or the motive. This leads him to believe they might be dealing with two unrelated cases. The murder of Jocke and the murder of Tore.

The cab turns into Seilduksgate.

"Just drop me off at the lights over there," Henning says, pointing across the passenger seat. The driver switches off the meter at the junction with Markveien. A receipt is printed out on which Henning scribbles his signature in a handwriting even he can't decipher.

Outside the tarmac is hot. Glumly, Henning kicks a pebble along the dusty pavement and hobbles to the door. What kind of story can he write about the things he has discovered today? Has he discovered anything at all?

He is about to unlock the door when his attention is drawn to a picture of a cat that has been stuck to the wall above the door bells. *"Have you seen Måns?"*

No, I haven't, Henning says to himself as he goes inside. But Måns has given him an idea.

Thorleif had forgotten how quiet the mountains can be. After they moved to Oslo, the ever-present traffic foisted itself on them like an invisible family member, even though the street they chose—Nobelsgate—is relatively quiet. But the number 13 tram is always rumbling and squealing past and then there are the sirens from emergency vehicles that frequently run up and down Bygdøy Allé.

In the mountains the silence is interrupted only by the wind and sporadic signs of people nearby. Under different circumstances Thorleif would have embraced the change, relished the opportunity to step away from the pressures of everyday life and simply immerse himself in the magnificent landscape that surrounds him. And even though it is difficult to think of anything other than the mess he has ended up in, he can feel with his whole body the value of having a place to go to, just the four of them, to fish, to ski, to feel their cheeks glow in front of an open fire after a long day outdoors.

Thorleif has tried to read *The Mourning Cloak* by Unni Lindell, but every time he reaches the bottom of the page, he can't remember the words he has read or what happened. His thoughts keep straying and he thought of every imaginable way he might contact Elisabeth without finding one that would be safe.

Thorleif closes his eyes and begins to relive the long car journey from Julie's nursery to Larvik that day. Did the man with the ponytail give anything away? Thorleif shakes his head.

Every time he asked him a question he would receive no reply or the man would simply change the subject. Nor can Thorleif remember if the man spoke on his mobile or if he—

Thorleif opens his eyes.

The mobile.

At one point the man received a text and had to remove his glove in order to press the keys. And Thorleif remembers that he didn't put his glove back on straight away, but texted a reply on his mobile and then put his arm on the armrest. He rested his hand in the same place, not for long, but possibly long enough for him to leave a fingerprint?

Agitated, Thorleif sits up. It's not much, but it could be enough. It might be just what he needs to extricate himself from this nightmare.

70

Iver Gundersen feels pressure at the back of his eyes as they leave the Colosseum Cinema. He should have checked with her in advance as to how long the film lasted. Over two and a half hours where he couldn't move and added to that wearing 3D glasses, which involve a completely different strain than the muscles of his eyes are used to. They are worn out now. As is Iver. Nora, however, looks anything but.

"What did you think?" she says, beaming.

Iver hesitates.

"It wasn't bad."

"Not bad? It was absolutely—"

Nora lifts her head toward the dull evening sky while she searches for the right word.

"Magical," she exclaims, enthralled, and looks expectantly at him. Iver doesn't reply, he sees no need to ruin her experience. Then he takes her hand and says:

"I'm glad you liked it."

Nora smiles and weaves her fingers into his.

"Are you hungry?" he continues.

"More nauseous. I ate far too much popcorn."

"A proper meal will soon fix that—"

Iver is interrupted by his mobile ringing. He takes it out and looks at the display. He lets go of Nora's hand.

"It's Henning," he says and looks at her.

She takes one step away from him.

"Hi, Henning," Iver says.

"Did you enjoy the film?"

"Eh?"

"There aren't many places where people turn off their

mobiles these days so I assume that you've been to the cinema. Am I right?"

Iver is silent for a few seconds. Then he says:

"It wasn't too bad."

Iver glances at Nora who doesn't look back at him. Henning spends the next minutes telling him what he has found out about Thorleif Brenden, his behavior at home, the drawing he left under Elisabeth Haaland's pillow, and the man Brenden referred to as Furio.

"Wow," Iver says when Henning has finished. "I'm impressed."

"If you're still planning to visit Åsgard later, then ask if they know a hit man or enforcer who is tall as a tree and thin as a beanpole and looks a little bit like Furio."

"Do you really think anyone will tell me that?"

"No, but you'll probably be able to think of a slightly more elegant phrasing than I can."

A short distance in front of him Nora is studying a shop window.

"I spoke to TV2 earlier today," Iver says.

"What did they say?"

"That Brenden had been acting very strangely in the last couple of days. Guri Palme thought it was because he had been ill—he threw up outside the prison after Pulli's death. And the footage he shot was completely out of focus, as if he wasn't paying attention at all while he was filming."

"That's probably true if his mind was on other things."

"Brenden is one of their best cameramen, according to Guri. They're very worried about him."

"I could include that quote in my story and I'll run it with a double byline. Have fun at M."

"Eh?"

"Café M. That's where you're going, isn't it? You should try the halibut if they still serve it. It's delicious. Grilled with some sort of apple."

"We're not—"

"Catch you later."

Iver has no time to reply before Henning hangs up. He sighs and looks at his mobile as if it could explain to him how Henning knew where they were going.

No. Just no.

He takes hold of Nora, but this time he doesn't seek out her fingers.

"Listen," he says while they wait for the lights at Majorstua junction to turn green. "Why don't we go somewhere else for dinner?"

71

A smiling green-and-red-painted troll is holding up a sign outside the entrance to Ustaoset Mountain Hotel. This time, fortunately, the door is open.

Tentatively, Thorleif walks across the gray slate floor in the reception area where a white fireplace dominates the lobby. To his left black leather chairs have been arranged around an oval coffee table. Further in, past a wall that sticks out into the long corridor, there is a sign for the Usta Restaurant.

The woman behind the reception counter is talking on the telephone. She looks up at him and smiles warmly. Her dark brown hair is tied back in a ponytail. Her lipstick is bright red and her skin lightly tanned. Around her neck, just above the white blouse, is a pendant with half a heart.

Thorleif takes a step forward when she hangs up.

"Hello," she smiles. "How can I help you?"

"I was wondering if you have Internet access here?"

"Indeed we do. We have wireless Internet in the whole lobby area. Guests or anyone else can connect. The network is free and you don't need a password."

"Ah," Thorleif says, grateful for anything that will save him money. The woman serves up her best service smile. He looks around again.

"Is there a computer I can borrow?"

"No, unfortunately. We don't offer that. But if you have WiFi on your mobile then you can use that."

"I don't have a mobile, either," Thorleif says and shakes his head. "Is there a telephone here I could use? I'll obviously pay the cost of the call and—"

"I'm sorry, I—we—we don't have that, either."

Thorleif looks down. A tortuous silence fills the room.

"Are you a guest here?" she asks.

Thorleif looks at the wall further away where notices and posters have been put up at random.

"No. I live—in a cabin further up the mountains."

"And you didn't bring your computer or your mobile?"

"No."

Another silence. What does he do now? Go to the nearest library?

"You could borrow my laptop if you want."

Thorleif looks back at her, sees that she is holding up a laptop bag and smiling at him again.

"I always bring my laptop to work. At this time of the year there isn't much to do in the evenings."

"Really? You would lend me your laptop?"

"As long as you sit where I can see you, so that—"

She smiles and points to the black leather chairs next to the fireplace.

"You never can tell, isn't that right?"

"Absolutely," Thorleif says, drawn to her warm smile. "Thank you so much. You've no idea how grateful I am—"

He stops and looks at her.

"I can see it in your face," she replies.

"Can you?"

She nods eagerly.

"I'm a writer, you see. Or—at least I'm trying to become a writer. That's why I always bring my laptop to work in case I have some spare time and then I can write. And I'm used to studying faces. But please don't tell my boss. He's in my book, you see."

She giggles. Thorleif smiles, but feels his smile freeze instantly. The thought that this helpful woman has memorized his face hits him like a punch to the stomach. He takes the bag as she lifts it over the counter and tries to look appreciative.

"I've always wanted to write a book," he says, mostly to say something.

"What a coincidence."

Thorleif nods.

"I'm Mia, by the way."

"Hi, Mia."

She looks at him in anticipation.

"My name is—Einar."

"Will you be staying here a long time, Einar?"

"Well, I . . . I don't really know."

"I work here every night, so just drop by. The restaurant is open on weekends."

"Okay," Thorleif says, unwillingly. "I'll . . . I'll remember that."

He turns around and walks over to the leather chairs where he sits down facing Mia so she won't be able to see what he is doing. The screen wakes up the moment he opens the computer.

"My laptop remembers the network here, so surf away."

Thorleif nods in response to her charming smile and thanks her with his eyes.

Ever since he remembered the potential fingerprint he has wondered who to contact and how to go about it. The police are out of the question since the man with the ponytail said that they had infiltrated them. Thorleif has considered contacting someone from work, but since the gang knew that Thorleif was part of the team that was meeting Tore Pulli, he can't trust anyone at work, either. He has to find someone else.

Out of habit he visits TV2's website first and sees an advert that frames the homepage, but initially there is nothing about Pulli's death. Nor can he find anything about himself. In the news section he finds an interview the news editor has done with Guri Palme. An edited video with the final images of Pulli has also been uploaded. That must be Reinertsen's footage,

Thorleif assumes, but he can't bear to watch it. He checks the other newspapers and sees that *VG, Dagbladet, Aftenposten,* and *Nettavisen* are all running stories on Tore Pulli, but they don't mention Thorleif's disappearance, either. He goes to 123news. When the ads at the top half of the page have downloaded themselves, his eyes widen. One of the top news stories reads:

TV2 CAMERAMAN MISSING

Eagerly he clicks on it and reads the introduction:

There has been no contact from TV2 cameraman Thorleif Brenden since Thursday morning. His family is worried.

Everything that has happened in the last few days becomes even more real as he reads about himself online. Fortunately, the story is not accompanied by his photo. Below the introduction he sees the names of the journalists who wrote the article.

Henning Juul and Iver Gundersen.

Strange, Thorleif thinks, that 123news is reporting his disappearance when nobody else is. Perhaps he isn't officially missing yet? It might be too soon. So why and how did 123news know?

He rereads the final sentence and feels his stomach lurch when it dawns on him that the reporters have spoken to Elisabeth. Thorleif reads on:

> Respected TV2 cameraman Thorleif Brenden has gone missing. Thursday morning Brenden was at work and according to a colleague went to fetch something from his car at the end of a recording. He never returned.
>
> "We dread to think what might have happened to him," says reporter Guri Palme to 123news. She was working with Brenden just before he disappeared.

Brenden's girlfriend, Elisabeth Haaland, is also anxious as to what might have happened to Brenden.

"It's not like Thorleif to behave like this," she said in tears to 123news.

His disappearance has been reported to the police who have initiated a search for him.

In tears, Thorleif thinks, poor Elisabeth.

In a box to the right of the main text are links to various stories about the death of Tore Pulli. Thorleif clicks on them in turn and sees that Iver Gundersen wrote all of them. He is also the first to report that Thorleif is missing.

Thorleif opens another window and logs onto Hotmail.com.

72

"Okay, thanks for your help."

Ørjan Mjønes hangs up and puts a despondent hard line through the name of Jan Ivar Fossbakk. Above him four other names have already been crossed out: Benjamin Røkke, Syver Ødegård, Idun Skorpen-Wold, and Sverre Magnus Vereide. Mjønes leans back and stretches out his arms, turning his head from side to side so the bones creak.

He gets up, shuffles across the shiny floor, and enters the kitchen. From the fridge he takes out a carton of milk, finds a clean glass in the top cupboard, and fills it up. He downs the milk in a couple of big gulps. He has more ticket inspectors to call, a task he never would have started if he didn't know that they are trained to recognize faces.

Mjønes returns to the living room and sits down at the circular table where his laptop is open. Lying next to it is the list Terje Eggen was kind enough to provide him with, which gives him the NSB ticket inspectors' names, their mobile numbers, and the specific train line they were working on the day in question. Mjønes picks up the sheet and finds the next name on the list. Nils Petter Kittelsen.

"Hello, yes?"

"Detective Inspector Stian Henriksen, Oslo Police," Mjønes says in a commanding and grave voice.

"P-police?" Kittelsen stutters. "Has anything happened?"

"I'm sorry for disturbing you on a Friday evening, but I'm investigating a murder that took place in Oslo yesterday."

"I-I see?"

"We have reason to believe that the killer left Oslo on the train to Bergen, the train you are responsible for, around lunchtime yesterday. We're trying to find out where the killer got off and I hope that you can help."

Mjønes hears Kittelsen swallow.

"I'll do my best."

Mjønes looks down at the picture of Thorleif Brenden.

"The man we're looking for is approximately thirty-five years old, he's just under six foot tall and he was wearing dark blue shorts, a white T-shirt, and probably a hat or a cap when he left Oslo Central Station yesterday. Do you recall seeing a man who fits that description?"

There is silence for a while.

"I really couldn't say."

"Think carefully. It's very important."

"I'm thinking" Kittelsen says, intently, as he breathes hard into the mobile. Then he sighs despondently. "I'm sorry, I don't think I saw him."

"He may not have been on your train," Mjønes says, trying to hide his disappointment. He takes the tip off the black felt tip pen.

"Was he wearing sunglasses?" Kittelsen suddenly asks. Mjønes stops and looks at the picture of Brenden.

"He was."

"And a black baseball cap?"

"He might well have done. Did you see him?"

"I think I might have," Kittelsen says, eager now. "Pale skin, a goatee?"

"That's him!" Mjønes exclaims, unable to suppress the elation in his voice. "Do you remember where he got off?"

Another silence.

"There are so many passengers," Kittelsen says, defensively.

"I know. But please try."

"I'm sorry, I—"

"Do you remember if he was on the train for a short period or a long time?"

Another pause for thought.

"He was there for some time, certainly."

"How long, do you think?"

"A couple of hours, at least."

"Okay. More than three hours? Four hours?"

"I don't know," Kittelsen says, despairing at himself. "I'm quite sure that I saw him when we stopped at Flå, but I don't think he was there when we got to Finse."

"How many stations are there between Flå and Finse?"

"Six," Kittelsen replies immediately.

"Okay. That gives us something to go on. Thank you so much, Mr. Kittelsen. You've been a great help."

"Don't mention it."

73

Iver Gundersen is strolling down the small steep hill where Bogstadveien meets Josefinesgate, when his eyes are drawn to a sign on the right. A castle with a heart that frames the name Åsgard. Iver smiles to himself. Something of a trite fantasy to sell, he thinks.

It's still early in the evening, it has only just gone ten o'clock, but it makes it less likely that the club will be busy.

Nora was unhappy that he had to work after their dinner and she sulked even more when he refused to tell her why. They have had this conversation before. Iver doesn't mind discussing stories they are both working on as they unfold, but it's another matter when he is out chasing his own scoops. Then he never shares information with her. Nora has never quite accepted it, she thinks he ought to trust her, says that she wouldn't dream of stealing a story or an angle from him. But as far as Iver is concerned it's a matter of principle. Besides, he doesn't really believe the scene of tonight's assignment would have done much to lighten her mood.

Iver notices a red carpet that sticks out from the entrance to the strip club. He walks under a canopy and heads for the door. Two doormen in matching black suits and black T-shirts are standing outside. Bulging muscles. Earpieces in place, of course.

Iver walks up some steps and into a room that opens diagonally to the left and offers booths where customers can seek refuge or simply sit and gawp without anyone seeing the beads of sweat on their foreheads or their throbbing groins under the table. The bar stretches deep inside the room before breaking off to the left at an angle of ninety degrees. The stage is bathed in a pink and purple light and it is small, no bigger than a kitchen floor. The traditional dance pole, longing to be caressed by sensual fingers, is mounted near the front. To the right there are more booths, some tables and chairs, and pictures of naked women on the walls. A spiral staircase leads up to the next floor where Iver imagines a similar layout, perhaps a private room—or twelve.

Iver nods to the bartender and introduces himself.

"Even Nylund, is he here?" Iver says and holds up his press card as if he worked for the FBI and the card automatically opened every door to him. The bartender, a man who proudly wears a white T-shirt with the Swedish flag emblazoned on his chest, says in Swedish:

"I'll check. Wait here."

Iver makes himself comfortable on a bar stool, puts down his notepad, and takes out his mobile, mainly to have something to do while he waits. He looks at two solitary men at separate tables some distance from the stage.

"He's just coming. What can I get you?"

"A beer, please."

The bartender turns around, takes a glass, and starts filling it from a green spout. Iver notices the camera fixed to the ceiling above the bar and pointing at the booths. The lens stirs as if distracted by the rhythm pounding out into the room and suffusing the atmosphere with a sticky sensation of foreplay. A few minutes later a man sits down heavily on the bar stool next to him. Iver is caught off guard and spins to the left.

"Oh, hi," he says. "Iver Gundersen, 123news."

"Even Nylund."

Right palm meets right palm, hard. Iver instantly regrets it, unsure as to where Nylund's hands have been in the last few minutes.

"Thanks for talking to me."

"Uffe, get me a Coke, will you?"

The bartender obeys without nodding.

"So," Nylund says. "How can I help you?"

Iver studies Nylund and decides that the man conforms to the stereotype of shady club owners, which Iver had expected to find. Nylund's hair is water combed and sticks to his scalp in a failed attempt to disguise a bald patch; the hair at the back is gathered in a thin ponytail. He is skinny, but has still chosen to wear an unbuttoned black linen shirt that reveals chest hair of the same color and reminds Iver of pubic hair. Nylund's stubble makes his ruddy face a shade darker.

"Has there been any vandalism to the club recently?"

Nylund shakes his head sullenly.

"Not that they've given up yet, those FASB bitches. If I had caught any of them red-handed, I would bloody well—"

Nylund clenches his fist.

"No, I don't know what I would have done if someone had keyed my car, either." Iver says.

"And they sprayed fire extinguisher foam into my car."

"And you are sure that the FASB was behind it?"

"On the fender someone had left a note saying Front Against the Sale of Bodies. What do you think?"

Iver smiles and nods.

"What annoys me the most is that the politicians don't distance themselves from that kind of behavior."

"I heard that one of your doormen got into serious trouble?"

"Yes," Nylund says, looking down. "He did."

"What happened?"

Nylund sighs.

"It was the eighth of March though you probably already know that since you ask. There was a mob outside the club. A bunch of feminists in need of a good lay who were going on and on about International Women's Day and all that. The usual rubbish. Petter got angry, he tried to scare them off, but they wouldn't budge. And then he lost it."

"He went to prison, didn't he?"

"Yes. He got a couple of months inside. There were a lot of witnesses, as you might expect."

"Where was he sent?"

"Botsen Block, Oslo Prison. Why do you want to know?"

"I'm just curious. I'm working on a story about Tore Pulli."

"Right. So that's why you're here, is it? Not to write about the vandalism and the attacks on my business?"

"No. But I'm interested in that, too," Iver lies. "I might do a story about it later. I agree with you. They shouldn't be allowed to carry on like that."

Uffe puts a glass filled with ice cubes and Coke in front of his boss. Nylund takes it and drinks in big gulps.

"It's a real shame about Tore," Nylund says.

Iver nods and waits for Nylund to continue, but he doesn't. Iver reflects on this for a while before he decides to cut straight to the chase.

"We think he might not have killed Jocke Brolenius."

Nylund bursts out laughing.

"Oh, I get it," he says. "You're one of those reporters who sees conspiracies everywhere, aren't you? Who can never take no for an answer, but always take *no* to mean *I'm lying*?"

"Not at all," Iver smiles.

He loves reporters like that.

"What makes you think Tore didn't do it?" Nylund asks.

"There were several anomalies in his case that no one paid attention to. But there's no point in dragging that up here. You followed the trial, I presume?"

"On and off," Nylund says. He puts an ice cube in his mouth and sucks it. "I'm sorry, I can't help you," he continues and puts down the glass on the counter as he crunches the ice cube between his teeth. This was a bad idea, Iver thinks. And a bad strategy.

"Did Tore have any enemies here?"

"No."

"That no came very quickly."

"Here we go again," Nylund sighs.

"What?"

"The *no* that really means *I'm lying*."

"Are you?"

"No."

"Are you lying now?"

Iver holds up his hands and smiles apologetically.

"Sorry, I couldn't resist that."

He tries to laugh it off, but Nylund isn't amused.

"It's no secret, Nylund, that you employ people who have links to criminal gangs. You wouldn't happen to know a man in that business who is slim, tall, and always wears his hair in a ponytail?"

Nylund looks at him, smiles wryly.

"Did you say your name was Gundersen?

"Yes."

"You ask some strange questions, Gundersen."

"Someone has to."

"Are we done?"

"So you don't know anyone who fits that description?"

Nylund shoots him a condescending smile.

"Sorry," he says. "I don't think I can help you."

"Okay. Thanks for your time."

Nylund abandons his still half-full glass and walks up the spiral staircase to the first floor. This is taking too long, Iver frets. How the hell does Henning get these people to talk? Just for once he would have loved to tell Henning something he didn't already know.

74

Henning is munching a slice of crisp bread and rereading his own article about Thorleif Brenden when his mobile rings. It is Bjarne Brogeland. The inspector skillfully ignores pleasantries.

"I've seen the video footage," he says. "What did you want to talk to me about?"

Henning swallows and tells Brogeland his suspicions about Brenden's clenched fist and Pulli's sudden, perturbed look.

"It's not a particularly good camera angle, but something happens while Brenden has his hands on Pulli's back," Henning tells him.

Silence. He reaches toward the windowsill and turns off the fan. The hum in the kitchen stops and the heat immediately starts sticking to him.

"Have you discovered the cause of Pulli's death yet?" he asks.

"The preliminary autopsy report provided no answers except that—"

Brogeland stops.

"Except what?"

"I can't tell you, Henning. Sorry, I—"

"Come on, Bjarne, you know I won't write anything that would harm your investigation."

Brogeland exhales.

"They found an abnormal lesion on his neck."

"From what?" Henning asks eagerly.

"They don't know. But it could be a tiny prick. From a needle or something similar."

"A needle," Henning mutters, remembering what Dr. Omdahl told him about nerve toxins. In which case it must have been a highly poisonous substance.

"Clever," Henning says. "Tore Pulli was a diabetic. And he used to have loads of piercings."

"So what?"

"When we met, I asked him if he had grown used to needles and injecting himself with insulin. He said that he hardly noticed it these days."

Henning smiles to himself. It was a clever plan.

"I spoke to his girlfriend earlier today. She showed me the drawing Brenden left under her pillow. Was she any help?"

"What do you mean?"

"Have you produced an E-fit of this guy Brenden is talking about? Do you know who he is?"

"Not yet," Brogeland replies. "But we're working on it."

Henning nods.

"So when can I write that Tore Pulli was murdered?"

"We're not sure about the cause of his death yet, Henning. And you can't start speculating, either, or we run the risk that whoever could have been behind it will disappear."

"Okay," Henning sighs.

When they have ended the call, Henning listens to the silence in the flat. He has a bad feeling about this. Even though Brogeland refuses to be drawn, it looks very much as if Pulli was murdered, probably poisoned. But will they be able to detect which kind of poison was used? The final autopsy report won't be ready for two months, at the earliest. And even if they do find evidence of poisoning, how will they trace it back to the people who made Brenden kill Pulli?

Henning logs onto FireCracker 2.0 again, but 6tiermes7 isn't online. Then his mobile vibrates. A text message from Iver.

Sorry. Small catch from Åsgard. Iver.

Henning rings Iver immediately. Two heads are better than one, he thinks and presses the mobile to his ear while he waits. It takes only a few seconds before Iver's recorded message can be heard from the handset. He must be on another call. Perhaps he is talking to Nora, arranging to go over to hers when he has finished work. Or perhaps he is asking if he can go over there straight away.

Thinking about Nora and Iver shouldn't hurt so much. Not anymore. But he can't dodge the punch that hits his chest every time. He can't just erase his ex-wife like a typo.

Henning waits a few minutes before he tries Iver again. Same result. He looks at his watch. A quarter to eleven. Glumly, he hobbles to the bathroom and cleans his teeth, changes the compresses under his feet, and tries calling Iver a third time when he has finished. And yet again he gets Iver's voicemail.

Never mind, Henning thinks and decides to call it a night.

75

Iver takes a deep breath as soon as he leaves Åsgard and instantly feels better for it. Cleaner, too, now that he thinks about it, even though the summer night is still humid.

He tries to look inconspicuous, desperate to avoid meeting anyone he knows on his way out of a club no one can claim is selling anything other than fantasies and orgasms. He decides to head home. Right now the thought of crashing with a cold beer in front of the television is more tantalizing than a night-time visit to Nora's.

Iver crosses Bodstadveien and continues into the darkness down Josefinesgate where the tall buildings and sloping wilderness gardens with swings and sandpits are partly lit up by the full moon. He passes Josefine where he has spent many a Tuesday night listening to live music on open-mike night when the management allows both the talented and the not so talented to have a go. A few hundred meters further ahead the left wall of Bislett Stadium curves toward the roundabout. Iver takes out his mobile and sends Henning a text about tonight's small catch.

The footsteps appear out of nowhere. Heavy footsteps from boots with hard soles, but Iver doesn't have time to turn around before he feels an iron grip on his neck. He can't move his head as he is dragged into a yard and brutally thrown on the ground. He can feel shingle under his body, crunchy sharp pebbles, his legs dig into them as they kick out, but it doesn't get him anywhere. He is flipped onto his back as if he weighs nothing at all. His eyes close instinctively when a fist comes hurtling toward his face. He hears it make contact, feels his jaw and cheek give, and everything starts to throb. The blows rain down on him with a speed that takes his breath away. The back of his eyes begin to sting, a pricking light appears, and he hears nothing, he feels only intense pain.

The blood is running from his mouth and mingles with saliva and tears. Iver tries to raise his arms to protect himself, but they refuse to obey and fail to ward off the blows landing on him. Soon he no longer feels the pounding, the punches simply make contact and fling his head from side to side. But he is able to think that if this assault doesn't stop soon, the ending will be terribly, terribly bad.

76

The smoke is different this time. The opening stretches further. Henning sees fumbling hands in front of him trying to wave away the smoke. Somehow they succeed. The contours of a CD rack appear as he coughs and splutters. He stops and turns to the left where the stripe of light continues. But then the smoke thickens again, the light disappears, and even though he swings his arms frantically, it makes no difference. Everything in front of him goes completely black.

Henning sits up with a start, quickly wipes his face, and looks around for the flames. But he can't hear the crackling of fire and the door is still intact.

Those infernal dreams again.

He lets himself sink back onto the pillow and waits for the smoke detector above him to flash. In the distance a siren wails. There is always a siren somewhere, he thinks, there is always someone whose life is about to be changed forever by something happening at this very moment. There is no guarantee which promises us that we can close our eyes safe in the knowledge that we will open them again. Life, as we know it, can change in an instant.

Jonas once asked him a question, as he often did—especially at bedtime. It could be a simple one, such as why the walls were white, or more complicated questions, such as what was wrong with the man they saw on their way home from nursery, the one who was sleeping on a bench in Birkelunden Park. But it might also be something more profound, thoughts Henning could easily see would baffle his son without Jonas finding the time to think them through or remember them long enough to articulate at the time they crossed his mind. But the questions would come at night when everything calmed down.

"Daddy, do you hate Mummy?"

There is nothing unique about what happened to Nora and Henning. It happens every day, all over the world. People meet, they fall in love, they fall out of love, fall in love with each other again. They do stupid things or experience something that makes it impossible for them to go on living together. So they part, often to start over with another person. Or not. It's not unique. And yet, from time to time, the thought of why it had to happen to him absolutely chokes him. Why did it have to be them? Why did it have to be Jonas?

"Did Mummy say that?"

"No, but—"

Henning turned over, rested on his elbows, and looked at Jonas. But the more he thought about it, the harder it became to come up with an answer. The moment stretched out, it became too long for him to contain it, and all he could finally say was:

"I don't hate Mummy, Jonas."

No explanation. Just a brief statement, like when a child says "because" when you ask them to explain why they cut up the newspaper with a pair of scissors. And Henning doesn't know how long he lay there, on his elbows, looking at Jonas's searching eyes, but it felt like forever.

A persistent buzzing sound and a sharp light bring him back to the present. His eyes dart to the bedside table where his mobile is vibrating. Henning leans across and picks it up.

"Hello?"

"Hi, it's—Nora."

Henning can hear voices in the background. He sits up.

"What is it?"

"It's Iver."

A note of panic has entered her voice.

"He's in the hospital. He was attacked and beaten up."

"What?"

"He's in a coma."

Henning's jaw drops. His eyes flicker from side to side.

"Where are you?" he asks.

"At Ullevål Hospital."

"Okay," he says and stands up. "I'm on my way."

77

Iver, in a coma, beaten senseless. Given what he was investigating, it can be no coincidence, Henning thinks and throws two hundred kroner onto the passenger seat for the cabdriver. He rushes inside the hospital. Walking as fast as he can manage, he makes his way to emergency admissions. The highly polished floor swims in front of his eyes as he goes through two doors, passes waiting next of kin, sees white walls and randomly displayed pictures with equally random motifs, and notices doctors and cleaners, but he doesn't look anyone in the eye. Not until he sees Nora.

She gets up from a chair and comes to meet him. Even from a distance he can see that her eyes are red. She doesn't stop walking until he embraces her and then she clings to him.

Christ, how she clings to him.

He holds her for a long time and feels his body grow hot all over. Old memories are reawakened, images he doesn't want to see and certainly doesn't want to relive. But he is incapable of suppressing the memory of their time together, which is so distant now that nothing can bridge the gap between them. And he hates himself because it hurts him so much that she is crying and even more that she is crying for somebody else.

"What are the doctors saying?" Henning asks and holds her out from him.

She sniffs and shakes her head at the same time.

"They don't know very much yet."

"He's still in a coma?"

She nods and dries the tears from her eyes. They walk over to a seating area and sit down.

"Who found him?"

"An old lady who lives near by. The noise woke her up so she decided to have a look outside."

"But she didn't see who did it?"

Nora shakes her head again, lifts her hands to her mouth, and squeezes her eyes tightly shut. Fresh tears roll down.

"How did you find out?"

"Iver briefly regained consciousness when he was brought in here."

"Did he say anything else?"

"Not that I know."

Henning nods. A nurse marches past them.

"Have the police been here?"

"Yes, but they've gone again."

Henning breathes in deeply, stays in his seat and looks around without taking anything in.

"Have you been to see him?"

"Only for a short visit."

"What did he look like?"

Nora looks at him for a long time. Then she says in a voice that breaks:

"Bloody awful."

Henning returns her gaze, watches her tears.

"Are you staying here until he wakes up?" he asks her.

She nods.

"It could be a long time, you know that, don't you? The doctors never try to rush this. You must let nature take its course. Iver will wake up when he is ready."

She looks at him with eyes that well up.

"*If* he wakes up."

Henning doesn't know how Nora reacted when she was told that Jonas was dead. Nor does he want to know. But he heard that she lost fourteen kilos in the four weeks that followed. Several of them are still missing, but she is slowly starting to recover. And if there is anything left of the Nora he knew, then she has been balancing on a knife's edge every single day since.

Henning considers a sentence that is forming itself inside him. He never thought he would say it, let alone mean it.

"Iver is a fighter, Nora. He'll be all right."

She looks at him.

"I hope so."

"He will."

"I can't bear to lose—"

Henning is grateful that she doesn't complete the sentence. He pulls his jacket more tightly.

"Give him my best when he wakes up," he says and stands up.

"Where are you going?"

"To work."

"Now?"

"Yes. I've a story to write."

78

The duty editor raises an eyebrow when Henning lets himself into the office and presses the button for black coffee. Henning gives him a quick update before he sits down at his desk.

On his way to the office he wondered how he should approach the story. The headline was obvious: *Famous journalist in coma*. He knows that anyone awake at this time of night will click on it. Given the headline it could be anyone in the media, an industry fond of turning its own into celebrities. And celebrities sell. That's just the way it is. If the story is also placed on the front page where the introduction can't be seen so that the readers won't automatically see which celebrity it concerns, the story will generate loads of hits.

It's macabre, Henning thinks, to take such things into consideration at a time like this, but he is sure that Iver wouldn't have minded. On the contrary—he would have insisted on it.

Henning starts to write. When he was at the hospital, he couldn't take it in. Nor did it sink in when he was talking to the duty officer at the police station to get some quotes. But when he types the word "coma" and writes that Iver Gundersen is hovering between life and death, the brutal truth that Iver might actually die finally dawns on Henning.

Ørjan Mjønes turns toward the morning sun, shielding his face with one hand as he peers toward the entrance door that only stays closed for short periods. Passengers with bags and suitcases on wheels are walking in his direction. Mjønes looks at his watch. The train leaves in five minutes.

He lights another cigarette and sucks it greedily. He is

about to ring Jeton Pocoli when both Pocoli and Durim Redzepi come shuffling down the platform. Their tired faces grimace when the sun greets them.

Mjønes nods when they reach him and pulls them aside.

"Let's go over this once more: Durim, you get off at Flå, you take with you a picture of Brenden and start looking around. Check out shops, gas stations, hotels, post offices, and restaurants."

Redzepi grunts.

"And you," Mjønes says, looking at Pocoli. "You'll do the same at the next station. Nesbyen. I'll take Gol. And we'll keep each other updated."

More bleary-eyed looks.

"What about Flurim? Isn't he coming?" Pocoli asks.

"He's monitoring data traffic, you know that. This wouldn't have been necessary if you had done your job properly in the first place."

Pocoli looks down and makes no reply.

"If we aren't lucky at any of those stations we'll continue on to Ål, Geilo, and so on."

Mjønes looks at them. Nobody nods. A ticket inspector with a backpack passes to one side of them. Mjønes checks the clock on his mobile. Ten minutes past eight.

"Okay," he says. "We'll travel in separate compartments. I don't want anyone seeing us together."

79

It is just past nine o'clock in the morning when Henning rings Geir Grønningen's doorbell at number 13 Tøyengata. He presses the bell four times and keeps his finger on it extra long on the last ring. Soon afterward he hears a hello in a voice still thick with sleep. Henning can't be sure, but he thinks it's Grønningen.

"Henning Juul. May I come in, please?"

A few seconds of silence follow.

"Now?"

"Yes, now. I need to talk to you again."

"Are you kidding? At this time in the morning?"

"I wouldn't be here at this hour if it wasn't urgent," Henning barks.

Again there is silence. A morose snort can be heard from the intercom.

"Hang on a minute, I just need to put some clothes on."

Henning looks around while he waits impatiently for the door to buzz. Soon he is let in and he stomps up to the third floor. The smell of spices that hits him the moment he entered the stairwell grows less noticeable the higher he gets. Grønningen meets Henning in the doorway of his flat at the top of the stairs.

"Do you have any idea what time it is?" he says.

Henning nods while his tries to get his breath back.

"I was working until the early hours," Grønningen continues.

"In which case you went to bed just as I started work," Henning replies, unperturbed. "A colleague of mine was beaten up last night. I think you might know who did it."

"Me?"

"Did you see a man with long hair wearing a corduroy jacket talking to your boss yesterday?"

Grønningen scratches his head while he tries to remember. His eyes are still sleepy.

"When was this?"

"About ten thirty. Shortly afterward, on his way home, he was attacked."

"Dammit, Juul, I did tell you."

"Yes and I warned him not to be as cocky as he usually is, but I don't think he heard me. Are you going to let me in?"

Grønningen hesitates for a long time before he nods and pushes open the door.

"It's a bit of a mess."

"Do I look like a guy who cares?"

"No, I don't suppose you do."

"I wouldn't mind a cup of coffee if you could manage it."

"It'll have to be instant."

"Instant is fine."

Henning kicks off his shoes. In the hallway there is a mountain of shoes, socks, and coats.

"I don't bother tidying up when I have things to do," Grønningen says as he fills the kettle. Henning struggles to step over the mess.

"So what are you doing, then?" he asks.

"Writing the eulogy. For the funeral."

"Yes, of course. When is it?"

"Tuesday. In Tønsberg."

"That was quick."

"Yes, Veronica wanted it over and done with as soon as possible."

Henning indicates with a nod of his head that he will wait in the living room. There he tries to find a vacant seat on the worn black leather sofa. He just about manages it. He sits down and takes a look around. There is carpet on the floor with bits of crisps imbedded in the fibers, a beer cap, several empty bottles, bags of photo copies. A dumbbell marked 17.5 kg has made a hollow in the carpet under the coffee table.

On the wall are pictures of bodybuilders in various glistening poses. A poster of Arnold Schwarzenegger in *Terminator* appears to have the pride of place.

Grønningen comes in soon afterward and sits down in an armchair next to the sofa.

"Thank you," Henning says and slurps the hot coffee.

"So what happened?" Grønningen asks him.

Henning spends thirty seconds telling him about Iver's meeting with Kent Harry Hansen and the Åsgard visit later that same evening.

"According to Iver, Hansen was quite angry when he left."

Grønningen looks as if he has suddenly put two and two together.

"What?" Henning says.

Grønningen looks down.

"No, it's just that I—"

"What?" Henning says again after a fresh pause. Grønningen looks at Henning for a long time before he answers unwillingly: "When Kent Harry came to the gym yesterday, he was angry about something. None of us knew what it was."

"Did he say anything?"

Grønningen shakes his head.

"He just stormed into the office and slammed the door behind him."

"And you never found out why he was in such a bad mood?"

"No. I left soon afterward."

"And no one has been boasting about beating up some scummy journalist, either?"

"No. But I wouldn't tell you if they had."

Henning nods slowly before he decides to change the

subject to something he has been pondering since their previous meeting.

"Do you know if Tore made any enemies while he was inside?"

Grønningen looks up at him.

"Not that I know," he replies. "Why do you ask?"

"Because I can't work out why Tore was so keen to talk to me. There aren't that many journalists in Norway, certainly not crime reporters, so I can't ignore the fact that Tore might have known who I was before he was locked up. But how did he know that I was back at work?"

Grønningen keeps his eyes fixed on Henning for a few seconds before they glide away.

"Tore doesn't have access to the Internet in prison. And the only person to visit Tore, apart from Veronica, is you."

Grønningen meets his eyes again before they disappear out into the room.

"Did you tell him?"

"Me? No."

Henning makes no reply, but looks directly at Grønningen.

"Do you know if Tore knew who I was before he went to prison?"

"No idea."

Henning takes a deep breath. I'm getting nowhere, he thinks. Every door slams in my face.

"Okay," he says and signals that he is about to leave. "Thanks for the coffee."

Grønningen nods to indicate that Henning is welcome.

"I'll probably see you on Tuesday," Henning adds. "Good luck with the eulogy."

"Thanks."

80

The bell above the entrance to Fighting Fit chimes energetically as Henning arrives and steps onto the purple carpet. He walks up to the reception counter. The girl who was behind it before is also there today. Like the last time she looks up and pushes her chest up and out as he comes over. A Pondus cartoon, which he has seen before, briefly attracts his attention.

"Kent Harry Hansen?" he inquires and sees that the woman recognizes him. She manages a bored nod toward the back room before her fringe falls over her eyes again. Henning thanks her and as he starts to walk, the popular Prima Vera song about the Swedes starts to play on the loudspeakers. Henning doesn't bother knocking, he just walks straight into Hansen's office.

"I'll call you back," Hansen says and puts down the handset. He gets up and looks at Henning.

"Can I help you?"

"Yes," Henning says, aggressively and without introducing himself. "The man who interviewed you yesterday is in the hospital, beaten to a pulp."

"Is he?"

"Yes, he is."

Henning looks at Hansen's unruffled face and shifts his gaze to Hansen's hands. No evidence of recent fighting.

"Would you know anything about that?"

"Me? Why would I?"

Henning doesn't reply. Instead he studies Hansen's eyes, but he can't read anything in them.

"Sometimes he upsets people. He told me he had got on the wrong side of you."

"Yes, but I don't go round beating people up for that."

"No, I don't suppose you do. You have people who do it for you."

Hansen scoffs.

"As I said to that journalist, I don't know what you think we're doing in here. And I don't know who the hell you think you are, coming here, hurling accusations about—"

"My name is Henning Juul," Henning interrupts him. "I asked Iver to talk to you about Tore Pulli, I got him into this mess. I don't know what questions he asked you, but I gave him the ammunition. If you have a problem with the press or your operation here can't stand a little close scrutiny, then take it up with me. Don't beat up people in dark alleys."

"Listen, I don't know what you think you're—"

"It's either you or Even Nylund who sent some heavies to tell Iver to shut up and back off."

"I think you should leave now."

"Or you'll beat me up, too?"

Hansen looks at Henning for a long second before he quickly moves past the desk, grabs hold of Henning's upper arm, and pushes him out of the office. Prima Vera is halfway through the chorus, Henning can hear, as Hansen shoves him in the back and Henning has to take a step to the side not fall over.

"Get out of here," Hansen thunders.

"Thanks for talking to me," Henning says with sarcasm, but he does as he is told. Out of the corner of his eye he sees the for now gentle receptionist staring at him.

81

The sound of a car approaching is unmistakable. Thorleif sits up, goes straight to the kitchen window, and looks outside. Down the road an Audi comes to a halt before it turns left, toward the cabin. Thorleif's heart skips a beat, panicking he considers rushing to the larder to hide when he notices an estate agent's sign at the roadside by the crossroads. The sign wasn't there yesterday.

There must be a viewing at one of the cabins this weekend, he concludes. It could attract many potential buyers. Thorleif swears softly. He hears the car spray gravel as it comes down the road. He steps back behind the curtain as it drives past. With a sigh he sits down at the dining table where a notepad and pen are waiting for him.

When he came home last night he began to write, inspired by Mia, the hotel receptionist. He did it in an attempt to keep himself busy since he couldn't concentrate on reading and he realized at once how good it felt to express himself in the old-fashioned way again. Writing on a computer is so quick by comparison.

He started with the man who forced him to kill Tore Pulli, tried to describe him in as much detail as possible in case he'd need to remember it later. Then he tried to articulate what he had been through in the past week. At the end he realized that what he had written was a confession and an apology to Tore Pulli's family and to his own. It was as if the words took on a will of their own.

It's Saturday, Thorleif thinks, it's almost twelve hours since he emailed Iver Gundersen. Perhaps Gundersen was working last night or he is at work today? Worst-case scenario is he won't see Torleif's email until Monday. But he might get his emails forwarded to his mobile, he might be one of those people who can't help checking their messages all the time. It could mean that Gundersen has already taken action and contacted someone he knows or trusts.

There is still hope, Thorleif says to himself.

Never give up hope.

82

Henning finds Nora on a chair outside the intensive care unit where Iver is being monitored. Her skin is pale. The circles under her eyes have grown more noticeable, but she is just as beautiful as she always was. She stands up when Henning approaches her.

"How is he?" he asks. "Any change?"

She shakes her head.

"He hasn't regained consciousness yet?"

"No."

"So what are the doctors saying?"

"Not much. They're just waiting for him to wake up."

Henning nods and concentrates on her.

"And how are you?"

She looks up. Her eyes are swollen.

"Forget it," he says. "Stupid question. Have you had something to eat?"

She stares at him as if the concept of food is alien to her.

"You have to eat something, Nora."

There is silence for a few seconds. Then she says:

"You too, Henning."

They stand there looking at each other.

"Then let's do that," he says.

They sit in the hospital's café clutching warm mugs. Henning has coffee, Nora drinks tea. As always each has taken two sugars. He bought a ham and cheese baguette and had it heated up in the café's microwave oven, but neither Henning nor Nora is in a rush to sink their teeth into the chewy bread.

He studies her in brief flashes. He has never noticed until now how small vertical stripes appear to be carved into her lips with a careful scalpel. It feels weird to be with her again after everything that has happened. Nora stares at something vague with a glowing melancholy in her eyes.

"The police haven't found the person who did it," he says.

"What?"

"Iver's attacker. The police haven't got much to go on at the moment."

"Right."

Henning takes a sip of his coffee. He knows there are other people present, but the only face he sees is Nora's. It is like being caught in a force field. He isn't sure that he wants to, either. Sitting here opposite her with food and drink on the table between them makes it difficult not to remember the golden hours before everything became so bloody complicated. Before Jonas. And he knows deep down, in his heart of hearts, that they loved each other once.

For a while they eat in silence and though Henning knows that it belongs to their past life, he recognizes the feeling of companionship, the idea of a joint project where pauses are permitted so that the silence which follows each sentence can embrace them. But it doesn't happen now. And he knows that the longer they sit there without saying anything, the harder talking will be.

"There is something I need to tell you."

Nora takes a bite of her baguette and chews it absent-mindedly. Henning takes a deep breath.

"I've discovered a clue," he says, uncertain as to how to continue.

"What do you mean? What kind of clue?"

"A clue that relates to the fire?"

"The fire? What do you—"

Her mouth opens.

"I know that somebody set fire to my flat . . . our old flat . . . my place, on the day that—"

For no reason he makes a fencing movement with one arm.

"Henning, what are you—"

"Just listen to me, Nora, please," he interrupts her. "I know I'm right. And now I've discovered a clue that I believe changes the case. The day of the fire—Tore Pulli was outside my flat that day and—"

Nora's mug hits the table with a bang.

"Henning, what the hell are you talking about? What clue? What case? Tore Pulli? Are you sitting there telling me that someone caused Jonas's death? Is that what you're saying to me?"

"I—"

"What the hell does Tore Pulli have to do with anything?"

Henning searches for the start of a sentence that will extinguish the embers he sees in her eyes, but he finds nothing. Nora pushes the chair out behind her.

"Christ, Henning, I knew you were mad, but not that you had lost the plot completely."

"Nora, please—"

"Forget it. Just forget it. I don't want to hear another word about it, I can't bear it. And don't come here again. Please, don't come here again."

On her way out she knocks into her chair, which almost falls over. People stand back to make way for her. Henning sees that she is crying as she leaves the café.

He doesn't move for several minutes. You idiot, he says to himself. It has taken you almost two years to be able to breathe normally when Nora is in the same room as you. And then you go and ruin everything. And, honestly, what did he think would happen? That she would jump for joy and say: *Well done, Henning. I'm thrilled that you've found a clue. Come here, I always knew that one day you would discover who killed our son. My all time hero!*

He should have tested the waters first, found out what Nora thought about that day, if she shares his suspicions. When he thinks about it, he knows that she has crossed Jonas out. Not deep down because she carries him in her heart, but she applies correction fluid every day.

He shakes his head at himself. Great, Henning. Well played.

83

They ought to rename this dump Hole, Ørjan Mjønes thinks as he gets back on the train after spending three hours wandering around the center and vicinity of Gol. He is fed up with hotels and motels and bars and cafés, especially since none of the people inside them has seen anything of Thorleif Brenden. Durim might be right when he said it would be like looking for the proverbial needle in a haystack. Nor have the other two got anywhere in Flå and Nesbyen. They are on their way to Ål and Geilo now. Mjønes remembers what Langbein said. The clock is ticking.

He finds an empty seat by the window and updates Durim and Jeton before he rests his head against the wall and weighs up the situation. Brenden might have sat in this very seat. What did he think? What plans did he make?

Mjønes rings Flurim Ahmetaj, taking care to speak quietly into the mobile.

"Have you found out if Number One has friends or relatives or any other links to the area between Flå and Finse?"

"I haven't discovered any."

"He wasn't stationed here when he was in the army?"

"No. He did his military service in Jørstadmoen."

"Do a wider search on the guy, check his Facebook profile, see if any of his friends live around here."

Ahmetaj sighs.

"We should have wrapped this up two days ago. I have other things to do. If you need my services after today you'll have to stomp up some more cash."

"You'll carry on working until the job is done. That was the deal."

"Yes, and the job you wanted done finished last Thursday. Today is Saturday. So how much extra are you going to pay me?"

Mjønes sighs as he shakes his head.

"Let's discuss your fee when I'm back. In the meantime I want you to—"

"No."

"What did you say?"

"Discuss your fee? What the hell do you think this is?"

Mjønes takes a deep breath.

"What will it take for you or the three of you to stick with this job until it's done?"

"Twenty a day."

Mjønes shakes his head.

"I'll give you ten."

"Fifteen."

"Agreed. But then you had better come up with something useful."

"Now, now old man. I've got some news for you. I've lost the feed at Number Two's flat. The cops turned up and searched the place. They found the cameras and took them away."

Mjønes ends the call and feels like hurling the mobile against the wall. Soon afterward they pass Ål.

Ål. Gol.

Where the hell do they get these names from?

84

Henning walks under the ruby red canopy and stops in front of the two doormen outside Åsgard. He looks at them in turn.

"Which one of you is Petter Holte?" he asks.

The doormen exchange glances before the bigger one pushes his chest up and out.

"You don't seem to be answering your phone," Henning says.

Holte makes no reply, he merely stares at him blankly. The light above the entrance shines on the bald patch on Holte's head. There is a dense crescent of stubble around his pate.

"I've been trying to call you," Henning continues.

"And you are?"

"My name is Henning Juul."

Holte looks at him, but shows no signs of recognition.

"I don't know you."

"No, but I know you. You're Tore Pulli's cousin."

Holte doesn't reply.

"Are you going in or what?" the other doorman says.

"In a moment. I just need to have a quick word with Petter first. I'm a reporter."

"I don't talk to reporters," Holte says, far from impressed.

"Oh, you don't? But perhaps you beat them up?"

Henning watches Holte closely as his muscles tense and his face darkens. Henning reacts by straightening up.

"A colleague of mine was beaten up last night. Before that he had been here."

Henning has to narrow his eyes in order to see Holte's pupils.

"We don't know anything about that," the other doorman says.

Henning focuses exclusively on Holte.

"Why are you wearing gloves?"

Holte looks down at his hands before he takes a step forward. His tanned face has taken on a flushed undertone.

"What do you want?"

In another time the heavies in front of Henning would have intimidated him. "I want to know if you beat up my colleague last night."

Holte snorts. The light from the lamp above the entrance bounces off his right earring. The voice of the other doorman is softer.

"Petter has made it clear that he doesn't want to be interviewed. You need to respect that or we'll have to ask you to leave."

Henning looks at Holte for one more second before he holds up his hands and says "okay." Holte's colleague steps aside and opens the door. It would have been fun, Henning thinks, to accidentally bump into Holte's inflated shoulder, but it strikes him that he might have pushed his luck far enough as it is. In spite of everything, he would still like to leave in one piece.

Henning enters and the Swedish bartender tells him to go upstairs to Even Nylund's office. From the first floor Henning has a view of the small stage where a woman of Eastern European appearance tries to tantalize the sparse audience with sensual movements.

It is like entering an attic. The corridor in front of him has an opening that reminds him of a vagina. The lighting is subdued. On the wall to the left he sees an illuminated picture of a woman having sex with a fallen warrior. It must be Freya, Henning thinks and remembers from his school days how Vikings who died in battle would come to her. In Norse mythology this kind of death was depicted as an erotic encounter.

Henning walks down the corridor, stops in front of an open door, and peers inside. A man sitting on a chair with his back to him turns around.

"Ah, right. There you are."

Four TV monitors are mounted on the wall above Even Nylund. Nylund gets up as Henning goes inside. They shake hands.

"So you found it."

Nylund gestures to a chair. Henning sits down.

"Can I get you something to drink?"

Henning shakes his head even though his shirt sticks to his body and his throat is parched. He looks around. The walls are decorated with pictures of scantily clad women, advertising posters, and press cuttings. The images on the TV screens are replaced every few seconds. They are live shots from the bar, the stage, the whole room seen from a bird's-eye view plus pictures from outside. Petter Holte stands tall and tough with his thumbs hooked in his belt.

"I know who you are," Nylund says.

"Do you?"

"I spoke to Geir Grønningen earlier today. He seemed to think that you might be stopping by. I was sorry to hear about your colleague," Nylund says and shakes his head. Henning studies him, not sure what to make of Nylund's apparently genuine expression of sympathy.

"Your colleague said you have a theory that Tore Pulli was innocent?"

Henning holds up his hand in front of his mouth and coughs briefly.

"So he told you? Yes, I suppose we have. I wonder if that's why he was beaten up."

"Who by?"

"Well, that's the problem. You, possibly."

Nylund smiles.

"Look at me," he says. "I weigh sixty-eight kilos. Some of my girls can beat me at arm wrestling."

"Yes, maybe they can. But those who work for you have been known to beat people up."

Henning points to the screen where Petter Holte is holding up an authoritarian hand to a middle-aged man on unsteady legs who is trying to enter the club.

"I can assure you, Juul, that no one here is involved in the attack on your colleague."

"And you're sure that you know what your staff gets up to at any given time?"

"When they're at work, then yes."

"And you keep an eye on them from here?"

Henning points to the monitors.

"And in person—when I'm downstairs."

"Right. Do these monitors record?"

"Yes."

"So you can find out who left the club after my colleague did."

"I can."

"Would you do it?"

Nylund smiles.

"I'm sorry about what happened to your colleague, Juul, but my customers are entitled to a certain amount of privacy. I can't show you recordings of what happens in here just because you want me to."

"I could get the police to do it."

"Be my guest—the police can see the footage as long as they produce the right paperwork. And just to be clear, it's nothing personal."

"Mm."

Henning looks around again. One of the video cameras is pointing at a door with a sign saying Glitnir.

"Why the Norse theme?" Henning asks and turns to Nylund again.

"It was Vidar's idea."

"Vidar Fjell?"

"Yes. Some years ago when I talked about opening this

place we spent an evening discussing how we could make the club stand out. Vidar talked about Freya and the Vikings and all that, and I was fascinated by the Norse concept of sex. I think we all were. We decided it would be a good look for us, and that's how Åsgard was born."

"So Vidar was into Norse mythology?"

"Yes. In a big way."

Interesting, Henning thinks, as he remembers that Fjell's father is a professor of Nordic studies. This must be where his interest sprang from. Henning realizes he is excited by this discovery though he doesn't quite know why.

He sits for a while looking at the real-time clock at the bottom right-hand corner of one of the monitors. It makes him think about the nineteen minutes that left Tore Pulli shaking his head. If he really was innocent and he continued to insist that he had arrived on time—how could time pass so quickly?

The answer is obvious, Henning thinks, and it irritates him that the thought hadn't occurred to him earlier: time doesn't run fast unless someone makes sure that it does.

Someone must have tampered with the clock on Pulli's mobile. Someone with easy access to it.

85

Mia is working today as well. Thorleif smiles to her as he enters the hotel lobby.

"Hi," he says.

"Hello, you."

"I was wondering if I could borrow your laptop for a little while. Just for a couple of minutes," he says, apologetically.

"Of course you can."

"Thank you so much. There was just something I wanted to check."

"Take as long as you like. It's fine."

Mia smiles and lifts the bag with the laptop over the counter. He takes it.

"Thank you. How is the book coming along?"

"Not too bad. I'm working on an escape scene at the moment. It takes place in a hotel," she says with her most conspiratorial smile.

"Oh, good," Thorleif says. He realizes he would genuinely like to hear more about Mia's other experiences as a budding writer, but suppresses the urge. He can't allow himself to get to know her or anyone else here. Instead he sits down in the same seat as yesterday and throws his denim jacket on the adjacent chair. The hotel's homepage glows at him as he opens the screen. Thorleif straightens his cap, opens his newly created email account, and waits with bated breath as it downloads. There is no reply from Iver Gundersen.

Thorleif slumps a little in the chair, but decides he might as well check the newspapers as he is already online. He finds an article which informs him that the preliminary autopsy report on Tore Pulli provided no answers as to his cause of death. Apart from that there are no interesting stories about Pulli.

Most newspapers have produced their own, practically identical stories about Thorleif's disappearance, but none of them is accompanied by a picture. This is one of the advantages of being behind the camera, he thinks. You're practically invisible to the public.

"Mia?" he calls out.

"Yes."

"Where are the lavatories, please?"

She leans over the counter and points to the right.

"Go past the piano and you'll find the lavatories on the other side."

"Okay. Thank you. Is it all right if I leave your laptop here while I'm gone?"

"Yes, as there is no one else around—"

Mia smiles again. Thorleif gets up and walks past the fireplace, he passes a lobster tank by the entrance to the restaurant and turns the corner by the dark brown piano. After the smell of the old earth closet in Einar's cabin, it is a treat to enter a fragrant room. There are gray tiles on the floor. The walls are white.

Thorleif relieves himself and spends a long time washing his hands in one of the two square sinks in front of the mirror before he dries them with a paper towel which instantly disintegrates and sticks to his fingers. He is about to return to the lobby, but stops at the sight of a man at the reception with his back to him. The man is wearing a black leather jacket. And he has a ponytail.

Ørjan Mjønes looks around as he gets off the train. A gas station, a hotel, a shop, and a kiosk. Is that all this place has to offer? he wonders. In that case it will be a brief visit. If I was

Thorleif, he thinks, and I had got off the train here, where would I have gone? What would I have needed?

Mjønes tries the shop by the gas station first, but finds it closed. The kiosk, however, is open, but the woman behind the counter has never heard of Brenden. Mjønes walks down the steps and out into the evening heat. This sky above him is turning as dark and gloomy as he feels.

The hotel, red and built in the eighties, looms large in the landscape. I might as well stay here for the night, he thinks. The last train back to Oslo left long ago.

He enters the lobby and smiles to a friendly girl behind the counter. He takes out the folded photo of Brenden and introduces himself as Detective Inspector Stian Henriksen.

"I'm looking for this man," he says. "Have you seen him?"

86

Thorleif stands rooted to the spot. His breath has stopped somewhere at the back of his throat. He can't move. Mustn't move.

How the hell did the man with the ponytail get here?

Thorleif looks around, panicking. He can't risk running into the restaurant from where soft music and muffled conversation drift out toward the lobby. It's too near reception. Nor can he go back inside the lavatory because there is no way out from there. He turns around and sees a door right behind him. And above the door there is a green exit sign.

His only chance.

He backs toward the door as calmly and quietly as he can. He sees the man lean across the counter, but it is impossible to hear what he is saying to Mia. Thorleif holds his breath as he takes tiny steps backward. When he can no longer see the man, he turns around and narrows his eyes as if that will prevent the door from making a sound. As noiselessly as he can, he pulls the door open and enters a bright room with art on the walls. He closes the door carefully behind him. Without looking back he starts to walk, softly to begin with, then faster until he finally starts to run.

He passes a gray staircase that splits into a right and left branch and continues toward the Plenary Hall, but decides to follow the green exit sign past a bench, two chairs, and a table in pale pine that have been placed in front of a window. He reaches a corridor with no windows, but there is a door at the end of it. He tears it open and steps out into the evening as he gasps for air.

To his right is a covered wooden walkway with red doorframes and green doors leading to the new holiday apartments. It gets darker and darker further down the corridor. Don't go that way, Thorleif tells himself, you don't know if there is a door at the other end. Instead he steps out onto the gravel, sees hundreds of cabins up to his left and a mountain that has shed its misty veil. He runs past first one cabin, then another before he reaches the road that leads either to the gas station or further up the hillside, past Presttun. I can't go back to the village, he thinks. The man could come out of the hotel at any moment and he would have no trouble spotting me out here in the open. But does he know that I'm here? Or is he just trying his luck?

Then he remembers it. The denim jacket. The laptop. And Mia would have recognized me, Thorleif thinks, if the man gave her a description or showed her a picture. But perhaps she has guessed the man is a villain—after all, she is obsessed with studying faces. What are the chances that the man would then give up, try the next village, and never come back?

Thorleif swears to himself. It's Saturday night. The last train is bound to have left long ago. He looks up toward Einar's cabin.

Then he starts to run.

Ørjan Mjønes stares at the girl behind the counter.

"I'm not sure," she says nervously and looks furtively over his shoulder. Mjønes turns around; on a low table he sees a solitary laptop whose screen is facing them. There is a thin black denim jacket on the sofa. He gives her a look before he walks over to the laptop, bends down, and reads the newspaper article displayed on the screen.

The story is about Thorleif Brenden.

He is here, Mjønes thinks and glances at the jacket. The stupid prat is in Ustaoset and he was here a minute ago. Mjønes walks back toward the girl.

"Y-yes, I have seen him," she stutters as she points to the lobby area. "His name is Einar and he has just gone to the lavatory."

Einar, Mjønes thinks and looks around. The corridor is empty. He turns to her again and looks briefly at her anxious eyes before he thanks her and marches briskly past the dark brown piano. Inside the lavatory all he finds are two urinals, two sinks, and a cubicle. The door is closed, but Mjønes pushes it open.

No one there.

He goes back out into the lobby, checks the restaurant and sees a solitary couple engrossed in conversation at a table. But no Brenden. He must have seen me, Mjønes thinks. Otherwise why wouldn't he be in the lavatory? And he left his jacket behind. Mjønes returns to the corridor where he discovers the gallery. Brenden must have gone that way, he thinks. It is the only way out from there.

Mjønes opens the door and enters. It's as if he can see Brenden's footprints on the dark gray slate floor. He continues across the bright room, looks around, stops and listens. No footsteps anywhere. Mjønes follows the exit sign through the gallery. Soon he is outside. He scans the landscape. No Brenden in sight, only more buildings and cabins that block his view. At that moment his mobile rings.

"Yes?"

"Hi, it's me again," Flurim Ahmetaj says. "Why are you whispering?"

"Because I'm hot on his heels. Number One is in Ustaoset."

"That makes perfect sense. One of Number One's Facebook friends is called Einar Fløtaker. His family owns a cabin in Ustaoset.

Einar, Mjønes thinks, and at that moment he hears the sound of pieces falling into place.

"Right," he whispers. "Email me everything you've got."

"Okay."

Mjønes thinks about the girl behind the hotel reception. She has seen his face and she knows who Brenden is. And if Brenden turns up dead in Ustaoset in the next few days she might put two and two together.

He turns to the door he has just come out of and looks through it. Then he shakes his head. One thing at a time, he says to himself. First things first.

87

Once he is back inside the cabin, Thorleif realizes that he hasn't drawn breath for a long time. With a gasp he hunches his shoulders, exhales deeply, planting his hands on his thighs as he does so in order not to fall. He stands like this before he slumps down on the floor and leans against a kitchen cupboard. He looks up at the ceiling and closes his eyes.

He sits there in deep despair, panting, before he stands up on wobbly legs and creeps over to the window. Carefully, he twitches the curtain and looks outside. The evening is matt and dark. There is not much left of the moon in the horizon, only a torn nail that offers little light. There is no one on the road below.

It was possibly a mistake to return to the cabin, Thorleif thinks, but he couldn't think of anywhere else to hide. As he surveys the landscape and can clearly see both the roads and the cabins, he realizes that it was actually quite a smart move. He can easily see anyone approaching. All he has to do is stay where he is and keep a lookout. Stay awake and wait. But what does he do if the man should turn up?

Thorleif looks around, he can't remember if he saw any weapons in the toolshed. There must be an ax, he thinks. Next to the tap he sees a set of kitchen knives. He takes the biggest one, the one that looks the sharpest, and feels the edge. Yes, it's nice and sharp, he decides. He knows that he must get the first strike right. No mistakes. He has covered several crime stories where the victim tried to use a knife against a burglar or boyfriend only to fall victim to their own weapon.

Thorleif puts down the knife on the table and looks outside again. In just a couple of minutes the sky has grown darker.

But he sees no one. He hears no one. He blinks and runs a hand over his sweaty face, his T-shirt sticks to his body. Take it easy now, Thorleif, he says to himself. Stay alert.

You have been in worse situations than this.

A dark Mercedes saloon stops in front of the red information board cut in the shape of a cabin, complete with ridged roof and windows. Ørjan Mjønes, who had been leaning against the left wall of the Mix kiosk while he listened for the sound of the engine, steps forward and goes over to Jeton Pocoli and Durim Redzepi as they emerge from the car.

"What's happening?" Pocoli asks.

"He's up there," Mjønes says and nods in the direction of Hallingskarvet as he takes out his mobile and opens an email from Flurim Ahmetaj. The email contains a jpeg file with a map of all the cabins in Ustaoset. One of the numbered cabins has been circled in red.

Pocoli and Redzepi move closer.

"Here is the road," Mjønes says, pointing. "It bends to the right a little further up."

He turns toward the gas station and gestures to the right, to the back of the brown building.

"And you can see the cabin up there."

He points toward the red cabin.

"There are tons of cabins here, but I bet my life that's where he is."

"But won't he see us if we take the road?" Pocoli asks.

"Yes, and that's precisely why we won't do that. We'll split up. Before the hill begins there is a road called Nystølvegen to the right. You'll take that and follow it for a while.

"But won't he still be able to see us from the cabin?"

"Yes, possibly. But he doesn't know who you are. He has only met me."

Pocoli nods.

"So we take the long way round and approach the cabin from the rear?"

"Yes. Spread out so you cover as much of the back as possible. Don't get closer to the cabin than fifty meters. And take as much time as you like. There is a greater chance that he will be less vigilant if he doesn't see anyone apart from you on the road.

"And what will you be doing?"

"I'll stay here until you're in position. Once you are, I'll start to walk up the hill. If he sees me, he might try to run away, away from me."

"And then he will run right into us."

"Exactly."

Pocoli nods again.

"It sounds like a good plan."

88

Ørjan Mjønes waits for fifteen minutes until Jeton and Durim have reached Nystølvegen before he walks back to the hotel. He enters the lobby and nods to the girl at reception.

"Hi," he says and pretends to be out of breath. "I didn't find him."

"Oh," she stutters, nervously. "What a . . . shame."

"You don't happen to know where he lives, do you?"

"No, it . . . I've no idea. He never mentioned it. He never really said very much about anything."

Mjønes nods, turns around, and sees that the laptop is no longer on the table.

"It was my laptop," she says by way of explanation. "I let him borrow it. He didn't have a mobile or a laptop with him."

Mjønes nods.

"Did he say why he wanted to borrow it?"

"No, all he said was that he . . . he had to check something."

Another nod. He fixes his gaze at her. She is sweet. Sweet, innocent, and naive like a young girl.

"What's your name?" he asks.

"Mia. Mia Sikveland."

"Okay, Mia, I need to have a look at your laptop."

She hesitates.

"I just need a quick look," he assures her.

She still appears reluctant.

"Don't you need a court order or something in order to do that? Or a green light from the public prosecutor?"

Mjønes has to think quickly. Mia is clearly not as gullible as she looks. He closes his eyes in an overbearing manner as if he is explaining something very simple to a small child.

"This is an active investigation," he lectures her. "In which case it's my decision whether I need to obtain a warrant from the court before I carry out a search or confiscate potential evidence."

She looks at him for a few seconds.

"Besides it's late. I can't call anyone in Oslo now."

"But I . . . I thought you were from Geilo Police?"

"No, I've been following Br . . . Einar all the way from Oslo."

She nods slowly.

"This isn't unusual. And you could help me save time," he says with a hint of irritation in his voice. "Time could be of the essence here."

"Okay, it's just that I—"

He looks at her.

"Nothing."

She hands him her laptop bag over the counter.

"Thank you. And I'll need your telephone number and address in case I need to speak to you again."

"Okay," she says, unwillingly.

"Thank you," Mjønes says and smiles at her.

Thorleif blinks hard in an attempt to stay awake. His legs can barely manage to keep him upright. He has no idea what time it is except that it must be late. The sky is dark, but there are no clouds to cover the twinkling stars.

Thorleif drinks a mouthful of water from a glass he has filled up several times. He will have to go to the lavatory soon. Surely it would be safe to go now? He hasn't seen a living soul since the two men he noticed further down the road for what must now be several hours ago. He runs to the lavatory, pees, but doesn't wash his hands before resuming his position behind the window.

His eyes widen.

Only one hundred meters away he sees a figure striding purposefully up the road. Thorleif snatches a pair of binoculars he found in a drawer in the living room and puts them to his eyes. He gasps.

Frantically, Thorleif grabs the knife and raises it, ready to strike. The man with the ponytail is close now. What the hell am I going to do, Thorleif panics. The man can't possibly know which of these cabins I'm in, he says to himself in disbelief.

Or can he?

He takes a step back as he considers his options. What is better: making a run for it now in the middle of the night or hiding somewhere in the cabin and waiting for the right moment to attack? He mutters a string of expletives. He can't stay behind the window in case he makes a movement that attracts the man's attention. He looks around while his thoughts rage. Then he grips the knife harder and slips into the living room.

89

It is quiet. Thorleif holds his breath, looks at the knife, feels the weight of it. He has never held a knife like this before nor thought what he is thinking now. Even the idea of stabbing another human being fills him with revulsion. But then he thinks: you have done it before. You've already killed another human being and you did it to protect your family. Now you have to do it again, this time to protect yourself.

He tilts his head. The footsteps are right outside the cabin. Damn, he thinks. Somehow the man must have discovered that Thorleif has a friend who owns a cabin in the area. Thorleif exhales and waits. A drop of sweat runs from his forehead down to his temple. He lifts his T-shirt to his face, wipes it off, dries the handle of the knife as well and grips it once more.

Then he hears the sound of the door.

And the floor squeaks.

Even though he hasn't been out in the hallway, he remembers the sound from when he was here with Einar. His heartbeats throb inside his head. Thorleif closes his eyes, he hears the rustling of clothes. Light footsteps. Controlled breathing. He tries to concentrate, telling himself he must be ready to strike at the right moment without fear or hesitation.

The footsteps stop right outside the door behind which he is hiding. Thorleif holds his breath again and stares at the door handle. Slowly it starts to move. The door is opened, calmly, it conceals Thorleif who makes himself small. He sees an arm, an arm that isn't holding a weapon, and at that moment Thorleif lashes out as hard as he can, he flings out his arm from behind the door, feels the knife take hold and sink in, a voice cries out, loud and shrill, and Thorleif is about to stab the intruder again when he feels a hand around his wrist. He is pulled out from his hiding place behind the door and stares right into the man's angry eyes, he sees that the knife stabbed him in the shoulder and that blood is pouring from the black leather jacket. Summoning up all his strength, Thorleif grits his teeth and tries to force the knife toward him again, but he fails, the man is too strong. Next Thorleif kicks out and feels his foot hitting the man's shin, but the man doesn't even move, he merely roars in anger and pushes the knife out and away from himself. Thorleif tries desperately to find some extra strength, but he can feel that he is almost running on empty, that he is being forced back into the bedroom. He tries to gain a foothold with his trainers, but the man overpowers him and pushes Thorleif backward as he twists his wrist. The pain is intense. He tries to resist the man's force and ignore his own agony, but it hurts so much, so much, it feels as if his arm is about to be snapped off. The knife slips out of his hand and falls to the floor.

Thorleif feels the man's eyes on him. They shine, ice cold and hostile, and the next moment Thorleif receives a blow to his stomach that knocks the wind out of him. He buckles, clutching his stomach, and feels another blow, this time to his back, and his legs collapse under him. He hits the floor knees first. There he stays, struggling to get air into his lungs and finally manages it with a gasp.

Drops of blood fall onto Thorleif's neck and back. He hears more footsteps enter the cabin, but no voices. The bedroom becomes crowded and claustrophobic. Thorleif looks up at two men of Eastern European appearance.

"You're bleeding," one of them says.

"Of course I bloody am," the man with the ponytail snarls.

Thorleif is still on his knees, wheezing. His eyes look around for the knife, but it is beyond his reach.

It's over, he thinks. This time it really is over.

"Take him outside," the man says. "And clean up the blood. Damn!"

It grows dark in front of Thorleif, one of the men towers over him. He closes his eyes and waits for the sharp blow to his back or his neck or perhaps an arm tightening around his throat. But the man helps him to his feet. Thorleif opens his eyes again and looks straight at a man slightly shorter than himself.

"Come with me," the man orders him

Thorleif looks at him apathetically, but allows himself to be led outside.

"W-where are we going?" he stutters.

Neither of them replies. Soon Thorleif is outside in the night air. Above him the stars are twinkling.

"What do you want us to do with him?" one of the men asks.

Thorleif watches as the man with the ponytail glances around before looking up the mountain. He makes a nod with his head.

"You're joking?"

"No," he says and pulls a face. He clutches his shoulder. Blood drips from his hands.

They stay where they are until the third man comes outside. Even in the faint light Thorleif can see the bloodstained paper towels in the plastic bag the man is carrying.

"You'll have to finish him off without me. I've got to get this seen to," the man with the ponytail says, pointing to his shoulder.

Thorleif looks up at the mountains with acceptance. If he concentrates he is sure he can see Pål's face up there. His son is smiling and laughing with that special light that radiates from his eyes when he is happy. Julie is next to him with dimples in her cheeks, Thorleif sees her now, she is waving eagerly to him. Just like she does at nursery. Behind them Elisabeth is happy, beautiful, and gorgeous. She holds up the bookmark he gave her, the first token of his love after they started going out, a red heart-shaped bookmark with no wording. *So you'll always know where you are and where you have me,* as he said to her. And there is the Ketch shepherd with his blasted dogs. But Thorleif knows that throwing stones at them won't help him now.

Slowly they fade away. Thorleif looks at the moon, or is it the sun? Or perhaps it's Morocco?

Yes, it's Morocco, he thinks.

And he knows with a conviction stronger than anything he has ever felt that it *is* possible to love someone as far as that.

Part III

90

It is five minutes to one in the afternoon. It means Petter Holte is unlikely to be at home, Henning thinks, since Sunday workouts are sacrosanct. He stops outside a block of flats in Herslebsgate and presses the doorbell for Tore Pulli's cousin. There is no answer. Henning tries again and waits thirty seconds before he accepts defeat. Then he presses all twelve buttons on the intercom betting that at least one of the residents will do what he himself always used to do, which was just to let people in.

Seconds later Henning closes the door behind him with a satisfied smile and enters a hallway where three prams block the stairs. Arabic music wafts through the keyholes upstairs. Henning battles his way up. On the third floor he stops and knocks on Holte's door. He tries the bell, too, but without success. Henning inspects the door and the lock. It is a regular Yale lock.

Some years ago he wrote a story about how easy it is to break into someone's home. It took only a few Internet searches to learn that the most effective way to pick a standard lock was through a method known as lock bumping, a technique invented by a Danish locksmith a quarter of a century ago. The secret lies in using a blank key, known as a bump key, and cut it so its teeth glide into the lock. But rather than push the key all the way in, you insert the key one notch short of full insertion and then you give it a firm whack with a hammer or something similar. The friction created when the teeth are bashed bumps the pins in the lock the same way balls on a snooker table scatter when you break. This allows you to turn the key and open the door.

Henning tested the method first on his own front door

and later at some friends' house. When his friends eventually accepted that he had done them a favor by breaking into their home, they were happy to provide quotes for his article. Henning has kept the blank key on his key ring ever since and he decides that now is the right time to put it to use again.

He isn't sure what he hopes to find in Holte's flat, but it's impossible to get these people to talk to him and he has to find out more about who they are.

Henning puts on a pair of latex gloves, takes out the hammer he brought from home, slides the key in place, and gives it a whack that echoes against the walls. Then he turns the key and opens the door. Piece of cake.

The silence that follows confirms that he is alone in the flat. In the hallway two pairs of identical boots are lined up next to a pair of worn trainers. A black Alive Force leather jacket gleams at him from a hook. A white horizontal line across the chest and some white squares decorating the middle of the upper sleeve make the jacket look like something out of a science fiction movie. Henning can easily imagine Holte wearing it.

Henning starts to explore the flat. There is a small kitchen to the left filled with dirty plates and glasses. The cooker is speckled with food splashes and fat stains. Empty bottles under a blue wooden table. Beer and Coke Zero, a couple of bottles of tequila, empty jars of Metapure Zero Carb. The walls are unfinished. No burglar alarm as far as Henning can see.

He goes into the living room where two heavy dumbbells lie on the floor next to the fireplace. In front of the television is a messy pile of DVDs, a mixture of action movies and exercise videos with muscular men on the cover. At the center of the room a clotheshorse laden with socks, underwear, and T-shirts dominates the space. On one T-shirt three monkeys are covering their eyes, ears, and mouths respectively while appearing to find something hilarious, *That's what friends are for* it says on another. And a Metallica one, of course. The T-shirts are a size "small," presumably so they will cling to his body as tightly as possible.

Henning stops and listens again, but he can't hear any noise coming from the outside. He starts on the shelving unit in the living room, rifling through the drawers and finding takeaway menus, cables, and a box with a video camera inside it. He opens the drinks cabinet, checks behind books, looks in the drawer under the TV unit, behind the sofa, under the sofa, inside every cupboard, but he finds nothing of interest.

In the bedroom he is met by the smell of stale sleep, but resists the temptation to open the windows. Methodically, he searches the cupboards and drawers in there as well, but discovers only what he assumes to be a jar of steroids. Under the bed all he finds is dust, a vacuum cleaner, and a transparent plastic box with spare duvets and pillows. On the bedside table a book by R. N. Morris is gathering dust. Henning has difficulties imagining a man like Holte devoting much time to literature, but then again crime fiction is considered light entertainment by some.

The bathroom smells of mold. The cupboard above the sink reveals only toothpaste, shaving foam, some lotions, and dental floss. In the laundry basket he catches sight of a blood-stained T-shirt. Iver's blood, he wonders? He is tempted to take the T-shirt with him, but he decides to photograph it instead.

He spins around when a bang echoes from the stairwell. He rushes back to the hallway and leaves the flat as quietly as he can. The footsteps come closer. Henning looks around for another way out. As the noise coming from below grows louder, he kicks off his shoes and tiptoes upstairs. When he reaches the fifth floor he leans against the wall and holds his breath. The footsteps stop. Henning can't be sure, but he thinks that someone is outside Holte's flat. Perhaps he didn't go to the gym after all?

There is a jingling of keys. Henning hears a key being inserted and turned, but the door doesn't budge. It appears to be jammed.

He hears grunting coming from below, but he can't identify the voice. The door finally opens with a bang before it is slammed shut again. Henning seizes his chance and doesn't wait to put on his shoes but races down the stairs. His socks are so slippery that he nearly skids down several steps and he has to cling to the banister for support. It's not until he is back on the ground floor that he stops and breathes a sigh of relief as he quickly glances upward.

No one is there.

91

Light. Is that a light?

Dots far away. They are black and they dance up and down. Something beeps. A pounding sound comes closer. His eyelids slide open. Yes, there is light. Something white appears. Gradually everything comes into focus, but he doesn't recognize his surroundings. Where is he?

A fan whirrs in the ceiling. He senses movement by his side. He tries to turn his head. Movement is impossible, but he sees a bright, smiling face.

"Hi, Iver. I'm glad you're finally awake."

The grip on his neck. The exploding pulse. Something hard hitting him in the face. He didn't manage to dodge the punch. Damn.

"My name is Maria."

"Hello, Maria."

His voice is alien. As if it belongs to someone else.

"I'll let the doctor know that you're awake and he'll come to have a look at you."

She appears to float across the floor, away from him.

"Wait," he says in a rusty voice.

Maria turns around and comes back. Nice face. Pretty smile. He still can't move.

"Have I been paralyzed?"

A warm smile.

"Oh, no. No danger of that. You're in plaster and you have some bandages that will make it hard for you to move for a while. But you're going to be fine."

Iver feels himself sinking back into the mattress.

"How long have I been here?"

"Since Friday."

"And today is—"

"Today is Sunday."

Iver nods, gingerly. He remembers straight hair combed back, a man with stubble. A man who spoke Swedish. Jacob Aalls Restaurant. Dinner. The text message. To Henning.

Maria is about to leave the room when Iver calls out again. "Yes?"

"Please would you do me a favor?"

Henning has only just stepped back out into the Indian summer when his mobile rings.

"Hi?" he says in a hopeful voice.

"Iver is awake," Nora says.

"He is?" Henning exclaims. "That's brilliant. Is he—is there any permanent damage?"

"I don't think so."

"Has he said anything yet?"

"No, not very much."

"Have the doctors said anything about his injuries?"

"No, I'm on my way to the hospital now. But—he wants you to come as well."

Henning stops.

"He said that?"

"Yes, you were—the first person he asked after."

Henning hears an element of disappointment in her voice, but he doesn't want to address it at this moment in time. So instead he says: "Okay, I'm on my way."

92

After regaining consciousness, Iver has been moved from the intensive care unit to a side ward. Henning spends a long time asking for directions until he finds the right door, and when he finally arrives he hesitates outside it for a few seconds. Going in feels intrusive, like entering someone's bedroom while they are still under the duvet. That Nora now shares a bed with Iver doesn't make it easier, but he tries to ignore the image that conjures up.

Henning knocks on the door, opens it tentatively and enters. Nora is sitting on a chair by Iver's bed. She lets go of his hand. Henning can barely see Iver's eyes because of the swelling to his face. His lips look dry.

"Hello," Henning says, sheepishly.

"Hello," Iver and Nora reply in unison.

"How are you?" Henning asks him.

"Good, I think. Or good enough."

Iver's voice is slow and feeble. His lips curl into a thin, crinkled smile. Henning looks around for a spare chair, but finds none. His eyes stop at a vase with fresh, long-stemmed flowers on the table.

"I think I'll go get myself a cup of coffee," Nora says, standing up. "Would anyone else like one?"

"No, thank you," Henning says, shaking his head simultaneously.

Nora looks at Iver.

"I don't think I'm allowed to drink coffee yet," he says.

Nora nods. Henning waits until she has closed the door behind her before he approaches Iver's bed.

"I should have brought something, but—"

His sentence hangs in the air.

"What would that be? Flowers?"

Iver's lips stretch again. They look as if they might tear open at any moment.

"Sit down, would you please. I get stressed when people stand."

"Oh, yes, sorry, I forgot."

"Don't worry about it."

Henning smiles.

"Christ, you look Swedish," he says as he sits down on the chair. The seat is still warm.

"Why?"

"Your face is blue and yellow."

"Ah."

Iver's lips crack into a smile again. A bad time to make jokes, Henning thinks. The silence starts to stick to the walls. Henning looks at Iver in the knowledge that he looked very much like him almost two years ago. But with one crucial difference. The chair by his bed wasn't warm.

"Do you remember anything that happened?" Henning asks in an attempt to shake off the memory.

"I remember being lifted up as if I weighed nothing at all and then there was a bang."

"Did you see who it was?"

"No, but he was strong. I wanted to wriggle free, but I never got the chance."

Iver maneuvers one arm toward a cable that lies across his stomach, lifts up a handset, and presses the button marked *up*. The bed starts to hum and slowly he is raised to a sitting position. Henning takes out his mobile.

"Do you recognize this T-shirt?" he says, turning the display to Iver. Iver tries to focus.

"I don't know. It happened so quickly."

Henning nods and puts the mobile back in his pocket.

"I think the man who beat you up was Petter Holte," he says.

"Pulli's cousin?"

"Yes."

"Why?"

"I don't know. But Petter is or was an enforcer once. He also works as a doorman at Åsgard."

Iver nods. So far so good.

"Did you know that he went to prison?" Iver says, trying to make himself more comfortable.

"No?" Henning replies, surprised. "What for?"

"Last year on International Women's Day there was a demonstration outside Åsgard. Petter was a bit heavy-handed with one of the feminists. Got a couple of months inside for it."

"Really? Did his serve his sentence at Botsen?"

"Yes."

"Do you know if he was in contact with his cousin while he was inside?"

"That I don't know. There are hundreds of cells there, but they probably met in the yard. I believe inmates are entitled to one hour of fresh air every day."

Henning nods. If Holte and Pulli were in prison at the same time something could have gone down between them.

"The doctor has probably told you to take it easy," Henning says. "So I don't suppose we should be talking shop."

"That's just something they say in the movies, Sherlock."

Henning grins.

"Has the doctor said anything about how long you will be in here?"

"No, but I think it'll be a while. I'll be bored out of my skull. You'll have to keep feeding the monster yourself while I'm out of action. I know you'll struggle without me, but—"

Henning laughs.

"Are you still able to send text messages or do you need help with that as well?"

"I haven't tried yet."

Nora enters the room, which instantly grows hotter and more claustrophobic. Henning gets up.

"Do you know where my mobile is?" Iver asks.

"No," Nora replies. "But I can find out."

"Yes, please, would you?"

She disappears out the door again. Henning follows her with his eyes before he turns to Iver.

"I need to leave," he says.

"Where are you going?"

"I'm going—I'm going home."

"Okay."

There is another silence. Henning starts to walk toward the door.

"Henning?"

Henning stops and turns around.

"Has it gone?"

"Has what gone?"

"The cocksure look."

Henning looks at his colleague, seriously this time.

"Yes, Iver. It has. How does it feel?"

"It hurts like hell."

Henning's face creases sympathetically.

He hasn't felt like smiling this much for a long time.

93

Henning's mobile rings as he is about to go into the hospital newsagent to buy a paper.

"You just can't manage without me, can you," he mutters, feigning irritation.

"Henning," Iver says eagerly. "I think I got an email from Thorleif Brenden."

"What?"

"At first I thought it was spam, but the contents suggest that it's him."

"I'll be with you in a sec," Henning says, tossing down the newspaper. A few minutes later he is back in Iver's room.

"What does he write?" Henning asks, agitated, as he rushes toward the bed. In a brief moment he registers that Nora isn't there.

"Read for yourself," Iver replies. Henning takes the mobile and starts reading:

From GulvSprekk <gulvsprekk@hotmail.com>
Subject: <<missing TV2 cameraman>>
To: Iver Gundersen iver.gundersen@123news.no

Hello. I see that you are writing about me.

I am contacting you because I don't know who to trust. I hope I can trust you. I am still alive and I am still sane— though I have good reason not to be.

I need your help. I was forced to commit a murder. I killed Tore Pulli. I had no choice. And now I am on the run from the people who made me do it because I think they want to kill me.

Henning spends some minutes reading the rest of the email before he looks up at Iver.

"Bloody hell," he says. "This is—"

"I know," Iver nods. "Forward the email to yourself or take my mobile with you."

"I'll forward it to myself. Write a reply and see if you hear anything back from him."

"That's a bit difficult," Iver says, looking at his hands. "I needed Nora's help to ring you in the first place."

"Oh, right," Henning says, flustered. "I didn't think—"

"Don't worry about it," Iver says.

Henning forwards the email and gets ready to go.

"Keep me updated," Iver calls out after him.

"Of course," Henning replies. While he half-runs down the corridor in the direction of the lift he takes out his own mobile and finds Brogeland's number.

"There are no new developments," Brogeland sighs, wearily.

"Oh, yes there are. Are you at the station?"

"Yes."

"Come downstairs and meet me in reception in half an hour. I have something to show you."

Thirty-five minutes later Henning is in Brogeland's office. He puts his laptop, which he picked up from home on his way to the police station, on the inspector's desk. Brogeland sits down and moves his chair closer to the table. Henning reads the email over his shoulder. He pays particular attention to the second half.

> I don't know if this can be used as evidence, but the man who forced me to murder Pulli might have left a fingerprint in my car on the day he tested me to find out if I could be ordered to kill. The fingerprint is on the armrest on the passenger

side. I parked my car in Kirkegaten. It has probably been issued with several parking tickets by now. But if you can get someone you trust from the police to check this out for me I think it might be possible to discover the man's real name.

I hope you can help me. The way things look now you are my only hope. At the moment I don't want to say anything about where I am, but I hope you will help me so I won't have to remain in hiding for very much longer.

Please would you also contact my girlfriend Elisabeth Haaland and let her know that I am all right? But please do it discreetly. I have reason to believe that our flat is under surveillance.

Yours sincerely,
Thorleif Brenden

Henning waits impatiently for Brogeland to finish.

"Have you already swept his flat for bugs?" he asks.

"Yes," Brogeland replies. "We found masses of high-tech equipment. Video and audio."

"Did you now?" Henning says.

Brogeland nods. The next moment there is a knock on the door. Sergeant Ella Sandland appears. She sees Henning standing behind Brogeland and she makes a gesture with her head to indicate that she needs to speak to her boss. Brogeland returns soon afterward with a grave expression on his face.

"What is it?" Henning asks.

"We've just had a call from Geilo Police. A body has been found at the foot of Hallingskarvet. From the description it's likely to be that of Thorleif Brenden."

94

Henning goes home and lies down on his sofa. He stares at the ceiling and thinks about Elisabeth Haaland, of the news awaiting her—if she hasn't been told already. And he feels for the children, only eight and four years old. A difficult time lies ahead of them.

Henning checks the time on his mobile. It's too soon, he thinks, to write anything about Brenden except the fact that a body has been found. It will take a couple of hours to confirm Brenden's identity. Then the police will inform his next of kin, and out of respect for the bereaved, reporters should really leave family and friends alone for a couple of days. But very few members of the Norwegian media care about that these days.

You should seriously consider a change of career, he tells himself, given how much you loathe your own profession. There is hardly any decency left among reporters. But deep down Henning knows he is exactly like them when he smells a good story. Is this really the kind of person he wants to be? Is this truly how he wants to feel?

That's the problem. He doesn't know what he wants.

In the tender infancy of his journalist career he had an idea—or it may have been more of a fantasy—where he would position himself in the same place in the city for six months, say, and look out for people who repeated the same actions every day. He wasn't interested in people commuting to and from work, but those who went there just to have somewhere to go. He would seek out those who avoided eye contact, who hid themselves away, who preferred walking close to the wall rather than the curb. Henning believed that they each had a story that needed telling. Something had made them like this. Something unique to each of them.

But he never found the time. There was always a new story, always something of greater urgency. And before Henning returned to work, after Jonas's death, he had himself turned into someone who walks in the shadows.

Perhaps I'll find my way back one day, Henning thinks. When everything is over.

A sudden flash of inspiration makes him sit up. Before he has thought it through, he is on the phone to Iver.

"What's happening?" Iver asks, answering after just a few rings. "I've got some headphones and a remote control now," he adds, happily, before Henning has time to say anything. "At least I can call people now."

"Don't do it."

"Eh?"

"I don't want you to talk to anyone. Especially not the media. Has anyone called you today?"

"Why would they do that?"

Henning tells him about the coma article and the discovery of Brenden's body.

"Many people know you're in the hospital," he continues. "And several reporters will probably check how you are, maybe not today, but definitely tomorrow when everyone is back at work. The thing is, I don't want anyone knowing that you've regained consciousness yet. If the people who killed Brenden are aware that he sent you an email, and if they also check up on you and discover that you're in a coma, then they may believe that Brenden's email was never received. We can buy ourselves some time."

"Okay," Iver says. "I get it."

"You need to tell Nora."

"I'll try."

The stab wound sends spasms of pain from his shoulder and down his arm, even though he cleaned the cut with whatever he could find and applied a makeshift bandage. There is an agonizing pounding coming from the point of entry. Perhaps it has already become infected, Ørjan Mjønes thinks, since he feels feverish all over. The knife was unlikely to be sterile.

The public telephone rings at eleven o'clock exactly, just as it did three days ago. Mjønes steps inside and picks up the receiver with his left hand.

"Hello," he says. At the same moment the throbbing in his shoulder escalates.

"Is everything taken care of?"

"Yes," Mjønes says, clenching his teeth. The pain feels like flames brushing his forehead.

"And you're quite sure of that?"

"Yes. There are no loose ends this time."

The handset is filled with white noise for a few seconds.

"Good."

"Which means only one item is outstanding," Mjønes says. "But there has been a change of plan. I want the balance paid into my bank account."

Silence. Mjønes wipes the sweat away with the same hand that is holding the handset.

"Why?"

"I have my reasons."

There is silence again.

"Okay?"

"I have a bank account in Sw—"

"Not on the telephone," Langbein cuts him off. "We need to meet."

Mjønes frowns. Why? So that Langbein can shoot him dead and avoid paying the two point five million kroner he owes him?

Mjønes makes it a rule never to ask his employers about

their motives. He takes on a job and he sees it through, mostly without getting his own hands dirty. But now that he thinks about this particular assignment, his curiosity is aroused, especially since Langbein hadn't been in touch since newspapers the world over commemorated the anniversary of 9/11. Prior to that date he and Langbein regularly did business, but for much lower fees.

If you don't take the job then you become the job.

So Langbein would have had me killed, Mjønes considers, if I hadn't agreed to do this job. Or was this his plan all along? Get me to kill Pulli and send someone after me later? It might explain why it was so easy for me to push the price up from two to three million, he thinks, a sum that, even to begin with, was considerably higher than is usual for this line of work. Perhaps he is walking right into a trap? Given his knowledge of Langbein's previous operations it's not unthinkable, even though he doesn't know who Langbein is or who he works for.

"We're not going to do that," Mjønes says. "I'll contact you the way you contact me. The advert will appear sometime tomorrow morning and the numbers you'll need will be in it. If the money hasn't reached my bank account by Tuesday, I'll charge interest."

"Are you in a hurry?"

"Yes . . . or—no."

"You're not thinking of disappearing, are you?"

Mjønes hesitates.

"Oh, no," he lies.

95

Henning can't sleep. In addition to Pulli's nineteen minutes, another question is vexing him, so he sends a text message to Frode Olsvik early the next morning asking for a few minutes of his time as soon as possible. The reply arrives immediately:

I have five minutes in Stockfleths by the Courthouse at 8:30 am.

Henning agrees with Heidi Kjus that he will come into the office a little later and squashes himself in with all the other morning rush-hour commuters on the number 11 tram to the Courthouse. In Stockfleths he orders a double espresso and takes a seat by a window while he waits for the lawyer. A few minutes past eight thirty. Olsvik appears, but rather than go up to the till to order, he nods to the waiter behind the counter who returns his greeting with a smile.

Olsvik maneuvers his large body into a chair by the table and holds out his hand to Henning.

"Thank you for agreeing to meet with me at such short notice."

"Not at all."

In the course of the next minute Henning learns that Olsvik has been informed about what has happened both to Pulli and to Brenden and that police are looking for the hit man who was probably paid generously for arranging Pulli's death.

"How can I help you, Juul?" Olsvik says and straightens one of his braces. Henning takes a breath, but decides to hold off sharing his suspicions about the time on Pulli's mobile. He needs to test his hypothesis first.

"In the last couple of years no one had more to do with Pulli than you. I would bet that you knew him better than most."

"I suppose you could say that."

"Did he make any enemies during the time he spent in prison?"

A patronizing expression spreads across Olsvik's face. Henning braces himself for a lecture.

"My relationship with my client is purely professional, Juul. Our conversations mainly revolved around his case. And my client is still entitled to a duty of confidentiality even though he is dead."

"Even though he was killed?"

"Even though he was killed. Especially if the person asking the question is a reporter."

"Even though it was you who tipped off Tore Pulli that I was back at work?"

Olsvik looks at Henning as a cup of steaming hot coffee is placed in front of him.

"Thank you," he says, looking up at the waiter. "Put it on the company account, would you."

"Sure."

Olsvik waits until the waiter is out of hearing range. Then he pins his eyes on Henning.

"What are you talking about, Juul?"

"The only people to visit Tore while he was inside were you, Geir Grønningen, and Veronica Nansen. And I know that neither of them told Tore that I had returned to 123news."

Olsvik smiles wearily.

"I don't know what you're talking about, Juul. There are many ways to get information in a prison, even if you don't have visitors every day or access to the Internet. The inmates speak to the prison guards, with other inmates, and they're entitled to make twenty minutes' worth of telephone calls every week."

"I thought all telephone conversations were monitored?"

"In theory, yes. But no one listens in to every word that is said. They do spot checks, primarily to determine if any communication relating to drug smuggling or similar is taking place. And I regret to have to tell you, Juul, but no alarm bells would start ringing if someone, in an aside, happens to mention that you're back at work. People have more important things to worry about."

Feeling a tad humbled Henning has to admit that the lawyer is probably right.

"Do you know if the prison keeps a record of which numbers an inmate has called?" he says, trying to shake off his embarrassment.

"I imagine that they log outgoing calls. And Tore might have tried to get someone on the outside to help him by calling or writing a letter. He is not the first inmate to believe he was unfairly convicted. Some write to the press, others to private detectives."

"So you and Tore never discussed if a third party might be able to help him?"

"I really can't tell you what I did or did not discuss with my client—"

"Please, Olsvik," Henning interrupts him. "I know you have attorney client privileges and rules to observe, but we're not talking about information that is sensitive to your client's case. And I'm asking you because I'm still trying to help him—even though he is dead."

"And you can do that by finding out how Tore knew that you were working again?"

Henning hesitates for a second.

"Among other things."

"You have to explain the logic in this to me."

Henning takes a deep breath.

"In parallel with working on Tore's case, I'm also trying to find out what happened on the day my son died. Tore claimed that he—"

A thought occurs to Henning that almost takes his breath away. Pulli contacted him in the hope that Henning could help exonerate him. The bait was the truth of what happened the day that Jonas died.

What if that was the reason Pulli had to die?

"Pulli claimed what?" Olsvik asks him.

"That he knew something about the fire in my flat," Henning says, distracted.

"And you think your son's death relates to Pulli's?"

"Yes. Or—I . . . I don't know," Henning admits without looking up.

He remembers what Elisabeth Haaland told him about their burglar alarm packing up on a Sunday. That must have been the day after Pulli called me, Henning concludes, since he met the fire investigator Erling Ophus on a Saturday. In which case someone must have acted with extreme speed. First they would have to identify someone who could get close to Tore Pulli, a job that would surely require time and research, then they would need to get hold of the surveillance equipment for Brenden's flat—on a Saturday—and install it when the Brenden family left the house the next day.

Henning shakes his head. There wouldn't be enough time.

"I know nothing about this," Olsvik says. "I haven't heard anything."

Henning nods slowly. But the thought refuses to go away. And there is another option, he thinks, which Olsvik also touched on. That Pulli had been in contact with someone else regarding the same subject before he called Henning.

I need to get hold of those call logs, Henning says to himself.

96

Normally it takes the police five to six weeks to get an answer when they send off a fingerprint to Kripos. But after locating Thorleif Brenden's car in Kirkegaten and successfully lifting a fingerprint from the armrest on the passenger side, Brogeland persuaded forensic scientist Ann-Mari Sara to convince her bosses to give the sample top priority and run it through AFIS, the Automated Fingerprint Identification System. It took only ten or twelve seconds before she got a hit. And after the result had been checked manually there was no doubt that the fingerprint belonged to a man called Ørjan Mjønes.

Brogeland remembered Mjønes from his plainclothes days. His name also appeared on the long list Nøkleby gave them after Elisabeth Haaland had described "Furio"—the man who pretended to interview her.

It really is ridiculous, Brogeland thinks, that so few staff within the police force have access to the Indicia database, where all information about everyone—obtained both officially and unofficially—is collected and stored. If you have a description of a person and if information about someone with similar features has previously been entered, everything relating to them, including any criminal record, appears in a matter of seconds. In some cases the level of information stored about the person includes the smallest details. All mapping of Eastern Europeans, for example, in connection with Project Borderless is being entered into Indicia.

Brogeland studies the fact sheet on Mjønes that Nøkleby has printed out and given to them. His criminal career began in his teens and he has two previous convictions. The first is for a robbery in Majorstua, where a car was used to ram raid a jeweler's, while the other conviction relates to possession of an illegal weapon in a bar in Oslo. When police searched his remarkably tidy home, they discovered several other weapons as well as explosives and burglary equipment. While he was suspected of being the brains behind a string of minor and major robberies in his early twenties, things quietened down around him at the end of the nineties and at the start of the new millennium. For that reason Mjønes was suspected of having made the transition from petty to organized crime and moving into an even more lucrative and discreet career as a fixer. This could mean anything from providing persuasive heavies to carrying out actual hits. But even though the rumors flourished, the police never found anything concrete they could arrest him for.

Yesterday Brogeland had called one of his former colleagues at Organized Crime, Njål Vidar Hammerstad, to ask if they had come across Mjønes in recent years. Hammerstad said that they didn't have him under surveillance, but that his face popped up from time to time. They knew, for example, that Mjønes had befriended several people in the criminal Albanian community. But Hammerstad didn't know if there was a link between Mjønes and Tore Pulli.

In an ideal world, Brogeland thinks, plainclothes officers should have followed Mjønes and his cronies every day all year round. But it's too expensive. Every year Oslo Police spends billions of kroner fighting organized crime and yet it's still not enough. It doesn't even scratch the surface. Norway is an attractive country for criminal gangs because we're an affluent nation, he thinks. With a chronically understaffed police force.

Sometimes his wife asks him if he misses his old life as a plainclothes police officer. His reply is always no, but that's a lie. Of course he does. He misses the buzz of the chase, even though there might be long boring intervals in between. He remembers the endless hours sitting in cars or trying to blend in on the street. And then the high when everything kicked off at last, when he would explode into action, give his all without hesitating. Not for one second. But he couldn't live that life once he had a family. The level of risk and the generally anti-social working hours were intolerable in the long run.

Brogeland heaves a sigh and looks at an old photograph of Mjønes. A man who has stayed in the shadows in recent years, but who has now emerged to carry out a hit. The chances that he has already left the country are considerable—unless something went wrong. But what would that be?

97

Ørjan Mjønes feels cold even though he is sweating. He puts one hand on the tiled wall in Durim's bathroom for support and stares at his face in the mirror. It's white. His arm dangles limply by his side. It's as if a heavy lump is trying to force its way out from inside of his shoulder and paralyze him totally.

Mjønes blinks hard and watches as the damp creases in his face fill with sweat trickling from his forehead and eyes. I'm burning up, he thinks, and splashes himself with cold water. It helps. For now.

The night on Durim's sofa was one of the worst that he can recall. At one point the ceiling transformed into an ocean where a gigantic wave came crashing toward him. When he blinked, everything returned to normal. Then he started see- ing colors, yellow and purple, pink and blue—all mixed up. In a lucid moment he realized that he must be hallucinating. Early the next morning he called the doctor. A man whose name Mjønes doesn't know, a man who makes house calls at short notice to provide medical assistance to people who pre- fer to avoid hospitals. It's an expensive service, but the com- bination of lifesaving first aid and discretion is usually worth the money.

Durim opens the door when the bell rings. A few minutes later the doctor enters. Mjønes stands up on trembling legs. A chill washes over him. The doctor comes toward him. Tall, well-groomed, newly shaven, hair neatly combed.

"And here's the patient," the doctor says and smiles.

He carries a small suitcase in his hand. He stops in front of Mjønes, puts the suitcase on the floor, and inspects the bandage on Mjønes's shoulder. The doctor starts to ease off the makeshift dressing, slowly persuading the fabric fibers to release their hold on the scab. Mjønes cries out in pain when the sticky skin finally lets go. A crust has formed at the edge of the wound, but the cut itself is still open and weeping. Mjønes estimates that the cut is between four and five centimeters deep and sees that the area around it has grown redder and even more swollen overnight. Judging from the color of the bandage the wound has become infected. The skin around it is hot.

"We need more sterile surroundings," the doctor mutters. "We should really cut around the wound and then rinse it with a saline solution."

"Can't you do that here?"

"No. That would only make it worse. You need to go to an operating theater."

"I don't have time for that."

"You could become very ill, do you realize that? The infection you've acquired could spread to the bones in your shoulder and your blood might become infected with bacteria. That could lead to septicemia. Worst-case scenario you could die."

"Just do the best you can, would you. And spare me the melodrama."

"There isn't very much I can do. I presume the cut is more than eight hours old?"

Mjønes nods reluctantly.

"Then I can't stitch it. All I can do is clean the wound and keep it open so the pus can drain out. And I'll give you a course of antibiotics.

"Sounds good to me."

The doctor puts his suitcase flat on the floor and opens it. Mjønes sways.

"What about traveling with this thing?" he says, pointing to his shoulder.

"I wouldn't recommend it for a couple of days, at least not until you have the infection under control."

The thought of running away, leaving Norway behind, makes him remember the safe in his flat where the ampoule is stored. You have to collect it first, he tells himself. Get rid of it and anything else that links you to the murder of Tore Pulli.

But first you have to get better.

98

Henning sits down at his workstation and rubs his face with his hands. The chair opposite him is empty. Thank God Iver is going to be okay, he thinks, relieved. Even though he knows that Iver is entirely responsible for his own actions, he would never have been in the hospital if it hadn't been for Henning.

He stares into the air. Given that the police now believe Tore Pulli was murdered, they may already have requested the call logs from Oslo Prison to find out what kind of contact he had with the outside world. Or perhaps they haven't. They think that Ørjan Mjønes is behind Pulli's death. So why bother with the logs? They are going to be more interested in who Mjønes was talking to.

On his way back to the office Henning calls Knut Olav Nordbø at Oslo Prison and learns that an inmate's telephone records are deleted if they die or when they are released, and that this happens in a matter of days. In other words it may already be too late. He will never be able to access the logs himself, but the police could if they obtained a court order.

So Henning rings Nøkleby. From her tired, fed up voice he realizes that skipping the social niceties is a wise move. He also resists the temptation to ask if she still believes that Tore Pulli was guilty of the murder of Jocke Brolenius.

"I'll be quick," he begins. "As far as Tore Pulli is concerned, have you allocated all your resources to Ørjan Mjønes now or are you still pursuing other leads?"

"Still pursuing other leads."

Henning waits for more, but nothing comes.

"Can you tell me anything about the leads you're following up?"

"Not at this moment in time, no," she says in a guarded tone.

"Do you have any theory as to why Tore Pulli had to die?"

"No comment."

Henning hesitates.

"What about Tore Pulli's telephone records from prison, have you asked to see them?"

Nøkleby doesn't reply immediately. Then she says:

"I can't discuss specific details of the investigation with you, Henning."

He sighs.

"I think it might be a good idea if you were to look at those logs."

"Yes, I imagine you do."

Henning lets the slightly ironic remark pass unchallenged.

"I have nothing else. Oh, yes, are you going to the funeral tomorrow?"

"We haven't decided yet."

"I see. Well, I'm going."

"Okay. Do let us know if you see anything you think might be a good idea for us to follow up."

"I'll—"

Henning breaks off and smiles wryly. And when Nøkleby ends the call shortly afterward without saying good-bye, his smile is even broader.

99

The light that seeps through the windows of Solvang Church casts a cold, blue sheen across the floor. It matches the covers on the chairs, Henning thinks, as he stands at the entrance looking down the rectangular room. In the middle of the floor, in front of the pulpit, Tore Pulli's coffin sits white and beautifully decorated with flowers. Long white ribbons with golden letters express grief and last messages.

Henning knows that he ought to go inside to get a proper look, but he can't bear being present during the actual ceremony. Afterward, however, he mixes with the mourners at the graveside. Partly because he wants to see how Pulli's friends will behave, but also because Heidi Kjus asked him to document the event with his camera. So he takes some close-ups as discreetly as he can, without becoming intrusive. He wants to get some poignant pictures of big, hulking men struggling to keep their tears at bay. Petter Holte runs a hand over his shaven head and breathes heavily. The clothes he wears look as if they might burst at any moment. Geir Grønningen lets his long hair hang freely over his eyes. For once his heavy torso has been defeated by gravity. The eyes of Kent Harry Hansen are also shiny. The sunlight makes his white, stubbly hair glow like a torch.

Henning shoots some group photos as more mourners emerge. A man Henning thinks he recognizes from somewhere approaches them. His muscles are tightly packed under his black suit jacket and he moves lightly across the gravel, looking over his shoulder as if ready to lash out at any moment.

Suddenly there is movement in the crowd as Petter Holte pushes his way to the front and walks right up to the new arrival, who takes a step back. Holte jabs an agitated index finger against the man's chest. Henning lifts his camera and lets it shoot.

"You've got a bloody nerve showing your face here today," Holte hisses.

"Tore was my mate, too, you asshole," the man says.

Geir Grønningen and Kent Harry Hansen intervene. Grønningen locks his arms firmly around Holte who resists.

"Not here," Grønningen tells him. "Not at Tore's funeral, show some respect."

Hansen deals with the newcomer whose mood has also turned ugly. The man adjusts his jacket without taking his eyes off Holte. Eventually Holte backs down.

It takes several minutes before the crowd calms down again. Henning tries, unsuccessfully, to find the face of the man Holte took offense at, but the crowd closes up and the gap disappears. The incident is over, but Henning is incapable of paying attention while the vicar performs the committal. Grønningen stands close to Holte, towering over him by a head, at least. Nearby Veronica Nansen clings to an older man with the same eyes and mouth as her. The butch girl from Fighting Fit is there, too. Everyone seems to be here. At last Henning spots the man who incurred Holte's anger, further back among the sea of people. His head is bowed. Where have I seen him before?— Henning racks his brains.

Soon the first handful of earth falls on Pulli's coffin. Henning hides behind the camera and takes some more pictures. He sees Holte reach up toward Grønningen's ear and whisper something before clenching his fist as if he is ready to punch someone.

After the earth has been thrown, a line of people forms in front of Veronica Nansen. She shakes hands with everyone who has come to pay their respects. Henning joins the back of the queue and sees how Nansen grows more and more exhausted the closer he gets. But she carries on, smiling bravely. When it is Henning's turn, he stops right in front of her.

"My condolences," he says, holding out his hand. Nansen takes it and pulls him closer, almost as if she is on autopilot.

"Thank you for coming," she says.

"How are you?" he asks as they glide away from each other. Nansen shrugs her shoulders.

"It's strange," she sniffs. "It feels as if I've lost a huge piece of myself."

She speaks slowly without looking at him.

"A part of me has gone, and yet, somehow, that part still hurts. Do you know what I mean?"

Henning looks at her with eyes that are starting to well up, too. He would never have thought that a woman like Veronica Nansen could articulate a feeling he has lived with for almost two years.

"Phantom pains," he says quietly.

"What?"

"I know what you mean."

"Yes, of course you do," she says and shakes her head. "Sorry."

The man he presumes to be Nansen's father comes over to them and nods to Henning.

"There is a get together afterward for Tore's friends," she says as they start to walk. "It would be nice if you could join us."

"That's very kind of you, Veronica, but I don't know if I can call myself a friend of Tore's. Or if my presence there would be wildly popular. It didn't look as if everybody was equally welcome."

"No," Nansen says and looks down. "Petter, he is—"

She shakes her head in resignation.

"Who was the other man?" Henning asks as they reach the car park.

"That was Robert," she replies. "Robert van Derksen."

100

The doctor's efforts helped Ørjan Mjønes get a good night's sleep, but the next morning he still woke up early and feeling restless. The body of Thorleif Brenden had been found far too quickly. Nosy little Mia Sikveland, the receptionist at Ustaoset Mountain Hotel, will probably raise her eyebrows when she reads about Brenden in the newspaper, even though his death is likely to be recorded as an accident. She will wonder why Brenden used an assumed name and she certainly won't understand why a police officer failed to correct her when she referred to Brenden as Einar. That had been a mistake. A big one. And if he had had a little more cash on him, he would have dispatched Durim to Sikveland's small flat in Geilo and made sure she was silenced, too.

Fortunately, they had had a stroke of luck with Brenden. The email he had sent from Mia Sikveland's laptop had—according to Flurim Ahmetaj—been addressed to a journalist who was now in a coma. And as far as Mjønes is aware, he has yet to regain consciousness. As long as I move quickly, he thinks, there shouldn't be any problems. He even has the money now. Two point five million kroner have been transferred to his account, adding nicely to the substantial sum he already had there. It will last him a long time. And as his money arrived without delay—despite his misgivings—neither does he need to worry about Langbein. His suspicions were unfounded.

So far so good.

After lunch Mjønes books a one-way ticket to Marrakech using one of his false identities for no other reason than he has always wanted to go there. He takes the number 13 tram to Sandaker Shopping Center, gets off and walks down to

Thorshov Sports. He checks the cars parked on both sides of the road, but there is no sign of drivers surreptitiously waiting for someone. Nor can he see anyone behind the windows or on the rooftops. He walks down Sandakerveien and past the recycling plant on Bentsehjørnet, which the buses going to Sagene rattle past before turning one hundred eighty degrees and repeating exactly the same exercise. With exactly the same outcome.

Even so he feels increasingly uneasy the closer he gets to the flat where he has lived for the last six months. If this had been a hit or a burglary he would have called it off by now. He always used to back down at the first sign of bad vibes. It's one of the reasons he has stayed out of prison for the last seven or eight years.

Mjønes glances around again. You have to go to the flat today, he tells himself. You have to get rid of the evidence. It will only take you a few minutes.

He looks around one last time before he lets himself in.

Inside the flat a wall of heat hits him, but he refrains from opening the windows in case the place is under surveillance. Instead, he makes a mental list of everything he needs to take with him. All the research he did for the Pulli hit might be retrieved by IT experts, even though he did his best to erase every trace from his laptop. Even if he doesn't take the whole machine he should at least take the hard drive.

Mjønes enters the bedroom where the roof slopes toward the floor. The fetid and stale air sticks to him. The smell reminds him of Durim and the pigsty of a flat he lives in. Mjønes puts these thoughts out of his mind, goes over to the large white wardrobe, and opens the door. He kneels down, enters the four-digit code that unlocks the gray safe inside, and starts stuffing bundles of euros into his backpack. Then he takes out the box where he put the ampoule for safekeeping. He opens it and looks at the shiny transparent liquid inside.

It had required considerable ingenuity and a touch of creativity to work out how to kill Tore Pulli in a quick, discreet, and effective way. The fact that Mjønes had to travel all the way to Colombia to pick up the murder weapon only added to the fun. He likes the exotic, the primitive and yet simultaneously sophisticated.

He is about to close the box and the safe when he senses movement on the floor behind him.

"Ørjan Mjønes?" he hears an unknown voice say.

What the hell?

The sound of footsteps. Several pairs of shoes. Cops, he thinks. Damn. He considers his options. He should have brought a weapon, as it is he has no way of defending himself. Yes, he is holding one in his hands, but he is lacking the most important thing. A needle or something with which to penetrate the skin. The box with the piercing needles is still in the safe, but he knows he doesn't have time to remove the wrapping from the needle, open the ampoule, and dip the needle in the poison. Besides, he would need to do it twice. And he is aware that he will never be able to take on two cops with only one working arm.

Mjønes swears again.

"Get up, slowly."

Mjønes does as he is told, turns his head and sees a police officer he thinks he recognizes from somewhere. Big. Tall. Muscular. And behind him, a man with a similar physique.

"Who are you?" he says, his mind racing.

"You're under arrest," the blond police officer says.

"Why?"

"You're suspected of conspiracy to murder."

Mjønes doesn't reply, but looks at them in turn and sees them take up positions. Mjønes thinks about his shoulder, his money, the box with the ampoule. Think quickly, he says to himself. That's what you're good at. Thinking on your feet.

Discreetly he takes out the ampoule and slips it into his trouser pocket. Then he turns to the police officers.

"What is that?" one of the police officers asks, pointing to Mjønes's hand.

"It's just a box," he says.

"Put it down on the table."

Mjønes obeys him.

"Take it easy," he says, holding up his hands to indicate his cooperation. "I'm coming of my own free will."

Mjønes takes one step toward them and tries to make eye contact. Lose the ampoule before you reach the police station, he thinks. Drop it in the road, anywhere it will disappear by itself, under a car tire, in between some bushes.

And without resisting he allows himself to be led out of the flat while reminding himself of two point five million reasons not to say a single word for a very very long time.

101

Henning can't stop thinking about the incident in the churchyard. Why was Petter Holte so mad at Robert van Derksen? Had he done something to Pulli?

Henning considers the obvious explanation, namely that van Derksen was responsible for the murder of Jocke Brolenius, but it strikes him that Holte would hardly have reacted as he did if that was an acknowledged truth among Tore's friends.

On his way back Henning tries to call Geir Grønningen, but all he gets is his voicemail. He sends him a text message, but that doesn't produce a response, either. He realizes why when he remembers that Grønningen is giving the eulogy.

Henning winds his way through the rush-hour traffic in his rental car and decides to drive up to visit a source who so far has proved to be the most reliable in her insight into human nature. This time he catches up with Vidar Fjell's girlfriend as she is leaving her house.

"Oh, hi," Irene Otnes say. "You again?"

Henning doesn't have time to say anything before she tells him that she is on her way to the shop.

"Perhaps I could ask you a couple questions first?"

Otnes closes her front door and locks it.

"If you don't mind walking down to the car with me," she says in a cheerful tone.

They start to walk. Above them the clouds are moving swiftly.

"I didn't see you at the funeral today," he remarks.

"Did you come here to ask me that?"

"Yes and no."

"I hate funerals," she says, though she strolls along as if Pulli's death hasn't dampened her mood noticeably.

"I find them upsetting. And I spoke to Veronica on the telephone yesterday and she said it was okay that I didn't go."

Henning starts.

"Would you know why Petter Holte has a problem with Robert van Derksen?"

"Oh, yes," Otnes smiles. "I can tell you that. Robert stole Petter's girlfriend while he was inside. Or rather she dumped him, I think, but she dumped him for Robert. You don't do that to your friends, you know."

Otnes starts walking down the steps. Henning follows her doggedly. The scabs under his feet protest, but he ignores the pain.

"Poor Petter. He's always being teased about his small feet."

"What do you mean?"

"You know—small shoes, small—"

She points to her crotch.

"I thought that was a myth?" Henning says.

"I wouldn't know about that. Not that it made any difference to his friends. Petter has been made to suffer for years, believe you me."

"Was Tore Pulli one of his tormentors?"

"No, not Tore. It was Tore who told Petter that his girlfriend had started seeing someone else."

Henning thinks quickly.

"While they both were in prison?"

"Yes. I believe he felt that Petter had a right to know. That was one of the things I liked about Tore. He was decent to a certain extent. And he heard it from Veronica during one of her visits. Veronica and I—we tell each other everything," she says and laughs.

"But I couldn't help feeling sorry for Petter. He has never had much success with women, he has always been a loser.

Women never stay with him for very long, you see. We women like a challenge."

Otnes smiles and turns around when she reaches the car.

"Anyway, I'm off to see a client now."

"Okay. Nice talking to you," he says.

"Likewise."

His image of Petter Holte is becoming increasingly complete, Henning thinks as he drives back toward the city center. Short fuse. A failed enforcer. Never managed to step out of Tore's shadow. Possibly envious of Geir Grønningen who became Tore's best friend instead of him. Even his girlfriend walked all over him.

The question is: how deep are those scars?

102

The evening wind wafts through the open window and brushes Robert van Derksen's glistening face. He takes a deep breath, leans back in the sofa, and stares at the ceiling. It has been a long day. Going straight from the funeral to teach a demanding maga class full of students who expect him to deliver is not to be recommended. It requires energy to perform, especially given how the funeral went.

Tore Pulli—dead as a dodo. Just thinking about it feels weird. In their eyes Tore was immortal, the man who could do nothing wrong. And then his life fell apart. First he was sentenced and jailed, then dead long before his time.

Van Derksen thinks about what the reporter said to him that day, that it made no sense that a man as clever as Tore would leave behind his calling card at the crime scene. It was a valid point and van Derksen had himself pondered this anomaly shortly after Tore's arrest—especially once Tore put a reward of one million kroner on the table for information that could help free him. But then Tore was convicted and everybody stopped talking about it after a while. Nor had Robert given it much thought, until the reporter called. And that in turn prompted him to make a call straight afterward. Now when he reruns the short conversation it strikes him as really quite odd.

"I've been thinking about something: you didn't teach anyone else the Pulli punch, did you?"

There was silence for a while.

"Why do you ask about that?"

"No, I was just wondering. A guy just called me suggesting someone other than Tore had killed Jocke and elbowed his jaw. To make it look as if Tore did it."

Again there was silence.

"What kind of guy?"

"A journalist."

"Name?"

"I don't remember."

"For God's sake, Robert, of course you do."

He thinks hard.

"Juul or something like that."

Another silence.

"Henning Juul?"

"Yes, it could be him. Do you know him?"

Long silence.

"I know who he is."

What if the reporter was right? Robert wonders. What if Tore really was innocent? In which case the list of alternative suspects is very short indeed.

The next moment someone rings the doorbell. Van Derksen gets up, gives the punch ball suspended from the ceiling a Pulli elbow, and goes over to the intercom on the wall. He asks who it is, but receives no reply. Through the handset he hears hard footsteps on the stairs.

"Hello?" he calls out. Downstairs, the front door slams shut. Probably a cold caller, he thinks and goes back to the living room. He has barely sat down when there is a knock on his door. Wearily, he gets up again and goes out into the hallway. He opens the door and stares at a face that makes his blood run cold. He instinctively takes a step back. And at that moment he knows he is going to die.

103

Bjarne Brogeland is roused from a chaotic dream. He contracts his abdominal muscles and sits up, finds the luminous instrument of torture on his bedside table, and answers the call before the ring tone wakes Anita. The duty officer in the control room briefs him while Brogeland registers Anita's grunting and stirring.

"Okay," he whispers. "I'm on my way."

He tiptoes out of the bedroom as softly as he can and closes the door behind him. Yet another murder, he sighs and knows immediately what the next few days will look like. The initial phase is the most important. The first twenty-four to forty-eight hours are about building the best possible foundations for the investigation. In practice this means that huge resources are reassigned without delay, forensic technicians, investigators, and as many officers deployed as possible—in consultation with the head of the Violent Crimes Unit. Everyone drops whatever they are doing and heads for the crime scene. Everybody knows their role and the job they have been trained to do. Fortunately, it is a well-oiled piece of machinery.

It takes him fifteen minutes to reach Vibesgate. Red-and-white police tape has been stretched around the whole block. Nosy onlookers have congregated as usual, even though it is past midnight. Cars are parked along pavements, illegally, but no one cares about that now. Brogeland nods to a crime scene technician before he bumps into Detective Constable Emil Hagen.

It doesn't surprise Brogeland that Hagen is already there. There is competition to be the first at a crime scene, or at least there is between Hagen and Detective Constable Fredrik Stang.

But Stang hasn't arrived yet as far as Brogeland can see. And it irritates him that Hagen always looks so bloody bright-eyed and bushy-tailed. His footsteps are bouncing, his mouth half open. The gap between his front teeth makes him look so damn young.

"What happened?" Brogeland asks.

"Man in his early thirties, shot five times."

"Five times?"

"Yes. I've just spoken to one of the neighbors, but he heard nothing."

"He didn't hear five shots?" Brogeland says in disbelief.

Hagen shrugs.

"Silencer, possibly."

"Hm. Caliber?"

"Nine millimeter. The flat belongs to a Robert van Derksen and it's very likely that he's the victim."

Brogeland walks around in a small circle. The name sounds familiar, he thinks, as they enter the courtyard. Neighbors peer down from open windows. The flower bed next to van Derksen's stairwell appears to have been dug up by a dog. There is scattered soil in front of the entrance.

"Have we found any evidence upstairs?"

"We found a shoe print outside his front door."

"Which doesn't belong to van Derksen?"

"That remains to be seen," Hagen says, shaking his head. "But I don't think so. It looks like a smaller shoe size."

Henning gets the message from Heidi Kjus just as he is about to leave his flat. *"Murder in number 2 Vibesgate. Can you go straight there?"*

Henning rings her immediately rather than reply to her text message. Neither of them bothers with small talk and Kjus gives him a quick update.

"So are you going over there?" Heidi asks.

"Okay," Henning sighs.

He had been chatting with 6tiermes7 the night before and had intended to start the day by breaking the news about Ørjan Mjønes, but that will have to wait now. He is confident that the news won't reach anyone else until he has finished in Vibesgate.

Before he leaves, he visits the Yellow Pages website and types in *2 Vibesgate* in the search field. It will be some time before the police confirm the victim's identity, he assumes. He gets two pages of hits and prints them out. As he picks up the sheets, he quickly skims the names. And then he stops and looks up.

"Oh, to hell with it," he says, softly.

Henning sees that several of his colleagues are already there and he goes up to the police liaison officer, a tall man in uniform who looks stern-faced and gray as he answers the standard questions according to the book. Henning asks a few of them himself, but gets no useful information. *It's too early to say. We're working on securing evidence.* The usual.

A little later Brogeland emerges and marches resolutely down a side street. Henning makes sure that nobody follows him and catches up with Brogeland just as the inspector is about get into a patrol car.

"You're kept busy these days," Henning begins. "First you arrest Ørjan Mjønes, the man who arranged the murder of Tore Pulli, and then one of Pulli's friends is killed on the same day he has an argument with one of Pulli's friends at Pulli's funeral."

Brogeland looks sharply at Henning.

"What's on your mind?"

Henning tells him about the altercation between Robert van Derksen and Petter Holte.

"It's the body of Robert van Derksen you've found, isn't it?"
Brogeland sighs.

"You can't write that it's him, Henning. Not yet."

"I know. So when can I?"

"I don't know. We haven't even told his next of kin."

"Okay, I'll hold fire until you give me the go ahead, but I want to know before you issue a press release."

Brogeland looks hard at Henning for a long time until he gets into the car. Before he turns the key in the ignition, he glances up at Henning and nods.

104

The patrol car drives off without sirens, but at high speed. Henning watches it disappear around the corner before he takes out his mobile and calls Heidi Kjus. He knows that she hates to act as a switchboard for reporters in the field, but this time she accepts instructions from a field agent without asking questions. Nor does she express an opinion on the quotes from Robert van Derksen's horrified neighbors. Instead she asks him when he is coming in.

"I haven't finished here," Henning lies.

There isn't much more for him to do in Vibesgate, but he has other plans. Plans he doesn't want to share with Heidi.

Henning flags down a cab and goes to Niels Henrik Abels-gate. It doesn't take him long to establish that Veronica Nansen isn't at home so he continues to Ullevål Stadium. There he locates the offices of Nansen Models AS on the second floor, next door to a clinic for allergy and respiratory diseases. Strange juxtaposition next to a business that provides scantily clad entertainment, Henning thinks but dismisses the thought as he enters a reception area and nods to the woman behind the shiny, boomerang-shaped glass counter.

"Veronica Nansen?" he says.

"What's it about?"

"I need to speak to Veronica. She knows who I am."

"She is a bit busy right now."

"Just tell her Henning Juul needs to speak to her," he says. "And that it's important."

The secretary scowls at him before she slips the handset under her long hair and utters some sentences Henning fails to catch. Isn't it a bit odd, he thinks, that Veronica is back at work so soon? Then again he knows that many people need distraction at a time like this, and try to pick up their old routine as quickly as possible.

"It's that way," the secretary says, pointing down a corridor. Smiling, he thanks her for her help and knocks twice on the door with Nansen's name in large silver letters. A voice on the other side asks him to wait a moment. Then he hears footsteps. The door in front of him is opened.

"Hi, Henning," Nansen says, surprised.

She steps aside to let him enter. Then she walks around her desk and sits down. Henning spends thirty seconds breaking the news to her. When he has finished, Nansen leans forward on her elbows. Her hair falls in front of her eyes.

"What the hell is going on?" she says and looks at him.

"Christ knows," Henning says and sits down.

The room gets claustrophobic and quiet. He lets her have a moment to digest the information.

"It's tempting to point the finger at Petter in light of what happened yesterday," he begins. "He has threatened Robert's life before."

He puts it as a question, but Nansen doesn't reply.

"Do you know what Petter did after the wake?"

"Some of the guys went to the gym to work out, I think, but the rest went home."

"They worked out yesterday?"

"Yes, they're always at the gym. Petter thought it was the best way to honor Tore's memory," she says and rolls her eyes.

Henning runs through the deaths in his mind's eye. Jocke Brolenius was killed with an ax, Tore Pulli appears to have been poisoned, and Robert van Derksen was shot. And since Ørjan Mjønes has been arrested, he can't have orchestrated the latter unless he planned it a long time ago.

There must be several killers here, Henning concludes. There have to be.

"Do you know anything about guns?" he says and hears immediately how loaded the question is.

"Why do you ask me that?"

"No, I was just curious."

"I don't believe that. You're never just curious."

Henning tries to evade Nansen's probing eyes.

"Do you know anyone who has a gun?"

"They all do, I think."

"What about Tore? Did he?"

"Yes."

"Have you ever used it?"

"Yes, a couple of times. A long time ago."

"So you know how to shoot?"

"Yes."

Her face instantly darkens.

"But I didn't shoot anyone last night, if that's what you're asking me."

"That's not what I'm asking you," Henning replies and lowers his eyes.

But it occurs to him that no one had better access to the knuckle-duster than her. And she could have had a million reasons to want her convicted-killer husband dead. What if van Derksen knew something? What if that was the reason he had to die?

105

The Command Center—CC—lies halfway between the red and green zones on the fifth floor of the police station. The Violent Crimes Unit holds all its joint meetings at the CC, in addition to eight o'clock conferences every morning with the Institute of Forensic Medicine where that day's autopsies are prioritized.

The room has a golden glow thanks to the Scandinavian furniture and the pale yellow linoleum on the floor. Bjarne Brogeland sits down on a chair with a black floral pattern and pours himself a cup of coffee from a metal pot. The duty officer, a man in uniform with thick blond hair and a noticeable double chin, is standing in front of the whiteboard with an uncapped marker pen in his hand. Before he writes Robert van Derksen's name in capital letters, he hoists his trousers up well over his hips, but they soon slide down again.

The duty officer spends some time presenting the facts of the case. The soil from the flower bed, the size 6½ shoe print found outside van Derksen's flat, and the bullets. When he has finished, Brogeland takes over and briefs them on what happened at Tore Pulli's funeral.

"Interesting," Chief Inspector Arild Gjerstad says. "How did you find that out?"

"Henning Juul told me," Brogeland replies. "He was there. We should have been there, too."

Brogeland looks at Pia Nøkleby who looks away. An ominous silence falls on the table. Gjerstad rubs his mustache with two fingers before he clears his throat.

"We need to map Petter Holte's movements after he left the funeral. Bjarne—take Emil with you and pay him a visit."

Brogeland and Hagen nod.

"Sandland, you find out what kind of people van Derksen mixed with. Unless we get lucky, we'll have to interview the lot of them."

Sandland nods.

"We'll probably have to do that in any case," Nøkleby interjects.

"And we also have to consider other possibilities," Gjerstad continues. "If it was a burglary gone wrong, what—if any—valuables he had and anyone he was in contact with in his last twenty-four hours. We also need to go back and speak to potential witnesses. Neighbors. See if there are any CCTV cameras nearby that might have picked up any vehicles that we should check out. We also need a list of cabs in the area. Pia, do you want to add something?"

"I can run his name through Indicia and see if anything crops up."

"Yes, please," Gjerstad says, getting up. "Right, let's get to work."

Seconds later the CC is empty.

Brogeland and Hagen park next to the pavement outside the redbrick building in Herslebsgate. Three dark-skinned men standing by the greengrocers on the corner turn to look at them. We should have taken Hagen's car, Brogeland thinks. Patrol cars attract too much attention. And his own car is in the garage. Again. Bloody fan belt.

They get out and quickly walk up the stairwell until they reach Petter Holte's flat on the third floor. Soon they hear heavy footstep on the other side. The door opens. A man partly covered in shaving foam appears and gives them a puzzled look.

"Petter Holte?" Brogeland asks.

Holte, whose face looked happy bordering on blissful when

he opened the door, immediately puts on his hard man expression.

"I'm Detective Inspector Brogeland and this is Detective Sergeant Hagen and here's my warrant card," Brogeland continues, unperturbed. "Could we come in for a moment, please?"

Holte's eyes grow even darker.

"Why?" Holte says and inflates his chest.

"It's about Robert van Derksen."

"What about him?" Holte says, provocatively.

"He's dead."

Holte makes no reply, but continues to glare at Brogeland with the same scornful expression.

"May we come in, please?"

Holte doesn't budge. Thin white trails of foam find their way from his scalp to his temples. Long moments pass before his face suddenly changes, as if the news needed a minute to hit home. Reluctantly, he steps aside. Brogeland is the first to enter, but he stops immediately. Lumps of soil are scattered across the floor. Hagen and Brogeland exchange looks before Brogeland turns to Holte and enters without taking off his shoes.

"What the hell happened?" Holte asks.

"Firstly, I need to advise you that I'm recording our conversation," Brogeland says holding up an MP3 dictaphone. Holte gulps and nods.

"Where were you last night?"

"I . . . I went to the gym for my workout."

"Was anyone else with you?"

"Kent Harry and Geir were there. And a couple of other guys."

"But not Robert?"

"No, Robert and I, we—"

Holte stops, searches for the words, but doesn't find them in the next thirty seconds.

"How long was your workout?"

"I was there until—"

Holte looks away from Brogeland while he thinks

"Until eight or nine o'clock, I think."

Brogeland nods. Preliminary examinations suggest that van Derksen was killed sometime between nine or ten.

"What did you do after your workout?"

"I went home."

"Alone?"

"Yes."

"Have you been here ever since?"

"Yes, I—"

Holte doesn't complete the sentence. His eyes flicker.

"What shoe size do you take?"

"What size—what the hell do you want to know that for?"

His tone is instantly aggressive.

"Just answer the question, will you."

Holte lowers his head.

"Six and a half," he mutters.

"What did you say?"

"Six and a half."

Hagen and Brogeland look at each other again. Then Brogeland says:

"We would like you to accompany us to the station."

106

All the text message from Brogeland says is *OK,* but Henning needs nothing else to write his story, name the victim, and highlight his link to Tore Pulli. Suddenly it's no longer a straightforward murder. Henning even includes the arrest of Ørjan Mjønes, though he doesn't mention him by name.

He notes with satisfaction that the story receives top billing on 123news's homepage and not surprisingly their competitors are quick to pick it up. In a way this is unhelpful, Henning thinks, since it will lead to added pressure on the police. It could also make it considerably harder to cover the rest of the story. But he had no choice. News is news. And if he is lucky, the extra pressure from his competitors will result in more information coming to light.

Henning calls Brogeland to hear if there are any developments, but gets no reply. Nor had he really expected one. Instead he writes him a text asking the inspector to ring him when he has a moment. When Henning has sent it, he starts to think about the killing of Jocke Brolenius. Robert van Derksen looked like the prime suspect right from the start, though Tore Pulli was quick to dismiss this possibility. And Henning agrees to some extent. A man with such a massive need for recognition wouldn't be able to keep a secret for two years. But could he have known something all the same—without being aware of it?

The air is stuffy and clammy even though Bjarne Brogeland and Petter Holte have only just sat down in Interview Room One. A thin white microphone hangs from the ceiling. A camera is pointing at them from its position above the door in the neutral gray room. Brogeland knows that Gjerstad and several of his colleagues are probably sitting in the CC following events via a screen. He could have talked to Petter Holte in his own office, but everything becomes more onerous in an interview room.

"Do I need a lawyer?" Holte asks.

"Do you think you do?"

Holte doesn't reply.

"We can get you a lawyer if you want one."

"I haven't done anything wrong so why would I need one?" he replies, defiantly. Brogeland looks at the compact body in front of him. As always it is encased in a layer of aggression, but there is something more. He's scared, Brogeland realizes.

"Do you own a gun?" he asks.

"I've a weapon, yes."

"What kind of weapon?"

"A SIG nine."

Nine millimeters, Brogeland thinks. With the type of barrel that takes a silencer.

"Have you got a license for that?"

"Yes, of course I do," Holte sneers.

"How long since you last used it?"

"Awhile," Holte replies and starts picking his nails. Tiny beads of moisture have found their way up through the brown and partly polished scalp.

"Why did you argue with Robert van Derksen at Tore Pulli's funeral yesterday?"

Holte looks down.

"Robert nicked my girlfriend when I was inside. Besides, he was no friend of Tore's anymore. Him showing up was disrespectful."

His voice grows more outraged.

"Did you go over to his flat after your workout yesterday?"

"No."

"There was a lot of soil in your hallway."

"Yes, what about it?"

"There was a lot of soil in Robert's hallway, too."

"What's so unusual about that?"

"Nothing, possibly, but we found a shoe print outside his flat that matches the size of your feet."

Holte looks up. His face takes on a frightened expression.

"There's no way that's my shoe print," he says, getting angry now.

Brogeland doesn't reply, but watches Holte for a couple of seconds. The air becomes even more oppressive.

"Okay," Brogeland says and gets up. "Wait here, please."

He goes over to the workstation where he pauses the recording, steps out onto the red floor, and goes to the CC. Gjerstad and Hagen turn around as he enters.

"What do you think?" he says.

"There is enough to justify a search warrant," Gjerstad replies.

107

Searching a suspect's home has never been Bjarne Brogeland's thing—trawling through drawers and bookcases, wardrobes and bed linen, hunting the one piece of evidence that will crack open or close a case. He appreciates the importance of this work, of course he does, but he is pleased that it's rarely something he has to undertake himself. It simply makes him irritable and impatient.

Being in the field was another matter. They had no other choice than to be patient if they were to catch criminals, or as they call them, villains. And this type of work offered a completely different level of tension. Observing the interaction between the villains from afar, reading their codes. Who delivered what to whom and where? Who was talking to whom and when? In this way patterns would emerge that the police could use as a starting point for further investigations, to determine who was worth following and who wasn't. But evidence found in a flat, fibers on the body. It's too fiddly for him. Too feminine.

However, he took part in the search of Petter Holte's flat because Holte was his collar. It was his information that led to Holte being remanded in custody, almost in record time. And the evidence found in Holte's flat was more than enough to nail him for the killing of Robert van Derksen. That's why Brogeland experiences a pleasant sensation all over as he returns to his office and lets himself fall into his chair. He takes out his mobile and discovers that he has a long list of calls and texts from known and unknown numbers. Brogeland realizes without having to check the Internet that Henning Juul has broken the news about Robert van Derksen.

For a brief moment he feels the taste of disloyalty in his mouth. Nøkleby and Gjerstad want to manage the flow of information themselves, and in theory Brogeland can live with this. In fact, he is delighted that someone else is prepared to deal with communication. However, Juul is a special case. Even though he can be an absolute pest, he is a pest with a nose. And surely the bottom line is getting results. Like now.

Brogeland scrolls through his text messages and sees that Juul has asked him to call. He glances at his watch. He is about to resume interviewing Petter Holte and he needs a little time to prepare. But I can manage a quick call, he says to himself and presses the green button. Juul replies a few seconds later.

Brogeland tells him about the arrest and the imminent charging of Petter Holte on the condition that none of this information ends up in print.

"Are you quite sure it's him?" Juul asks.

"We found a weapon in his flat that was definitely fired yesterday."

"Really? And what does he have to say about that?"

"We haven't confronted him with it yet. But it will be difficult for him to wriggle out of it given the other evidence."

"What other evidence?"

Brogeland hesitates before telling him about the soil in the hallway and a footprint that matches Holte's size 6½ shoes. When Brogeland has finished there is silence.

"What is it?" he asks.

"No, it's just that I . . . I just think it sounds a bit odd," Henning replies.

"Why?"

"I don't see why Holte would make it that easy for you. And moreover I think there is a link between the murder of Jocke Brolenius and the murder of Robert van Derksen, though I can't put my finger on it yet."

"There is nothing to suggest it, Henning. We need evidence.

Like the missing murder weapon, for example. And, ideally, we need to place that ax in the killer's hands whether that person was Petter or someone else."

Brogeland hears a sigh down the other end of the telephone, but Henning doesn't elaborate on his frustration.

"And there is always the possibility that Pulli really did kill Jocke. You mustn't ignore that."

"No," Henning replies, glumly. "I won't. I just can't get it all to add up."

108

Suddenly everything is happening at once, Henning thinks. Even the weather seems to be changing. An ominous dark cloud has appeared out of nowhere. Could Petter Holte really be responsible for the death of Jocke Brolenius as well? Henning can't quite imagine how a man who has failed at practically everything in life could plan and execute such a sophisticated murder only to screw up completely when killing one of his oldest friends.

So Henning rings Geir Grønningen repeatedly that afternoon. Finally he gets hold of him and Grønningen reluctantly agrees to meet for a chat outside the supermarket in Grønland Torg. By the time Henning arrives it has started to rain. Grønningen has taken shelter under an umbrella, but Henning is oblivious to the downpour.

He decides to cut straight to the point.

"The police have arrested Petter," he announces.

Grønningen reacts with disbelief.

"Bloody idiot," he says, squeezing the handle of the umbrella hard. "I don't know how someone can be that stupid."

Grønningen shakes his head and looks ready to punch the first person he sees. Instinctively, Henning takes a step back.

"What did he say to you after his row with Robert yesterday?"

Grønningen looks down at Henning, then he scans the surroundings for anyone who might see or overhear them.

"I saw him whisper something to you when the earth was scattered on the coffin," Henning says to prompt him. "And afterward he clenched his fist."

"Yes," Grønningen replies. "But that had nothing to do with Robert."

"Then what was it about?"

"Petter said that if anyone dared to knock over Tore's gravestone he would—"

Grønningen imitates Holte and clenches his fist. Henning remembers printing out an article about how Vidar Fjell's grave was desecrated though he can't remember the details.

"But at the wake afterward he started mouthing off again," Grønningen continues. "Said he was going to get Robert and blah-blah-blah."

He shakes his head again.

"But you need to know that's just Petter. Even though he has a temper and does the first thing that comes into his head, he is still a tough guy. He has had plenty of opportunities to have a go at Robert, but he never did anything about it."

"Why not?"

"Probably because he knew that he couldn't have handled it. Robert may not have been as strong as Petter, but he was much better technically. In close combat, for example, there is no doubt who would have had the upper hand."

"Perhaps that was why Petter chose to shoot him."

"Yes, but he could have done that any time. Why yesterday when the whole bloody congregation had just seen him argue with Robert? It's . . . it's like asking to be caught."

Henning nods in agreement.

"Did he know the Pulli punch?"

Henning lifts up his elbow to demonstrate. Grønningen hesitates.

"I think he might have practiced it, but like I said Petter was no technical genius. He was just muscle."

Exactly, Henning says to himself. And if Petter was too scared to take on a guy like Robert van Derksen, he was unlikely to have tried it on with Jocke Brolenius in the first place.

Something here isn't right, Henning thinks.

Again his thoughts return to Tore Pulli.

"Did you work out with Tore on the night that Jocke was killed?"

"Yes, we always worked out together."

Henning looks at him closely.

"Did you have separate lockers?"

"Yes."

"And you would lock them while you worked out, obviously?"

"Yes, of course we would, we're not idiots."

"Where did you keep your locker keys?"

"That depended. People who had been members a long time were allowed to leave them behind the reception or in Kent Harry's office. What Tore did depended on who was on duty. Tore put his trust in people rather than locks. Why do you ask?"

Henning ignores the question and mulls over the information he has just been given.

"So when you worked out, how would you know what time it was?"

"We would check the clock on the wall."

Henning looks up at him.

"The clock behind the reception counter?"

Grønningen nods.

"None of us wears wristwatches these days. We check our mobiles instead."

Pulli probably did exactly that when he had finished his workout, Henning thinks, excited, to see if he had any messages or missed calls. That's the first thing Henning does when he has been asleep or had a shower. So it can't just be the time on Pulli's mobile that was wrong, Henning surmises.

The clock at Fighting Fit must have been wrong, too.

Henning thanks Grønningen for his time and heads straight to the gym. He expects the place to be packed given everything that has happened, but it is practically deserted. He assumes the group must be in shock.

Henning takes a step onto the purple carpet. The tall woman behind the counter looks even more surly than usual when she sees who it is. Henning ignores her attitude and asks if Kent Harry Hansen is around.

"Didn't he make it clear that you're not welcome here?"

"Yes," Henning replies. "But I still need to talk to him. Where is he?"

"Dunno."

Henning nods, but his attention is drawn to the wall behind her. He takes out his mobile and compares the two clocks. They show practically the same time. No wonder, he thinks. If someone deliberately changed the clock the night Pulli was meeting Jocke Brolenius, then that person would have had to change it back again either later the same evening or the following morning at the latest. Anything else would have been a giveaway.

But who could have done it?

"That clock up there," he begins. "Has it—do you know if it—"

Henning hesitates, unsure as to how to phrase the question.

"Is it always precise?" he asks and realizes instantly that his question is blatantly obvious.

"I think so," she says without taking her eyes off the magazine in front of her.

"Do you know if it has been too slow—in the past?"

Henning groans inwardly at his atrocious questioning. Behind him the weights clang against each other.

"No idea," she says, sounding bored.

"I'm only asking because I was wondering if it was very slow on the twenty-sixth of October nearly two years ago."

She lifts her head, slightly less bored now.

"That was the night Jocke Brolenius was killed," Henning informs her. "Were you working here that night?"

She snorts.

"Do you think I can remember that?"

"No, but please could you check who was? There is probably a list on your computer. A duty roster, possibly. Time sheets. Payroll. How many people work here?"

"You need to talk to Kent Harry," she says and looks down again. "Though I very much doubt he'll be willing to help you."

Henning stares at the clock behind her again, at the wall surrounding it before he looks back at her. His eyes stop at the T-shirt she is wearing. At chest height three monkeys appear to be having a whale of a time.

"Is that yours?" he says, pointing to the monkeys.

She looks up and follows his finger.

"Jesus, of course it's mine. What kind of stupid question is that?"

Henning nods slowly while he studies her. Her mouth is downturned, exasperated. She eyeballs him back.

"Don't you have an Axe T-shirt as well?"

She searches his face for a reason for this question.

"What's it to you?"

Henning doesn't reply. They lock eyes.

"No reason," he says, eventually. "Nice talking to you."

109

Bjarne Brogeland sits down on his own in the canteen with a cup of coffee in front of him. The light still streams strongly through the large windows. He massages his face trying to rub away the tiredness in his eyes. The last few days have been full on. Tore Pulli, Thorleif Brenden, Ørjan Mjønes, Robert van Derksen. Even so, he shouldn't be feeling this exhausted. It should all be in a day's work for him. So what the hell is going on? The first signs of old age? Is his body telling him to start to slow down?

No, he says to himself. He will never show signs of weakness. For him it's all or nothing. Until the day he drops.

Brogeland picks up his mobile just as a text message from Anita arrives.

> Hi, honey. Please would you get dinner tonight? Oda Marie is coming home with Alisha after nursery. Get something healthy and tasty. J xxx

Brogeland quickly replies *OK*.

He switched his mobile to silent while he was interviewing Petter Holte, and now he sees that seven unanswered calls were received in the meantime. He checks the list of callers. Reporters. Henning Juul, twice. It appears he has also left a message on Brogeland's voicemail.

Brogeland sighs as he recalls the rebuke in Gjerstad's voice at the meeting they just had. As usual it was about leaks. And Gjerstad's eyes more than hinted that he was blaming Brogeland since he had referred to his conversation with Juul at the joint meeting earlier. His boss warned them against further contact with the press and threatened repercussions if anyone were to disregard this order.

Brogeland stares at the letters in Juul's name. Then he shakes his head and puts down the mobile. Time to call it a day.

Henning tries to call Kent Harry Hansen on his way home to Grünerløkka, but there is no reply even after numerous rings. Henning thinks about Petter Holte remanded in custody while the evidence against him stacks up. Just like Tore Pulli. And just like his cousin, Holte insists that he didn't do it. History is repeating itself, Henning thinks. But if Holte really should turn out to be innocent, then it means that someone else had a reason for killing Robert van Derksen. Why did he have to die? And why did Petter Holte have to take the blame?

Henning is reminded of something Irene Otnes said the last time they spoke. He rings her up and asks her to explain what she meant when she said that Petter Holte wasn't much of a challenge for women.

"Well, he's a wimp, to put it bluntly," she replies.

"Yes, I remember you saying so, but what did you mean? Give me an example."

Henning presses a finger into his other ear to block out the noise from the torrential rain.

"There was no doubt who wore the trousers when he was going out with Gunhild. Every time she was near he turned into a puppy."

"Gunhild, did you say?"

"Gunhild Dokken. His ex-girlfriend. And if the rumors are to be believed he's still trying to get her back—not that he's getting anywhere, from what I hear. For Petter's sake I hope it never happens. Gunhild was no good for him."

Henning nods as he passes the Deichmanske Public Library in Thorvald Meyersgate.

"I've always felt a bit sorry for Petter," she continues. "And it can't be easy for him, either."

"In what way?"

"Have you been to Fighting Fit?"

"Several times."

"Then you've probably met Gunhild," Otnes says. "She works in reception. And Petter works out almost every single day."

The sour-faced girl, Henning thinks, and hurries across the junction by St. Paul's Church before the green light changes to red.

"And when she isn't at work, he sees traces of her everywhere."

"What do you mean?" he asks, eagerly, and stops outside Probat. In the shop window a white T-shirt with an old photo of the Swedish singer Carola Häggkvist beams at him. The caption under her happy-clappy Christian face is: *Stranger, what do you hide from me?*

"Gunhild designed the gym's logo," Otnes says.

"The logo for Fighting Fit?"

Henning tries to visualize it while his thoughts race.

"Gunhild was one of the first people Vidar helped when he started working with recovering addicts. She had hit rock bottom after a life of thieving, drug abuse, and God knows what else. Vidar helped her get back on her feet, got her doing graphic design. She became quite good at it. And when Vidar decided to open Fighting Fit, he gave her the job of designing the logo."

"Right," Henning says, slowly.

"He helped her get a couple of other jobs, too. A strip club in Majorstua was one of them."

"Do you mean Åsgard?"

"How did you know that? Have you been there?"

"Yes. But not in the way you think."

"Yeah, right, that's what they all say. But I shouldn't be so hard on Gunhild. She hasn't had it easy. And her finding Vidar's body that morning hasn't exactly helped, either."

Henning is about to say something, but instead he continues to stare at the vintage print T-shirts stacked on the square shelves. Without Henning being aware of it, he lowers his arms, including the one holding the mobile. For several minutes he gapes at the shop window until he realizes that he hasn't understood anything at all.

Not until now.

110

Henning calls Brogeland straight away, but the inspector doesn't reply. Henning tries to contact him via the police's central switchboard, but is told that Brogeland isn't available. The same goes for Nøkleby and Gjerstad. They're probably in meetings, Henning thinks and rings Brogeland's mobile for the umpteenth time and leaves the world's longest voice mail message. When he has finished, the inside of the display is covered with condensation. Henning tries to wipe it off, but the wet clothes he is wearing only succeed in spreading the moisture.

Back home, having changed his clothes, he paces up and down the kitchen floor while he thinks of the pieces of the jigsaw that have been right in front of his nose though he has been unable to fit them into the bigger picture. But the pieces fit. He sees that now.

The clothes he saw drying on the clotheshorse in Holte's living room belonged to Gunhild. It was she who came to Holte's flat the other day and nearly caught Henning redhanded. Irene Otnes told him that she believed that Gunhild Dokken still has a key to Holte's flat, even though they are no longer together. It would be easy for her to go there and pick up his gun and a pair of his shoes that would probably fit her. She already had experience planting evidence. And she had every possible motive to kill Fjell's murderer and frame anyone who refused to avenge him. And no one had better access to the clock at Fighting Fit than her.

But what the hell can he do about it? He can't get hold of anyone. And the question remains, is any of what he has discovered useful if they don't have the murder weapon? As Brogeland said to him: they need evidence.

In the stairwell Gunnar Goma is stomping up and down, wheezing and undoubtedly bare-chested. Further down the front door slams shut before the sound of clicking heels mixes with the slapping of Goma's naked feet. The acoustics in the stairwell transform the solid seventy-six-year-old army voice into a mishmash of low sounds. Judging from the steps, Henning assumes that someone is visiting Arne who lives upstairs. Soon afterward a door closes.

His mobile rings. Henning answers it immediately hoping that it might be Brogeland or one of the other officers at the police station returning his call, but he is just as excited when he sees that it is Nora.

"Hi," he says in a voice that ends up high-pitched.

"Hi," she replies in a dull and unwilling tone.

She doesn't continue. Something must have happened, Henning thinks.

"How is Iver doing?" he asks, now worried.

"I would have thought you would know that better than me," she says, tartly.

Henning exhales with relief.

"I haven't visited him since yesterday," he says.

"Oh, really? He's better," she says, quickly.

Henning goes to the kitchen and takes out a carton of juice from the fridge.

"Have you been to the hospital today?" he asks her.

"I've just left it."

"What did he say?"

"Only that he was wondering if I knew how this story the two of you are working on is going."

She is upset, Henning thinks as he takes a glass from the top cupboard, opens the carton, and fills his glass. But there was something else, he can hear it in her voice. He swallows some juice. Another long silence passes.

"If he asks you again, please tell him that I've cracked it," Henning says, mainly to keep the conversation going. "I think the police will make an arrest sometime tonight. If Bjarne Brogeland gets a move on."

Henning waits for her to quiz him, but she merely says:

"I visited his grave today."

Henning stops in his tracks and puts down the glass. So that was what he heard in her voice. The seconds pass and then he slowly closes his eyes.

"And I've been thinking about what you said to me in the hospital yesterday," Nora continues, but struggles to finish what she has started. Henning keeps his eyes closed as he listens. Even though Nora speaks in a calm and normal voice, the sentences elongate and turn into long, strangling hands.

"And I know you, Henning. I know you wouldn't have said what you said about the fire if you didn't have a reason. I know you weren't trying to hurt me."

Henning is incapable of speech.

"I haven't visited Jonas's grave for . . . for a long time. And I felt bad about it."

Henning nods as the silence returns. He hasn't managed to visit the grave . . . his—

Then he opens his eyes.

Nora's voice continues in his ear, but he is no longer listening to her. He turns on the speakerphone and puts down the mobile on the kitchen table, bends down to the pile of papers on the floor next to the printer, and flicks through the messy heap of articles about Rasmus Bjelland, Tore Pulli, Jocke Brolenius, and Vidar Fjell. Nora carries on speaking without Henning paying attention to a word she says. He finds the article he is looking for. His eyes race across the lines as he reads:

MURDER VICTIM'S GRAVE DESECRATED

"It's a complete nightmare," Irene Otnes says.

Only a few weeks ago she buried her boyfriend, Vidar Fjell. Tuesday morning she woke up to the news that someone had overturned his gravestone and vandalized the plot. She is in no doubt as to who the perpetrator is. Last Friday night the man who is believed to have killed her boyfriend was himself found murdered in an old factory in Storo.

"It's an act of revenge carried out by his friends," Otnes says to *Aftenposten*. She is being comforted by Gunhild Dokken, who discovered the desecration early Saturday morning when she went to put flowers on Fjell's grave. It was she who alerted the police.

"It's despicable," she says.

Henning looks up before he examines the photograph of Irene Otnes and Gunhild Dokken by Fjell's overturned gravestone.

It's despicable.

"Do you understand what I'm saying?" Nora says.

Henning doesn't reply, but continues to stare at the photograph that accompanies the article. He concentrates on Gunhild Dokken's eyes.

And then he runs out of the flat.

111

Henning races down the stairs and out into the late afternoon where the rain pelts down on the tiles in the courtyard. In a flower bed he finds a small spade, which he bends down to pick up and put in his green shoulder bag, but as he stands up, his mobile slips out of his breast pocket and lands in a puddle, facedown. Henning swears, quickly retrieves it and wipes it down. He presses a random key. It's still working, he sees, relieved. Then he straightens up, finds his Vespa, and sets off. He doesn't mind the weather. On the contrary, he thinks it might even be to his advantage.

The early-evening traffic is light and easy to navigate and it takes him only ten minutes to reach Gamlebyen Cemetery where Vidar Fjell lies buried along with seven thousand other souls. Henning drives onto the pavement and parks up against the fence by Dyvekes Bru. The tall spruce trees growing along the length of the fence make it almost impossible to see into the cemetery from the road. Cars driving past spray water from the puddles, but Henning marches resolutely toward the nearest entrance while he takes out his mobile from his inside pocket to call Brogeland one more time.

But this time the mobile is dead.

Incredulously, he stops and stares at the gray, damp display before he turns it off and turns it on again. Nothing happens.

"Damn," he swears out loud and returns the mobile to his pocket as he enters the cemetery. A fine layer of mist creeps toward him and envelops the trees and the bushes. From his recollection of the photograph in the newspaper, Fjell is buried near a rectangular fountain. Henning follows the gray flagstones where grass grows in between. The smell of wet autumn and fresh flowers follows him as he walks. Around him the gravestones rise like tall dark teeth, surrounded by flowers that have started to succumb to the beating of the rain. He reaches two medium-sized trees, sees tall bushes lined up at intervals to form an avenue leading to a fountain. That must be it, Henning thinks as the mist comes ever nearer.

Once Henning reaches the fountain he stops and looks around. The flagstones spread out. He tries unsuccessfully to conjure up the details in the photograph, so instead he begins walking around the fountain and reading the gravestones. Name after name after name. Further away tarpaulin covers what must be an open grave. A pile of earth nearby has also been covered. When Henning has walked all the way around the fountain, he stops. Under a tree, well hidden by bushes, he sees the name *Vidar Fjell* on a gray stone. Henning goes over to it and spends a moment contemplating the letters and the numbers that make up the life that has ended. Above him the rain increases in volume.

A desecrated grave always attracts attention, Henning thinks. Everyone thought the vandalism was an act of revenge from someone close to Jocke Brolenius. There was no reason to ask questions. No one thought twice about the overturned soil, what else could it conceal but a coffin? No one would ever believe that a girl Vidar Fjell had brought back to life would dream of doing this to her benefactor's grave.

It's the perfect hiding place for a murder weapon.

Henning puts down his shoulder bag next to Fjell's grave and looks around again. There is no one nearby, no one mad enough to venture out in this dreadful weather. He kneels down and examines the ground in front of the grave, he touches the grass. It is moist and firm. And so it should be since the vandalism occurred nearly two years ago. He gets up and looks down the avenue. All he hears are car tires against the wet tarmac outside the cemetery mixed with the splashing of raindrops drumming against the flagstones and the water in the fountain.

Are you really going to do this? he asks himself. Wouldn't it be better to wait until you have convinced someone that it's absolutely essential? He takes out his mobile and tries to wake it up, but it is still dead.

Henning glances around one last time before he grabs his shoulder bag and takes out the small spade. For a few seconds he squats down with the spade in his hand. It not only feels like a violation, that's exactly what it is. But he has to find out if he is right.

Do it, he tells himself. Do it with respect.

He presses the spade into the soft grass. It goes in easily. He repeats the movement and marks out an area roughly half a meter square in front of the gravestone and starts removing the turf carefully. He places it neatly to one side. Then he starts to dig deeper. A feeling of revulsion surges in his stomach the further down he gets. He has never believed in any kind of God, never understood how people can anchor their life in faith, but there is something about disturbing a person's last place of rest. Despite his honorable intentions, nothing can change the fact that he is violating both a life and a creed. Henning tries hard to convince himself that the end justifies the means.

At regular intervals he stops and looks around, but visibility has deteriorated even further in the last few minutes. He tries to wipe away some of the water from his face with one hand, but it makes no difference. He carries on digging, plunging in the spade as deeply as he can, checking if he hits anything other than pebbles and earth, but he hasn't.

He has been digging for fifteen minutes when he stands up and peers into the square hole he has made in front of Vidar Fjell's gravestone. The coffin itself must be another meter and a half further below, he thinks. He got soaked through long ago, but when he kneels down again, it's as if the wetness also penetrates his skin. He is out of breath now. Could I have been wrong? he wonders as he resumes digging more furiously than before.

Then the spade hits something other than earth.

Henning inserts the spade into the ground again, right next to the place where he just was, making small, cautious movements just a few centimeters apart. He can feel that he has found something; it could be a large stone or an object of some sort. He starts to remove the soil.

Then he sees it.

The handle of an ax.

Feeling reenergized now he clears away more soil. Part of the blade comes into view. Henning digs faster and faster while reminding himself not to do anything to damage his discovery. With a little bit of luck the police now have the evidence they need.

Henning is about to stand up when he senses movement right behind him. He spins around. But all he has time to see is something black hurtling toward him. And he barely hears the blow.

112

Bjarne Brogeland stretches out on the sofa. On the floor next to the coffee table Alisha has set out a plastic toy castle that Oda Marie is making a concerted effort to destroy. He hasn't got the energy to tell them off, all he wants to do is close his eyes and go to sleep.

His father always used to lie down after dinner with one leg resting on the back of the sofa. It never took more than a couple of minutes before the family would hear the low hum coming from his nose. Brogeland remembers how he always hoped that his father would play with him. But he hardly ever had the energy. And now he has become exactly like him.

"Do you want some coffee, honey?" he hears from the kitchen.

"No, thank you."

A doll dressed in pink hits the floor with a bang. Brogeland scowls at the girls as Anita enters the room. She signals to him to move so that she can sit down next to him on the sofa. He shifts a few centimeters.

"You look exhausted," she says and places a warm hand on his forehead.

"I'm just tired," he says and strangles a yawn.

She smiles.

"You're allowed to say you're worn out."

Brogeland looks at her slender neck, the little spot where the neck turns into the chest. He traces her throat with his finger up to her cheek. Soft and smooth.

"I think you should try and take a couple of days off," she says. "It's not good to work as hard as you do."

"I can't," he replies.

"Of course you can."

"No, we're in the middle of—"

Brogeland is interrupted by his mobile buzzing on the coffee table. Anita sends him a look of disapproval as he sits up.

"Please, would you move?" he says to her.

Reluctantly, she does as he asks. The number is unknown. It could be the station. It could also be a nosy journalist, he thinks, but he has no desire to continue the discussion with Anita so he answers it.

"Is this Bjarne Brogeland?" a quick and anxious female voice says.

"Speaking."

"My name is Nora Klemetsen, we've spoken a couple of times before."

Brogeland tries to put a face to the voice.

"I work for *Aftenposten*," she begins.

Brogeland is about to interrupt her, but she gets there first.

"But I'm not calling as a journalist. I'm Henning Juul's ex-wife. And I'm calling you because I'm . . . because I'm quite worried about him."

"Aha?" Brogeland says and straightens up.

"I was speaking to him on the telephone earlier when he suddenly stopped talking. I've tried calling him back a couple of times since, but there is no reply. I'm outside his flat now, but he doesn't come to the door when I ring the bell. I don't know if he has fallen over or what could have happened to him. You haven't spoken to him, have you?"

Brogeland wrinkles his nose.

"No."

"Just before he hung up, he said that he was waiting for you to get a move on or something like that and that he had found out who did it."

"He said that?"

"Yes."

"And now you can't get hold of him?"

"No."

Brogeland stands up while he thinks.

"Okay," he says. "I'll ring you back in a moment."

He ends the call and opens the inbox on his mobile. Out of the corner of his eye he can feel Anita looking at him. He ignores her and opens Juul's text message, which is nothing but a request to check his voicemail. Brogeland rings his voicemail and waits impatiently for the prerecorded female voice to finish. Then there is a beep. Juul's agitated voice fills the handset. Brogeland, who is trying to put on his shoes while still holding the mobile in one hand, stops as he hears the conclusion to Juul's argument.

"Bloody hell," Brogeland says to himself. And then he starts running.

On his way to Henning's flat in Grünerløkka, Brogeland calls Gjerstad to tell him what has happened. Then he gets hold of Fredrik Stang and tells him to contact someone from Fighting Fit who might know where Gunhild Dokken can be found if she isn't at home. He tries to ring Juul, too, but his call goes straight to voicemail. Brogeland can't remember that ever happening before.

Twenty minutes after Nora Klemetsen's call Brogeland parks outside Mr. Tang and meets her in front of the entrance to 5 Seilduksgate.

"Have you heard from him?"

"No."

Brogeland tries Juul's doorbell, but to no avail. Then he rings the other doorbells. Several respond. He identifies himself. Soon the door buzzes, he pulls it open and enters a corridor that stinks of cat and rubbish. He has reached the courtyard when he notices that Nora is lagging behind until she comes to a complete stop.

"What is it?" he asks. Nora is deathly pale and staring wildly into space. "What is it?" Brogeland says a second time; he has to go right up to her before she reacts.

"This is where it . . . happened," she says.

"What did?"

"Jonas," she says with an apathetic stare. "Over there," she adds, pointing without looking up. Brogeland follows her finger toward an area where three posts have been screwed together to create a football goal with no net. A slide stretches from a ladder toward a fenced-off graveled patch. Brogeland's gaze stops at the flagstones further in, under a balcony.

He turns to her again. For a brief moment he wants to ask Nora why the hell Henning decided to live here, in this very place, after the accident, but it strikes him that she is unlikely to know. And right now they don't have the time.

"I'm coming," she says, feebly.

Brogeland hurries to the next door and presses every single button on the intercom. Soon the door buzzes open again. He takes the stairs three steps at a time, he hears Nora follow him and the door slam downstairs. New doors open, curious faces look out, but Brogeland ignores them. On the second floor he knocks on the door to Henning's flat, but there is no reply. He takes hold of the handle. Locked. Brogeland tries to contact Henning on his mobile again as Nora comes up the last few steps toward him. He lifts his index finger to his lips. She stops.

No sound.

"Damn," he mutters and ends the call. "You wouldn't happen to have a key, would you?"

"Me?"

At a loss Brogeland looks around before he rings another number. Nora watches him while he waits for the call to be answered.

"This is Detective Inspector Bjarne Brogeland from the Violent Crimes Unit in Oslo. I'm at number 5 Seilduksgate in Grünerløkka. I need assistance opening a door. And get a bloody move on."

113

Gunhild Dokken looks at Henning Juul with contempt as he lies on the wet upturned soil with blood pouring from his head. She pushes the dripping wet fringe away from her eyes, takes a step forward and plunges the spade in the soil. She reckons he is dead. The rain washes away some of the blood flowing from his skull. She smiles with satisfaction and looks around. They are alone.

She should possibly have kept him alive long enough to make him tell her how the hell he knew where to look for the ax, but ultimately it makes no difference. You can't have everything in life. She got to him in time. Let that be enough, she says to herself. Now move on.

She made up her mind the moment Henning left Fighting Fit, after the business with the clock and—not least—his comment about her T-shirts. She didn't even go home first to pick up a weapon, she just followed him. He had got too close. And if it hadn't been for that old half-naked codger in Juul's stairwell she would have rung the doorbell, forced her way in, and happily strangled Juul in his own flat. Much simpler, too. Many more potential weapons as well. Now she has had to make do with a spade she found in the cemetery.

But where can she hide the body?

You should possibly have thought about this before you whacked him, she says to herself, not that there was ever likely to be an ideal solution. She would never be able to haul him from the cemetery without being seen, no matter how atrocious the weather.

Her only regret is not dealing with him earlier. She should have known that he was a threat. Robert was a threat, too, but in a different way. She trained with him for years and he taught her the Pulli punch. And when he called her that day and asked her if she had shown others how to do it, she realized that Juul had managed to sow seeds of doubt in Robert's mind. And to prevent that seed from germinating, she had to kill him. The perfect opportunity presented itself when Robert and Petter were at each other's throats at Tore's funeral. Petter, that moron, was the perfect fall guy.

Dokken checks Juul's pockets and finds a mobile that appears to be switched off or dead. She can't know for sure if he had time to share his suspicions with anyone, but it is possible. She certainly needs to make allowances for it. This means she must act quickly. So what can she do? Leave him there?

No. Not right next to Vidar's grave. On the other side of the fountain she notices a mound of earth covered by tarpaulin. The rain drops bounce off the plastic.

The door to Henning Juul's flat bursts open with a crash. Bjarne Brogeland nods to the fireman who destroyed the locks with a few well-aimed whacks of his ax and then forced the door open for them. Brogeland steps inside with Nora on his heels. It takes them only a few seconds to establish that the flat is empty.

"Who was he looking for?" Nora asks.

"I can't tell you anything about that," Brogeland replies.

"Henning said he had found out who did it," Nora continues and walks closer to the kitchen table. "Did what?"

Again Brogeland declines to answer. Instead he narrows his eyes, annoyed at himself for not talking to Juul earlier that day when he had the chance. At that moment his mobile rings. Brogeland quickly takes it out from his inside pocket.

"Hi, it's me," Fredrik Stang says. "According to a Telenor

aerial in Gamlebyen, Gunhild Dokken is in that area right now. Or she was there a moment ago."

"Gamlebyen," Brogeland mutters and feels someone elbowing him. He turns to Nora, who is holding up a printout of an article from *Aftenposten*. Brogeland sees the photograph of Irene Otnes and Gunhild Dokken in front of Vidar Fjell's overturned gravestone. Under the photo there is the caption about the desecration of a grave in Gamlebyen only a few days after the murder of Jocke Brolenius.

"Bloody hell," Brogeland swears and looks at Nora. He issues a quick order to Stang. Seconds later they are on their way out of the flat.

114

Gunhild leaves the ax where it is, grabs hold of Juul's feet, and drags him away. The guy weighs next to nothing, she thinks and looks over her shoulder to make sure she doesn't back into the fountain. She smiles to herself. Juul's lifeless head bumps against the flagstones. If he had been alive she imagines that might have been quite painful.

Soon she reaches the mound of earth. A thick sheet of tarpaulin is stretched across the grave that will probably be filled tomorrow. She lets go of Juul's feet and glances around again. Still no one around. She swiftly flings the tarpaulin to one side. Water pours into the two-meter-deep hole. Feet first she pushes Juul closer to the edge and peers down. She smiles again and looks at Juul.

Earth to earth. Ashes to ashes. Dust to dust.

Brogeland drives as fast as he dares down Toftesgate, frightening the life out of a woman with a pram who starts to cross the road by the entrance to Sofienberg Park, even though he has switched on both the siren and the flashing blue lights. The windscreen wipers swish back and forth at full speed sweeping the rain aside. Next to him Nora is clinging to the door handle and pressing herself into the seat as the buildings fly past.

Minutes later he drives under the ring road and turns into Schweigaardsgate. He turns off both the sirens and the blue light without taking his foot off the accelerator. Through his mobile he receives constant updates of where the rest of the units have positioned themselves and who will do what when they get there. Further down the road several patrol cars are driving across Dyvekes Bru. Brogeland runs a red light and follows them.

"There is his Vespa," Nora exclaims, pointing.

Brogeland hits the brakes without skidding and comes to a smooth halt.

"Are you sure?" he says.

"Yes."

Brogeland alerts everyone over the radio, forces the car's tires onto the pavement and stops. They both jump out. The trees by the fence provide some shelter against the powerful downpour, but even so they are soaked in seconds. Brogeland opens the boot and unlocks the gun case, takes out the police's standard hand weapon—a Heckler & Koch HK P30—and runs as quickly as he can to the nearest entrance to the cemetery. Nora follows right behind him.

Gunhild Dokken half-runs back to Vidar Fjell's grave, picks up Henning's shoulder bag, the ax with which she killed Jocke Brolenius, and the spade. As soon she gets back to the open grave, she removes the tarpaulin that covers the mound of earth and starts shoveling it into the hole.

There is a limit to how much earth I can put in, she thinks, since there is probably going to be a funeral the next day. It's likely that Juul's body will be found quickly, but she will win herself time. No one coming to the cemetery will think of looking into the hole, not once she has put the tarpaulin back over the opening. And even if anyone were to do so, all they would see is a layer of soil.

She peers into the grave and sees that she has managed to cover most of Juul's body. Only his head, hands, and part of one foot remain visible. She plunges the spade into the upturned soil again and flings the next load into the hole. She misses Juul's head, but carries on shoveling. This time she gets him. The soil covers almost all of his face. Satisfied, she registers that the next shovelful will hide Juul's hands and that the following two will cover his foot and all of his head. She waits for a few seconds to make sure that Juul isn't moving. Then she resumes digging. Just to be on the safe side.

Brogeland glances at the article they brought with them from Juul's flat as he moves quickly down the flagstone path. In the distance he can just about make out the fountain in the mist. Around him officers are approaching with their weapons aimed straight ahead. They don't have time to wait for Delta Force now. Every second could mean the difference between life and death.

They move with stealth. To the side of him a man he can only just make out the contours of raises a clenched fist. Everyone stops. Fresh signals are given, some officers spread out, but Brogeland walks right ahead, stops again, all he can hear is the sound of rain hitting the ground. Then he sees something further ahead. A dark figure holding a spade, briskly shoveling soil from a pile in front of her. He sees the fringe that keeps flopping over her eyes. There is no sign of Henning Juul.

Slowly, they approach. Brogeland recognizes Gunhild Dokken, but she doesn't notice them. They stop again. The mist makes it difficult to see how far away they are, but he guesses ten or fifteen meters. Dark shadows draw near from various angles through the mist. They have got her. She is surrounded. There is nothing she can do.

Dokken carries on digging. Brogeland looks at his boss to his left a few meters ahead and gets the go-ahead. He takes off, screaming at the top of his voice like he always does when he wants to surprise someone, he hollers and hopes that the shock itself is enough to stun her so that she won't have time to use weapons, destroy evidence, or flee, and he gets exactly the reaction he was hoping for. Gunhild Dokken is taken by surprise and remains rooted to the spot. He can see her look of incomprehension, baffled how anyone would know to look for her in the cemetery, and she stands like a statue until Brogeland flings his arms around her, topples her to the ground, and locks her in an iron grip.

115

Down in the grave a foot sticks out through the soil. While Brogeland pins down Gunhild Dokken, Emil Hagen jumps in, landing softly next to the foot and quickly removes the earth covering Henning Juul's face. Brogeland leaves Dokken to his officers, but resists the urge to leap into the grave as well because the space is limited. He sees Hagen find Juul's mouth and nose and soon the rain helps wash the soil off his face. Hagen places two fingers on Juul's neck.

"There is no pulse," Hagen calls out.

"Call an ambulance," Brogeland shouts.

A voice next to him replies that it is already on its way. Four, five minutes, Brogeland estimates and it will be there. He can see that Juul has sustained a heavy blow to the side of his head, probably with the spade, but with the flat side, not the edge. If that had been the case Hagen's resuscitation attempts would very likely have been pointless. Hagen takes a deep, controlled breath before he gets to work starting with fifteen heart compressions, then he blows into Henning's nose and mouth twice. He repeats this routine several times, but there is no sign of life. They hear the sound of sirens. Hagen carries on with his desperate attempt to revive Henning Juul, who continues to lie there with his eyes closed and an almost serene expression on his face as the rain pelts him.

The sound of a roaring engine comes closer and stops nearby. Shouts and orders ensue, then the hole in the ground is filled with another man who takes over the resuscitation. Hagen is asked to leave to make room for more people in red-and-green fluorescent uniforms and he does as he is told. He jumps, gets hold of the edge, and pulls himself quickly out of the grave. Still panting, Hagen joins Brogeland and together they watch the backs of the ambulance crew. Behind them a stretcher is being prepared. Brogeland takes a step to the side and bumps into Nora who is gnawing her fingers without blinking.

Then something happens in the grave. One of the uniformed men calls out and Henning is hoisted up. He is coughing, first deep in his throat then higher up in his mouth. His face contorts. Someone puts their hand on his back to support him and he sits up, leans forward while saliva and damp soil dribble from his mouth. At the edge of the grave Nora cries out and covers her mouth with her hands. Then she closes her eyes.

116

Five days later

Trees and plants, singed by an Indian summer without rain, have regained some of their original color. Henning Juul stops outside Ullevål Hospital. A few days ago he was a patient there. The doctors refused to discharge him until they were sure there were no complications. X-rays showed that he had a fractured skull, but there were no signs of blood clots.

He would clearly have died under the soil in his unconscious state if Emil Hagen and the ambulance crew hadn't arrived when they did. Henning has since learned that they would never have got there so quickly if it hadn't been for Nora and Brogeland. Exactly how he feels about that is something he hasn't dared to address yet. There has been a lot going on.

Except for the first night, which he spent at the hospital, he has been at the police station for several interviews. He has also filed a number of stories despite the doctors telling him to take it easy for a while.

Henning walks into Iver Gundersen's room and finds his colleague sitting up in bed. His hands are clamped around his mobile and he appears to be using it as a steering wheel. The sound of screeching tires and potentially fatal collisions cease the moment he spots Henning.

"Hi," Iver calls out happily and chucks the mobile aside. "The man of the hour, back from the dead, if I'm not mistaken?"

Henning smiles. The bandages around Iver's head are gone, but his face is swollen and still the color of the Swedish flag in places. His movements, however, are quicker and more alert.

"How are you?" Henning asks as he takes a seat.

"I think I should be asking you that question?"

"I'm all right," Henning says. "My head hurts a bit, that's all, but I'm fine."

"I'm not, far from it," Iver replies. "Lying here is driving me up the wall. I'm not used to it, you know. I spend most of my time racing cars."

Henning nods and smiles.

"Go on then. Tell me all about it. I was hoping you would show up yesterday or the day before, so what has kept you?"

"I've been a bit busy lately."

"Yes, so I've noticed," Iver says and holds up his mobile. "I bet The Eagle is thrilled. I bet she doesn't nag you about scoops anymore, does she?"

Henning smiles again.

"No, she has mellowed in the last few days. She says hello, by the way."

"Hm. Right then, come on. I'm going mad in here!"

"What do you want to know?"

"Everything!"

Henning laughs.

"I've read about Dokken's key to Petter Holte's flat and the clock at the gym, but I haven't seen anything about how she killed Jocke Brolenius. I'm really curious to know that. I mean—a girl versus a tough enforcer—it's an unlikely match no matter how angry she was."

Henning makes himself comfortable in the chair.

"Gunhild Dokken went to the factory before Jocke and Tore. She went inside the building but left the door open so Jocke would think Pulli had already arrived. He was famous for his punctuality. And Jocke swallowed the bait. Dokken was waiting for him behind a pillar. As he walked past her, she attacked him quick as lightning, hitting him on the side of his neck, here, roughly," Henning says, demonstrating on himself. "The first whack nearly took his head off. The rest was easy. She hit him thirteen times in total. Back, shoulders, arms, and another blow to the neck."

"Good God," Iver says. "That's a lot of anger. And afterward she broke his jaw?"

"Yes. But she needed something more to link Pulli to the killing, and this is where the knuckle-duster comes in."

"I still don't get it. Wouldn't it have been easier to just shoot Jocke like she did with Robert van what's-his-name?"

"It might have been safer, yes. Dokken has, as far as I know, not said anything about her choice of weapon yet, but I've a theory about that. Have you heard about Forsete, the Norse god?"

"No, but I prefer two seaters, anyway. Much cooler."

They both laugh.

"Through his father Vidar Fjell had developed a passion for Norse mythology, a world he probably introduced Dokken to during the years they knew each other. Remember, she designed Åsgard's decor where everyone is having Norse sex all over the place. Dokken's plan was to avenge the murder of Vidar Fjell, she wanted justice for Vidar. Forsete was the god of justice in Norse mythology. And he had an ax."

"What about the knuckle-duster? How did she get hold of that?"

Henning scratches his forehead.

"When Tore Pulli quit debt collecting, he hung the knuckle-duster on the wall of his study at home as a symbolic gesture. I believe he made a big deal of it and it was something everyone who knew Tore would know about. One night when the Fighting Fit gang was back at Pulli's discussing what to do about

Jocke Brolenius, Dokken stole it. She used to live on the streets and had nicked plenty of things in her lifetime."

Iver nods. He is impressed. They sit for a while in silence.

"However," Henning says and gets up. "I haven't come all this way just to make small talk to an invalid like you."

"No, I didn't think so."

"I have a question for you. From Petter Holte."

117

A week after Gunhild Dokken's arrest, Henning meets Veronica Nansen outside Sognsvann station. She gives him a long, warm embrace.

"Good to see you, Henning," she says.

"Likewise. How are you?"

"I'm not too bad. How about you? I hear you've been a busy boy recently."

"Yes, there turned out to be a lot of stories to tell," he says and smiles reluctantly.

They pass the Norwegian School of Sport Sciences and walk down toward the lake. People with prams and men and women in tracksuits stroll up and down past them.

"I didn't think Petter would ever have agreed to talk to the press," Nansen says. "And what's more, to be so open and honest about being in custody, how he thought about what had happened to Tore and dreading that he, too, would be fitted up for something he hadn't done. You did a great job, Henning."

"Thank you," he says, blushing. "And it wasn't the only thing he came clean about."

Henning tells her how the same fear prompted Holte to put his cards on the table and admit to the assault on Iver Gundersen. Kent Harry Hansen was fuming when he returned to Fighting Fit after being interviewed by Iver. Holte went into his office and Hansen told him what had happened. Later that night when Iver visited Åsgard, he met Holte at the door. Holte decided to take matters into his own hands. He saw an opportunity to protect his friends and increase his status in their eyes. But he never intended to injure Iver quite so severely. He just wasn't very good at knowing when to stop.

"That's so like him," Nansen says. "What's going to happen to him as far as that charge is concerned?"

"I'm not really sure. I asked Iver if he would consider drawing a line under the whole business and he said he would think about it. But even so, Holte could still be charged."

Nansen nods and takes Henning's arm. They turn onto a broad path. Henning kicks a pinecone that jumps up and rolls away. A runner passes them, wheezing and checking his pulse monitor.

"I heard it was a T-shirt that led you to identify Gunhild as the killer?"

Henning starts to laugh.

"I think that's a case of telephone. But it's true that I saw a T-shirt in Holte's flat, which I guessed must be hers. It turned out that Gunhild's washing machine had broken down, and Holte being the wimp he is had offered her the use of his."

"Poor guy. I bet he thought it might help win her back."

"Yes. And I'm sure he believed he had succeeded when she turned up at his place after killing Robert van Derksen. But she went there purely to put back Holte's gun and his shoes, which she had taken earlier. I spoke to one of the officers who arrested Holte, and he said that Holte's face was practically euphoric that morning."

"So Gunhild spent the night with him?"

Henning nods.

"One night probably made no difference to her."

Nansen shakes her head.

"I've tried to look back," she says after a pause. "I've tried to remember if Gunhild ever did anything that I should have noticed so that some of this might have been avoided. But . . . I haven't been able to think of a single thing."

Henning nods while he recalls the book he saw on Petter Holte's bedside table. *The Gentle Axe* by R. N. Morris. And he thinks about the T-shirt Gunhild wore the first time he met her. With the logo for *Axe—deodorant for men*. There was something provocative about the way she pushed her chest up and out, almost as if she wanted him to notice her. It might have been a coincidence. Or it could have been Gunhild's substitute for heroine, surrounding herself with subtle hints of what she had done while believing that nobody would ever be able to expose her. Henning realizes that he is inspired to explore not just her wardrobe, but her whole life for other references to the murder of Jocke Brolenius. Though this would be purely to satisfy his own curiosity.

"Don't beat yourself up, Veronica," he says. "It won't make it any easier."

She looks at him as she attempts a smile.

"I'll try not to."

They walk for a while in silence.

"How is the investigation into . . . into what happened to Tore going?"

"Slowly," Henning says. "The man they arrested, Ørjan Mjønes, hasn't said one word during interviews. But the police have found incriminating evidence on his laptop. Mjønes appears to have carried out extensive research about an extremely deadly nerve poison called batrachtoxin. It comes from a frog in Colombia. Choco Indians dip their darts in it. The frog is actually called the poison dart frog and a single frog contains enough poison to kill anywhere between fifty and one hundred people."

"And that was the poison given to Tore?"

"The Institute of Public Health is still checking it, but it very much looks like it. There will be a story about it in the paper tomorrow. One hundred micrograms are enough to kill an adult and all you need to do is scratch the skin."

Nansen nods pensively.

"Imagine if they ever came to Norway."

"The frogs, you mean? That's the fascinating bit. They can't produce their poison anywhere except the western slopes of the Andes because the ants and the insects on which they feed form a unique chemical bond in the frog that creates the poison."

"Mjønes went to South America?"

"Most probably. But . . . he isn't saying anything. Not yet, anyway."

"Isn't that unusual?"

"Yes, perhaps. But I'm guessing he's keeping his mouth shut because he's banking on the evidence against him being purely circumstantial. However, it would take a lot for him not to be convicted. A receptionist at the mountain hotel close to where the body of Thorleif Brenden was found has said that Mjønes impersonated a police officer looking for Brenden. A chalet girl in the area also alerted them to a break-in in a cabin where Brenden's notes were later found. In them he describes Mjønes and the events that happened in the days leading up to Tore's death in considerable detail. That plus the frog poison will weigh heavily against him in court."

There might be two other reasons, Henning thinks, why Mjønes won't talk. First, he knows that the money he was paid for killing Pulli is waiting for him somewhere once he has served his sentence. Second, he might also be scared that what happened to Pulli could happen to him, even though he might not know the identity of his employer and so couldn't give him up even if he wanted to. Most orders for hits are made in code and under fictitious names.

The smell of a disposable barbecue wafts toward them. Soon they reach a gravel path. The sunlight sparkles in the water. In the distance a red kayak slices through the dark blue surface. Nansen and Henning sit down on a bench overlooking the lake.

"I need to ask you something," he begins. "You usually visited Tore once a week while he was inside. During that time did he ever seem—how can I put it—more tense or nervous than usual?"

She turns to him.

"His mood varied, but I can't think of anything in particular. Why do you ask?"

"Because—"

Henning looks down and thinks about Pia Nøkleby. When he spoke to her a couple of days after the arrest of Gunhild Dokken, he asked again if the police had put in a request for Pulli's telephone records from the prison. Her reply had been no, they hadn't prioritized it. And Knut Olav Nordbø from Oslo Prison confirmed the same day that it was now too late.

"I think Tore was killed because he knew who was behind the fire in my flat," Henning says. "I don't think Tore contacting me was the direct cause, but he might have been speaking to someone else about it *before* he called me."

"Why would Tore have done that?"

"I don't know. Because he thought it might be to his advantage?"

"How?"

"If Tore knew who torched my flat, he might try to use that knowledge as leverage against that man or whoever that man works for. People who are in the same line of business that he used to be in, who might be coerced into helping him."

"Tore would never have threatened anyone," Nansen says, shaking her head. "Not any more."

"Are you sure about that, Veronica? Prison is hell, and it's even worse if you're innocent. I don't have a problem believing Tore was desperate—especially since his appeal was about to be heard. I can easily imagine that the person or persons who were responsible for the death of my son didn't want that information to come out."

Nansen looks at him before she bows her head.

"And now we'll never know what it was," she says.

"No," Henning sighs. "I don't suppose we will."

118

Special offers from supermarkets, requests from real estate agents looking for a property just like his, furniture sales— Henning fails to catch all the junk mail that spills from his mailbox as he opens it. He bends down, picks it up, and flicks through his post with lukewarm interest. But he freezes when he sees the name Erling Ophus and his address in Leirsund written on the back of an envelope.

The police report, Henning thinks.

He runs up the stairs as quickly as he can and opens his brand-new front door. Once he has sat down on the sofa, he tears open the envelope and pulls out two sheets. He reads:

VENUE AND FIRE INVESTIGATION REPORT

REMIT

Commissioning party: Chief Inspector Tom Arne Sveen, E-section, Oslo Police Station

Remit: Location investigation following a fire at 23 Markveien, Oslo, at approximately 20:35

Date of request: Tuesday 12 September 2007 at 08:10

Investigators: The scene of the fire was examined by Engineering Inspector Rune Olsen, Oslo Electricity Board; Fire Chief Nicolai Juve, Oslo Fire Service; and Chief Inspector Tom Arne Sveen who prepared this report at 10:00 on 12 September 2007.

Conclusion

After examining the scene of the fire and considering other information relating to this incident, it is my opinion that:

— the fire originated in the hallway behind the front door of the second-floor flat belonging to HENNING JUUL, but that
— the cause of the fire remains unknown.

Location of the fire
23 Markveien is an apartment block containing thirteen flats and a full basement. The flat on the second floor is accessed through a communal front door.

Additional information
The front door leading to the second floor was unlocked. The communal front door at street level was also open.

Investigation of the scene of the fire
The fire started in the hallway behind the front door to the left when viewed from the landing outside. There is most damage to the surface of the internal west-facing wall. Here the internal wall has completely burned away and there is substantial damage to the back of the external wall.

The wall between hallway and the stairwell was badly damaged as the internal wall had been destroyed, but the fire damage was considerably less on the back of the panel.

Having removed debris from the floor in the hallway near the stairwell, we noticed that the floor covering (linoleum) and chipboard flooring were badly charred and there were some burn marks to the surface of the underlying wooden floor. This damaged area extended across the whole floor, all the way to the walls.

Samples taken
A section of partly charred woodwork was taken from the internal west wall.

Examination of material
This sample will be sent to Kripos to be tested for accelerants.

Observations
The photo shows that the fire started low, in the hallway right inside the front door leading to the flat. The damage was relatively major and the fire spread to large parts of the flat.

The open kitchen window caused the fire to spread quickly.

The front door showed no signs of forced entry.

Chief Inspector Tom Arne Sveen

Henning puts down the report. So the kitchen window *was* open, he thinks, though he can't remember why. Perhaps they had been frying eggs, Jonas and him, and needed to air the room. If only they had eaten crisp bread instead.

He looks inside the envelope and discovers a yellow Post-it note that must have fallen off the report. He takes it out. The note says *ring me when you have read the report* and Ophus's initials and mobile number are written below the message.

Henning rings him immediately and introduces himself when Ophus answers.

"Oh, hi," Ophus says. "It's you, is it? You've got the report, I gather?"

"Yes."

"I didn't get the chance to send you the photographs and they wouldn't have been very helpful either, as photocopies. Black and white, you know. Everything looks like soot."

"Hm."

"But I wanted to ask you about your front door. I remember us talking about how you always locked it, but that you couldn't remember if you had locked it that day. Is that right?"

"Yes?" Henning replies, intrigued.

"The report says that your front door was unlocked and that there was no sign of forced entry."

"I can only imagine that I didn't lock it."

"Yes, that was what you said. But something puzzled me when I took a closer look at the photographs of your door. Had you attached something to it? A picture or a piece of paper—something like that?"

"No. Or—I don't remember. I don't think so. We always stuck things on the fridge. Oh, yes, I put up a picture Jonas had made at nursery, a picture of him and me, but that was on the front of the door."

"And you're quite sure that you never stuck anything to the back?"

"Quite. I certainly never had before. What's on your mind, Ophus?"

There is a short silence.

"There was a drawing pin stuck to the back of your door. Like the door itself, it was badly burned. And that's why I wanted to know if you had stuck anything there."

"I can't imagine."

"But if you're right that someone was trying to frighten you, it might be that this person stuck a note to the back of your door that you were supposed to see as you left. That sounds plausible to me," Ophus says, keenly.

Yes, it does, Henning thinks and tries to visualize the scene. He closes his eyes. When he opens them again it's like he is back in the dream. He is awake, but he isn't waving his arms in front of him to clear the smoke. This time the smoke stands still. The flames sting and burn his face. There is a beam of light in the smoke, an opening he can peer through. The light grows stronger and brighter with every second and suddenly a picture emerges. For a brief gripping moment he observes himself looking at the door while the flames lick the walls and consume him with intense heat. He is about to take a step back in the run-up to jumping through the wall of flames, but he pauses. And that's when he notices a piece of paper on the door. A standard white sheet. And now he sees that there is writing on it:

first and last warning

119

That evening Henning sits in front of his laptop for hours waiting for 6tiermes7 to log on. It is nearly midnight before he gets a response.

Henning immediately brings up the warning note.

6tiermes7:
And you didn't notice anything? You didn't hear anyone enter?

MakkaPakka:
No. I was woken up by Jonas's screaming.

6tiermes7:
Do you think it could have been someone looking for Rasmus Bjelland?

MakkaPakka:
No idea. Right now I just don't know.

6tiermes7:
I haven't found any updated info on Bjelland, by the way.
It's not going to be easy if he has got himself a new identity.

MakkaPakka:
Okay. But please carry on looking.

6tiermes7:
Will do.

Neither of them has anything to report for a while, but they don't leave the chat. Henning thinks about the people who want to get Bjelland, but he can't convince himself that B-gjengen or Svenskeligaen—whatever is left of them—would torch a flat to obtain information. They would have chosen a physical approach, aimed directly at him because flames are difficult to control. Even so, Henning has a distinct feeling that Bjelland is important. He just doesn't know why.

> **6tiermes7:**
> By the way, I have something to tell you.

It takes a few seconds before the continuation comes.

> **6tiermes7:**
> I wasn't going to tell you at first, but I've reached the conclusion that I have to.

> **MakkaPakka:**
> What is it?

> **6tiermes7:**
> Your son died on 11 September 2007, didn't he?

Henning sits up.

> **MakkaPakka:**
> Yes, why?

> **6tiermes7:**
> After what you told me about Tore Pulli and the fire, I checked him out. And I found out something interesting. A traffic warden in Grünerløkka contacted the police the following day because of a car with a man inside that had been parked outside your flat several nights in a row. The traffic warden thought it suspicious and a patrol car was dispatched. The man in the car was identified as Tore Pulli.

MakkaPakka:

But Pulli has already admitted to being there. Are you saying he sat there for several nights?

6tiermes7:

Yes. But I haven't found out anything about what he was doing there.

MakkaPakka:

So nobody challenged him?

6tiermes7:

I certainly found no information to that effect. And neither the officers nor the traffic warden are named in the incident so there is not much to go on.

MakkaPakka:

Is that normal procedure?

6tiermes7:

It's not certain that whoever entered the incident into Indicia knew which officers were dispatched. And the traffic warden could have requested that his or her name be kept out of it to avoid possible repercussions.

MakkaPakka:

Quite. But does it say anything else?

6tiermes7:

No. That's it.

Henning sits for a while thinking, but he isn't sure how to interpret the information he has just been given.

MakkaPakka:
But if someone entered information about Pulli being
in my street on the 11 September 2007, surely his name
should have cropped up during the fire investigation?

6tiermes7:
Not necessarily. We can't be sure that an Indicia search
was carried out in connection with the fire. Many swear
by the old systems. And Pulli was never called in for an
interview.

Dear God, Henning thinks. Is that possible?

MakkaPakka:
But why were you reluctant to tell me this?

6tiermes7:
Because the entry has been edited. And I think that
important information has been deleted.

MakkaPakka:
What makes you think that?

6tiermes7:
Because there is hardly anything there.

MakkaPakka:
But why would anyone do that?

6tiermes7:
Why do you delete information?

MakkaPakka:
Because it's wrong?

6tiermes7:
Or because it's sensitive.

The sentence he is staring at sends a shiver down Henning's back. His head spins.

MakkaPakka:
You're saying that someone who works for the police probably deleted information about what Tore Pulli was doing outside my flat that evening?

6tiermes7:
That's how I interpret it, yes.

Henning leans closer to the table.

MakkaPakka:
What's the point of deleting some of the information— wouldn't it make more sense to delete the whole entry?

6tiermes7:
That's probably the biggest mistake you can make. Pulli was a celebrity and it wasn't just the traffic warden and the officers in the patrol car who knew that he had been spotted outside your flat. It was known in the control room, the duty officer probably knew about it and it's likely that several staff members discussed it that night. It would look more suspicious if a well-known incident about a recently deceased celebrity disappears from the system than if only bits of information are missing.

MakkaPakka:
Okay, so tell me who edited the log?

6tiermes7:
This is the part that makes me uncomfortable.

The continuation, when it comes a few seconds later, takes Henning's breath away.

6tiermes7:
It was Pia Nøkleby.

Acknowledgments

I have pestered numerous people during my work on *Pierced*. Knut Erik Rønningen, Jørn Lier Horst, Vibeke Ødegård Sør-Reime, Kristin B. Jenssen, Grete Lien Metlid, and Arild Kai Erland—I can't thank you enough.

I also thank warmly Silje Hovland, Jan Ove Årsæther, Fredrik Brodwall, Sverre Arild Olstad, Petter Anthon Næss, Hege Enger, Henning Enger, Torgeir S. Higraff, Kari Ormstad, Gustav Peter Blom, Liliana Bachs, Gunn Kristine Smeby, Agnar Gerner, Nils Petter Granholt, Asle Skredderberget, Morten Ø. Karlsen, Espen Skaar, Marius Vik, Inger-Brit Vindeg, and Trond Hugubakken. Thank you also to the friendly people in Ustaoset.

Among the books I read in the course of my research, I would like to make a special mention of *Politi & Røver* by Kjetil Østli.

Benedicte, you deserve the greatest praise for reading, crossing out, thinking, and making suggestions. And for being you.

Thank you, Theodor and Henny, for reminding me daily of what really matters.

Oslo, May 2011
Thomas Enger